EXIT

At first I thought [that someone had, per]haps
maliciously, throw[n] [the] [the]se kimono into a heap in the middle of his dressing room
floor.

But no, the back of a head covered thinly with lank
strands of grey hair protruded from the neck of the
kimono. Incongruously small white-stockinged feet
stuck out below the hem. It was Pooh-Bah himself who
lay crumpled facedown on the grey carpeting in his
black kimono splashed with yellow peonies. One of the
peonies had changed color to an ugly red. From its
center, like an obscene stamen, projected the elaborately decorated hilt of the authentic antique aikuchi
dagger.

Oh, no, please no! It had to be a joke, a horrible practical joke. A mannequin, a splash of red paint . . .

I stepped farther into the room.

From my left a voice said, "Don't touch 'im, Phoebe.
He's dead."

Critical Acclaim for Karen Sturges and

DEATH OF A BARITONE

"A standing ovation for Karen Sturges's DAZZLING
debut mystery . . . Phoebe Mullins is a sleuth to
cherish." —Carolyn Hart

"This one rocks along to the strains of 'Cosi fan tutte'
with nary a sour note. BRAVA . . . and let's have the
encore quickly." —*The Washington Times*

Please turn the page for more acclaim.

Books by Karen Sturges

DEATH OF A POOH-BAH
DEATH OF A BARITONE

DEATH OF A POOH-BAH

KAREN STURGES

BANTAM BOOKS
NEW YORK TORONTO LONDON SYDNEY AUCKLAND

DEATH OF A POOH-BAH
A Bantam Book / November 2000

ISBN 0-553-58131-7

Published simultaneously in the United States and Canada

Bantam Books are published by Bantam Books, a division of Random
House, Inc. Its trademark, consisting of the words "Bantam Books"
and the portrayal of a rooster, is Registered in U.S. Patent and
Trademark Office and in other countries. Marca Registrada. Bantam
Books, 1540 Broadway, New York, New York 10036.

PRINTED IN THE UNITED STATES OF AMERICA

10 9 8 7 6 5 4 3 2 1

DEDICATED IN LOVING MEMORY TO
MY PARENTS, JOHN AND DOROTHY DUKE,
WHO TAUGHT ME TO LOVE
WORDS AND MUSIC

ACKNOWLEDGMENTS

Northampton, Massachusetts, is, of course, a real town, and some of the scenes in this book are set in real places. Others are not. Do not, for example, go looking for The Old Church Theater, or for Portia's house or Sam's pizzeria or Irene's craft shop—they exist only in my imagination and soon, I hope, in yours. The same is true of all the characters who appear in this story. It's fiction, folks.

That said, I have tried to remain as true to the probabilities of real life as I could, and in this endeavor many people have helped me. Anything I've gotten right is due to them. Whatever sounds unlikely should be chalked up to my own stubbornness. My very sincere thanks to:

Detective Lieutenant Kenneth Patenaude and Lieutenant Brian C. Rust of the Northampton Police Department; Peter Boruchowski of Valley Sport Center in Easthampton, Mass.; John Ebbets and Anna-Maria Goosens at the *Daily Hampshire Gazette;* Kathy Udall, R.N.; C. Richard Hinckley, M.D.; Osa Flory; Carol V. Paul; Joan Cart; Faith Foss; Nancy Taylor; Samuel Crompton; Ellen Schleicher; Adrienne Auerswald; Morgan Lindley; and Anne Eliot Crompton.

Deep gratitude to my supportive agent, Ruth Kagle, and to my skillful editor, Tracy Devine.

And lastly, special thanks to my husband, William Sturges, who patiently serves as consultant, comforter, and cheerleader, and who also feeds me.

THE NORTHAMPTON REPERTORY COMPANY PRESENTS

THE MIKADO

or THE TOWN OF TITIPU

Book by W. S. GILBERT   *Music by* ARTHUR SULLIVAN

Directed by HARRY JOHNS
Musical Director NADINE GARDNER

Production made possible through the generosity of
Portia Carpenter Singh

Dramatis Personae

THE MIKADO OF JAPAN	Arnold Zimmer
NANKI-POO *His son, disguised as a wandering minstrel,* *and in love with Yum-Yum*	Mitchell Kim
KO-KO *Lord High Executioner of Titipu*	Derek Bowles
POOH-BAH *Lord High Everything Else*	E. Foster Ballard
PISH-TUSH *A Noble Lord*	Carl Piquette
YUM-YUM	Ardys Feldman
PITTI-SING *Three Sisters, Wards of Ko-Ko*	Jane Manypenny
PEEP-BO	Beth Rosario
KATISHA *An Elderly Lady, in love with Nanki-Poo*	Lydia Hicks

Setting by PETER BOWLES
Costume and Props Coordinator IRENE POLASKI
Choreography by PHOEBE MULLINS

1

. . . a victim must be found . . .

THE THREE LITTLE MAIDS HAD TWIRLED THEIR PARASOLS without dropping a one. Ko-Ko, the Lord High Executioner, had been successfully persuaded to drop from his "little list" his more scurrilous inventions involving key segments of the local population. The Mikado had remembered almost all of the words to his big song. The audience had eaten it up.

In fact, the debut performance of the Northampton Repertory Company, presenting Gilbert and Sullivan's *The Mikado,* had come off with a smoothness I was not at all sure it deserved. The combined sighs of relief from those reponsible ought to be enough, I reflected, to blow away the sulky clouds that had been hanging over the valley for the past two weeks. Even, perhaps, to disperse the metaphorical bad weather that had been hanging with equal persistence over the members of the Northampton Rep themselves. The rehearsal period had not, in the main, been a happy one.

Now, however, buoyed by the crowd's approval and heady with the relief of having actually pulled the thing off, most of the company had taken themselves off to the cast party in an unwonted atmosphere of good cheer and togetherness. A few of the stage crew were still about, tinkering with a set piece which had almost, but not quite, fallen apart during the second act. And since, as stage manager, I was in charge of locking up, I was obliged to stay around until the building was cleared.

I wandered among the pews (real pews; the Old Church Theater was not named on a whim), picking up programs to recycle at tomorrow night's performance. I had barely had time to glance at them earlier—they had arrived at the theater a half hour before curtain—and now I took a closer look.

Quite handsome, I thought: a red and black design on buff featuring a Mikado who, rather than appearing menacing, had a rather jovial look. Circling his picture were smaller sketches of the other principal characters: Nanki-Poo and Yum-Yum making goo-goo eyes under her parasol; Ko-Ko, bent under the weight of his huge executioner's axe; Pooh-Bah, Lord High Everything Else, looking down his nose; Katisha, her headdress sporting pins the size of small swords.

I turned to the inside pages. Directed by Harry Johns . . . production made possible through the generosity of Portia Carpenter Singh . . . potted biographies of the cast, acknowledgments, production crew—ah yes, there I was. Twice. Choreography by Phoebe Mullins, and on the following page, Stage Manager: Phoebe Mullins. I shook my head, asking myself for the umpteenth time how I'd allowed this to happen. But I knew, of course. I had gotten sucked in by a combination of curiosity, flattery, and the charms of Gilbert and Sullivan. And, most essentially, because of my Aunt Portia, a difficult lady to deny, and of whom, in a very short time, I had become deeply fond.

Speaking of Portia, where was she? I'd assumed she'd be waiting for me to drive her to the party, but a quick visual sweep of the now shadowy interior of the

Old Church's main space turned up no aunt, nor indeed anyone else. Perhaps she'd gotten a ride from Harry or one of the others. I hoped they'd keep an eye on her. Since she'd recently had the cast removed from her arm and graduated from a four-pronged institutional metal cane to a handsome ebony stick, Portia had become entirely too frisky to please me.

I took my stack of programs—those that hadn't been rolled, folded, sat on, or otherwise mutilated—to the table behind the last pew. From there I started back down the aisle, intending to tell the remaining stagehands to give it a rest for the night. But a glimmer of light coming from the staircase at the far right side of the auditorium just left of the red EXIT sign gave me pause. The stairs led down to the basement, where the dressing rooms were located. I'd already checked that area and thought I'd made sure everyone was gone and the lights were out. Wasted electricity was not within the budget of the Northampton Rep. I reversed course and headed for the stairway.

At its top, the metal folding chair with a neatly hand-printed sign reading NO ACCESS taped to its back had been shoved aside. And down below, sure enough, a bare lightbulb hanging from the ceiling—all twenty-five watts of it—was doing its best to penetrate the murk. Damn! how had I missed that? I trotted down the stairs and was reaching up to switch off the bulb when I saw another streak of light at the far end of the looming open space that constituted the main area of the church basement. There, in the region under the stage (formerly the chancel), beyond the big central area where the chorus dressed and made up, were located the principal dressing rooms. The light was coming through the half-open door of room number one, most convenient to the stage and therefore quickly comandeered by Dr. E. Foster Ballard, our Pooh-Bah, ostensibly on grounds of seniority but basically out of a sheer bloody-minded inability to consider anyone's comfort but his own.

How like him, I thought crossly, to take off without bothering to turn out his lights.

On second thought, how *unlike* him not to have made sure his door was closed and locked with the padlock that he had insisted the company install after the broken mirror incident. Besides, was he not contributing to the production his own, authentic Japanese kimono, as well as his authentic antique Japanese aikuchi knife? He surely couldn't be expected to leave them unsecured.

Thanks to E. Foster, I thought as I picked my way across the cement floor, I now knew more about Japanese aikuchi knives than I really cared to. A variety of dagger, he'd expounded, with an etched blade and elaborately decorated hilt and scabbard. Carried during the Toku-something era by persons of rank. Also used in committing hara-kiri. Ugh! had been my basic reaction, not having a fondness for weapons of any variety.

E. Foster, however, set great store by his treasured knife, and would never have left it in an unlocked dressing room. Therefore, he'd either taken it with him, or he was still on the premises. And yet I was positive that when I'd checked the basement twenty minutes ago the door to Pooh-Bah's dressing room had been closed, with no light showing underneath. Well, he must have returned for some reason.

Just short of my goal, I stepped on a small object that crumbled under the sole of my shoe. Probably a cylinder of makeup charcoal or some such thing, I thought. Too bad. If people couldn't take care of their stuff . . .

"Foster, are you still here?" I called out, and when there was no answer I pushed the door all the way open.

The bright glare of a row of makeup lights above the dressing table on the opposite wall momentarily dazzled me, and it took me a startled moment to realize that the image floating above the jars and pots and boxes of Kleenex was my own reflection in the wide mirror. My second impression was that someone had carelessly, or perhaps maliciously, thrown E. Foster's authentic Japanese kimono into a heap in the middle of the floor.

But no, the back of a head covered thinly with lank strands of grey hair protruded from the neck of the kimono. Incongruously small white-stockinged feet stuck out below the hem. It was Pooh-Bah himself who lay crumpled facedown on the grey carpeting in his black kimono splashed with yellow peonies. One of the peonies had changed color to an ugly red. From its center, like an obscene stamen, projected the elaborately decorated hilt of the authentic antique aikuchi dagger.

Oh, no, please no! It had to be a joke, a horrible practical joke. A mannequin, a splash of red paint . . . I stepped farther into the room.

From my left, a familiar voice said, "Don't touch 'im, Phoebe. He's dead."

I whirled to face my aunt Portia where she stood in the shadow just beyond the open door. Both hands gripped the silver handle of the ebony stick and she was breathing heavily. She stared down with an unfathomable expression at the man on the floor. Clearly visible on one cuff of her long-sleeved white silk shirt was a smudge of the same color that stained the yellow peony.

It was easily the fourth worst moment of my adult life.

2

Wafted by a fav'ring gale . . .

THE CHAMPION WORST WAS WHEN I KNEW THAT THE child I'd carried for five and a half months would not make it into this world, and that for me there would be no other. The second was when they came to tell me that my husband of twenty-five years was dead. At the age of fifty-five, Mick (to me; to the *NY Times* et al. "famed conductor Michael Mullins") had collapsed from a heart attack on the podium where he'd been leading a rehearsal of the Brahms 2nd Symphony.

On a sunny and brisk day in mid-October, a little more than three weeks prior to my discovery of Pooh-Bah's lifeless body, not only that fourth worst moment but also the third were yet to come.

On that day I was driving slowly along a street in Northampton, Massachusetts, looking for my aunt's house. It was a curving and rather narrow street, lined on both sides by substantial houses set close together. Between the houses and the street, immense old trees—maples and beeches and chestnuts and the occasional heroically surviving elm—reached to touch each other overhead in a patchwork canopy of gold and russet, orange and red. Along the curbs, accumulations of fallen leaves streamed like fantastically Crayola-colored rapids.

It was scenes such as this that were no doubt responsible for much of the traffic that had accompanied me along the Merritt Parkway and up Route 91. New England was putting on its annual show and the leaf peepers were out in force. I, however, while enjoying the dividend, had not been motivated by the glories of nature. In my shoulder bag resting on the seat beside me was the letter that had brought me here. I knew it by heart.

My dear Phoebe (it read):

Perhaps you'll be surprised to know that you have an aunt, alive and living in Massachusetts. My fault, if so. But I hope that your mother, my sister Helen, may have mentioned me to you from time to time. I'd always thought that Helen & I would have time together in our later years. But then she died. Regrets, I find, are even more useless than they are reported to be.

I would like you to visit me. This is a big house & you can have all the privacy you want. Lately I fell off my bicycle and broke my left arm and hip, so for the time being I can't get around much. But I think, on your own, you'll find Northampton an interesting town. I'd very much like to meet my niece. Maybe you'll have some curiosity about me. You can stay for as short or long a time as you wish.

Last time I saw you, you were three years old. You told me my dress was pretty & that I had a big nose. I hope you've retained your forthright nature, & that you won't hesitate to tell me whether this invitation is or is not agreeable to you.

I look forward to your reply.

Sincerely, your aunt,
Portia Carpenter Singh

The letter had arrived at a particularly opportune time. I had recently returned to New York City after three months of employment at a summer opera colony on Long Island's East End. The summer had been in some parts traumatic, but also hugely liberating. After a lifetime of living in the shadow (and in the service) of others—first my pianist father and then my conductor husband—I had found myself emerging, at the age of forty-eight, into a Phoebe Mullins I hardly recognized. A person who could function very nicely on her own, thank you. A person who could hold down a job and drive a car. Whose years of dealing with overwrought artists, their public, managers, and hangers-on had, it seemed, developed in her talents she hadn't fully appreciated. I had, over the course of that summer, run a complicated business office; been the recipient of so many highly personal confidences that I had finally to assume I was good at it; served as a box-office manager, program designer, stage manager; been romantically pursued by a quite attractive cop; solved a murder.

Heady as it had all been, however, at the end of it, back in New York and with the rest of my life to consider, I couldn't quite see in this mishmash of accomplishments anything that might be termed a career direction. I needed a job, but what? I really didn't want to be someone's secretary, no matter how delightful the boss or exalted the title. Since I was without a college degree or any other credentials, listening to people bare their souls, while fascinating, was not likely to lead to paid employment. My introduction to detection had been too painful to tempt me in that direction, not to mention my total lack of training (see above).

From childhood on my ambitions and energies had centered on my dream of being a professional dancer. My mother's death when I was eighteen had put an end to that. My father needed me, and then my husband did, and it was off to the world of the touring musician—of hotels and lost luggage and preconcert

nerves and postconcert euphoria/depression/exhaus-
tion. Of autograph seekers and celebrity groupies, of
shirts that were either over- or under-starched, rooms
too hot or too cold, of tantrums, diplomacy, and hand-
holding. True, I could recognize, and even hum extended passages of, much of the standard Western
classical music canon. But short of someone coming up
with a highbrow—and highly paying—version of
Name That Tune, it was an accomplishment of little
practical value.

Now I was forty-eight. Most dancers of my age were
already well into their retirements. Teach? I'd kept up
taking class during those years whenever and wherever
possible. But where was my track record, my list of
achievements, my professional history? In spite of the
love and admiration I'd had for both my father and my
husband, there were times when I contemplated those
years spent cosseting the male artistic temperament
with something uncomfortably like bitterness.

The arguments went in circles, always smacking up
against the intractable fact of my lack of formal training
in anything smiled upon in the marketplace. The
process was beginning to seriously undermine my recently won self-confidence; and then came my aunt's
letter.

Of course I would go. My God, I had an aunt! I was a
niece! The younger sister my mother had told me about
who had gone "abroad" at an early age and never returned, from whom came the occasional photo or
Christmas card, was not the semimythical person my
young mind had conjured. She was real. Alive and
living in Massachusetts. I, who had lost a mother at
eighteen, a father at twenty-two, a baby at twenty-six,
a husband at forty-seven, had come to accept that I was
not a person destined to have relatives. And now I had
an aunt! The fact of it alone instantly overrode any little
concerns I might have been having about how I would
justify the rest of my life.

Over and over I studied the letter. It was, I decided, most intriguing for what it didn't say. "Singh"? An Indian name, I thought. Was there a Mr. Singh? Did I perhaps have cousins? What was Portia Carpenter Singh doing in Massachusetts, in the town she and my mother had grown up in, and how long had she been there? "Fell off my bicycle" . . . I did the calculations. My aunt Portia was now in her early sixties. Not, it seemed, a woman planning to drift gently into her golden years.

And above all, *why* the long exile? A "falling out" with their parents, my mother had said with the sort of vagueness that told me I wasn't going to learn any more. Some falling out, to create such a breach! And now she had made a deliberate return to the scene of whatever dire happening had caused a lifetime of estrangement. Why, why, why?

The next day I sat down and replied to my aunt's letter. Portia was obviously not a waster of words, and I followed suit. Yes, I would very much like to visit her. I named a date for my arrival, leaving the extent of my stay unspecified. (We would know quickly, I was sure, if the relationship was going to be a happy one.) I told her I had long since outgrown the habit of making personal remarks, and was glad she had not taken mine amiss. Within days I had her reply, consisting of a brief expression of pleasure in anticipation of my arrival, and some concise travel directions.

Which I was now following, and which seemed to indicate . . . no! that couldn't be it! But it was: a great Victorian pile, set away from the street on a grassy slope, surrounded by rusted wrought-iron fencing, and painted a bilious green. An open porch, rich with gingerbread, stretched across the front, and bulged out into a semicircle at the corner. Over the bulgy part a shingled roof swirled to a point, topped by a spike that looked as if it had come off a German helmet. Another two stories of house was capped by a gabled roof.

Beyond that I had a jumbled impression of bay windows, a variety of scalloped siding, and swatches of stained glass. Well, I reminded myself, still goggling, she'd said "a big house."

Now that I was actually here, I had a cowardly moment of wanting to turn and run. I was about to meet, as far as I knew, my only living blood relation. What if she didn't like me? What if we had nothing in common? How quickly could I decently say thanks so much and withdraw? What, I wondered, was she expecting of me?

I looked down at my brown slacks, moccasins, and yellow pullover. Was this what one wore into a house that reeked of elaborate, if seedy, Victorian splendor? In the rearview mirror my eyes stared blackly back at me, emphasized by the paleness of my face. What had happened to that charming summer tan? I rooted in my bag for blusher and lipstick, ran a comb through the short curly dark hair that had started the day under control and was now beginning to frizz.

Ah, hell, Phoebe, you're being ridiculous. I took a deep breath, put my hands on the wheel, and turned my little red Toyota through the opening in the iron fence. A driveway angled steeply up, then leveled and widened to accommodate several cars. Two others were already parked there: a Honda Civic of a jaunty metallic green and an elderly black Volvo. Pasted to the Honda's passenger-side window was a flyer announcing a production of Gilbert and Sullivan's *The Mikado*. Bumper stickers on the Volvo proclaimed, "Hate is not a family value," and "Every mother is a working mother."

As I got out of my car and started along the path leading to the front entrance of the house, the door opened and a young woman came out. Under one arm she carried what looked like a pillow roll. A large leather bag on a strap hung from one shoulder. She was slim and ponytailed and wearing a long paisley skirt. At the top of the porch steps she stopped to adjust her load, and in so doing dropped the leather bag, which clunked noisily down the steps and landed at my feet.

I bent to pick it up, but quickly changed my mind.

"Good Lord, what have you got in here? Bricks?"

"Weights," the woman said. "For exercise." She came down the steps and took hold of the bag's leather strap. "I'm a physical therapist."

"Ah," I said, enlightened. "You're giving Mrs. Singh physical therapy for her hip."

The woman sniffed. "I'm trying." She glanced back toward the door, then said in a somewhat lowered voice, "Mrs. Singh has some issues with . . . um . . . following instructions." She heaved the bag onto her shoulder, and added, with exasperation, "Hell, actually she has issues with anyone trying to tell her anything. You from the Visiting Nurses?"

"No," I said. "I'm Mrs. Singh's niece."

"Oh," said the woman, "I'm sorry." She shrugged and turned away down the path toward the car park.

Had I just received an apology, I wondered, or a commiseration? With an even more heightened sense of expectation, I mounted the steps and pushed the doorbell.

3

I'm much touched by this reception.

"WELL . . . *PHOEBE,*" MY AUNT SAID. THERE WAS SATIS-
faction in her tone and on her lips the hint of a smile. It
seemed that, initially at least, I had passed muster.

We were sitting opposite each other by a deeply
curved bay window in a room that stretched a good
thirty feet down the side of the house. I had been led
here by a small Indian lady wearing a green and gold
sari, who, on opening the door to me, had said only,
"Ah, you are Phoebe. Come this way, please."

"This way" turned out to be through a vestibule into
an entrance hall and then through the second of two
doors on the right. I processed in passing lots of pol-
ished oak woodwork, an ornately banistered staircase
that rose to a landing and then angled off to the right,
looming pieces of furniture, oriental carpets spread over
parquet flooring, a liberal use of color in wall hangings
and drapery, an odor of burning incense. And as we entered the long room, at its far end a harp (a *harp?*)
gleaming goldly in a shadowy corner.

Halfway down the room, three people appeared to
be in confab, heads together, two of them leaning over

the third, who sat in a large brown leather recliner. On my entrance, the two standing figures straightened and moved slightly away, and I could see that the person in the recliner was a woman indubitably my aunt. And despite the place's distracting admixture of Victorian and oriental clutter, it was she who was the room's compelling center.

Through the mullioned window to her left, early afternoon sunshine, filtered through a mass of hanging greenery, dappled her substantial figure and lit with silvery fire a carelessly piled-up mass of white hair. A navy-blue denim skirt reached almost to the tops of white anklets rising from a pair of well-worn running shoes. Atop the skirt she wore a man's cotton shirt in royal blue. The left sleeve of the shirt had been cut short to allow the passage of a cast that extended from wrist to elbow. A utilitarian white sling was draped over the chair's arm—removed, perhaps, in my honor? Atop the blue shirt, my aunt's quite remarkable face now regarded me, as I sat facing her on a rose velvet settee, with an expression I could only describe as smug.

Portia Carpenter Singh's face, I decided, had either grown into its nose or my tastes, since the age of three, had broadened. It was certainly a strong nose, and it sat in a strong face: large, level, intensely blue eyes, wide mouth, large teeth, long chin. On first seeing her, I had looked for a reflection in her features of my mother's face, but had found none.

She must have done the same, because now she said, "You take after your father, Phoebe. Can't see Helen there at all." She turned to the taller of her two companions, a man who now stood by the window, absently fingering a philodendron leaf. "Fortunately, Phoebe's daddy was a good-lookin' son-of-a-gun. Skinny, curly hair, like Phoebe. Greek, y'know. Gave our parents fits." She barked a short laugh. "Named their daughter after a Greek, but God forbid she should marry one!"

From a corner of the room came a soft, sibilant sound. I had almost forgotten the Indian lady. After bringing me to my aunt, she had quietly taken a seat at a little distance and picked up some knitting.

My aunt hmphed and said to me, "Anandi doesn't approve of my bad-mouthing the progenitors. *Bene, bene . . . scusi,* Anandi."

For my part, I was fascinated and bewildered in equal parts. Was I at long last going to learn something about those shadowy figures, my maternal grandparents? Why was my aunt speaking in Italian to the Indian Anandi? Who *was* Anandi?

The man at the window grinned at me. He had a round, high-cheekboned face under a head of wiry, greying curls and one of those thin-lipped mouths that you wouldn't think would be attractive, but is. He'd been introduced to me as Harry Johns. The other person—a Derek something . . . Bowles, that was it—had wandered away to the far end of the room where he stood picking out a desultory tune on the harp strings. I had no idea what either of them was doing here.

"Harry's directing our production of *The Mikado,*" my aunt said. "And Derek's playing Ko-Ko."

"Oh, yes, the flyer in the car window," I said, trying not to look spooked and grateful to have found something I could make sense of. "How is it going?"

"Thanks to Portia, very well," Harry Johns said. "She's been extremely generous."

"Absolutely could *not* be doing it without her," said the person named Derek Bowles. He had left the harp and now came and perched familiarly on the arm of the recliner. The *Mikado*'s Lord High Executioner was a small man, at least three inches below my own five feet five. He was also slight, with a boyish, almost pretty face. Silky fair hair fell with a kind of calculated insouciance over a smooth, broad forehead. Full lips curved winsomely. Not my idea of a Ko-Ko.

He placed a hand with what seemed like genuine affection on my aunt's shoulder. "Our angel in every sense of the word." His voice was a surprisingly resonant baritone. A knowing twist of the full mouth indicated a self-deprecating humor. I adjusted my assessment. Maybe he could be a Ko-Ko after all.

My aunt hmphed dismissively, but she looked pleased. "Always liked G 'n S," she said. "Was goin' to play Katisha myself until I broke m' damn bones."

I noted the deep voice, the clipped, carrying delivery, and something else . . . a sense of banked—even dangerously banked—energy. Katisha! Of course! The most formidable of all of Gilbert and Sullivan's formidable middle-aged ladies. I'd bet my Aunt Portia would have done her proud.

"Your aunt would have been a fantastic Katisha," Harry Johns said to me. "The gal we've got is okay, but . . ."

"Well, well, let me see 'em," Portia said. Harry Johns retrieved from a nearby chair a large manila envelope and joined me on the settee. Derek/Ko-Ko dropped onto a hassock beside the recliner. "Photos," my aunt explained. "Head shots. For the lobby. These two were just about to show 'em to me." She cocked her head at Harry. "I s'pose we *have* a lobby?"

"Oh, indeed. Quite plush, actually. Red carpet, paneling, stained glass."

"The theater's in an old church building," Ko-Ko explained to me. "Absolutely too marvelous."

I said to Portia, "And you've never seen it?"

She grimaced. "Was on my way there when I fell off m'damn bike. Hospital, then a rehab. Now the fool doctors won't let me go down the steps of m'own house for another week. Not to mention sending 'round some female new-age type to fuss over me. I hear the word 'holistic' one more time I'll puke on 'er damn crystal."

The physical therapist I'd met on the doorstep, I

deduced. I began to appreciate the problems she must be experiencing with my redoubtable aunt.

There was another sound—a kind of gentle tut-tutting—from Anandi's corner.

"Yes, yes, Anandi, I know. Own best interests, etc., etc., and I'm doin' the fool exercises, aren't I? Don't have t'pretend to like it. And the damn woman's always turnin' up at inconvenient times." She gestured to the envelope in Harry's hand. "So . . . let's see what I'm payin' for."

As Harry Johns pulled out a sheaf of eight-by-ten glossies, I scrambled to orient myself in what was still, to me, a bewildering landscape. My aunt's tendency to ellipsis was obviously not confined to the written page. It seemed that Aunt Portia was underwriting to a significant degree a local theatrical production. Taken together with this enormous house, indications were that my aunt was a wealthy woman. Where did the money come from? And how long had she been living in Northampton to have become so deeply involved in such a project? How had she linked up with Harry Johns and Derek Bowles?

All were questions that I had to assume would eventually be answered. For now, I turned my attention to the pictures which were being handed one at a time from Harry to Derek to Portia and then, with what I thought rather a blithe assumption that I would be interested, to me.

Harry and Derek kept up a running commentary. Harry: "Our Katisha, Lydia Hicks. Big voice, good presence." Derek: "*Quite* formidable. She'll do—since we couldn't get the best," with a smile at my aunt.

I glanced at Portia to see how she reacted to this bit of good-natured sucking up, but she was studying the photo critically and only commented, "Good. Looks strong."

"Mitchell Kim, the Nanki-Poo. Really nice tenor."
"Yum-Yum . . . pretty girl, very young. She'll take some work." "Pish-Tush . . ." "Pooh-Bah . . ."

In spite of myself, probably in response to my aunt's obvious enjoyment of the process, I had begun to study the photos with some interest. I knew *The Mikado* well. Although by the time I reached high school the obligatory yearly Gilbert and Sullivan operetta had long since given way to the likes of *Oklahoma!* and *Finian's Rainbow,* my mother had been a real buff. I remembered sitting beside her on the piano bench, both of us belting out with gusto "I am the Captain of the Pinafore" and "A policeman's lot is not a happy one" and "Tit-Willow," while my father shook his head and retreated to a far room. You were either, it seemed, a G&S enthusiast or you couldn't stand the stuff.

Now I fitted the various faces to the characters they were to portray. Nanki-Poo, for instance, the tenor, the romantic lead. Actually, in this case, being played by an Asian . . . Kim, was it? Korean, probably. A nice fillip. And here was Derek/Ko-Ko, looking quite dashing. From the head shot, unaware of his diminutive stature, you would have said a perfect juvenile lead. I wondered how much he minded . . .

"Who's this?" my aunt said abruptly. I looked up. She was staring at the picture in her hand with the expression of someone whose cat has just deposited a mangled mouse on her foot.

"That's our Pooh-Bah," Harry Johns said, "he's—"

"Yes, I know," my aunt said. "What's his name?"

"Oh, uh . . . E. Foster Ballard." Harry Johns's attractive face had assumed a wary expression. It seemed the *Mikado*'s benefactor was unhappy about something.

He and Derek exchanged a quick look and Derek said, "He's a little old for it maybe but he's awfully good in the part. Is there a problem?"

My aunt gave what could only be described as a snort. "E. Foster. Well, well." She gave the photo another long look before handing it across to me. "No, no problem, 'course not."

But there was a pause before she reached for the

next one, and a tenseness in the muscles around her mouth that betrayed a more than passing emotion in connection with the face in the photo.

To the casual eye, I thought, it was not a particularly remarkable face. I judged the man to be in his sixties. Thinning grey hair combed straight back, pale, heavy-lidded eyes, fleshy cheeks, nose, and chin. Conveying in an infinitesimally raised eyebrow a message of superiority; in the tilted line of the closed lips one of self-satisfaction. In other words, a perfect Pooh-Bah. Had he been posing for this purpose, I wondered, or was this the authentic E. Foster Ballard? Had those pictured indications of a less than agreeable personality been enough to cause my aunt's reaction? I didn't think so. I thought she knew him.

However, she wasn't saying. And while consumed with curiosity, I certainly wasn't asking. Neither was Harry Johns nor Derek/Ko-Ko, who continued their thumbnail descriptions of each actor with only slightly dampened enthusiasm. My aunt continued to nod and make the occasional comment, but she was obviously distracted.

Perhaps a change of subject would lighten the atmosphere. I turned to Harry. "You'd probably be a good one to ask: is there a dance studio in town where I could take a class while I'm here?"

"Oh, certainly," he said, "there are several in the valley, I can give you some names—" He broke off, as if struck with a new idea. "I didn't know you were a dancer."

"Well, I'm not, really, not anymore, I just like to keep up . . . keep in shape, get some exercise—" I broke off in turn, annoyed at my own automatic response of ambivalence and defensiveness.

But the *Mikado*'s director wasn't listening, being absorbed in his own thought processes. "Then you probably know about fans—handling them, I mean."

"Yes," I admitted cautiously, "I know something."

Derek Bowles said with enthusiasm, "Oh, *super*. Because we've got all these marvelous Japanese fans and nobody seems to know what to do with them. *I* certainly don't."

Harry Johns leaned toward me. "Would you mind awfully coming to a rehearsal and giving us some pointers?"

A whiff of woodsy aftershave penetrated the gentle redolence of jasmine and musk that hung in the air. My sensory organs went on alert. I had wondered whether Harry and Derek were a couple, but something now told me that they were not.

I had been a widow for well over a year. I had loved my husband and he had been my only lover. Until a couple of months ago, I had thought that my sexual side had died with him. Then I had discovered, with some chagrin but more joy, that this was not the case. Since then I had found myself reacting with a sometimes embarrassing enthusiasm to those stimuli I had previously thought myself immune to. In other words, my grown-up self told me sternly, like a randy teenager. Fortunately, I told myself in return, I was a mature woman of discretion and common sense.

Harry Johns's eyes were a true grey with flecks of gold and green. I returned their gaze with my most mature and commonsensical expression. "Yes," I croaked, cleared my throat and started again. "Yes, I suppose I could do that. That is, if . . ." I turned to my aunt.

Portia, who had lost her distracted expression, was smiling broadly. "Great idea," she said. "Give Phoebe somep'n interestin' to do, make her want to stick around a while."

Oh Lord, what had I gotten myself into now?

4

Must have a beginning, you know.

"YOUR AUNTIE THOUGHT YOU WILL LIKE THIS ROOM," Anandi said. "It is nice and big, you see."

I put down my two suitcases, which I had only just prevented the tiny Anandi from attempting to carry up the stairs. The room was indeed big, with its own bay window—a twin, I judged, of the one in the living room below. There was a queen-size bed with a carved filigree headboard, a night table holding a white Princess phone, a dresser, a couple of comfortable-looking armchairs, and several small tables. Anandi skimmed across the room-size carpet—unless I was much mistaken, an antique Karistan—opening closet doors and demonstrating how to work the window curtains.

"And here, you see, is your own bathroom." Her voice was high and soft, the lilt of India giving it a special charm. I thought of what a contrast it made with my aunt's deep-voiced abruptness. She paused in front of me, hands folded at the waist of the green and gold sari. Head slightly cocked, she looked up at me (she barely came to my shoulder) as if awaiting with some anxiety a word of approval. Although her hair, parted in

the middle and pulled back into a thick coil, was still
only partially streaked with grey, her oval, nut-brown
face was deeply creased. But her dark eyes were clear
and bright, and full of intelligence. How old was
Anandi, I wondered? More to the point, *who* was she? It
seemed if I wanted the answer to that one, I'd have to
use the direct approach.

"The room is wonderful," I said. And then, "I'm
sorry, but I don't really know what your . . . um . . .
what you and my aunt—"

Anandi's high-pitched giggle rescued me. "Ah, your
Auntie Portia is not always so clear, am I right? I am
your aunt's sister-in-law. She has married my brother
Ram, oh, twenty . . . twenty-three years ago. Now he
has died, and so she has decided to come home. And
she has asked me to come with her."

"Then Aunt Portia's been living in India all this
time?"

"In India, yes. Mostly. At first in Italy, that is where
we met, in Italy."

Evidently she considered that with this all had been
explained, because she glanced at the slender silver
watch that encircled her small wrist and said, "We are
having our supper in an hour. In the kitchen. You will
find it down the stairs and then to the back," gesturing.
She started toward the door, hesitated and came back
to me. Her head made its characteristic tilt. "You must
understand, Phoebe, that your Auntie Portia is very,
very glad that you are here. I say this only because I
know her so well, and I know that she is not always so
easily letting her feelings show."

She nodded once or twice and then went quickly
out the door. Wait! I wanted to cry. *Italy?* And where
was Portia for the twenty-some years before that?
What was this Mr. Ram Singh's business and where
did all the money come from? And India? My mind
boggled at the image of Aunt Portia as a member of
an Indian household, which in my understanding

involved a good deal of feminine subservience. And why had she returned to her girlhood home and what was the relationship with the E. Foster Ballard whose photo had so discomposed her? And what, finally, was she expecting from me?

Well, I thought, I will simply have that many more questions for my Aunt Portia.

But it was not to be—at least not yet.

We sat, the three of us, at one end of an immense oak table in the big, old-fashioned kitchen. Old-fashioned, that is, except for a six-burner stainless steel range, matching double sink, and black-fronted dishwasher. Otherwise, I thought, the room probably looked much as it had a hundred years ago. Dark, waist-high wainscotting; cupboards in the same dark-stained wood lining the high walls—so high that Anandi, I imagined, would have a stretch even to reach the lowest shelf; an ancient Welsh dresser painted green. At some point the countertops had been layered with that newfangled linoleum, but the pine flooring had escaped the march of progress and lay scrubbed and bare.

Off a small, square mudroom, a half-glassed door gave access to the backyard and a garage. On the wall beside the opening to the mudroom hung a black chalkboard, listing, in bold capitals:

MILK—<u>NOT SKIM</u>
<u>EARL GREY</u> TEA
OREOS

And in a smaller and less aggressive hand:

    lettuce
    carrots
    wheat flour

My aunt was already ensconced when I arrived, in a large padded wooden chair at the head of the table. Her left arm now rested in the white sling. A no-nonsense four-pronged metal cane stood nearby. Even so, I thought, she must need a good deal of help with bathing, dressing, getting in and out of bed. Since I'd seen no evidence of any other resident caretaker, I assumed that Anandi must be stronger than she looked. At least, I thought, here was an area where I might make myself useful.

But I was given no chance either to make that offer or to talk about much of anything else except myself: my childhood, marriage, travels, and, in detail, the events of the past summer in which I had been involved with two murders that had caught the attention of the national press.

By the time I had completed that narrative, the lamb curry, rice, and chipatis had been consumed, and Aunt Portia was beginning to look a little pinched around the nostrils. My offer to do the dishes was gently but firmly refused ("we have, you see, a dishwasher"). But I was allowed to help my aunt from her chair and, with Anandi, accompany her slow progress, leaning with her one good arm on the cane, from the kitchen to the room at the front of the house which was serving as her temporary bedroom.

At the door she straightened and said to me, "Didn't invite you here to be my nursemaid. Anandi can take over now." She reached her hand to touch my cheek—the first gesture of physical affection she had offered. "Glad you came, Phoebe. Hope you'll stay. Long as you want, y'know. Okay, Anandi, let's do it."

She turned, bent again to the cane and thumped her way across the threshold and into the room. Anandi, murmuring a soft "Good night," closed the door.

·   ·   ·

It had been arranged that Harry Johns would pick me up the next evening to take me to the rehearsal of *The Mikado.* I had assumed that Aunt Portia and I would spend the day getting acquainted, but again I was mistaken. The physical therapist, it seemed, would not be put off a second day and the Visiting Nurse was also scheduled to make an appearance. "Tiresome people," my aunt informed me over the breakfast table, "but the doc's threatened to put me back into rehab. So they come and hassle me for two hours and then I'm wiped out and have to rest."

She reached into the right pocket of a voluminous robe in threadbare burgundy silk that looked as if it originally came from some Large and Tall Men's department, and produced a set of keys which she handed to me. "Here, Phoebe, take my car. Ought to be driven, been sittin' in the garage too long. Get a look at the country. 'Sposed to be peak season, shouldn't miss it."

Well, that was true enough. Like yesterday, the weather was near perfect—brilliantly sunny with a delicious bite in the air. Okay, if that's what Aunt Portia wanted. But I promised myself that after today I would *not* be put off any longer.

Walking briskly, I followed the driveway back behind the house to the two-car garage, and was reaching my hand to the door handle when I collided with a bear that had appeared without warning from around the corner. I yelped. The bear stepped back and began to apologize profusely. I now saw that the bear was in actuality a large bearded man wearing a fuzzy brown pullover sweater.

"I *am* so sorry," the Bear said yet again. He reached down to retrieve the keys I'd dropped, handed them to me, and stood irresolutely running a hand through a thicket of black hair, causing it to stand up in peaks. "I didn't hurt you, did I?"

He looked so truly distressed that I bit back any remark I might have been going to make about people
who go barging around corners without looking. "No,
really, I'm fine. Just startled."

I turned back to the garage door, but the Bear fore-
stalled me by grabbing the handle and heaving the door
up on its metal runners until it came to rest with a
clang. "You see, I rent half the garage from Portia . . .
Mrs. Singh." He stuck out his hand. "Ben Solliday."

"Phoebe Mullins. I'm Portia's niece."

"Ah, yes. I've looked forward to meeting you." He
smiled, the grey-streaked beard parting to show a nice
set of normal-size, unbearlike teeth. "But not exactly
like this."

"Yes . . . well . . . I'm taking Aunt Portia's car out." I
looked at the two vehicles sitting side by side: a silver
Subaru station wagon and a brown Porsche. Again, my
aunt had been skimpy with details. Judging her to be a
practical person and one not given to status symbols, I
headed for the wagon.

The Bear watched as I backed the car cautiously out
and around and started down the driveway. When I
glanced into the rearview mirror he was still standing
there, staring after me.

So Mr. Tubby drove a Porsche. The less attractive
side of Phoebe, nose still smarting from the collision
with two hundred and fifty pounds of careless male,
wondered for what, exactly, he was compensating.

Harry Johns was not chatty as we drove to the rehearsal
that evening. I wondered if he was regretting having
asked a virtually unknown entity who claimed to be a
dancer to horn in on his territory. I knew something
about how jealously the various members of a performance company guarded each sphere of authority,
however small. Especially, God knew, the director. It
would be "his company," "his actors," "his production."

Well, Mr. Johns needn't worry. I had no intention of doing anything more than giving a brief demonstration of fan technique and then dropping quickly from the scene.

On the theory, though, that people respond better to Authority wearing the right uniform, I had dressed accordingly: black leggings and a green silk overshirt cinched with a narrow silver belt, character shoes, hair held back with a green print scarf, and one of my favorite pieces of clothing, a swirly loden green wool cape. Harry Johns, at any rate, had reacted appreciatively. Perhaps on the same theory, he was wearing jeans, a tweed jacket with elbow patches, and a faded-blue shirt with a paisley ascot tucked jauntily into its open neck.

We had been driving for a minute or two past the Smith College campus—brick dorms appropriately ivy-draped, a white chapel with a soaring spire, a pair of grey stone pillars—when he reached up to give his right earlobe a pull, then said, "Have you ever been involved with a community theater before?"

I considered. School productions. A South American tour with a minor opera company early in Mick's conducting career. Last summer, the Varovna Opera Colony which, while essentially a school, was on a pretty professional level.

"No, I suppose I haven't. Why, is it so different? As in really mediocre?"

The director shook his head vigorously. "No, thank God, in this case the quality's very good. All these colleges to draw from." He brought the car to a stop at a crosswalk where a gaggle of students was negotiating a passage across Elm Street. "And there are a number of professionals around who've opted out of the strains of the big time either for academia—like me, I teach at a community college nearby—or just for the area itself. It's one of the best small arts communities in the country, you know."

The car moved on and I waited for the "but." He didn't disappoint me.

"But I've been surprised at the amount of . . . um . . . personality clash and—oh, you know, prima-donna behavior. It seems there's a good deal of history between some of the cast members."

I couldn't see any significant difference here with any professional company, and said so.

He glanced over at me, the thin lips parted over small, even teeth in a wry smile. "I guess my problem is how to deal with it. In a professional situation you can fire people—God knows there'll be a dozen hungry actors falling over themselves to jump in. Or in school you can hold a bad grade over their heads. Here you have to establish authority without any kind of threat to back it up. Doesn't sound nice, I know, but that's the truth."

I had visions of a company in anarchy, every actor his own director, every actress a mistress of upstaging. I was torn between wanting to give Harry's curly head a sympathetic ruffle and wondering if I had been recruited for some more complicated purpose than the stated one. "Heavens," I said, "is it that bad?"

"No, no, no," the director said hastily, with another sideways glance. "I'm exaggerating, sorry." Perhaps, I thought, he had suddenly remembered that I was the niece of the company's financial backer. I hadn't heard him express any of these concerns to Aunt Portia. "Mostly it's going fine," he went on, "good people, very cooperative. Problem is, it only takes a few." He paused. "Actually, it only takes one."

Another pause, another sideways look, another pull on the ear. Then he said, a shade too casually, "I thought Portia . . . um . . . may have recognized one of the actors. When we were looking at the photos?"

Yes, I had thought so too.

"I thought she seemed . . . disturbed. Would you have any idea what that was about?"

"None at all," I said. "You have to remember, I hardly know my aunt. We've only just met, and she hasn't been exactly forthcoming with personal information. But I like her a lot," I added, wanting to make clear where I stood.

"Oh, absolutely," Harry Johns said. "Portia's a re-markable lady. Well, here we are."

We had pulled up in what appeared to be a mixed business and residential neighborhood on the other side of the Smith campus and not far from downtown Main Street. A large rectangular three-story building of dark red brick looked as if it had once been a factory. Now a sign out front announced it as Riverview Apartments as well as listing a number of doctors' and lawyers' offices. Farther along on the same side of the street was a ram-bling, white-clapboard house with a big wraparound porch, badly in need of a paint job.

Between these and set diagonally to the street was another red brick building with a wooden, peak-roofed tower, and more angles than you'd have thought a structure that size could cram in. Beyond a narrow front, where a flight of stone steps led up to an arched, green-painted double door, walls veered off in an ex-travagance of planes, corners, crooks, and bulges. Atop this agglomeration, pink-tiled roofs of various slants el-bowed each other, jostling for air space. In a wall to the left, a fifteen-foot-high stained glass window, depicting a biblical scene I couldn't immediately identify, pro-claimed the building's ecclesiastical origins.

"Wow!" I said. "What a marvelous place for a the-ater!"

"Isn't it, though!" Harry said. After jockeying the car into a minuscule space at the curb, he had done me the courtesy of assuming I was capable of opening a car door on my own while he rummaged in the Honda's backseat. Now he joined me on the sidewalk. Under one arm was a jumble of notebooks, clipboards, and a score of *The Mikado,* under the other a motley collection of umbrellas. "For practice," he explained, "until we get the parasols."

Lights glowing through the big window, and a size-able collection of cars crammed bumber to bumper on both sides of the street indicated that the *Mikado* company was gathered and awaiting its director.

So here I am again, I thought, the outsider about to be thrust among a group of strangers. How many times had I played out the role? Hundreds, surely. The groups might vary—symphony boards of directors, moneyed patrons of the arts, music school faculties, community cultural organizations—but the process was the same. First the identification ("That's the daughter." "She's the wife—the one in black"), then the sizing up, friendly or hostile or dismissive, depending on individual tempera-ment. On the part of the outsider, a conscientious as-sumption of the cordial smile, the gracious interest in listening and responding to the same observations and questions as on the like occasion two days ago or last week or the days and weeks stretching back and back. "Oh yes, my father/husband and I are enjoying being in (fill in the blank) so much. Such a very beautiful/inter-esting/exciting town/city/country." "The travel? Well, it does get tiring but it's also so . . . um . . . stimulating, you know." "Your daughter plays the piano/cello/glock-enspiel/tuba? You must be very proud. Well, I'm sure the maestro would be . . . but unfortunately we have to leave first thing in the morning."

Because of course my real function at these affairs— basically my function in life—had been the guidance and protection of the artist of the moment. To this end I made it my business to learn all I could ahead of time about who was who and what was what. Thus equipped, I could drop a discreet whisper of reminder as to the name of our host; warn against inquiries about spouses either divorced or dead since last we passed this way; identify the Really Important People who would require at least a minimum of kowtowing; make sure gratitude was expressed (by me if no one else) not only to the glitter couple nominally responsible for the event's success but also to the quiet woman in the corner who had done all the real work.

This time, though, I had only brief glimpses of some photographed faces, an introduction to one other company member, and Harry's rather amorphous misgivings to go by. As we walked together up the path toward the steps and the green double doors, I felt the familiar small thrill of nervousness, the momentary quick stiffening of the backbone. Yes, here I was again. Only now I was no longer simply an adjunct to the main event. Now I *was* the event.

The circumstance was new enough still to take me by surprise.

5

If you want to know who we are . . .

"OH, EXCELLENT!" I EXCLAIMED, AS EIGHT LARGE YELLOW fans wielded by eight masculine hands snapped open in unison.

The wielders exchanged gratified glances, and a flurry of applause came from the remainder of the company scattered among the pews of the Old Church Theater. Derek Bowles, perched on the back of a second row pew, grinned and gave me a thumbs up. He was wearing a pink-and-white-striped pullover and looked, given the setting, like an anorexic cherub.

What had Harry Johns been talking about? From the moment of the director's brief and businesslike introduction of "the fan expert," to our present triumph of synchronism, all had been geniality and cooperation. Any discomfort I might have felt from the initial curious scrutiny of twenty-some pairs of eyes had quickly dissipated in the hands-on practicality of fan management. The chorus of eight "gentlemen of Japan," ranging in age, I estimated, from late teens to early fifties, had responded with enthusiasm, and here we were.

Here I was, too, really getting into it. "Hey, it might

be a nice effect, for variety, to do them in sequence: you know, snap, snap, snap. That is . . ." I looked to Harry, sitting in the front pew.

"Sure, sounds great. Try it."

I faced the gentlemen again. "Okay, on my count, starting at that end. One" (snap), "two" (snap), "three . . ."

A whooshing and then a thudding noise startled me into turning around. The sound had come from the opening and closing of the heavy swinging doors leading from the lobby into the theater proper. "Mr. Director," said a voice which carried easily over the considerable distance to the stage, "I'm late, and I *do* apologize. Oh, sorry, don't let me interrupt."

Since the speaker had already done just that—and could easily have seen exactly what was going on through the window set at eye-level in each door—the speech struck me as more than a little fatuous. A woman sitting by herself in a pew to my left muttered to no one in particular, "If we knew *you* were coming we'd've baked a cake." She was a generously proportioned lady in her fifties, defiantly strawberry blond and with a humorous, intelligent face. I recognized her from her photo—it was the actress playing the elderly Katisha.

The new arrival sauntered down the middle aisle, divesting himself as he did so of a navy blue cashmere topcoat and grey silk scarf. Under these he wore a navy blazer and sky blue turtleneck pullover with grey slacks. The pullover had to do some stretching to cover a pronounced paunch. I noted the smooth, fleshy face, eyelids at half-mast, the expression that said, "I am here." Pooh-Bah had entered the building.

He had been eyeing me as he progressed, and having reached the front pew he said, "Well, well!" and raised an inquiring eyebrow at Harry. The director, who had an air of holding himself severely in check, explained my connection and my mission. Pooh-Bah extended a plump and manicured hand which, standing as I did on a platform some four feet above him, I had to bend over to grasp. "Delightful," he said. "Dear Portia's niece. Imagine that!" His eyes, I realized, were fixed on the V neck of my green silk shirt. I resisted an urge to direct the toe of my shoe to the tip of his chin and settled for straightening up quickly enough to send him slightly off balance. He didn't so much as blink, but dropped into the seat next to Harry and intoned, with a gracious wave of the hand, "So sorry to interrupt, do carry on."

But the momentum was gone. The Gentlemen of Japan tried gamely to follow my count, but although they got close it never quite came together. Finally I said apologetically to Harry, "Well, with practice . . . you might want to use it."

"Absolutely," Harry said. "It's a great idea, we'll work it in, I'm sure."

"Not *quite* the Rockettes," Pooh-Bah observed, and then laughed as heartily as if he'd said something truly clever. To my surprise, his laughter was echoed by a handful of others. Evidently His Pooh-Bahness had his adherents among the company. I couldn't imagine why.

Harry, after thanking me warmly, now took the rehearsal in hand. He moved a few rows back, and a frizzy-haired young woman with a clipboard and either a bad cold or a chronic smoker's hack took up a position beside him. I drifted off to a back pew feeling dissatisfied, not to say resentful. I had just started to enjoy myself, and now it was over. Well, wasn't that what I'd wanted? Get in, do my duty by my aunt Portia and the nice director, and get out. Yeah, but . . .

Anyway, removed from my instructional role I now had a chance to take in my surroundings, and I did so.

The interior of the Old Church Theater carried out the promise of its quirky outside. The floor of the gently curving sanctuary sloped at an angle of about fifteen degrees down to the former chancel, now the stage. Four sections of pews, stained a dark mahogany and equipped with red velveteen cushions, rested on successive levels which, at the aisles that separated them, formed broad and shallow sets of red-carpeted stairs. A second immense stained glass window balanced on the opposite wall the one I had glimpsed from the outside. Now I could see that one depicted Christ as The Good Shepherd; the other The Prodigal Son. Nurturing and forgiveness, I thought; a church I could have warmed to.

The sanctuary walls were wainscotted in the same dark color as the pews to a height of about six feet. Beyond this, white plaster intersected by curved beams swept upward to a shallow dome painted gold and blue. From this hung three gilded chandeliers with candle-shaped bulbs which worked on rheostat switches located at one side of the swinging doors. (When Harry and I had first come in, the couple of dozen bulbs in each fixture were ablaze. He had lowered them with a muttered, "These guys seem to think God's paying the electric bill.")

Behind where I sat, pillars supported an ornately carved balcony which I assumed to have once served as a choirloft. If there had been an organ there was no sign of one now. I wondered where it might have gone, and how long ago, and what had caused the congregation who had worshipped here to give up a building which had been raised (seventy-five, a hundred years ago?) with such an evidently loving, not to say lavish, hand.

Whatever the case, its present transformation into a theater had been accomplished with remarkably little modification. The obligatory red EXIT lights had been installed over the main entrance and the panic-bar-equipped outside doors on both sides of the auditorium. The stage area, some thirty feet across, had been built to curve out into a modified thrust. On it were scattered several small platforms of various sizes and heights. Black masking flats delineated the back and sides of the playing space; beyond these I glimpsed a couple of doors that presumably led to areas that could be used for costume room, scene shop, and dressing rooms. A baby grand piano stood below the lip of the platform at stage right. It was presided over by a tall young woman with dark red hair that fell in Burne-Jones ripples halfway down her back. Theatrical lights were hung on four tall standards at the sides of the hall and along the railing of the balcony. Otherwise the church appeared to be in pretty much its original condition. A certain mustiness lingered in the air, as from cushions and carpeting left too long unheated, and the white plaster walls could do with a coat of paint. But structurally the building appeared sound, and must be so if public performances were being permitted.

Even so, lekos, Fresnels, and spots, lumber for the stage, heat and electricity would not come cheap. Let alone sets and costumes. And surely Harry Johns was getting paid, and probably the music director. How much of this outlay, I wondered, represented the contribution of my aunt Portia?

The frizzy-haired cougher, clutching her clipboard importantly, had been making some announcements inaudible to me. Now the redhead at the piano was calling everyone up to the stage for a vocal warm-up. Actually, I thought, there was nothing to stop me from slipping quietly away and walking home. The evening was clear, my cape was plenty warm, the exercise would do me good.

I was in the act of rising from my seat when an interesting bit of byplay caught my eye. A set of steps stage left gave access to the platform from the floor of the auditorium. As the cast members converged on it, creating the inevitable jam, Pooh-Bah and Katisha came face-to-face at the bottom step. Pooh-Bah made an exaggerated bow and waited for Katisha to go first. It would have been a more effective gesture if he hadn't at the time had an avuncular arm around the shoulders of a willowy blonde who looked to be several years under the age of consent. Katisha glared, mouthed a short comment, and stomped up the steps. My lipreading skills were good enough to be pretty sure the words "damn fool" figured in her remark.

Almost immediately, Derek Bowles, who had vaulted neatly onto the stage without benefit of stairs, appeared at Katisha's elbow, smoothly steered her away from the egregious Pooh-Bah and said something to her in an undertone that made her laugh.

I settled back down. Like the Elephant's Child, I am cursed with a " 'satiable curiosity" about the vagaries of human behavior. The potential before me was too rich to resist.

I began trying to identify the members of the company. On stage, besides the principals, were some fifteen or so chorus people, but I should be able to pick out the ones whose photos I'd seen. The willowy blond jailbait, for instance, that was definitely Yum-Yum. Flanking her were the other two Little Maids. One was a chunky, dark girl with enormous eyes, about the same age as the blonde; the other a wiry little woman at least a couple of decades older: Pitti-Sing and Peep-Bo, though I wasn't sure which was which.

There was the Korean Nanki-Poo, slim, serious, wearing glasses with thick black rims and exuding sex appeal. Although the cast were now, under the direction of the redhead, running through one of the choral numbers and therefore supposed to be grouped according to vocal category, at least three members of the female chorus had jumped ship and hovered in limpetlike proximity to various facets of the Nanki-Poo anatomy.

A stocky middle-aged man with a goatee and a hairline that had receded about as far as it could go I recognized as Pish-Tush.

Pooh-Bah . . . Ko-Ko . . . Katisha . . . yes, that completed the roster of principals. Except for the Mikado of Japan himself, who appeared to be absent—no doubt because the character doesn't appear until Act II and hadn't been called for this rehearsal.

And so what? Why was I taking all this trouble? It wasn't as if I were going to be seeing these people again . . .

Who was the redhead at the piano? Evidently the musical director, and she had prepared the singers well, but she looked awfully young—surely not more than college age. In the few words I'd heard her speak, I thought I'd detected a slight British accent. A sense of familiarity tickled at my consciousness and then retreated. I knew I'd never seen her before.

"Okay, men's chorus, Pish-Tush, opening number," Harry said. "Try to remember the staging we set last time and bring the fans open on"—he consulted his copy of the score—"the measure before 'We figure in lively paint.' I'll cue you."

The stage cleared, the men's chorus secreted themselves behind the back masking flats, then entered to the lively piano introduction, took their poses, and sang lustily: "If you want to know who we are, We are gentlemen of Japan." And by golly, at the appropriate measure, on Harry's jabbing his hand in the air eight fans flared open with one jaunty accord. Harry grinned back at me. I beamed. The Gentlemen carried on with only an occasional false step, following the movements their director had set, and I began to fidget. So much more could be done with those fans. There . . . right there, they should be closed . . . then held just so . . . then a pose straight front . . . ah well, I could hardly interfere . . .

"Phoebe?" Harry's voice startled me and I jumped guiltily. But here he was gesturing me to join him—"I'm sure you have some ideas about this choreography— not really my forte." And here I was sitting beside him, making my suggestions, jumping up to demonstrate, having a glorious time, while the Cougher shot me baleful looks.

We worked together well enough and with enough dispatch so that we managed in the next hour to sketch out two more numbers, and Harry called a break. The oldest Little Maid—Pitti-Sing, as I now knew—with the help of Nanki-Poo and several hangers-on, trundled out from the region behind the stage a cart holding an industrial-size coffee urn, paper cups, mugs, and two plates of cookies.

It was quickly surrounded. Harry gallantly braved the crush and brought coffee and two cookies apiece to the Cougher and me, then went off to speak to the musical director. Thus mollified, the Cougher became a fraction more cordial. She turned toward me a face strongly reminiscent of the Andrews Sister with the biggest mouth. "Jane Manypenny makes the cookies," she volunteered.

"Manypenny?'

"Pitti-Sing. And does the coffee and all, and cleans up. I mean, as Harry's assistant I'd be happy to do it, we're all doing a bunch of different jobs. But she seems to enjoy it, you know? Like, she's the kind of person who has to be doing something *every minute*." She turned aside to deliver a particularly violent and phlegmy series of hacks. "Sorry," she said, "I've had this thing for *weeks*. From the pollen, you know, it's not contagious."

Maybe not, but it sure was disgusting. To make up for which unkind thought, I searched for something pleasant to say. "That's a pretty coffee mug," I offered, "is it your special one?"

The Cougher looked gratified at having her yellow polka dots admired. "Yeah, we mostly bring our own. It's better than drinking out of paper." She pointed at the cup in my hand, blue with the legend in white, "Directors Do It With Gestures." "That one's Harry's."

Which seemed to remind her of her original grievance with me, because she got up abruptly, moved away, and began talking in undertones to a passing chorus member.

Since I had been putting out a good deal of energy

over the past hour, I sat and rested and sipped my
coffee and wondered where, in my own case, all this
was leading.

That hour had expanded my knowledge of at least
several of the *Mikado* cast. Nanki-Poo, I'd learned, pos-
sessed a sweet, light tenor, perfect for G&S. If his acting
was a tad stiff, no female in the audience over the age
of six was going to give a damn.

The balding Pish-Tush was one of those workhorses of
the theater: always reliable, always letter-perfect, always
adequate, always unexciting. I wondered if he knew, or if
he minded. He seemed to be enjoying himself.

The blond and nubile Yum-Yum had a small, effort-
less soprano and a personality that appeared to consist
of being the prettiest girl in her vicinity—any vicinity.
Her sidekick and evident acolyte, the stocky teenager
playing Peep-Bo, had twice the vivacity and three times
the appeal and would probably take years to discover
the fact. I sighed for the pain of being seventeen.

Pitti-Sing, whom I now knew as Jane Manypenny,
was the only member of the cast attempting an English
accent. To me it sounded way over the top and out of
place and I wondered why Harry wasn't telling her to
stop it. No doubt if I did end up hanging around for a
while I'd find out.

I hadn't gotten much of a look at Derek Bowles's Ko-
Ko, as Harry had been skipping around to the big ensemble numbers. I also had the impression that at least
for the moment Derek was keeping his performance
under wraps. At the very least, he and Katisha would
make a comic visual image, she being at least a head
taller.

But the real revelation had been Pooh-Bah. Pooh-Bah
represented the definitive meeting of role and personality,
a triumph of typecasting. Every sneer, every pomposity,
every hypocrisy rolled from him as if he were coining the
words on the spot. And yet . . . and yet . . . I had to be fair.
This E. Foster Ballard was also a consummate actor.

Timing, projection, body control—he had them all. As well as musicality and a strong, if past-its-prime, baritone. It made for an interesting dilemma: how self-aware was Mr. Ballard? Did he recognize how genuine a Pooh-Bah he was? Was it conceivable he was actually capable of laughing at himself?

At any rate, my mind was set at rest on one point. I had been wondering what made Harry Johns put up with the creep. Now I knew.

Harry called "five minutes." That wiry little bundle of energy Jane Manypenny whisked away the trolley holding the coffee urn, the used mugs, and empty plates. And shortly the company was launching into a musical run-through of the first act finale. I thought someone was missing, and then noticed Jane, drying her hands on a piece of paper towel, slip in from backstage just in time to deliver Pitti-Sing's first two solo lines.

A choral section came next, and then Pooh-Bah began his solo: "As in a month you've got to die, if Ko-Ko tells us true . . ." Something's wrong, I thought, why is he so pale? He soldiered on with the next line, however: " 'Twere empty compliment to cry, 'Long life to Nanki-Poo' . . ." then broke off, frowning, put a hand to his forehead, and was suddenly and hugely sick all over the sky blue turtleneck, the floor, and the shoes of those unlucky enough to be standing nearby.

In the ensuing hubbub no one, of course, including me, gave a thought to those distinctive and individual coffee mugs. The mugs which now, owing to the ministrations of the compulsive Jane Manypenny, sat sparkling clean in a rack in the Old Church's utility room. Those thoughts would come later.

6

Why, who are you who ask this question?

THERE WERE SIX OF US IN THE HIGH-BACKED WOODEN booth at Sam's, a downtown Northampton pizzeria and bar. It was an old-fashioned place, dark-paneled, wood-floored, dim-lit, smelling of oregano and cheese and beer and—but no, something was missing. Ah yes, of course. The blue haze and consoling aroma of tobacco smoke. No smoking, I'd been told, in Northampton restaurants. An initiative I applauded, and yet . . . I was beginning to think that living in an atmosphere of such exemplary purity might be a tad taxing to the merely mortal.

I sat between Harry Johns and Derek Bowles. Across from us were Katisha, Pish-Tush, and a member of the female chorus called Irene. In a booth across the room, Nanki-Poo and the red-haired pianist had just been joined by several other members of the company. I caught the redhead's look of annoyance as she scooted over to make room for the new arrivals. Yum-Yum and Peep-Bo were not among them. Peep-Bo's father had arrived on the dot of nine-thirty to collect the two teenagers—the only terms, Harry had told me, under which they'd been allowed to participate at all.

For the umpteenth time, Harry Johns said, "But what could it have *been*? He'd been perfectly fine and then . . ."

"Barf city," Katisha said gaily. With one purple finger-nail she tucked a stray lock into her blowsy pile of pinkish hair and with the other hand poured the re-mainder of a bottle of beer into her glass. "Poor old Foster, the *last* thing he'd want. His precious dignity smashed all to hell, and in front of the teenyboppers, too. Tsk, tsk." She raised the glass and took a large swig. "To say nothing," she went on with satisfaction, "of falling prey to the Manypenny."

For it had been Jane Manypenny, a veritable steam-roller of solicitousness, who had led the unhappy Pooh-Bah to a seat on one of the stage platforms, who had flown to produce wet towels to press on the stricken brow, who had sponged his clothes, who had insisted, despite his feeble but heartfelt protests, on driving him home.

"Oh come on, Lydia," Derek Bowles protested, "you have to feel a little sorry for the guy."

"Nope," said Katisha. She winked at me, then reached out her hand. "These boors you're with never introduced us properly. Lydia Hicks."

I smiled and shook the proffered hand. "Phoebe Mullins."

"And," she went on, "this handsome fella practically sitting in my lap and trying to pretend he doesn't have the hots for me is Carl Piquette. Carl's a scientist. Teaches all those little dears at the high school. Have to watch out for scientists, Phoebe. 'Sposed to be so cere-bral, but what they are, my dear, is *of the earth, earthy*. Right, Carl?"

"Whatever you say, Lyd," Pish-Tush replied with equanimity. His eyes, in an otherwise unremarkable face, were a very clear blue. Their look, as they met mine across the table, was friendly. "And this multi-talent," he said, putting an arm around the woman named Irene, "not only sings but she's our costumer and prop person. She's responsible for scaring up those fans you were working with."

The costumer had been sitting quietly, sipping a ginger ale and seeming to pay close and grave attention to everything that was said. She was a fair, plump woman of about forty with small, neat features. She wore a full skirt and embroidered peasant blouse that might have been resuscitated from the days of the hootenanny. Her cornstalk-blond hair, streaked with silver, was pulled back into a single thick braid. At the braid's end was a tiny blue and white bouquet made of silk flowers.

She smiled now for the first time since we had sat down, and said, "Hi, Phoebe, I'm Irene Polaski. That was lovely, what you did with the fans. Welcome aboard."

"Oh, well, I'm not really—"

"Don't!" cried Derek Bowles. He grabbed my arm. "Don't say it! You can't desert us now, when you see how we need you!"

On my other side, Harry said, "It *would* be great, Phoebe, if you could hang in for a while at least."

I turned to him. "You," I said, "have got to be the least ego-ridden director I've ever known. Or else the most secure. You really want me meddling on your turf?"

Harry Johns grinned. "Call it saving my bacon. I've never done Gilbert and Sullivan before, I'm not much of a musician and I'm sure as hell no choreographer. You, Ms. Mullins, are a goddam answer to prayer."

I didn't voice the obvious, which was why, then, he had taken on the job, but I must have looked it.

"I roped him in," Derek Bowles said, "because I knew him and knew he could do it. Don't be fooled by all that modesty, Phoebe, Harry's a terrific comedy director. And of course Nadine's a wonder." He nodded toward the redhead in the booth across the room. "And now we have a choreographer to die for—" he held up both hands with fingers crossed—"it's almost scary how well everything is coming together."

"Ah," I said, "then it's you who's the mover and shaker—producer, is it?"

"Mover and shaker indeed," said Lydia Hicks, who had been murmuring to Pish-Tush during the foregoing and now turned back to us. "Don't know how he does it. Our very own tiny tornado."

"Dear, wonderful Lydia," Derek Bowles shot back. "Always *so* descriptive."

He turned away from her with some deliberation, and said to me, with his tilted smile, "Responsible as charged. All my own idea. Came up here to visit Harry, loved the town, saw the church—said 'My God, what a great place for a theater!' Got a bunch of people interested, your wonderful aunt among them . . . and voila!"

"Then this is the first production?" I said, surprised. "And by the way, how did you meet—"

"Oh, there you are!" Jane Manypenny had appeared at the end of our booth, bringing with her an atmosphere, which I was beginning to realize was permanent with her, of crisis barely controlled. I hadn't seen her up close before and was surprised at what a pretty woman she was: round-faced under a smooth cap of auburn hair, with dark-lashed green eyes and piquantly snubbed nose. Only two permanently etched vertical lines between her brows spoiled the ingenue effect. She said in hushed tones, "I thought you chaps would be here. I just wanted to let you know that Dr. Ballard is going to be *perfectly fine.*"

My question about why Harry hadn't told Jane Manypenny to lose the exaggerated British accent had its answer: that *was* her accent.

"Whoop-de-do," observed Katisha.

Jane, who had been addressing herself to Derek Bowles, gave Lydia Hicks a small forgiving smile accompanied by a gentle head shake. She turned back to

Derek. "By the time I got him home he was actually *quite* recovered. Quite chipper. He didn't even want me to come in, but of course I wasn't going to just *leave* him there. But he insisted he was feeling quite the thing again, so I only stayed a short time."

"Thank you, Jane," Derek said with warmth, "that was good of you. And thanks for letting us know. Hey, won't you join us? Pull up a chair?"

"Oh no," Jane said quickly, "I have to be at my office early tomorrow and then at five I have one of my groups at the hospital and then the rehearsal, of course. Thanks awfully anyway."

She started away and then came back. "Dr. Ballard has *no notion* what made him sick." And then somewhat defensively, "It couldn't have been the biscuits, everybody ate those."

"Of course not, Jane, nobody thought—" Derek began. But Jane Manypenny was already walking away toward the door.

"*Doctor* Ballard?" I said.

"*Ohhh* yes," Lydia Hicks said. "*Biiig* doctor. *Biiig* pediatrician." She was well into her third bottle of beer and the contours of her face were taking on a slightly melted look.

I couldn't help it. *"Pediatrician?"*

Lydia cackled. "Hard to believe, huh? 'Course he's been retired for ten years. When he started out, there were enough women still around who fell for the Big Smart Doctor Knows Best act." Her voice deepened in an uncanny imitation of Pooh-Bah's orotund and patronizing tones. " 'Now, little mother, you just leave it all to me and don't worry that pretty head.' If the kids didn't like him, what did they know? And ol' Foster, he didn't have a clue. Thought he was wonderful with children, couldn't tell the difference between an awestruck kid and a kid that was scared to death. Know where his own kids are now? One in Alaska, two in California. Think he makes the connection? Not a chance."

My glance had chanced to stray toward Irene Polaski during this mini-tirade. Her light, round eyes were fixed as if on a scene far from the convivial hum and funk of Sam's pizzeria and bar. For a moment I thought I saw them fill with tears. But then she blinked and came back, and I decided it must have been a trick of the light.

Nevertheless, a change of subject seemed like a good idea.

"What is Jane Manypenny's background?" I asked. "Has she been over here long?"

Carl Piquette chuckled. "Don't let the accent fool you. Janey's been around for years."

"Sounding more like Bertie Wooster with each one that passes," Lydia put in. " 'Biscuits,' for gawd's sake. Y'd think she never heard of a cookie. Her little gesture of defiance to us colonials in favor of Queen and Country."

Irene Polaski said in her quiet voice, "Jane has a good heart, Lydia. She really does try to help people. Even if," with a wry twist of the lips, "her judgment isn't always . . ."

"As in all that fawning over the Great Doctor?" Lydia said, with real venom. "Being a pompous ass prob'ly qualifies 'im as an honorary Brit to our Janey."

Carl Piquette put a hand on her arm. "Come on, Lyd. When you start ragging on Foster it's past time to go home."

Katisha batted her eyes. "When you say 'home' . . . ? Nah, I know. 'Home' as in drop old Lyd off at her house and run back to the wife and kiddies. Ah Carl, Carl, if you only knew what you're missing!" But she was already shrugging into her coat and it was obvious her heart was no longer in it.

"Phoebe Mullins?"

I looked up, startled, and at first had to struggle to place the large and solid presence standing hesitantly by the booth. Then I remembered—of course, the Bear who shared Aunt Portia's garage.

The Bear smiled widely. "I thought that was you!" He wore a brown corduroy jacket over a striped shirt. At the shirt's open neck tufts of dark chest hair seemed to be attempting a rendezvous with the beard just inches above. I was aware of Katisha staring with unabashed approval at the new arrival. Myself, I had never fancied the massive and hairy type, but the Bear had seemed like a nice enough guy.

"Hello," I said, "I'm . . . uh . . . sorry, I don't remember your name."

"Ben. Ben Solliday."

"Oh yes, of course." I made the introductions, and explained about *The Mikado*.

The Bear nodded. "Ah, Gilbert and Sullivan," he said. Something in his tone told me that Mr. Solliday was not an enthusiast.

But he also didn't seem in a hurry to leave. Ever genial, Derek Bowles said, "Will you sit down?"

"No, no," the Bear said, "I'm here with . . . um . . ." he waved a vague hand toward another part of the room, "that is . . . um . . . no, but thanks, some other time maybe," and with another nod he took himself off.

Lydia Hicks said, without rancor but with a certain edge, "Phoebe, just how long have you been in this town, anyway?"

I had to think back. It didn't seem credible, but, "A day and a half," I told her.

She raised her eyebrows. "Hunh!" was her only comment. Then, "Come on Carl, take me home. I'm obviously out of my league."

I thought of telling her she was wrong, it wasn't what she thought, I didn't even *know* the Bear, he was just being polite. But decided it would be pointless.

When they had gone, Irene Polaski, who had risen to let them by, said to Derek Bowles, "I have to be going too, but I just wanted to—" she gave an apologetic grimace—"well, I'm afraid it's about our friend Ballard again. It's about his costume."

"But the costumes haven't even come yet," Derek said. "Hey, Phoebe, wait till you see—we're renting the *most* beautiful costumes. Irene went to New York and picked them out herself. Drapery that won't stop, brights and pastels, she brought back pictures."

"Yes, well that's the problem," Irene said with a sigh. "Foster is insisting on wearing his own 'authentic' outfit he got on some Asian trip. He showed me a photo, and, Derek, it's *black* with big splotchy yellow flowers. It's not going to fit in at all! But of course," with a certain grimness, "he's not going to listen to *me*. I thought you should be forewarned." She bent down, patted his hand, said "good night" and left.

Derek moved over to the other side of the table, plopped down, and sighed in his turn. Seeing him there, his pink and white sweater a small, pale swatch against the dark expanse of the high settle-back, made me newly aware of his diminutive size. I knew that the physical dimension of the shoulders had nothing in reality to do with their ability to carry a metaphorical burden. Still, I felt a protective pang of sympathy. And quickly suppressed it, being sure it was a response Derek would hate.

He smiled gamely. "Shit, if *something* wasn't going wrong I really would be concerned. If the worst we have to worry about is a costume—"

"Excuse me, are you Derek Bowles?"

The speaker was a tall woman with greying hair pulled back into a ponytail. She wore a long flowered skirt and above it a shapeless black jacket. Behind her a second woman might have been taken for her twin, except that her jacket was grey and her ponytail black. What *was* it about our little group that was attracting all this variety of attention?

"Yes?" Derek said with understandable caution.

"You haven't seen fit to respond to any of our phone messages," said the first woman in an accusatory tone.

"*Or* our mailing," put in the second.

"Excuse me?" Derek's bewilderment was patent.

"We represent WAGS," the first woman said.

"*WAGS??*"

The surreality of the exchange was affecting Harry and me in the same way and we both struggled to suppress giggles.

The first woman glared. "Women Against Gilbert and Sullivan," she pronounced. "And let me assure you, we take this extremely seriously."

"Extremely seriously," echoed her twin sternly.

Derek Bowles stared up at the two women, his face such a study in baffled incredulity that Harry began to snort again. I gave his arm a pinch and he managed to sober up. Derek said, "You've got to be kidding!"

"No, Mr. Bowles," said the first WAG, "if you insist on proceeding with this production of yours you will discover that we are not in the least kidding."

"But it's *Gilbert and Sullivan* for God's sake," Derek yelped. "Victorians! Pillars of rectitude! What possible objection—"

"Sexists!" snapped WAG number one. "Misogynists!"

"Woman-haters!" her companion chimed in, in case we hadn't gotten it.

"Middle-aged women held up to ridicule and scorn!" the first woman continued. She started ticking off on her fingers. "Ruth in *Pirates of Penzance*. Lady Jane in *Patience*. The Duchess in *Gondoliers*. And Katisha is the worst of the lot! Listen to the words, man! 'A most unattractive old thing.' 'A caricature of a face.' Well, we don't think it's funny and we're not going to sit by and watch our young people being indoctrinated into . . . sexist garbage!"

"Absolute sexist garbage," echoed her cohort.

"So don't say we haven't warned you," said the first, and the two WAGS turned as one and strode out of the bar.

The three of us looked at each other and burst out laughing. Derek sank his head in his hands. "Serves me right for crowing about how well everything was going."

"Did they really call you?" I said.

He shrugged. "It's possible. You know how every other call these days is some idiot trying to sell you something. If it's no one I know, I fast forward right through the message. Same with the mail, if I don't recognize it I toss it. *WAGS!?* I probably thought it was a begging letter from some animal shelter."

Harry said, "What do you suppose they're planning to do?"

"God knows," Derek said, "perhaps nothing. If we're lucky it's only these two and they've let off their steam and that's it. Anyway, on that delightful note, I'm off. Thanks for your work, Phoebe. Harry, if you don't persuade her to stay on, you're not the director I'm banking on."

Evidently Harry was that director, because over the course of the next five minutes I did promise to become the choreographer of *The Mikado* at least to the extent of the next couple of weeks of rehearsals. It seemed, I argued to myself, that Aunt Portia was expecting—hoping—that my stay would be for more than a polite night or two. It also seemed that I was not going to learn quickly what I so wanted to know—about my aunt, my family, and, in the end, myself. The fact that I had become intrigued by the welter of crosscurrents at play among *The Mikado*'s participants hardly influenced my decision at all.

Speaking of which: "What is it with Katisha . . . that is, Lydia . . . and Dr. Ballard?"

"That's an easy one. Lydia's his ex. Ex-ex-ex, actually. He's been married three times, they all divorced him, the other two got out of here. Lydia stayed, for some reason. That's pretty much all I know." Harry rubbed his chin thoughtfully. "It's as if she's picking on a sore . . . testing a tooth to see if it still hurts. Search me. I just hope they can keep it to a level where it doesn't screw up the show."

As we were leaving, Harry stopped at the booth where Nanki-Poo and the red-haired music director were still sitting—finally on their own—to check a scheduling matter. I, not feeling I was involved, was moving on when Harry pulled me back. "You'll be happy to know," he said to the two in the booth, "that Phoebe's agreed to be our choreographer. And since I don't believe you've all officially met . . . Nadine Gardner, Mitchell Kim . . . Phoebe Mullins."

Mitchell Kim gave me a firm handshake and a sweet smile with just enough reticence behind it to be madly intriguing. I could see now that he was older than I had thought, nearer to thirty than twenty, with the traces of old acne scars on his cheeks.

Nadine Gardner was staring at me, her mouth half open as if frozen in mid-greeting. She had the skin of the true redhead, pale and clear. It had suddenly become even paler, causing a previously invisible sprinkle of freckles to appear across her nose. Clearly something had startled her. She recovered quickly, however, shook my hand and expressed her pleasure.

Now what the hell was *that* about? I thought, as Harry and I headed for the door. It couldn't have been me, could it? Perhaps it was something or someone behind me she'd been looking at. And yet I had the impression . . .

We were outside before I remembered that I had meant to check and see who was with the Bear. Not that it mattered. Just another manifestation, I told myself severely, of the curiosity that was sure to get me into trouble if I started letting it run wild.

7

Ah, here it is at last!

ALTHOUGH ALL SHE ACTUALLY SAID WAS, "WELL?" IT WAS plain that Aunt Portia was itching to be told the outcome of my introduction to the cast and crew of *The Mikado*. Her expression, across the breakfast table, was so transparently eager that I had to harden my resolve: this time I would not be deflected from my own questions.

I nodded sagely. "Interesting," I said, and spread another dollop of marmalade on my toast.

"Oh?" said Aunt Portia.

"Um-hmm." I flirted with pursuing the possibilities of one-word conversational exchanges, but common sense intervened. "The production's going to be good," I said. "There's a lot of talent, people are working hard, Harry's a good director. And the theater is a gem."

"Ahh!" Aunt Portia said.

Lest she might be planning to enlarge on that remark in a direction away from the one I'd determined on, I cut quickly to the chase.

"The only . . . um . . . fly in the ointment, you might say, is the man playing Pooh-Bah. Dr. E. Foster Ballard?

He seems to be creating a good deal of friction one way and another." I took a breath. "I got the impression that you know him."

To my relief, Portia didn't seem particularly put out by this observation. She simply nodded. "Recognized his picture. Knew him in school. 'Cept back then he was plain old Eddie Balcowicz. Doctor, you said. Huh! So, what's Eddie been up to?"

Eddie Balcowicz!? On second thought, it seemed completely in character that Pooh-Bah should change his name from the solidly ethnic to the amorphously pretentious. I gave fleeting consideration to the determination that had to have accompanied Eddie Balcowicz's metamorphosis into Dr. Ballard. Then: So what? I'd've bet that the Big Creep was simply the Small Creep grown up.

"Up to?" I considered Portia's question. "Basically, I'd say it's more what he *is:* someone who likes to throw his weight around, be the big man. Insisting on providing his own costume, for instance, instead of wearing the one that will fit in with the rest. Then there's his ex-wife—she's the one playing Katisha. Acts as if she can't stand him, but if so why's she there?" As I spoke, it struck me that this litany didn't, in the end, add up to all that much and was sounding uncomfortably like ill-natured gossip. I stopped short of the elderly letch aspect of E. Foster's personality and added, "Incidentally, he's a perfectly marvelous Pooh-Bah."

"Good," Portia said. "Well, he would be. Boy was a rare little shit when I knew 'im. But a good actor. We were in *The Gondoliers* together in high school."

"Then you knew him well?" I ventured.

"Well enough," Portia said. She drained her coffee cup, then gestured to the machine sitting on a counter beside the big old country-kitchen range. "How about makin' us another pot, Phoebe? And put in plenty. This stuff Anandi gives me tastes like dishwater, she thinks caffeine isn't good for me."

I was sure there was more to the story of Eddie and Portia, but something in my aunt's tone told me I wasn't going to learn it now. Well, I'd made a start.

I pushed up the sleeves of my well-worn blue chenille bathrobe and went to rinse out the coffeepot. My aunt was again wrapped in her burgundy silk. I noted the fraying collar and cuffs, the few straggles of fringe dangling from the sash ends. Could it be that starting the day in tatty comfort was a family trait? Anandi, on the other hand, impeccable in a red sari, gold necklace and earrings, had already eaten and was now overseeing a team of cleaning persons who had arrived, as it seemed to me, at first light. I had had a strenuous couple of days and mornings have never been my time of choice.

Per my aunt's instructions, I got a brew going that, I judged, would have to be spooned into the cups. While the machine burbled sludgily, I sat down again and opened my mouth to ask my next question.

"So, Phoebe," Portia said, "leavin' Pooh-Bah aside, did you have a good time last night?"

Yes, I had to admit that I'd enjoyed myself thoroughly.

My aunt grinned with such evident relief that I felt guilty for not having made this clear right away. "Goin' to stay a while, then? See us through this thing?"

I admitted also that I'd pretty much promised Harry Johns at least the next two weeks of rehearsals. By that time, I thought, the stage movement should be set and my services no longer necessary. "But I will have to make a trip to New York to pick up some more clothes."

"Sure thing, you do that." My aunt, elbows propped on the table, leaned her impressive chin on her hands. Her large, sky-blue eyes gave me a considering stare. She said abruptly, "How're you fixed for money, Phoebe?"

Taken aback, my first impulse was to deflect the question with a polite generality. But then I thought, heck, she was family.

"All right for now," I said. "I saved some over the summer, and there's a small income from Dad's recordings. But I am going to have to get a job. In fact, I was trying to decide what direction to take when I got your letter."

"Hmm. Thought your husband was a big conductor. Don't they make a lot of money?"

"Yes, they do. And then they hire people to manage it. Unfortunately in our case the person turned out to be a compulsive gambler—who hadn't expected Mick to die at fifty-five. There wasn't anything left—no insurance, no investments, no pension. He was terribly sorry about it."

Portia nodded thoughtfully but made no comment except, "Thanks for tellin' me."

"So anyway, as I say, I am going to have to work at *something*. But in the meantime this is like a wonderful, unexpected vacation. On top of finding out I do have family after all. And very special family. I'm glad you asked me to come."

Portia had continued looking thoughtful. Now a faint pink came into her cheeks and she murmured something about "my pleasure" and "doin' me a favor." Evidently I had almost crossed the line into my aunt's version of a sentimental outburst.

To ease us through this emotional moment, I got up and busied myself with the coffee. Portia took hers black. I shuddered, cut mine in half with hot water and added milk.

When I had sat down again, I said, "Okay, now I have a question."

"Shoot," my aunt said.

"How did you get involved with *The Mikado*?"

"Simple. Derek put an ad in the local papers. New theater company, looking for backers. I met him, liked the boy, thought he had good ideas. Was lookin' for a way to get out in the community, meet people." She shifted in her chair, winced, and added, "Didn't know I was going to do somethin' stupid, miss all the fun."

"Then Derek Bowles is planning this as an ongoing project, not just a one-shot."

"Yup. Callin' it the Northampton Repertory Company. Hope he makes a go of it. Told him I'd underwrite the first production. I can do it, y'know." She glanced around the substantial kitchen, in acknowledgment of owning a large and desirable home in one of Northampton's pricier neighborhoods. "I'm comfortable. But not a bottomless pit. I let him know after this one he'll have to hustle elsewhere."

I was trying to find a tactful way of asking where the money came from when Portia said, a shade apologetically, "Married it, y'know. The money. Three times." She gave a dry chuckle. "Ran away to be my own woman, ended up three kinds of housewife. French, Italian, Indian. Not much to choose between 'em, really. As career moves, I mean. The men were all right. Ram was the best of the lot." Her eyes softened. "You would have liked Ram."

This sudden onrush of information left me momentarily speechless. Before I could untangle my brain enough to choose among a dozen possible lines of inquiry my aunt had veered onto another subject.

"What d'you think of Harry?"

I scrambled to reorient. "Harry Johns . . . well . . ." What, indeed? It wasn't as if I hadn't done some pondering on this subject. I liked him. I liked his curly hair and the way his thin lips tilted into a smile. I liked his lack of self-importance and the give-and-take way we had worked together. I liked his matter-of-fact acceptance of me as an adult and an equal—unhappily rare in men of my generation. And at the same time I'd enjoyed the touch on the elbow, the brush of a shoulder. I liked him a lot. And yet . . .

"I think he's a hard person to know. He's nice, very

nice. Affable, engaging. Attractive. And very guarded. Do you know him at all well?"

Portia shook her head. "Only met him a few days before I had m'accident. Divorced, Derek said. Took it hard, came up here lookin' for a fresh start, stability, that sort of thing. Good man, I thought." She eyed me speculatively.

Oh, right, just what I needed—Mr. Rebound. I drew a line through "Harry Johns" on my mental list of possibles. Then, realizing he was the only one *on* the list, I went back and added a question mark. You never knew.

I said to Portia, with a smile, "I'm sure he is. But if you were thinking . . . I'm not really in the market at the moment."

Well, it was almost true. And I certainly didn't want to encourage any matchmaking proclivities on my aunt's part.

Portia nodded solemnly. I didn't think she believed me.

The padded swinging door leading to the dining room was pushed open and Anandi glided in. She paused just inside and her eye went unerringly to the coffee cup sitting on the table in front of Portia. How did she know? I thought, then realized that from the pungency of the aroma filling the kitchen we might as well have been sitting inside a giant coffee bean. Portia's expression had become a cross between guilt and sly triumph. I was beginning to get a clearer sense of the relationship between these two.

Anandi, however, expressed no disapproval beyond a small shake of the head. She went to the coffee machine, poured herself a small amount, diluted it as I had done except with a lot more milk, and joined us at the table.

She said, "I believe I have seen from the upstairs window Mr. Ben on his way to the back door."

I had only time to give a fleeting thought to my

scraggle-haired, bathrobed, bare-faced state before there
was indeed a knock at the outside pantry door.

"C'mon in," Portia called out, and the next moment
the Bear had entered the kitchen. He'd had to duck his
head coming through the door (Victorian servants, I surmised, were expected to be undersized rather than the
reverse) and with his presence the over-big room seemed
to shrink to almost normal. He was dressed in corduroy
slacks, a green-and-blue-checked shirt, and a brown
sweater vest. I had the impression he'd trimmed the
beard since the last time I saw him. Actually he looked
quite spiffy. Fine for him, I thought sourly as I pulled my
faded chenille closer around the even more ratty cotton
beneath. He knew he was going to be seen in public.

Ben Solliday was carrying a plate covered with a
white napkin. As he approached the table, the glorious
smell of burnt sugar penetrated the concentrated
essence of caffeine.

"Sit down, Ben," commanded my aunt. "Ben Solliday,
my niece, Phoebe Mullins. Get the plates, Anandi."
But Anandi had already jumped up to retrieve plates,
forks, and a cake knife from the Welsh dresser. Evidently this sort of visit from the Bear was a familiar
event.

Portia whisked the napkin off the contents of the
plate: sticky buns, obviously fresh from the oven.
"Ahh!" she said, and began cutting them apart.

"Bribery," the Bear said to me. "It's the way I make
sure of keeping my half of Portia's garage. A convenient
parking space in Northampton is worth any amount of
groveling." The Bear's voice was appropriately deep
with a basso resonance that made me wonder if he did
any singing himself.

"Makes 'em himself," Portia said through a mouthful
of bun. "And Anandi's too polite to tell 'im not to be
bringin' me sugar."

Anandi gave me her gentle smile. "I am not so big an

ogre as your Auntie Portia is making you think. And
Mr. Ben's sticky buns are surely an exception to any
rule."

She had that right. I was so busy getting my mouth
around caramelized sugar, warm raisins, and fluffy
pastry that I almost forgot to be embarrassed at being
caught in terminal *déshabille*.

"Phoebe's goin' to do the choreography for *The
Mikado,*" Portia announced, when she was able to speak
clearly again.

"Yes, I know," said the Bear. "I saw her last night at
Sam's with some members of the company. They
kindly asked me to join them but I was stuck enter-
taining a supplier."

"Mr. Ben has a most beautiful shop," Anandi said.
"With wonderful objects from all over the world, from
India, from China. You must go to see it, Phoebe."

"Didn't know you'd already met," Portia said.

"Well, I hadn't really had a chance—"

"Phoebe was just beginnin' to tell me about the rehearsal," my aunt informed the Bear.

I shook my head. "I have an idea that Mr. Solliday is
not a big fan of Gilbert and Sullivan."

"Ben, please," said the Bear. "And you're right, I'm
more of a Puccini man. But educate me."

"Oh well," I said, nettled, "*The Mikado* is not
Madama Butterfly. But for what it *is,* it's the best. I mean,
poor Sullivan, everyone kept telling him—his friends
and patrons and so on, even Queen Victoria—that he
shouldn't be wasting his talents on this sort of thing, he
should stick to his 'serious' music. When the truth was
that light opera was what he was born to write. Listen
to the score of *The Mikado*—there's not one number
that isn't perfect in its way. The melodies, the choruses.
The music just . . . it just makes you smile, it makes you
feel light. Maybe that's what 'light opera' means—or
ought to mean."

"Hear, hear!" Portia said. "Feel that way m'self."

But I was on a roll now. "And old Gilbert, he was just as much of a genius with words, their sounds and sense and rhythms and rhymes. 'A wand'ring minstrel I, A thing of shreds and patches, Of ballads, songs, and snatches . . .' Don't tell me that's not great stuff!"

"I wouldn't dream of it," murmured the Bear. He had been staring at me with a combination of interest and bemusement, and I suddenly became newly aware of my disheveled state and the fact that I was very possibly making a fool of myself. Blame it on overdoses of coffee and sugar.

"Anyway," I concluded lamely, "the miracle to me is that those two got together. And stayed together as long as they did. Lucky for us and for them too. Anyone seen a production of Sir Arthur Sullivan's grand opera *Ivanhoe* lately?"

Smiles and nods of agreement. There was a silence, and since nobody seemed in a hurry to pick up the conversational ball I took it on myself to give it another bounce or two (the coffee again).

"Of course, Gilbert did have an unfortunate obsession with making fun of older women. Which for him seems to have been anyone over eighteen. Oh, I forgot!" and I described our encounter with the WAGS.

Aunt Portia laughed delightedly. "No such thing as bad publicity," was her assessment. "They'll have 'em comin' to the theater in droves!"

"I wondered about all the traffic over at your booth," Ben Solliday said. "I was envious, it looked as if you were having a much livelier time than I was."

"Traffic? Oh, right, Jane Manypenny, too. Only that wasn't quite so funny," and I described the unfortunate incident involving Pooh-Bah that had brought the rehearsal to a premature end.

Anandi shook her head sympathetically.

"Huh!" Portia remarked offhandedly, "wonder who put ipecac in *his* cocoa?"

"Coffee," I said automatically. And realized that my

aunt had only verbalized what had been lurking uncomfortably in the back of my mind. Why that sudden
and transitory illness so late in the rehearsal when he'd
seemed fine up to then?

Ben Solliday's expression had sharpened. "But wasn't
everyone drinking the same coffee?"

"Yes," I said, "but most people have their own cup
that they keep at the theater. I can't imagine Dr. Ballard
didn't have one."

"Hey!" Portia said, "I wasn't bein' serious!"

She was looking distressed, and I hastened to say,
"Oh, it was probably something he had for dinner. Or
one of those twenty-four-hour bugs that come on so
suddenly."

But given the dynamics I'd observed in my short
time with the Northampton Repertory Company, I
didn't find it at all hard to imagine that someone had
played a deliberate and quite nasty trick on E. Foster
Ballard. I only hoped it wasn't so.

8

Why who is this whose evil eyes
Rain blight on our festivities?

SINCE I NOW KNEW THE WAY, I DROVE MYSELF TO THAT
night's rehearsal of *The Mikado*.

The first thing that struck me was that since all the
street-side spaces were taken I had to park in the small
municipal lot about two and a half blocks from the Old
Church. Perhaps, I thought, someone in the neighborhood was throwing a really big party.

The second thing I noticed as I approached the
building was that a number of people were milling
around outside. Had someone forgotten the key? Then I
saw that several of the people were holding makeshift
signs. When I was near enough to make out that one of
the signs said "Gilbert & Sullivan Denigrates Women,"
all became clear. The grammar might be faulty, but the
sentiment was unmistakably that of the WAGS. The
Northampton Repertory Company was being picketed.

As I pushed my way past the group—about fifteen
strong and exclusively female—which was effectively
blocking the sidewalk, I was greeted by cries of "Don't
be exploited by chauvinists!" and "Think of the example you're setting for the children!" Three or four

men lounging on the porch of the ramshackle white house next door added to the general hullabaloo with whistles, catcalls, and guffaws.

Mitchell Kim was approaching along the sidewalk from the opposite direction, so I paused on the path leading to the church steps to wait for him. Over to one side, a very young man scribbled busily on a notepad. He obviously represented the press and was wearing a trench coat and fedora—a possible victim of too many viewings of *The Front Page*.

Before Mitchell could reach me, a short, plump woman wearing a green and white serape detained him with a hand on his arm. "How can you take part in a play that makes fun of the Japanese people?" she pleaded. I wondered if the organizers had failed to clue her in on the grievance of the moment.

Mitchell Kim looked down at her with a scowl. "I'm not Japanese, I'm Korean."

The woman was undeterred. "But as a member of an Asian minority—"

"Look," said Mitchell impatiently, "*The Mikado* hasn't got shit to do with the Japanese people. It's a spoof on Victorian England." He shook off her hand and started toward the steps, then turned. "And what makes you think I'd give a damn if it *was* making fun of the Japs? Geez, doesn't anyone read modern history?"

He turned again and bounded up the steps. The woman stared after him with a puzzled expression which changed to something softer as Nanki-Poo's nonexistent hips and tight little buns disappeared through the door of the Old Church.

The picket holding the "Gilbert & Sullivan Denigrates Women" sign planted herself in front of me. "As an intelligent woman, aren't you ashamed of allowing something like this to go forward?" she demanded.

Some snide little imp shoved aside my usually kindly persona. "You're right." I fished in my purse and pulled out a marking pen. Then I took the sign from her, carefully inked out the "s" in "Denigrates," and handed it back with an admonitory smile. "Think of the example you're setting for the children," I said.

Inside the Old Church Theater the air was humming with the confused chatter of a group of people who hadn't had time to decide whether to be outraged, sympathetic, or amused. Most of them, of course, hadn't known about last night's encounter with the WAGS, so the verbal assault outside the theater had come as a bewildering surprise.

Beth Rosario and Ardys Feldman (Peep-Bo and Yum-Yum), wide-eyed and giggling, grabbed me as I came in. Ardys said, "Are they still out there?"

I nodded, and Beth Rosario said, "My Dad wasn't going to let us come in. But then one of the women started to talk to him and I guess she like rubbed him the wrong way and he told us to go on. My Dad isn't, like, a real big feminist." She giggled again and trailed away after Ardys, who was making a beeline for Nanki-Poo.

Derek Bowles, down by the stage, spotted me, waved, and trotted up the center aisle to greet me. His choirboy face was wreathed in smiles. "Do you be*lieve* this?" he said. "If they keep this up we won't have to do any advertising at all! Oh, and Phoebe, Harry told me you'd agreed to stay on. I love you madly and I am *massively* grateful. Just wanted you to know," and he was off again. Obviously, Derek had decided with Portia that there was no such thing as bad publicity.

Lydia Hicks was sitting by herself in the front row, apparently studying her score. Since it was her role of Katisha that was being objected to, I wondered how she was taking it. I thought she seemed uncharacteristically subdued, but maybe she was just concentrating.

In the back rows, a small coterie of which Pooh-Bah was the center were engaged in inventing new acronyms

for the protesters—"*B*itches *A*gainst *G*ilbert & *S*ullivan"
and "*H*arridans *A*gainst *G*ilbert & *S*ullivan" were two
of the printable ones—and laughing loudly at their own
sallies.

I passed them by, feeling a wave of distaste. Mis-
guided as the cause and the tactics of the women outside
might be, they were undoubtedly sincere. And hadn't I
been noting just that morning W. S. Gilbert's mean streak
in regard to middle-aged women? And yet . . . and yet,
Gilbert and Sullivan were so lighthearted—so *funny*.
Where was their sense of humor?

Still, I found myself regretting what now appeared to
me as a childish and rather patronizing gesture in regard
to the sign.

I wasn't the only one with feelings of disgust for the
antics of Pooh-Bah and company. As I continued down
the aisle, I caught an almost startling look of repugnance on the usually serene face of Irene Polaski, the
costumer, who was standing by the piano and staring
up at the group in the back rows.

I was looking for Harry, and found him setting up his
command post in an aisle seat about halfway back. He
smiled on seeing me, but he looked harried.

"I'm glad Derek thinks being set on by a bunch of
humorless harpies is good news," he grumbled, as he
wrestled to attach a sort of desk affair to the back of
the next pew down. "As far as I'm concerned we do
not need this. It's going to ruin everyone's concentration." He straightened and ran a hand through the
wiry curls. "And on top of that, Cynthia's called in
sick."

Cynthia? Ah yes, the Cougher.

"It turns out she's been walking around with pneu-
monia for the past two weeks and now she's in the hospital." He grabbed my hands. "Phoebe, I hate to ask, but
could you fill in for tonight—take notes on the
blocking? If it doesn't get written down, I might as well
not bother doing it, my memory is so lousy."

The grey eyes were appropriately—and effectively—beseeching. "Sure," I said.

"Thank you." Harry squeezed my hands and in a quick gesture brought them to his lips. By the time my stomach had completed the tiniest of flips, those same hands were clutching a clipboard and I was ensconced in the seat next to Harry's.

"Listen to this!" Derek Bowles said, practically in my ear. He had appeared from nowhere to lean over the back of my seat and had startled the hell out of me. To the tune of Ko-Ko's patter song, "I've Got a Little List," he sang gleefully,

> And the humor-challenged feminist,
> Congenitally pissed,
> I've got her on the list,
> I've got her on the list!

"Sure, put it in," Harry said, "if you want to alienate half the population of Northampton."

"Spoilsport," Derek said. "Oh, well."

Harry rapped for attention with his clipboard on the wooden desk. "Heads up, group! I want to start with the dialogue leading up to Pooh-Bah and the girls, Number eight, 'So please you, Sir, we much regret.' Everyone else, if you have to talk, for God's sake go somewhere where I can't hear you."

Still seated in an attitude of gentlemanly repose, Pooh-Bah said, "By the way, has anyone seen my score? I think I left it here last night."

So get up off your butt and look for your own damn score, I thought crossly. But there was Jane Manypenny scurrying around, scanning the stage and the rows of seats and finally the back of the auditorium, where two long tables had once no doubt held church bulletins and pamphlets.

"Here it is," she cried triumphantly, and then immediately, "Oh, I say! Look what someone has done!"

She came slowly down the aisle to Pooh-Bah, holding the buff-colored book out in front of her as if it were something unclean. Even from where I sat I could see pages with jagged edges where they had been ripped almost in half hanging out from between the cardboard covers. The lines between Jane Manypenny's brows had deepened to dark ruts and she looked frightened, as if, being the messenger, she might be accused of the outrage.

But E. Foster took the book from her with aplomb, riffed through the ruined pages, and announced, "Well, well! The HAGS strike again!"

There was a ripple of relieved laughter. Then Jane Manypenny blurted, "But how would they get in? Isn't the theater always locked?"

Derek Bowles slapped his forehead and said, "I knew I should have had all the locks changed! Who knows how many keys might be floating around? I'll see to it first thing tomorrow."

Several other scores were offered, Pooh-Bah graciously accepted one, and the rehearsal began.

Wait a minute! I cried silently. If the WAGS had really been bent on sabotage to the extent of illegal entry, why stop at one inexpensive paper score? What about the flats, the piano, the theater itself? Besides, from what I'd seen of the group outside, anything as sneaky as breaking and entering was not their style.

Then Harry was murmuring to me, "Okay, we start with Pooh-Bah up on the stage left platform," and I was recalled to my new function. But as I drew my initials and squares and "x"s and arrows, I allowed myself the parting thought that no matter how much anyone else preferred to accept the convenient explanation, Phoebe Mullins definitely smelled a rat. A rat that was somehow connected with E. Foster Ballard.

·   ·   ·

Essentially there are three approaches to staging a Gilbert and Sullivan opera. The first is to aim for a replication of the original production—which in the case of *The Mikado* took place at the Savoy Theater in London in 1885. Sources are available detailing every traditional bit of business originally laid down by W. S. Gilbert himself, who was reportedly a terror of a director, given to dictating every vocal inflection of every line of dialogue. The result, of course, might as well be an exhibit in the Victoria and Albert.

The second is to employ the sort of flight of fancy that resulted, in the late thirties, in a jazzed-up, all-black version called *The Hot Mikado*. Or you could give the Gentlemen of Japan business suits and briefcases, put Ko-Ko on a skateboard and Yum-Yum and the girls in miniskirts. *The Mikado* now being in the public domain, you could even, if sufficiently demented, work in Pearl Harbor, Hiroshima, and the latest crash of the Japanese market. (This in spite of the fact, so pithily articulated by Mitchell Kim, that the essence of *The Mikado* is wholly British.)

The middle way is to stage the show as written, while acknowledging the past hundred-plus years of development in the musical theater, not to mention its audiences. This was the route Harry (and presumably Derek) had chosen. And here Harry's lack of experience in directing G&S was a plus, guaranteeing a freshness of approach that was met with enthusiasm by most of the cast, Pooh-Bah, naturally, being a holdout. Through a litany of "Excuse me, but this line is always done . . ." or "I hate to mention it, my dear fellow, but in the D'Oyly Carte production . . ." or "Awfully sorry to interrupt again, Harry, but don't you think . . ." Harry was a model of patience. "Just try it, please, Foster. Believe me, you'll get a laugh." And as the company obliged by howling at Harry's inventions, Pooh-Bah gradually simmered down. Somehow, though, he still managed to convey an air of indulging, in his superior wisdom, the inexperienced young director. It drove me crazy. I admired Harry's cool.

There was a member of the cast present I hadn't seen before. This was the actor playing the Mikado himself. His name was Arnold Zimmer. He was a big man, tall and running to fat and with a hesitant and apologetic air, as if surprised to find himself in such exalted company. Since the Mikado is supposed to be an overbearing and menacing type, whose entrance in the second act comes after one of the longest buildups in operatic history, I hoped that Mr. Zimmer was a better actor than his personality promised.

In spite of diligently attending to the nitty-gritty of my new position, as the rehearsal segued from spoken dialogue to musical number and back I began to appreciate fully another feature of the Old Church Theater: the acoustics were fantastic. From Pooh-Bah's oily tones to Jane Manypenny's crisp Britishisms to Pish-Tush/Carl Piquette's rather dry timbre, every word came winging to the ear as if on its own personally wired soundwave. From the way the sixteen voices of the chorus filled the space, they might have been thirty. Even Yum-Yum's pretty but small soprano floated easily to the farthest corners of the auditorium.

I knew this because during one of Harry's trips to the stage for some hands-on demonstration, I left my seat for a quick tour, moving from spot to spot to try to locate a dead one. There weren't any. Either by genius or serendipity, the builders of the Old Church had achieved, in their deployment of spaces, angles, and materials, the results that acoustical engineers of prestigious concert halls are paid large sums to attain, and frequently do not. No wonder Derek had glommed onto this space!

As I hightailed it back to my post, I caught, out of the corner of my eye, the music director, Nadine Gardner, staring at me with what appeared to be a kind of dogged fascination. It wasn't the first time that evening I'd intercepted such a look, and it was beginning to be annoying. What could it be about me? Or had it perhaps more to do with the famous man I'd been married to? It was quite likely that Nadine, being a musician, had heard of Michael Mullins, perhaps even attended his concerts. The classical music world, too, has its groupies. They tend to be somewhat older, a tad more staid, than their rock counterparts, but the guiding principle is the same. And while it is sometimes not a lot of fun being married to a sex symbol, I'd gotten used to it—including being eyed with a mixture of envy, awe, and resentment in my role as the Privileged One who got to sleep with Greatness. Fortunately Mick, who had a keen sense of the ridiculous, had not allowed his head to be turned into that particular avenue. We had often laughed together about one or another especially aggressive exemplar of the species.

But *Nadine*? She couldn't be more than twenty-one or-two. If she wanted to tell me how much she'd admired my dead husband, why not simply come to me and do so? Why the furtive glances?

When we took our coffee break I said to Harry, "What's Nadine's story?"

Harry took a swig from his "Directors Do It With Gestures" mug. (I had brought my own this time, from Portia's kitchen, plain blue and bare of cute sayings.) "Hampshire College," he said. "It's a new school in the valley, relatively speaking. Experimental. The kids more or less devise their own curriculum, and the last two years are given over to a major project. This is part of Nadine's. She's arranging the entire score for an ensemble she's recruited from the Five Colleges. The girl's enormously talented."

"I can see that," I said. "Where's she from?"

Harry frowned. "England somewhere. London?

Birmingham? But I get the impression she's been over here a while. Prep school and so on. We were lucky to get her."

I stole another glance at Nadine Gardner, who was standing and leaning with her elbows on the piano, her coppery head close to Mitchell Kim's dark one as they appeared to be in earnest conversation. Ardys Feldman, Beth Rosario, and three members of the women's chorus hovered nearby. As at that first time I'd laid eyes on the music director, I felt a flicker of something like recognition. It was as quickly gone.

Jane Manypenny had again been the one to organize the coffee and provide food—in this case, chocolate brownies. Pooh-Bah had helped himself from the spigot on the big urn and added, I noted, both cream and three spoons of sugar. He then spent the break wandering about the auditorium talking with various company members; even, to my surprise, as he passed the pew where his ex-wife sat not far from me, venturing a quiet word with she. Quiet on his part, that is. Lydia listened, flushed angrily, and snapped back with no attempt to lower her voice, "If that's what you think, you're an even bigger fool than I took you for." Pooh-Bah shrugged and moved on.

I had not kept this close track of his movements from idle curiosity: I wanted to see what he did with the coffee mug—an oversized one colored a dark green. What he did was to hold it closely to his chest when not actually drinking from it, and to put it back on the table only when Harry had called for the rehearsal to resume.

Interesting, I thought. Almost as if he were making sure that this time no one had a chance to tamper with its contents.

9

It's evident, very, our tastes are one.

THE WEEK PRECEDING THE THIRD WORST MOMENT OF MY adult life was deceptively calm. Even, I thought later, cruelly calm. There should have been a warning rumble off in the distance, or an occasional oh-so-slightly-sinister strain of background music. Instead there was only the rollicking good cheer and sweet melodiousness of the Victorian era's two masters of ironic playfulness. They do it better in the movies.

The day after my second exposure to the North-ampton Repertory Company, a Saturday, I drove to New York through a slow drizzle to pick up some more clothes. The big, prewar apartment on West End Avenue seemed even emptier than I remembered. I walked across its parquet flooring, past Mick's concert grand, past the rain-dappled windows overlooking the street five floors below, past the shelves crammed with books and scores and the eclectic furnishings—the things we had bought together and those we had inherited from his Irish/Russian family and my Greek/New England one. I had sublet the apartment last summer while I was at the Varovna Colony, and most of the personal stuff—photos and souvenirs and bric-a-brac—was still packed away in cartons in the building's basement. Even so, I was surprised at how little connection I felt to the place, how remote and sterile it seemed as opposed to the warmth and quirkiness of my aunt's establishment and the fascinating stew of emotions and personalities simmering away at the Old Church Theater.

I went into the kitchen, made myself a cup of instant coffee, and took it back to the living room. There I kicked off my shoes, curled up in a corner of the big crushed velvet sofa, and set to thinking.

What kind of person did it make me—a terrible one?—this lack of nostalgia for the home I'd shared with my husband of twenty-five years. But the fact was it had not been our home for more than a few months at a stretch. A repository, a base, but not a home. Home had been wherever Mick's wanderlust, his restless ambition and curiosity, had taken us. Because although, as his reputation grew, there were offers of permanent positions, Mick had never been able to contemplate such a clipping of wings. Home had been the rented villa outside Milan, the Paris apartment, the borrowed townhouse in London, a hundred hotel suites or, in the early days, tiny rooms in the sort of hotel popularly labeled fleabag, one memorable for actually having fleas. Home had been wherever we two were: we had been each other's home.

And I missed it terribly, that universe of two. Lovers, companions, confidantes, best friends. And yet, and yet . . .

I took a sip of the coffee. Yechh! Back to the kitchen, where I set Mr. Coffee to brewing a proper pot while I sat on one of the tall stools at the breakfast bar, elbows propped on its surface, chin resting on folded hands. Now where had I been . . .

Mick. With his mother's broad face and Slavic cheekbones, his father's thick, straight black hair and royal-blue eyes. I had loved him so much! And I had loved our life. Hadn't I?

Then why, after Mick's death, had I been so quick, so determined, almost without conscious volition, to put that life behind me? We had never stayed in one place long enough for me to form a network of close friends. But still, I knew a lot of people, people who would have been glad to be contacted, to be cordial to Michael Mullins's widow. Ah, that was just it! I said "our life." But the truth was that it was Mick's life—Mick's career, Mick's needs—in which I was a valued, even necessary participant. But not Phoebe's life, never Phoebe's. Perhaps if I had had a child. . . .

Over the past summer I had faced the knowledge that while Mick had been kind and supportive when our daughter was lost, there had been, for him, an underlying relief. How could I have catered to them both in the way Mick had become accustomed to? With that realization had come the first sense of distancing from the man I had loved and, for so long, lived through. The love, I knew, would always be there. But that life, I told myself as I poured coffee into a fresh cup, was then. This is now.

I wandered through the high-ceilinged rooms, sipping the comforting brew as I went. I really had to do something about the apartment, so ridiculously big for one person. It had mainly been inertia that had kept me here. Inertia and the arcanities of the New York City rent control laws. I could well end up paying as much for a studio apartment as I was now paying for six oversized rooms. Well, I'd deal with that later.

I went into the bedroom, dragged a couple of suitcases from the back of the closet and started to pack.

On Monday afternoon we sat around the big table in Portia's kitchen—Harry, Derek, Aunt Portia, and I—getting organized. At least that was what we were supposed to be doing. At the moment we were passing around a copy of the *Daily Hampshire Gazette* that

Anandi had brought in folded back to the page where a headline read: "Gilbert and Sullivan Insulting to Women, Local Group Says." Anandi, Portia explained with a touch of pride, regularly read the *Gazette* cover to cover and was an authority on such minutiae as the new promotions in the Police Department, how many jobs would be lost due to the latest bank merger, and who had paid how much for that really run-down colonial on Crescent Street.

Now Anandi hovered, keeping an eye on her newspaper, while Harry frowned and read aloud: "*Mikado* producer Derek Bowles said of the demonstrators, 'I'm astounded that anyone could take issue with a classic theater piece like *The Mikado*. Where is these ladies' sense of humor?'" He groaned and said to Derek, "*Ladies?* That's great, now they're really going to be mad."

"So?" Derek waved a careless hand. "The paper called me up, I had to say something." He grinned at Portia. "Couldn't pay for this kind of publicity, could we? First clipping for the scrapbook. Oh, say—speaking of publicity—"

"Excuse me," Anandi said. "Since you have now all read the article, I will cut it out for you when I have finished reading the paper, okay?" Harry handed over the *Gazette,* Anandi tucked it safely under her arm and disappeared with it through the swinging kitchen door.

"Listen," Derek said, "how about this? Harry and I dress up like G and S—cutaways, top hats, side whiskers, the whole deal—and we rent a carriage and horses and drive around town advertising the show." He beamed around the table.

"Absolutely not," Harry said. "Not with me. Jeez, Derek, we're trying to put on a decent show here, not stage a media event."

Aunt Portia said, "What would it cost?"

"I'll find out," Derek said. "I know there's a place in town or nearby that rents them out, the carriage and the horses. I've seen 'em used for weddings. Maybe Foster will play Gilbert if Harry won't."

"Can we get back to what we're supposed to be doing?" Harry said with some asperity. "Which I *thought* was nailing down a rehearsal schedule for the next two and a half weeks."

So we did. But the matter of the carriage was to arise with regularity between then and opening night.

As I've indicated, the remainder of that week was, in retrospect, an oasis of peace and productivity. Only the WAGS disturbed the calm. Unfortunately, they had not, as I'd half expected, figured they'd made their point and moved on to other challenges. A small group continued to show up each evening, waving their signs and occasionally breaking into chants of "Northampton Rep is out of step!" or (less successfully, I thought) "Send *The Mikado* incommunicado!" The short woman in the serape, whom I'd privately dubbed Ms. Clueless, was a faithful participant. I had a sneaking suspicion that she came mainly to watch Mitchell Kim walk down the sidewalk.

A couple of the guys from the rooming house next door occasionally appeared on the porch to offer a jeer or two, but in the main they seemed to have lost interest. Since I didn't imagine the WAGS had any thoughts of converting these gentlemen, and since there was virtually no other foot traffic in the area at this hour, it appeared that the hearts and minds of the *Mikado* cast and crew were the targets. If so, it wasn't working. In fact, the hearts and minds in question were becoming seriously ticked off. Lydia Hicks came to a near shouting match with one of the women I recognized from our encounter at Sam's, in which the words "stupid constipated bitch" figured prominently. I hoped that the WAGS would eventually wake up to the realization that nagging was not a persuasive technique and sensibly go away.

But I was more than ever convinced that the WAGS

had had nothing to do with the mutilation of E. Foster's *Mikado* score. Peter had announced to the company that the locks on the outer doors of the Old Church Theater had been changed, and everyone seemed to be accepting the WAGS-did-it version of that incident. With at least one exception, I was certain. I couldn't forget E. Foster's behavior with the coffee cup. And if he suspected—or even knew—that someone in the company was out to get him, why, given his propensity for throwing his weight around, wasn't he making a stink?

But as the week passed with no further acts of hostility directed at Pooh-Bah, I began to think that whatever the specifics, it was all a thing of the past.

Harry and I continued to work together with a smoothness that was, to me, little less than astonishing. We took to meeting in the late afternoons to go over the plans for the evening's rehearsal, so as to waste as little time as possible. Community theater productions, Harry pointed out, depended on the volunteer services of people who had already put in a full working day. You didn't want to wear them out, and you didn't want to piss them off by making them hang around while the director fussed over decisions that could and should have been made beforehand.

Owing largely, I chose to believe, to our sterling organizational skills, *The Mikado* was shaping up nicely. We were a good balancing act, Harry and I. When he became enamored of a bit of business that wasn't, to my mind, nearly as funny as he thought it was, I was generally able to talk him out of it. And in response to some of my wilder choreographic flights of fancy, Harry's response would be some variety of: "Lovely idea, Phoebe. But you know they'll never be able to do it."

Mostly, though, we were in agreement. When Ardys Feldman proved unable to make it through Yum-Yum and Nanki-Poo's duet, "Were you not to Ko-Ko plighted" (which she and Beth called "the kissy song"), without succumbing to giggles, no stern lectures from us about maturity and professionalism. Instead, Harry made Ardys and the long-suffering Mitchell Kim go through the number so many times in succession that no one, onstage or off, any longer found it remotely amusing. Arnold Zimmer, as the Mikado of Japan, we discovered, could sing, remember his lines, and walk, but not all at once. So we plunked him center stage, where he made quite an impressive figure, and let the action happen around him.

There was another balancing act going on, which I appreciated more and more as the week wore on: that between the level-headed Harry and the ebullient Derek Bowles. For one thing, it was Harry whose steadying hand was preventing—but only just—this particular *Mikado* from turning into *The Pooh-Bah and Ko-Ko Show*. I'd been right about Derek at those early rehearsals, he *had* been holding back. Now his full talents were on nightly display: the comic timing, the musicality, the dancer's control over his small, well-knit body, the expressive plasticity of that mobile face. Onstage he was riveting and hilarious, and after the first demonstration of that fact, E. Foster had revved up his own performance to meet the challenge.

The result was electric, but frequently careening way past the boundaries of theatrical etiquette. "Ditch the fluttering hankie, Derek, it's all anybody'll look at." "Foster, you *have* to be downstage on that line. Derek, the little jig is cute, but can it, we have to be paying attention to Pooh-Bah here." "Foster, no byplay with the dagger. Perhaps in another spot, but not here, this is Ko-Ko's scene."

All very well, I thought, during rehearsals. I only hoped that once unleashed in front of an audience they'd both have enough self-discipline to behave themselves. I wasn't counting on it.

One place, though, to which E. Foster Ballard would

not rise to Derek's bait was in the matter of driving
though town in a "horse-and-buggy" (as he contemptu-
ously dubbed it) playing the part of W. S. Gilbert. The
Ballard dignity, it seemed, drew the line at shilling in
public.

So Derek went back to nagging Harry, seemingly undeterred by his increasingly testy refusals to even consider the project. In this Harry was backed up by Aunt
Portia, once she'd learned the cost of hiring carriage,
horses, and driver. Derek, however, convinced that
Portia would change her mind if Harry signed on,
wouldn't let the matter drop, and at least once a day
managed to insert a wistful or pointed reference to
horses, sidewhiskers, or unrecognized advertising genius. I came to believe that he no longer thought there
was a chance of changing anyone's mind, but that an
essential vein of mischievousness in his personality
couldn't resist pulling people's chains and watching
them react. Depending on your mood, I decided, it
could either strike you as funny or drive you nuts.

In spite of the brisk pace of rehearsals, I managed
during that week to glean what seemed to me at the
time a good measure of insight into the psychology of
this particular group of individuals. Later, of course, I
wondered how I could have missed so much.

My biggest puzzlement had been to discover what it
was about Dr. E. Foster Ballard that appeared to command the respect, amounting to awe, of a sizeable faction of the *Mikado* company. This included about half of
the chorus members, Jane Manypenny, who practically
genuflected whenever his Pooh-Bahness deigned to
speak to her, and the Mikado himself, Arnold Zimmer,
who lurked at a respectful remove like an enormous
puppy, eager but uncertain of welcome. Harry was cour-
teous, but otherwise kept his distance. Derek, however,
seemed to enjoy (if that was the word) a special relationship with E. Foster, roaring at his jokes and frequently
pulling him aside for a sotto voce confab. When I

tackled him on this he laughed it aside with an, "Oh, E. Foster's not so bad. And we need him, you know, for the show. I'm the producer, after all, it's my job to keep people sweet."

Huh! At least, thank God, it wasn't mine.

It was Anandi, with her devotion to the *Daily Hampshire Gazette,* who finally clued me in. "Your Dr. Ballard," she observed to Portia and me at breakfast one morning, "is a big deal in this town. He is on boards, he sits on committees. And he owns real estate. The *Gazette* calls your Dr. Ballard a linchpin."

"He's not *my* Dr. Ballard," I said crossly, still in my less-than-charming, precoffee stage. "Calls him a what?"

Anandi went to fetch yesterday's paper from the pile in the blue plastic recycling bin by the back door. She searched briefly through its pages, then read out, "The Chamber of Commerce yesterday honored Dr. E. Foster Ballard. Dr. Ballard was cited as a linchpin of the entrepreneurship of the 1980s that fueled the renaissance of downtown Northampton."

"Hmph!" said Aunt Portia. "Little bastard always was a wheeler-dealer. Used to set up car washes, get other kids to do all the work, keep most of the money."

Okay, I got it now. Small pond, large, moneyed fish. It explained a lot.

Two small fish who were no longer dazzled by Pooh-Bah's attentions were Beth Rosario and Ardys Feldman. I came on them whispering together one evening in the corridor behind the stage. Beth looked close to tears. I stopped and asked what the matter was.

"It's *Eeeuuw* Foster," Ardys said. "He won't stop bothering Beth."

"Bothering?"

"He keeps patting my . . . uh . . . bottom, and then, like, pretending it was an accident," Beth explained.

"We told Jane about it," Ardys said, "because she's, like, with us most of the time. But she just said," and Ardys produced a pretty fair imitation of Jane

Manypenny's plummy accent, "O-ooh, you must be mistaken. Doctah Bal-lahd would ne-vah do a thing like that!"

"Like I don't know when someone's putting his hand on my ass," Beth said indignantly. "And I didn't want to, like, tell Harry or anyone, because I don't want to cause, like, this big fuss, and anyway maybe he wouldn't believe me either. And then if my father found out about it he'd, like, have a fit and pull me out of the show." Her dark, doe eyes stared up at me beseechingly from a face still childishly plump. If "Doctah Bal-lahd" had come around the corner at that moment I wouldn't have hesitated to punch him in the nose.

Since I wasn't granted that outlet, I took a deep breath. "Listen," I said, "when it happens again, this is what you do. You jump, like you're startled, and accidentally lose your balance and accidentally step hard on his foot. He wears those glove-leather slip-ons." I looked down at Beth's feet, shod in the sturdy work boots that I'd always considered a particularly hideous teenage fashion, and nodded in approval. "That should do it."

Beth was a quick and accurate study. Later that same evening, as the entire company trooped onstage for a run-through of the second act finale, I heard E. Foster give a yelp of pain. This was followed immediately by a girlish flutter of embarrassed apologies. Meryl Streep couldn't have done it better.

Nadine Gardner, on the other hand, had no need of my advice. Monday night, as I stood at the back of the theater, I had seen E. Foster leaning over her shoulder as she sat at the piano, ostensibly pointing out a passage in the score that sat on the rack. All at once Nadine's expression froze. She didn't turn, but her lips moved in what I took to be a few well-chosen words, because E. Foster backed away as if he'd stepped on a bee. After that he loftily ignored her. If forced to speak, owing to the fact that they were rehearsing the same show, he addressed her with exaggerated formality as "Ms. Gardner."

I had occasion, that week, to exchange a few words with Nadine from time to time, and as far as I could tell she was no longer directing at me those long, thoughtful glances from afar. Perhaps whatever her curiosity it had one way or another been satisfied. She struck me as a superserious young woman. When she and the equally serious Mitchell Kim were together, which they were often, there were rare smiles but seldom any laughter. I deduced, from certain nuances of body language, that they were sleeping together. Mitchell, I'd learned, was in real life a CPA. It seemed an unlikely pairing, perhaps one of those results of the ship-at-sea aspect of theatrical companies where odd and intense attachments flourish until landfall—or the end of the run—is reached.

Lydia Hicks, Carl Piquette, and Irene Polaski had co-alesced into another sort of alliance, based, it seemed to me, on a mutual distaste for E. Foster Ballard. Carl, as Pish-Tush, had several scenes with Pooh-Bah which he executed with perfect professionalism. Offstage, though, I noted that he never went near E. Foster, never spoke to him, never, that I could see, even looked at him. Perhaps he was only being loyal to his friendship with Lydia, of whom he seemed genuinely fond, but I thought it was more than that though I'd no idea what.

Lydia's antipathy was a lot more overt, but even she, during this period, was managing to limit herself to sporadic mutterings and eye-rollings. Since Katisha doesn't appear until the end of the first act, there were times when Lydia wasn't called, or could have come in late, but she showed up for the full length of each rehearsal. Afterwards, at Sam's pizzeria and bar, she would get quietly—or, depending on her mood, not so quietly—sloshed and Carl would drive her home. What she did with herself during the day, I had not yet discovered.

Most puzzling to me was Irene Polaski. While Jane Manypenny accomplished her contributions to the company with maximum bustle, Irene went about hers so quietly that it was surprising to total up their extent. Besides the fans, she had managed to come up with parasols for all the women as well as sundry other props. All of these were carefully set ready to hand on a table backstage before every rehearsal and locked up in an office at the back of the building each night. The cast's costume measurements, including shoe and wig sizes, obtained whenever she could find an opportunity in the course of rehearsal, were entered into a neat little notebook. From the small craft shop she ran in downtown Northampton had come enough silk cherry blossoms to decorate three *Mikado* productions. As a member of the chorus, she sang with energy and entered into the antics required with every appearance of pleasure. And she truly loathed E. Foster Ballard.

Was I the only one who could see this? Certainly E. Foster himself appeared oblivious. It must be the armor of his own self-esteem protecting him, I decided. Otherwise the sheer hatred beaming in his direction from those fixed and level eyes must have given him at least several moments' unease. Unless I was imagining the whole thing.

But I wasn't. I'd seen enough in my life of people assuming a mask of geniality to hide unpleasant or unacceptable emotions—hatred, envy, indifference, fear. Except in the case of genuine sociopaths, I didn't believe it could be done, not completely. And Irene wasn't even trying. Perhaps she felt protected by the general truth that in a theatrical company it is one's own emotions, not other people's, that are all-absorbing, leading to a sort of blinkered approach to the world. Or perhaps she just didn't give a damn.

All the same, I wondered why, given the degree of her hostility, Irene had chosen to become attached to any enterprise that involved being in the same room with E. Foster Ballard.

10

And I am right,
And you are right,
And ev'rything is quite correct!

ON SATURDAY MORNING AFTER BREAKFAST MY AUNT
said, "Phoebe, you ought to take a walk downtown.
Y'haven't had a real chance to take a look. Think you'll
like it."

The week following my return from New York had
passed with equal smoothness on the homefront as it
had at the theater. Anandi, Aunt Portia, and I had settled into a mutually satisfying routine: Anandi ran
things, and the three of us conspired in the fiction that it
was Portia who was in charge. Under Anandi's gentle
bullying, my aunt was persuaded to tolerate an acceler-
ated schedule of physical therapy. She was hoping to be
able to start attending rehearsals the next week. Judging
by the way she charged around the house, the four
rubber-tipped prongs of her cane leaving emphatic little
smudges on the parquet flooring, she was making good
progress. I was able to make myself useful by ferrying
Anandi, who didn't drive, to the supermarket and drugstore. And I had located a dance studio and joined an
adult class that met three times a week.

I had by now had enough experience of my aunt to

feel that we were genuinely becoming friends. We had several one-on-one conversations that week and I had gotten used to her elliptical style of communication and no longer expected much in the way of linear narrative. Nevertheless, I had learned a good deal about Jean-Luc, Marcello, and Ram, all three of whom Portia seemed to recall with only slightly varying degrees of fondness. She also spoke from time to time of her and my mother's childhood in Northampton and remarked on the changes in the town since then. But of the reason for her sudden departure and long exile, she never spoke, and I didn't ask. If and when she was ready, I decided, she'd tell me.

Ben Solliday continued to show up at breakfast time on most mornings, bearing some variety of baked offering. Since the conversation, in deference to my aunt's curiosity and proprietary interest, centered almost entirely on what had happened at rehearsal the night before, I couldn't imagine what his interest was. He never said very much and it seemed to me he must be bored to death. I had considered briefly that if this was going to keep happening maybe I should put on something more appropriate to company than the chenille bathrobe. Then I decided the hell with it. As far as I knew, he wasn't there on anyone's particular invitation and certainly not mine and it was his lookout.

As it happened, the Bear hadn't put in an appearance that morning. I speculated that, it being Saturday, he was more than usually required at his shop. Or perhaps he had finally given up trying to find amusement in our discussions of alternative lyrics for "I've got a little list" or how many encores of "The flowers that bloom in the spring" were appropriate.

I had driven through downtown a couple of times, found it slow going, and turned to alternate routes, about which Anandi was predictably knowledgeable. But Main Street had seemed lively, the day was promising to be another in a series of perfect autumn offerings, sunny

and crisp, and I decided to act on Aunt Portia's suggestion and take a closer look.

"A'course it's not what I remember," Portia said. "No
more Five and Ten, no department store, no soda fountain. All chichi shops now an' restaurants, fifty-eight
kindsa coffee. But the people are interestin'."

They were indeed. On the generous sidewalks bor-
dering the broad curve of Main Street the scruffy, the
prosperous, the academic, the young, the old, the ordinary, and the outlandish mingled with every appearance of mutual tolerance. They lounged at tiny tables
outside coffeehouses and delis or on the church steps or
the lawn of the courthouse, they walked briskly or
strolled or clustered in impromptu gatherings: long-
haired women in ankle-length India print skirts, hand-
holding couples of every sexual variety, parents pushing
strollers or with babies in backpacks, dogs meeting and
greeting at the ends of leashes, youths with their hair in
orange and purple spikes and with bits of metal
screwed into an astonishing range of body parts. People
in wheelchairs scooted up and down the ramps cut into
each sidewalk intersection. Dress was casual, with the
emphasis, for those who hadn't opted for the exotic, on
denim and T-shirts. As a result, the few folks wearing
business suits looked as if they were in costume. In
front of an establishment called Bart's, a dozen brawny
motorcycles lined the curb while their owners, outfitted
in the regulation metal-studded black leather, sat on
little plastic chairs indulging in ice cream and designer
coffee. The reason for the snail-like pace of traffic on
Main Street, I now realized, was that cars actually
stopped at crosswalks and waited until they were clear
of pedestrians. The sidewalks were remarkably free of
litter, and there was not one boarded-up storefront.

What *was* this place, some kind of theme park put
together by Mister Rogers and the ACLU? Presumably

there was, as everywhere, a dark underbelly to life in Northampton, but on this shiny day in October it looked to be very far under indeed.

Bumper stickers, I've found, are usually reliable indicators of a town's ethos. In my passage down Elm Street to where it merged into the downtown shopping area, I had been exhorted by the rear ends of cars to Boycott Nike, Homophobia, and Sexism, Question Assumptions, Visualize World Peace, and Free Tibet. I had been further instructed that Poverty is Violence, Meat is Dead, Anonymous is a Woman, and informed that the owner of a psychedelically decorated Volkswagen was Doing My Part to Piss Off the Radical Right.

As a nonsmoker who has never felt the urge to light up except when confronted with one too many NO SMOKING signs, by the time I hit the midpoint of Main Street I was starting to feel downright Republican. I was somewhat mollified, however, by reading that Age and Treachery Always Overcome Youth and Skills. And when a hulking SUV with New York plates sneered, "if i want your opinion i'll beat it out of you," my sense of balance was restored to the point where I could fully enjoy a shop window stocked with environmentally friendly Products for Holistic Living, and pause to listen with pleasure to a street musician coaxing mellow sounds out of a steel drum.

I had lived almost all my life in or near big cities. Was Northampton a place, I wondered, where I might put down belated roots? And would they flourish in small-town soil? Not that Northampton was *that* small, it was, after all, a county seat. But small enough so that a permanent resident would be unapt, for instance, to take a stroll downtown without running into some acquaintance or other . . .

. . . and by damn, wasn't that E. Foster Ballard himself emerging from a doorway several stores down from where I stood? Happily, he was headed in the opposite direction. I watched as he walked away with his characteristic saunter in his navy blazer and his soft Italian shoes, and was reminded of the web of small-town connections represented by the cast of *The Mikado*. Was this the sort of thing I wanted to become a part of? Well, it depended on . . .

Another familiar figure emerged from the same door. It was Jane Manypenny, attired in a businesslike shirt-waist dress with a linen jacket and low-heeled pumps, a neat black leather purse hanging over her shoulder. She started off in my direction, but at the crosswalk turned and made her way briskly to the other side of Main Street.

I dropped a dollar bill into the steel drummer's instrument case, continued on down the sidewalk, and stopped at the door in question. It opened, I discovered, onto a small lobby and a flight of stairs. A directory on the wall listed the building's occupants, which included four psychotherapists. One of them was Jane Manypenny, M.S.W.

Okay. But what had Pooh-Bah been doing there? I dismissed out of hand the notion that he might be a client of Jane's; the mind, as they say, boggled. I checked the other names on the directory. They belonged to three lawyers, an acupuncturist, two massage therapists, a mortgage broker, and a real estate company. A number of separate and logical reasons, then, why Pooh-Bah might have had business there and none at all to assume his visit was in any way connected with Jane.

Hmmm. I filed the incident away under "interesting coincidences."

Out on the street again, I found that the next storefront down was that of a pharmacy. It reminded me of something.

"Ipecac," my aunt had said almost automatically on hearing of E. Foster's sudden barfing episode. A remedy, I deduced, that had been common in her childhood. I remembered being given ipecac only once, swallowing down the sweet syrup and feeling mightily betrayed by the dire results. Was it still used?

I went into the pharmacy, passed by the toys, cosmetics, hosiery, candy, Halloween paraphernalia, etc., and began to browse the back aisles where the medical stuff was kept. I found it in the baby and child section: a small bottle of ipecac syrup whose label instructed, "For emergency use to cause vomiting in poisoning." The dose was one tablespoonful, to be followed by another "if vomiting does not occur within twenty minutes."

So . . . easily obtained, an unremarkable, over-the-counter purchase. Easily added to a cup of already highly sugared coffee put down for a moment in a setting of much casual movement and babble. It could have happened.

I looked at my watch. Getting on for lunchtime. I left the pharmacy and headed for home.

11

Life is a joke that's just begun!

"Jeez, does this happen every night?" inquired a lanky youth with shoulder-length hair and granny glasses. He had arrived, with some difficulty, at the door of the Old Church at the same moment that I did. Since he was carrying a guitar case, I presumed he was a member of Nadine's ensemble, which was about to have its first rehearsal with the company.

"No," I said, "not in these numbers. Must be a full moon."

The WAGS were indeed out in force, and I was smarting from an exchange I'd unwisely brought on myself with the one I thought of as the Head WAG. It had been a beautiful day and I was feeling an unwonted bubble of optimism about life in general: physically and mentally loosened by an hour-long dance class, comfortably sated with Anandi's tandoori chicken, and looking forward to tonight's musical rehearsal. I was less than usually in the mood to be jostled, hooted at, and have my feminist sympathies rudely questioned. When the Head WAG called out as I passed, "How can you be a part of this male chauvinist spectacle?" I whirled on her.

"Because I want to," I snapped. "Because it's a work of charm and beauty and genius and I love doing it! For God's sake, you've made your point and you're obviously not going to stop the show. So why don't you all just go away? You're making yourselves ridiculous!"

The woman stared. I noticed for the first time the depth of her large, pale blue eyes and the thickness of the grey hair pulled back into a ponytail and thought fleetingly, She must have been quite a pretty girl.

The Head WAG shrugged and shook her head. "You just don't get it, do you?" she said, and turned away.

The ensemble Nadine had recruited consisted of a flute, an oboe, two clarinets, trumpet, acoustic guitar, string bass, and a percussionist with an assortment of blocks, gongs, and drums. I had wondered at Derek and Harry's unquestioning confidence in Nadine's ability not only to arrange the music but to train her little group in its execution. From the first notes it was clear the confidence had been well placed. I doubted if Sullivan's music had often been played with more precision, clarity, and downright exuberance. The fact that the players sported, among them, three nose rings, one shaved head, two sets of dreadlocks, and four (visible) tattoos only added to the piquancy of the performance.

Since the main purpose of this rehearsal was to get the singers and the orchestra used to each other, the emphasis was on music rather than drama. The musical numbers were taken in order and those not involved sat out in front listening to performances that now took on new color and depth. Choruses sparkled. Soloists responded in their individual ways. Nanki-Poo and Pish-Tush turned in their usual solid jobs. Yum-Yum, on the other hand, positively bloomed. I suspected she had become bored with the attention of the same old crew; now there was a new one, all dedicated to her support and enhancement. It acted on the delicate-flower languor she'd begun to affect like a sudden dose of Miracle-Gro. Ko-Ko and Pooh-Bah's reaction was to ratchet their performances up yet another notch. Arnold Zimmer, the Mikado, was predictably thrown by the new sounds coming from the orchestra pit and had to be taken through his numbers virtually line by line.

Since it was Saturday night, everyone had been warned to expect to stay to the end of the rehearsal, whenever that might turn out to be. So it was relatively late in the evening when we got to Katisha's second major number, and attention among those not directly concerned had long since started to flag. They sat about the auditorium, some, veterans of marathon rehearsals, reading or knitting, some whispering together. I was standing at the back, my assignment being to listen for the balance of singer and orchestra, when Lydia began her song.

No matter how ludicrous the material provided by his cohort Gilbert, Arthur Sullivan was incapable of writing an ungraceful melody. In the case of "Alone, and yet alive! (Recitative and Song)," the dramatic situation is a typical one for G&S. Katisha is mourning the object of her passion, Nanki-Poo, whom she mistakenly supposes to have been executed. What makes the situation ludicrous is that Katisha (described in the dramatis personae as "an elderly lady") is easily old enough to be Nanki-Poo's mother, that he ran away from the Mikado's court to avoid having to marry her, and that in any case (as the audience is aware), he is still alive and only involved in an elaborate scheme to escape Katisha's clutches. Thus Katisha is that most risible of females, the old and unattractive woman lusting in vain after a young man who can't stand her.

Now Lydia stood on the stage, not in the character of Katisha as she would be with exaggerated makeup, bizarre and bristling headdress, and overdone histrionics, but dressed in jeans and a purple sweatshirt, singing simply, concentrating on the music. And now the song took on a genuine poignancy:

Hearts do not break!
They sting and ache
For old love's sake,
But do not die . . .

Sometimes during rehearsals a moment happens that a paying audience will never witness but that those who are present know is special and rare. This was one of those. Heads lifted, knitting needles stilled, whispered conversations broke off. Except, I noted, for Pooh-Bah, who sat in the last row murmuring to a member of the women's chorus, a thin woman with sharp features and a Theda Bara bob. The Chosen One whom, during the past week, he had singled out for attention. At least they were having the decency to keep it down.

Over a subdued accompaniment of guitar and muted winds, Lydia's still-resonant contralto rose on Sullivan's arching melody, singing Gilbert's words of mock despair:

Oh, living I!
Come, tell me why,
When hope is gone,
Dost thou stay on?

and they became real. When the song ended, the stillness in the place was absolute.

Until it was broken by a sudden bray of laughter from the back row. To do him a small justice, I don't think Pooh-Bah was reacting in any way to what Lydia had just done. I didn't think he'd even noticed—that the laugh was in response to some witticism from his partner in an unrelated context.

But the distinction, even if it mattered (better to be

deliberately insulted, or entirely overlooked?), was lost
on Lydia. Her face, lifted in the direction of that careless
laugh, flushed to a maroon that clashed cruelly with the
purple sweatshirt. And on it was an expression of such
bewilderment and hurt that I mentally kicked myself
for having been so blind. Incredibly (to me), Lydia Hicks
was helplessly, hopelessly in love with her awful ex-
husband. It had never occurred to me. Injured pride,
perhaps, disdain, irritation, even real enmity, yes. But
love? Yet there it was, emblazoned on that flushed face
under its strawberry blond pile with all the subtlety of a
billboard ad.

Or rather, there it had been. The company was ap-
plauding now, and Lydia responding with a smirk and
an exaggerated bow. She blew a queenly kiss or two,
turned, and exited behind the black flats. I had already
started down the aisle, and now I continued on, trotted
up the steps to the platform and followed after her. As I
reached the corridor backstage, I heard from the orchestra the opening strains of "Tit-Willow."

I found Lydia in the small room now being used as
the company office. She was standing behind the desk
and chair which were the room's only pieces of furniture, facing away toward the uncurtained window at
the back. Against the outside darkness, her reflected
image hovered—the ample figure, the arms tightly
crossed under her bosom, the tears running unchecked
and unheeded down her face. When my reflection appeared beside hers she turned. To my relief, she didn't
seem to mind my being there.

"I just wanted to say . . ." what *was* it I wanted to
say? "That was beautiful, what you did. It was just . . .
beautiful."

"Hunh," Lydia said. She heaved a large sigh and
dropped heavily into the desk chair, where she sat
staring at the surface of the desk while the tears continued to make glistening snail marks down her cheeks.
I stood in the doorway, unwilling to leave, but with no

idea what to say. After several moments, Lydia roused herself, grabbed a handful of tissues from a box on the desk and started mopping at her face. "Y'know something, Phoebe?" she said. "The frigging WAGS have it right. Old William S. was a misogynistic son of a bitch and we should be ashamed of ourselves." She blew her nose, pulled a compact out of her jeans' pocket and started to repair her makeup. "So instead, here we are aiding and abetting. Telling the world that any woman over the age of fifty—hell, over the age of twenty-one—is a pathetic, sex-starved harpy." She snapped the compact shut and stood up. "And you know something else? Screw 'em. I'm going to put on that god-awful warpaint and I'm going to play the hell out of Katisha. Because it's a great part, and how many of 'em are there out there for us harpies?"

"Tit-Willow" was coming to an end, and next up was Katisha and Ko-Ko's duet. Lydia came around the desk, and as we moved in the direction of the stage linked her arm in mine. "Don't get old, Phoebe," she said. "It's no fuckin' fun."

"Phoebe! Wait up!"

It was Nadine's voice, and I turned reluctantly and waited for her to join me on the sidewalk. It was late, I was tired, both physically and emotionally, and I just wanted to get to my car and go home. The incident with Lydia and Foster and then my conversation (if it could be called that) with Lydia had shaken me more than I could readily account for. What, I wondered, could Nadine possibly have to say to me that couldn't wait until tomorrow?

She came up to where I stood in the spill from a streetlight, breathing rather quickly. She was wearing an oversized navy peacoat which, though she topped my height by a couple of inches, made her slender body look positively frail. The harsh light of the halogen lamp paled the deep red of her hair and washed the little color from her face. She hugged her score of *The Mikado* to her chest, and when she spoke, the words, with their slight English accent, came in nervous little spurts. There was enough of a chill in the air to turn each word into a puff of vapor.

"I wanted to let you know . . . what you did, going after Lydia like that . . . after that bastard . . . God, he's the pits, you know? And nobody else made a move, but you . . . well, I was so glad that somebody . . ."

"I didn't really do much of anything. Lydia's a strong lady, she handled it. But thanks." I started to turn away.

"No, wait, I . . . there's something else."

"Yes?"

"It's something I've wanted to tell you ever since I knew who you were. But I didn't know whether I should. In fact, I'd pretty much decided not to. But then tonight . . . I mean, you were so sympathetic. But I'm afraid if I don't say it now . . ."

If Nadine's face, and the way she was clutching her score, hadn't expressed such an obvious level of anxiety, I would probably have pleaded exhaustion and told her to save it for another day. As it was, I said, "All right, Nadine. What is it?"

"Good night, Nadine. Phoebe."

It was Irene Polaski and Carl Piquette on their way to retrieve their cars. When they had passed, Nadine said, "Could we maybe go somewhere? I mean, like for coffee?"

Here I could draw the line. I shook my head. "Sorry, Nadine, but I really do need to get home. So why don't you just tell me what it is that's bothering you."

She fixed her eyes on my face, drew a shaky breath, and said, "Michael Mullins was my father."

I stared at the wispy small clouds that had issued from Nadine's mouth with these words. The crazy thought came to me that perhaps if I could catch them, gather them and stuff them back where they'd come from it would be as if they'd never been said. My second thought was to wonder, since I had just been hit in the chest with a large rock, why I was still standing. My third thought I spoke aloud. "I'm going to be sick," I said.

I pushed past Nadine to a space at the curb between two parked cars and threw up the remnants of Anandi's tandoori. When I turned around I saw Nadine, open-mouthed and looking frightened, and beyond her, Harry, who must have just come down the steps of the Old Church and was hurrying toward us.

"My God, Phoebe, are you all right?"

In other circumstances I might have been less tolerant of the human tendency at moments of stress to ask stupid questions. This time I was glad of the opening. "I'm fine," I said loudly. "I'm going home."

Harry was close enough by then to get a good look at me and he said, "Jesus, Phoebe, you look terrible. You shouldn't be driving, let me take you."

"*No,*" I said. "I'm perfectly able to drive myself."

Harry was now looking in bewilderment from me to Nadine. I gave Nadine a warning glare, turned my back on them both and walked away down the sidewalk.

Harry was right, of course. I had no business behind the wheel of anything more complicated than a kiddie car. When I pulled into Aunt Portia's driveway, I had no recollection of how I'd arrived there. But I had desperately needed to be by myself, to think, to calm myself, and that I had accomplished.

The one thought—the logical thought, you might say—that had *not* occurred to me at Nadine's flat and devastating statement was, Don't be silly, it can't be true. Because I'd known instantly that it *was* true. That periodic nagging sense of familiarity had not been an aberration, only unthinkable. Under the streetlight I had looked into Nadine's royal blue eyes and seen

Mick's eyes; noted the hands—long-fingered and deceptively delicate looking—clutching the *Mikado* score, and seen Mick's hands. I even knew who her mother was and that she had been married at the time and where she and Mick had met and when. I even remembered the extra tenderness that Mick had showed toward me around that time.

Nay-deen! I raged silently, what the hell kind of name was *Nay-deen*. *Our* daughter, Mick's and mine, would have been called Helen, after my mother.

I had to stop thinking.

Light glowed from the window of the small front room that housed the TV. I had to go in, make it past Anandi and my aunt and up to the sanctuary of my own bedroom.

"Hey, Phoebe, c'mere a minute," my aunt called as I crossed the band of light spilling from the open door of the TV room.

Portia and Anandi sat in matching armchairs, my aunt with her leg resting on an upholstered ottoman. As I stood in the doorway, my aunt gestured at the TV. "Take a look at this."

I went to stand by her chair and stared stupidly at the screen, where tiny figures in bright costumes gyrated to a familiar tune.

"It's the tape of that Canadian production," my aunt began, and then looked up at me. "Phoebe, what's happened?"

I tried to say, "nothing." I tried to say, "good night." I looked down at my aunt's face and reminded myself that this was a woman with a horror of emotional display.

I fell to my knees beside her chair, buried my face in her lap, and cried like a baby.

12

Dear, dear dear! This is very tiresome.

LATER, WHEN THE POLICE WERE PUMPING ME AND EVERY-
one else for significant incidents leading up to that
memorable opening night of *The Mikado,* I was to
wonder whether my personal turmoil had clouded my
perceptions of what was happening around me. One
thing though was clear: In contrast to the preceding hal-
cyon week, the remaining days of rehearsal were punctuated by smelly stuff hitting the fan with depressing
regularity.

The weather set the tone. It turned miserable
overnight, as if some cosmic dial had been switched
from Bright and Bracing to Wet and Dismal. The few
trees that had bided their time, waiting to become a
flashy coda to the fading season of brilliance, were
caught short. Their water-soaked leaves hung dispirit-
edly, or, wind-ripped from their branches, lay on the
sidewalks in sodden clumps. Kids mourned as Halloween promised to be a washout. TV weathermen,
trying in vain to hide their glee at finally having something to report, spoke solemnly of stationary fronts and

possible nor'easters. The temperature dropped twenty degrees and stayed there. It rained and rained.

On Sunday, Aunt Portia struggled out of bed, tried to stand, and promptly fell backwards, fortunately onto the bed. After Anandi and I had pleaded our way through several layers of medical bureaucracy with no success, Aunt Portia got on the phone. No, she didn't want any goddam ambulance to take her to the hospital so she could spend twenty-four hours waiting to see the goddam doctor. She wanted the goddam doctor here, now. Lawyers were mentioned, as well as certain significant contributions to the new Medical Center wing. The doctor came.

Aunt Portia, it appeared, in her eagerness to be sprung from house confinement, had overdone the exercising, straining the hip muscles that were in process of healing. With care, and a strict adherence to medical instruction, she should be able to make the *Mikado*'s opening night. On the bright side, the doctor opined that the arm cast could come off in a week.

Portia was not inclined to see a bright side. She had had her heart set on attending at least some of the final ten days of rehearsals. Now it seemed the investment that had been designed to launch her into the community had been a major bust. She was not happy. I got the feeling that in deference to my own fragile emotional state she was keeping up a good front with me, and that the brunt of her frustration was falling on Anandi. Anandi, who already blamed herself for not keeping a tight enough rein on her sister-in-law's activities, was thus doubly dejected.

As for me, I had not begun to come to grips with the sense of betrayal, anger, and confusion brought on by Nadine Gardner's revelation. Beyond a bare recital of the facts to explain my outburst of Saturday night, I was not ready to talk about it, even with my aunt. The three of us—Anandi, Portia, and I—ended up spending a lot of time tiptoeing around each other's various sensibilities; it didn't make for a comfortable household.

Therefore, when rehearsals resumed on Monday I was looking forward to a change, if only from one emotionally charged situation to another. Harry had phoned on Sunday afternoon, inquiring after my health. I'd told him it was a twenty-four-hour stomach bug and that I'd see him Monday night, and he seemed to accept that. From his tone, I was pretty sure that Nadine had not told him the cause of that peculiar scene under the streetlight, and for that, at least, I was grateful.

I was a few minutes late arriving at the Old Church. A sudden cloudburst, augmenting for a brief period the otherwise drizzly rain, had obscured the windshield to the point where I'd pulled the car over and waited it out. As I stood at the back of the auditorium, shaking out my umbrella and pulling off my poncho, I saw, sitting next to Harry in his customary command post, a familiar frizzy head. The Cougher had returned.

Harry looked over his shoulder, nervously I thought, and saw me coming down the aisle, my clipboard under one arm. He jumped to his feet.

"Oh, hi, Phoebe! As you see, Cynthia's back on her feet, so she can . . . um . . . take over doing the notes." His expression conveyed the equivalent of a helpless shrug.

From her seat beyond his, the Cougher favored me with a smug and toothy smile.

I smiled back. "Great!" I said. "Glad you're feeling better."

Harry grabbed my free hand. Uh-oh. There was more.

"The thing is, the person I thought was going to be stage manager has dropped out on me. And since you're the one who knows the show best . . . I really hate to ask, Phoebe, but could you?

I maintained the smile. What the hell? It would mean extending my stay by a couple of weeks but I had the feeling I'd probably need the time anyway to sort out my life before moving on. "Sure," I said. "There's a lot you'll have to fill me in on, but I guess I can handle it." I removed my hand from Harry's clasp, turned and continued down the aisle, but not before I'd noted an expression of immense satisfaction on the face of the Cougher. Ha! it said. Here *I* am at Harry's elbow and there *you* are banished backstage.

To my horror, I felt my eyes welling up. Oh, puh-*lease,* I scolded myself. It's not as if you have anything significant going with Mr. Charming-but-Cautious. Still, I could have used a bit of the closeness, camaraderie, friendly affection, whatever it was that we did have. First Mick, I thought, and now Harry. Over the past forty-eight hours my track record for inspiring male fidelity was reading 0 for 2.

I wrenched my mind away from that unpromising path and continued on up the steps and across the platform. If backstage was going to be my domain, I'd better give it a closer look than I'd done so far.

"For God's sake, Foster, you couldn't have missed the sign. I put it on the door myself. This room was supposed to be for Lydia and Jane."

I was halfway down the stairs that led from the backstage left side to the basement, where I knew the dressing rooms were being set up. It was Irene Polaski's voice I'd heard, but with an uncustomary edge.

There was an answering murmur with a placatory tone and when I reached the bottom of the stairs I saw Irene facing E. Foster, who stood in a doorway to my right. This door and two others beyond it presumably led to rooms located under the stage. Several others of the company were also standing around, including Lydia and Jane, the two teenagers, most of the female chorus, and Arnold Zimmer trying, with his usual success, to blend his bulk into the background. From above drifted the massed voices of the Gentlemen of Japan: "We figure in lively paint./ Our attitude's queer and quaint . . ."

From where I stood I was facing the main area of the basement, a large rectangular space interrupted by supporting columns. On the righthand wall was an old-fashioned porcelain utility sink. Next to it, an open door gave a glimpse of a lavatory sink and commode. A second sink on the opposite side sat next to a door that had been labeled with a cardboard sign reading WOMEN.

Around the perimeter of this space wires had been stretched in a rough circle and a start made in hanging on them makeshift curtains comprised of sheets. Another wire bisected the circle, presumably awaiting more sheets that would separate the space into male and female dressing rooms. A jumble of desks, tables, chairs, a random assortment of mirrors, and portable clothes racks with dangling hangers awaited arranging into some sort of order. The concrete floor had been thoroughly swept, but the characteristic basement smell of dust and damp still hung on the air. While a lot of work remained to be done, it was evident that someone, or more likely several someones, had been busy over the past two days.

No one, though, had been busier than E. Foster Ballard. Looking past him where he stood in the doorway, I could see against the opposite wall of the room a table covered neatly with white toweling. On top of the toweling lay an assortment of makeup items, two boxes of Kleenex, a jar of cold cream, a hand mirror, a small radio, and, at one end, an electric teapot. Propped against the wall was a four-foot-by-four-foot mirror, surrounded top and sides by banks of bulbs. A wire stretched across one corner supported, on separate hangers, E. Foster's own kimono, underskirt, and bulky sash. In front of the table sat a single folding chair. A collection of dusty pieces of sports equipment—a scuffed soccer ball, three or four heavily dinged baseball bats, parts of a croquet set, leftovers, I imagined, from a long-ago church youth group—had been shoved in an untidy heap to the far side of the room. A piece of grey carpeting lay in the space between door and dressing table.

Irene gave me an exasperated glance, then turned back to E. Foster. "Very cozy, Foster, but it's not fair. This is the biggest room and it should have at least two people in it and they should be Lydia and Jane."

"Now, now, dear lady," Foster drawled. "Age before beauty, you know. And I assure you, Derek is well aware that I absolutely need privacy before a performance. A silly quirk of mine, perhaps, but there it is."

"Oh!" cried Jane Manypenny, "I'm sure we can all understand how Dr. Ballard feels. I don't mind *at all,* Irene, taking another room. I'm sure Lydia and I can sort out . . ." here she faltered and looked anxiously toward her prospective roommate. Lydia, for her part, was leaning against the wall next to the second door, arms folded, wearing a look compounded of disgust and amusement. She raised her eyebrows, but said nothing.

Seeming to take heart from Lydia's silence, Jane burbled on, "The girls have already said they want to be with the others in the big space, and let's see . . . Mitchell and Carl and Derek have the third room, which is *quite* big, and Arnold—" She broke off, frowning.

"Arnold should share Foster's room," Irene said decidedly.

Arnold Zimmer, galvanized into speech by the temerity of this suggestion, stammered, "No, no, I wouldn't think of . . . I couldn't . . . I mean, I'd much rather dress with the chorus guys."

"Well, there then," Jane said brightly. "Bob's your uncle!"

Irene's scornful gaze swept over the assembled group. "My God, you people, you just let this man ride roughshod over you, have every damn thing his own way!" An angry flush had risen in her cheeks. Today she was wearing a dirndl skirt with a vest and had coiled her thick, fair braid around her head and fastened it with another silk-flowered barrette. The total effect was of Heidi, grown up and mad as hell. She turned to me. "Phoebe, aren't you the stage manager now? Maybe you can persuade *Doctor Ballard* to see reason."

It sure hadn't taken *that* bit of news long to make the rounds. Had I been the last to know? And here I was, faced with the first of what I was certain would turn out to be many proofs of why I should have turned the job down cold. So what's it going to be, Phoebe: wimp or warrior?

I had opened my mouth, still without a clue as to what was going to come out of it, when I was rescued by Lydia.

"Screw it, Irene, we all know ol' Foster's never going to change his stripes. Besides," with a kindly smile in Foster's direction, "perhaps he's right. Perhaps being the old man of the company does give him dibs on the best dressing room." She turned to the second door and pulled it open. "C'mon, Janey, let's see what we've got here."

Jane Manypenny, looking mightily relieved, scuttled into the room behind Lydia. The rest of the onlookers moved away—Ardys and Beth to the far reaches of the chorus dressing area, where their smothered giggles could still be heard.

E. Foster, who had looked considerably taken aback by his ex-wife's pronouncement, quickly recovered his aplomb. He put a hand on Irene's shoulder. "You see, my dear? No problem, everybody happy."

Irene Polaski swung her arm and caught Foster's a glancing blow, knocking his hand away. Then she turned, brushed past me, and ran up the stairs.

Foster rubbed his arm and said to me with arch ruefulness, "Ah, these artistic temperaments. Think you can handle it, little Phoebe?"

"Yes," I replied neutrally, "I think I can handle it."

He gave me an up-and-down look. "Care to come in? See what I've done with the room?"

My God, how had the old sleaze ever attained his vaunted position in the community? And in this correct new world, had the words "sexual harassment" not yet entered his vocabulary? I stared at him, while various phrases of righteous outrage battled it out for first choice.

And suddenly it was all too much. My capacity for processing heartbreak, anger, betrayal, and now repugnance had reached its limit and I burst into ungovernable laughter. I saw E. Foster's smooth, fleshy cheeks turn pink. Undoubtedly I had made an enemy, but what the hell? I flapped my hands helplessly and went to check the other dressing rooms, still giggling.

"Nadine," I said.

Rehearsal was over, and the music director was standing at the piano, gathering her score and other papers together. She was alone, the orchestra not having been convened for this rehearsal. She stiffened in the act of cramming her accumulation of material into a sturdy backpack, and turned on me a look both wary and resentful.

I didn't blame her. Whatever kind of reaction she might have been expecting with her revelation of Saturday night, it couldn't have been the one she got. What had she thought I'd do? Welcome with glad cries this living evidence of a husband's calculated deception? A dead husband, too, one beyond the reach of recrimination or even eventual reconciliation.

"I know we have to talk," I said. "But not . . . just yet."

Nadine's expression became marginally less guarded. "Okay," she said.

"And about Saturday night, well . . . it was a shock. As you no doubt noticed."

She didn't crack a smile, only nodded. It came to me how young she was. How was I ever going to be able to explain. . . . Whatever. It wasn't going to be now.

I started to go, then turned. "You have his hands," I said, then turned back and went quickly up the aisle.

13

*Don't let's be downhearted! There's
a silver lining to every cloud.*

ON TUESDAY THE COSTUMES ARRIVED, TO INITIAL CRIES
of delight. These lasted until people actually started
trying the things on. Derek had been right: the costumes were beautiful. They came complete with wigs,
were in a muted rainbow of pastels that would show
up wonderfully against the basic black background, and
did indeed involve "drapery that won't stop." It was
this last that was the problem.

The men, finding themselves in what amounted to
floor-length dresses with sleeves that drooped to their
ankles, suddenly became incapable of taking a step
without tripping. The difficulties were compounded for
the women by filmy, high-waisted overskirts designed
to billow out airily while they moved, then settle in
graceful swirls around the feet when still. One by one
the actors struggled up the stairs from the basement
dressing area, arms clutching excess yardage, to swell
the chorus of complaints. "How am I supposed to do
fancy things with a fan and . . ." "Whoever chose . . ."
"Look what happens when I try to. . . ."

There were a few exceptions. Derek Bowles and

Mitchell Kim were outfitted in pantaloons that stopped at mid-calf, so were not party to the general complaints. Derek, for the moment, was ignoring the to-do in favor of practising with glee the manipulation of a huge plastic executioner's sword. Lydia Hicks was quite sensibly exploring the movement possibilities of a three-foot train. Similarly, Carl Piquette had retired to a corner of the auditorium and was going over the steps for the opening number. And Arnold Zimmer, magnificent in red, black, and gold, had metamorphosed into the commanding figure the Mikado was supposed to be. He had taken a position center stage and was looking lordly as all get out. I made a mental note to assign a couple of chorus members to manage his train, which was even longer than Katisha's.

Into these thoughts erupted Pooh-Bah's oily tones, observing to no one in particular but loudly enough to be heard by all, "It appears that our esteemed choreographer neglected to take the small matter of costumes into consideration." I reflected sourly that it hadn't taken long for yesterday's little flight of lèse-majesté to flutter home to roost. He, of course, was wearing his own, authentic outfit, black splashed here and there with large flowers of a poisonous yellow, with a black underskirt that hung well clear of the floor. A wide yellow sash provided a showcase for the precious aikuchi knife. In contrast with the others, he looked like a crow who had wandered into a rose garden, but at least, I had to admit, he wasn't falling over his feet.

What made his remark really sting was that it was at least partly true. By the middle of last week I had begun to insist that everyone start wearing the socks and flip-flops that would approximate Japanese footwear. But I hadn't taken a close look at the photos of those costumes. Damn, damn, damn! However . . .

Standing just below the lip of the stage, I took a good look at the actors milling around on its boards, noting, in spite of their awkwardness, the basic elegance and flow of the costume designs, the fineness of the fabrics, and thinking it must be costing Aunt Portia a packet. And where was Harry during all this? Ah yes, sitting in his usual place, staring at the stage with a bemused expression while the Cougher murmured into his ear. I went over to him.

"I'm sorry about this, Harry. I should have been more aware of the costumes, how they'd affect the movement. But I don't think it's anything that can't be easily fixed."

The Cougher gave me an "Oh yeah, right" smirk, which I ignored.

"Okay if I work with them for a few minutes?"

"Absolutely," Harry said. As I turned to go, he caught my hand. "And by the way, I have no doubt about your being right. Just thought I'd give them a chance to vent a bit before you whipped them into shape."

He squeezed my hand before letting it go. The Cougher glared. I felt an unbecoming wave of triumph. What are you *doing*, Phoebe—competing like a teenager over a man you're not even sure you feel anything for beyond a passing itch?

Much as those in charge of boarding schools try to prevent it, students end up with a lot of free time on their hands during which many of life's more useful skills are acquired. I put two fingers in my mouth and delivered a whistle that produced a shocked and sudden silence.

"All right, people," I said, "For Pete's sake, chill out. This is not a big problem and we can deal with it right now." Before the mumbling could rise again, I turned quickly to Irene. "Is there any reason why the men's . . . uh . . . skirts can't be hemmed up an inch or two?"

Irene, who had been standing at one side of the stage with her lips tightly folded, shook her head. "No reason at all. If I get some help I can have it done by to-morrow."

"Good. May I have just the women on stage, please.

Okay. Now take the front edge of that gauzy stuff in your left hand—about halfway down, like this . . ."

If, previously, tentative lines had been drawn, from then on they were etched in cement. Of those who chose to socialize after the rehearsal, Pooh-Bah & Company now shunned Sam's pizzeria in favor of a rival bistro called the Grotto. On the Tuesday night of the costume flap, as Harry and I joined the group in a booth at Sam's, the tone was subdued.

"Thanks, Phoebe," Irene said as Harry and I slid in next to her. "I was getting so mad at those idiots I was about to lose it."

Carl Piquette said, "The costumes are fantastic, Irene. And it's not as if we're not getting them in plenty of time to work out any problems."

Beside him, Lydia said, "Mine makes me look like the wrath of God." Then, with a grin at Irene, "Which is what it's supposed to do. I friggin' love it."

There was a pitcher of beer on the table, but Lydia, I noticed, was sipping from a glass of clear liquid garnished with a lemon. At her elbow was a Perrier bottle.

"I just wish I knew what the hell is going on," Harry said. "I swear, I've never had to deal with anything like this before."

Carl said, with a bitterness which I hadn't heard in his voice before, "But then you've never had to deal with our Dr. Ballard. The man poisons everything he touches."

There was a pause, and I realized we were automatically waiting for some crack from Lydia. None came, though. She simply shrugged and continued to sip her Perrier.

"And now," Harry continued glumly, "it appears I've alienated my directorial assistant to the point where she probably won't want to talk to me. *That*'s going to make things awkward."

"Harry, if I—" I began, but he cut me off.

"It has nothing to do with you, Phoebe. Cynthia was a student of mine at the college. A 'returning' student, as they say, older than the others. She, um . . . seems to have developed a crush of sorts. I thought I'd made it plain how I felt or I'd never have asked her to join the company." He covered my hand with his as it rested on the table. "Believe me, I'm glad to be rescued. It's probably the only way she'd be convinced to lay off."

Hmm. Wonderful. So happy to be useful. I felt a glimmer of sympathy for the Cougher. Harry definitely needed work on making his feelings explicit.

Lydia shot me an amused and empathetic glance. No one offered any further comment, and we sat for a few moments in a kind of companionable gloom until Derek breezed in. He plopped down beside Carl, grinned at Harry, and said, "I think Foster's weakening. About the horse and carriage. I caught him just after rehearsal and painted him a picture of how devastatingly distinguished he'd look dressed up as Gilbert. He didn't actually say no."

Harry was not in the mood. "Portia *has* said no," he stated flatly. "And no wonder, after what she's paying to rent those costumes. Besides, as far as I'm concerned, no one in the cast needs any more distractions, including you. I assume you *are* working on the set pieces and the lighting design?"

"Oh well," Derek said airily, "I might even pop for the horse and buggy myself. The show is going to be marvelous, I want people to be there. And yes, Harry, the lumber's arriving tomorrow and Carl has rounded up a bunch of high school kids who he swears will know what they're doing."

Carl nodded an agreement as Derek burbled on: "And speaking of my *truly* Renaissance talents, listen to this." He jumped up, struck a pose, and sang to the tune of Ko-Ko's signature song, "I've got a little list":

"There's the double-dealing lawyer
And the others of his kind
Who slap your back with one hand
While the other steals you blind;
The pompous old professor
Who's an everlasting bore
But you're stuck 'cause he got tenure
Over twenty years before,
And that crystal-waving simpleton
The new-age therapist,
They'd none of 'em be missed—
They'd none of 'em be missed!"

There was applause from several directions, including the booth opposite ours where Nadine and Mitchell sat with three members of the ensemble. Derek smirked and bowed and turned back to us. "Well?"

Harry threw up his hands with a resigned expression. "Now I see why you want a big audience—so you can insult as many people as possible at one blow. Christ, Derek, lawyers and teachers and therapists? Have you looked around you lately?"

Derek pouted. "Shot down again. What always happens to us creative types. Ah, well."

He surveyed our five faces, chuckled, and said, "Cheer up, troops! I promise you, everything's going to be just fine. I'm just off to the Grotto. Up to me, you see, to keep everyone charming!"

He took himself off, and we exchanged expressions of disbelief. Carl articulated what we were all no doubt thinking: "If he's including Foster in that, I'd say his 'charming' expiration date is long past."

At least, we agreed, we had one thing to be thankful for. The bad weather had chased the WAGS from the door; no pickets had shown up so far this week. Perhaps they'd had their say and were satisfied.

14

Prepare yourselves for news surprising!

The flyer was egg-yolk yellow printed in black. It read:

JOIN US IN A PROTEST WALKOUT!

The Northampton Repertory Company has chosen as their opening production Gilbert and Sullivan's *The Mikado,* a musical that is REACTIONARY, SEXIST, and INSULTING to WOMEN. Let them know that Northampton WILL NOT TOLERATE this sort of SEXIST PROPAGANDA. Buy up their tickets, then join us in a WALKOUT that will leave the theater EMPTY! You CAN make a difference!

This flyer distributed by WAGS
Women Against Gilbert and Sullivan

Derek's face as he studied this missive was the face of an innocent newly introduced to the perfidies of the world. He looked up and around at the members of the company gathered at the front of the auditorium. Most of them also carried copies of the flyer. "Why are they *doing* this?" he wailed. "The damn things are all over town!"

No more insistence, I noted, that any publicity was good publicity. If the WAGS were successful, then good news at the box office could as easily be interpreted as bad news. I couldn't believe that the WAGS actually had enough sympathizers to make much of a showing, but then I didn't know Northampton all that well. At the least, they had achieved a breach in our producer's stance of dogged optimism.

Jane Manypenny said, "Well *I* think they've got some bloody nerve! Isn't this sort of thing against the law?"

E. Foster, lounging in a front row seat with his legs stretched out in front of him, stared thoughtfully at the ceiling and drawled, "You may have something there, Janey. Restraint of trade, perhaps?"

"I imagine," Carl Piquette said acidly, "that they're counting on that First Amendment thing. A big rule with us colonials, Jane. But then Dr. Ballard here has never been much bothered by rules."

It was the closest I'd heard him come to addressing Pooh-Bah directly.

Harry said loudly, "Okay, people, rehearsal time."

It turned out that four of the cast had called in sick: Mitchell Kim, Beth Rosario, and two members of the men's chorus. By the next night, Thursday, one week before the dress rehearsal, they had been joined by two more. A twenty-four-hour stomach bug, they said, that was "going around." From then on, rehearsals were conducted with a fluctuating roster of the sickening, the recovering, and the few who escaped entirely, who went on at boring length about the particular combination of diet, herbal remedies, and virtuous lifestyles to which they credited the superiority of their immune systems.

Harry succumbed, but turned up anyway and made it through with only one quick dash to the men's room. The Cougher sat three seats away from him and turned her head away whenever he leaned over to give her a note. Finally he gave up and took his own.

I came down with it in the small hours of Sunday morning, and missed the Monday rehearsal. But I was there on Tuesday when one of the high school girls on the set-construction crew came running up from the basement, wide-eyed, to announce to that evening's early arrivals that someone had taken a baseball bat to the mirror in Pooh-Bah's dressing room.

"Everyone stay where you are!" Harry barked, forestalling an automatic mass movement in the direction of the basement stairs. He jerked his head at Derek and the two of them disappeared behind the black flats.

Standing at the back of the theater, I did a quick recon of who was currently on the premises.

The girl who had made the discovery stood on the stage chattering excitedly to a group that included the other members of her crew—another girl and three boys—and Jane Manypenny. I heard the words, ". . . just passing by and I happened to . . ." and "I mean, it's, like, you know, totally smashed."

Irene Polaski sat on the lip of the platform, legs dangling, hands braced on either side, looking downward as her head shook slowly from side to side. She was wearing another of her Swiss Miss outfits. The jeweled barette anchoring her coiled braid sparkled with incongruous cheerfulness under the stage lights.

Lydia Hicks was at the piano, talking to Nadine. After a first startled reaction to the news, they had resumed their conversation, though I thought I'd detected a brief frown of concern from Lydia. The five musicians (out of eight) who were healthy enough to be on hand were busy setting up and appeared uninterested in whatever nonsense the actors had gotten up to this time. I was just starting down the aisle when Carl Piquette emerged from backstage, presumably from the large former Sunday School classroom where the scene shop had been set up. He was quickly clued in by his group of techies and I saw his look of disbelief and his mouth forming a muttered, "Ah, shit."

Pooh-Bah's entrance through the swinging doors at the back of the auditorium caused a momentary, almost guilty, hush. He surveyed the scene with raised eyebrows. "Talking about me, were we?" he said archly. "Do go on."

Jane Manypenny bustled to the front of the stage. "Dr. Ballard, I think you'd better . . . oh dear, there seems to have been some sort of . . . of *vandalism* in your dressing room." Her voice was high with distress. In another minute, I thought, she'd be wringing her hands.

"Indeed," Pooh-Bah said, smoothly. However, he wasted no time heading for the basement stairs, not even stopping to take off his coat.

Five minutes later he reappeared, followed by Harry and Derek. While whatever discussion that had taken place had been brief, it had patently not been harmonious. Harry's face was flushed, his mouth compressed into a thin line. Derek was running his hands repeatedly through his silky fair hair and glancing nervously from Harry to E. Foster and back. By now most of the cast—those that weren't home throwing up—had drifted in, been updated, and waited, agog, to be filled in on the latest bad news.

Harry said, tightly and without preamble, "Someone has smashed Foster's dressing room mirror with one of the baseball bats stored there. My feeling is that this was a deliberate piece of vandalism and that the police should be called."

Gasps from the listeners.

"Foster, however," barely acknowledging with a glance Pooh-Bah, who stood beside him looking properly grave and rocking slightly back and forth in his soft shoes, "does not agree with me. He thinks it was an accident—someone fooling around with some of the sports equipment in his room and hitting the mirror by mistake."

Here E. Foster directed a look of avuncular admonishment, accompanied by a small head shake, toward the group of high school students comprising the technical crew.

"Hey!" one of the boys said indignantly. "We didn't—"

"Please!" Harry interrupted. "Let me finish." He tugged on his earlobe, stared at the floor for a moment, then raised his head. "I'm not entirely happy with this decision, but I was outvoted." He glanced to his other side at Derek, who was biting his lip and actually looking subdued. "So this is the thing. From now on, nobody—*nobody*—goes into the basement except for me and the actors. And, of course, the stage manager," with a nod at me. "There's no reason for any of the rest of you to be there and for you it is out of bounds. Am I clear?"

Nods, and some muttered grumbling from the high schoolers.

"The only other thing I have to say," his voice just this side of pleading, "is that we have the makings of a wonderful show here. And it's been difficult with so many people sick. So we need a hundred percent from each of you to pull it together. Three days, guys."

It was a sobering thought.

I was in no condition, on that eve of the first (and final) performance of the Northampton Repertory Company's *Mikado,* to formulate a list of the questions that I had accumulated during the eventful weeks since my arrival at my aunt's house. But when I thought about it afterwards, I thought it would have included these:

What had caused the sudden turnaround in Lydia Hicks's behavior?

What was the background to Carl Piquette's evident loathing of E. Foster Ballard?

Ditto for Irene Polaski.

And while on the subject of who loathed E. Foster, what had really happened between him and Aunt Portia? And was it connected to whatever had caused her flight from her home?

Why was Derek Bowles so chummy with the horrible Pooh-Bah?

What did I actually know about Harry Johns, and was I in danger of falling seriously in love?

Was there some connection between Pooh-Bah and Jane Manypenny beyond their participation in *The Mikado*?

Who had put ipecac (or something) in E. Foster's coffee, torn up his score, and smashed his mirror? And why was he so determined to deny the implications?

What was I going to do about Nadine Gardner?

The answers to only two of those questions, as it turned out, would bear directly on the terrible aftermath of *The Mikado*'s opening night: Pooh-Bah lying crumpled on his dressing-room floor; me staring in horror at the knife buried in his back; my aunt's voice saying, "Don't touch 'im, Phoebe. He's dead."

15

A dignified and potent officer . . .

"IF YOU'RE READY, MS. MULLINS."

I stared at the man sitting across from me at the kitchen table. *Ready?* Hollow laughter of the metaphorical sort reverberated in my brain. No, I wasn't *ready*! Not for any of this.

How could it possibly be happening to me again? I absolved myself for ignoring that "it" had in fact happened to E. Foster Ballard: for the second time in less than six months I was facing a police interrogation in a case of murder and the person I was feeling sorry for was me.

The man at the other side of the table had been introduced to me as Detective Lieutenant Hal Griffith. The person who had done the introducing was Ben Solliday, the Bear, adding to my feelings of confusion and paranoia. What the hell was the Bear doing here? He hadn't even been at the theater last night, why was this any of his business?

Ben Solliday, it turned out, was a longtime pal of Lieutenant Griffith's. It had been thought that his presence might make my aunt and me feel more comfortable. He could assure us that the lieutenant was a really good man. A straight shooter. We had nothing to fear from talking freely to him.

Unless, of course, ran the unspoken subtext, it turned out to have been either Portia Singh or Portia Singh's niece who had plunged the dagger into Pooh-Bah's back.

At the moment, it was the niece's turn to face the Straight Shooter. The aunt, according to Anandi, was still sleeping off the effects of last night's trauma coupled with a hit of Demerol. Anandi had served coffee to the Bear, the lieutenant, and me, then quietly excused herself. The coffee, I noted, probably in deference to the double dose of testosterone on the premises, was good and strong.

If I had been asked to estimate Lieutenant Hal Griffith's age from his face I would have given myself a leeway of between thirty-five and fifty. Thin, almost white skin crisscrossed with spiderweb-fine lines stretched tightly across the bones of cheeks, jaw, and brow. His eyes were narrow, close-set, and very blue. His hair, at a guess, was a fading, perhaps greying, red, but cut so short as to be almost invisible. He was narrow-shouldered and wiry and, I noticed when they walked in together, a head shorter than the Bear. If their friendship was indeed close and long-standing, I wondered how many "odd couple" jokes they'd had to endure. The lieutenant took his coffee black, no sugar. I had a feeling he wasn't entirely comfortable with the situation. He had produced one brief, tight smile as he shook my hand and now sat straight-backed and sober-faced, as if to remind me, with an excess of formality, that this was not, after all, a social occasion. I wondered what sort of influence the Bear wielded to have been allowed to sit in.

The Bear was sitting at the head of the table in Aunt Portia's chair. The one time I'd glanced at him, his sympathetic brown eyes, gazing at me from above his exuberant tangle of facial hair, had been so full of concern that I'd looked quickly away. His intentions, I was sure, were the best, but if this was his idea of a reassuring presence, it needed work.

Lieutenant Griffith cleared his throat and pushed his coffee cup to one side. From the breast pocket of his grey tweed jacket he produced a minuscule notepad and a stubby pencil. I sighed.

"I drove myself and Mrs. Singh to the theater in my aunt's car. We got there at about six-fifteen. The call for the actors wasn't until seven, but as stage manager I needed to be there early . . ."

Let alone the fact that Aunt Portia had been dressed and ready since four in the afternoon, and in a state of such barely suppressed excitement that I'd been afraid another moment's delay might result in nervous collapse. The occasion was not only to be her introduction to *The Mikado* and the Old Church Theater. Aside from a couple of practice sessions in getting down the front steps and into the front seat of the car, followed by short drives into the countryside, it was her official reentrance into the outside world. Her eagerness let me know what a burden her confinement had been to her.

I had kept to myself the information that the dress rehearsal had been a shambles of miscues, botched entrances, bungled choreography, and plaints along the lines of "You must have changed that while I was out sick and nobody told me." The system of remote-control headphones had tested out fine at the tech run-through the night before. Now they crackled and hissed and faded in and out, making communication between me, huddled behind the stage-right masking flat, and the lighting crew in the balcony a hit-and-miss affair. Fadeouts came too soon, leaving singers warbling their final notes in the dark, spots appeared on the opposite side of the stage from the entrances they were supposed to illuminate. Harry, though trying to hide it, was clearly sinking deeper and deeper into gloom as the rehearsal progressed. Beside him the Cougher, from the sporadic glimpses I got, was taking a kind of grim pleasure in the whole debacle. Even Derek's determined optimism was beginning to ring hollow by the time the rehearsal limped to an end, though he gave a brave little speech to the exhausted and disheartened assemblage promising "a brilliant show" on the morrow. The WAGS's threatened walkout wasn't mentioned. Perhaps many were thinking, like me, that if, say, half the audience left, half the humiliation would go with them.

I had little faith in the dictum that "a bad dress rehearsal means a great first night." A bit of spurious folklore, I'd always thought, coined by a desperate director who had known that without it his actors would never be persuaded to take the stage at all in front of a paying audience. Still, among the chaos there had been glimmers of what could be. In spite of myself I hoped, for all our sakes and especially for Aunt Portia's, for a miracle.

". . . and after I'd seen my aunt to her seat, I went downstairs to the dressing rooms."

The lieutenant said, "And that was when you overheard the altercation between the victim and the director, Harry Johns. In Dr. Ballard's dressing room."

I nodded resignedly. If he'd already been told this stuff . . . ah well, I knew the drill. "Harry—Mr. Johns—had gotten a complaint from the father of one of the younger cast members, Beth Rosario. About Dr. Ballard. He—Mr. Rosario—was threatening to pull Beth out of the show. Harry was telling Dr. Ballard to, well, cut it out."

The lieutenant's barely existent eyebrows lifted. "It?"

"The pat on the bottom. The 'accidental' brush against the breast. Beth had told me about it earlier, and I'd given her a bit of advice about handling it. I didn't realize it was still going on."

"What did you tell her?" He sounded genuinely interested.

I explained about the foot-stomping ploy. The lieutenant grinned, a maneuver that sent the fine lines radiating into a burst of agreeable grooves. He shook his
head, and quickly reverted to sobriety. "You didn't
think of reporting the matter to the director, or to"—he
flipped back a few pages in his notepad—"the producer,
Derek Bowles?"

"No, I didn't. Look, Lieutenant, unfortunately that
kind of sexist power play is something young women
like Beth are going to encounter over and over. My
feeling is that if they don't want to be running off to
lawyers all the time they'd better learn to handle it on
their own. Up to a point, of course. And I thought Beth
could handle it. I was surprised to learn that she'd told
her father after all."

Lieutenant Griffith nodded thoughtfully. "How
angry would you say Mr. Johns sounded?"

The question caught me off balance—as it was no
doubt intended to do.

"Well, I only came in on the end . . . that is, they
stopped when I . . ."

I recalled Harry's voice, raised and with an edge I'd
never heard there before. "For God's sake, Foster, what
kind of fool are you? I had a hell of a time calming
Rosario down, he was ready to charge you with assault!"

And Pooh-Bah, the oil gone, the timbre pure steel:
"Careful, Johns. You're hardly the one to go around
talking about assault. I wonder just how much your
employers at that so-called college of yours know about
that business in—"

It was then they must have become aware of my
step on the stairs. By the time I reached the bottom
Harry was coming out of the dressing room and Pooh-
Bah could be heard humming the opening bars of his
first number. Harry's face was white, his lips set in a
grim line. I thought he was relieved to see it was me,
but all he managed as he passed was a quick grasp of

my shoulder and a muttered, "Can you believe that asshole?" as he headed for the stairs at the front end of the
basement.

In answer to the lieutenant's question, I said carefully, "I'd say he was appropriately angry. From what I
heard, Mr. Rosario was threatening assault charges. Not
the sort of thing a director wants to deal with on an
opening night. Besides the possibility of losing an important cast member."

"That was all you heard?"

"Yes," I said. After all, I had no idea what Pooh-Bah
had meant by "that business in" wherever. It could have
been pure bluster, though it hadn't sounded . . . no
matter. Time enough, I decided, to throw the cops a
bone in the shape of Harry Johns's perhaps dubious
past if and when Aunt Portia—or I, for that matter—
looked to be in real danger.

"Okay. And after that?"

"I checked the dressing rooms—mainly the central
area that was used by most of the cast, to make sure
there were enough chairs and so on, and I fixed a couple
of the curtains that were pulling off the clip-on hooks."

"Did you talk to Dr. Ballard then?"

"No," I said, with more emphasis than I'd intended.

In my peripheral vision I thought I saw the Bear's expression become even more anxious. I felt like patting
him on the arm and telling him I really hadn't done it.
The lieutenant, however, made no comment and only
said, "And what happened next?"

"Well, everybody started coming in—the cast and
crew and the musicians. A lot of excitement, of course,
being opening night. There were flowers delivered,
people giving each other presents, that kind of thing. And
then we did the show." I couldn't help adding, "It was a
wonderful show."

Because the miracle had happened. The adrenaline rush occasioned by heightened nerves, last-ditch

determination, and in some cases outright terror had produced a phenomenon of collective focus.

As the musicians played the opening notes of the overture with its "Mi-ya Sa-ma" theme ushered in by the quick boom-boom-boom-boom of the bass drum, my liaison in the balcony murmured into his headset— now working perfectly—the news that a grand total of four people had risen from their seats and stalked out of the theater. The applause that rewarded Nadine and her ensemble as the overture ended was hearty, with a smattering of bravos thrown in. Clearly, this was an audience prepared to enjoy themselves. Please God, I prayed, don't let us screw up too badly.

The Gentlemen of Japan took the stage. Through a tiny peephole in the flat I watched in awe as fans snapped on cue, kimonos swirled with authority, everyone remembered where to go, nobody fell down. And those eight voices, buoyed on the Old Church Theater's magical acoustics, rang like twenty.

Nanki-Poo made his entrance with his recitative: "Gentlemen, I pray you tell me . . ." When he reached "In pity speak—oh speak, I pray you!" I could have sworn I heard a collective feminine sigh rise from the house. The end of "A wand'ring minstrel, I" was greeted with the kind of high-pitched appreciation more commonly accorded to rock stars.

If E. Foster had been in any degree chastened by his encounter with Harry and the threats of Mr. Rosario, there was now no sign of it. His entrance received a burst of applause, which he acknowledged in character and then he proceeded to take command of the stage— unctuous, outrageous, and very, very funny. Although I hated admitting it, his costume even worked for him, emphasizing Pooh-Bah's apartness—in his own mind at least—from the hoi polloi with whom he was compelled to associate.

The women's chorus glided in, their drapery under

full command. Then the Three Little Maids, chipper as all get out and note perfect.

And when a portentous trumpet fanfare ushered in the diminutive Ko-Ko, dwarfed even further by the enormous sword he struggled to keep balanced on his shoulder, the howls of the audience almost drowned out the opening bars of "Behold the Lord High Executioner."

And so it went, from Act I to Act II to the standing ovation at the end. The miracle I had asked for. The golden moment forever made poignant when it turned out to be the one and only.

The lieutenant said, "I heard it was very good. My wife and I and Ben here had tickets for tonight."

Ben Solliday said, "I'm really sorry I didn't get to see it, Phoebe."

I turned to him. "I thought you didn't care for Gilbert and Sullivan."

The Bear looked hurt. "I'm not as hidebound as you seem to think. Besides, I could hardly listen to you and Portia talk about the show all this time without being curious."

Lieutenant Griffith cleared his throat. "What's your take on this organization that calls itself"—he consulted his notepad again and his expression became skeptical—"WAGS? I understand they'd been causing trouble for the production."

I shook my head impatiently. "They picketed and they threatened a walkout that didn't materialize, and that's all. In my opinion they were perfectly sincere and perfectly harmless."

"Not responsible, then, for these other . . . uh . . . incidents connected with Dr. Ballard? His playbook being torn up, mirror broken?"

"And putting something in his coffee? No, I'm sure not. Everyone seemed to want to blame them, but—"

"Wait a minute," the lieutenant interrupted. "Coffee?"

Rats! What had been that mantra I'd formulated? Answer questions. Don't volunteer. Don't complicate things. This time I was *not* going to get involved in matters that only guaranteed pain in one form or another to the involvee.

"It was probably nothing," I began, and then remembered that the Bear had been present that morning at the kitchen table when I had described in detail Pooh-Bah's sudden and graphic indisposition. I gave the lieutenant the short version. "At the time I thought it was odd—so out of the blue, you know. And then we were talking about it the next morning and Aunt Portia made a joke about somebody putting ipecac in his coffee—except she said cocoa, I think—and it started me thinking about how it would have been possible. But, as I say—"

"Ipecac?" the lieutenant said.

"It's an emetic—what you give people to make them vomit. A syrup, very sweet. A tablespoonful is supposed to work in under twenty minutes."

Lieutenant Griffith regarded me with, I thought, renewed interest. "You seem to know a lot about it."

Oh damn, why hadn't I kept my mouth shut? I sighed. "I was downtown the other day and I happened to pass a drugstore. I went in and found the ipecac and checked the label."

The lieutenant nodded. "I see. This was some time after the . . . uh . . . incident?"

The logical question hung in the air. I gave up and answered it. "I'd noticed that from then on, during the coffee breaks, Pooh-Bah—Dr. Ballard—after he got his coffee would walk around holding the cup close to his chest. He wouldn't put it down until it was time to clear up."

"Suggesting to you," the lieutenant said, "that he suspected it had been tampered with?"

I nodded.

The Bear spoke for the first time. "But wouldn't he have noticed the taste?"

"I don't think so," I said. "He took his coffee light with three sugars."

The lieutenant and the Bear exchanged a glance which, on the Bear's part, conveyed a sort of proprietorial pride. The lieutenant said, "You're a very noticing sort of person, Ms. Mullins."

"Well, I—"

"I understand you were involved in that case on Long Island this past summer. Where the opera singer was murdered. That you had something to do with solving it."

I shot the Bear what I hoped was an unmistakably dirty look. Here I'd thought he was looking out for my welfare while in reality he'd been throwing me to the wolves in the person of the Straight Shooter. How had the Bear (presumably the lieutenant's source of information) found out about my involvement in the Varovna Colony murders? My name had appeared in the newspapers only in connection with my role as near victim. I thought back to that first meal with Aunt Portia and Anandi, remembering the barrage of questions pushing me into ever greater detail about my part in the investigation. Oh, Portia, why did you have to tell? I was touched to think of the auntly pride that had prompted the telling, and at the same time seriously pissed at the outcome.

"It was mostly accidental," I protested. "I just happened to pick up a few things because of being around the Colony so much, getting to know the people . . ." I stopped. Again, not the right things to be saying.

Lieutenant Griffith said, "Uh-huh." It came out, Uh-*huh.*

There was a light tap at the door. The lieutenant said, "Yes?"

Anandi glided in. "Mrs. Singh is up now. She will talk with you whenever you are ready." She tilted her head toward the table and said, with a little ghost of a smile, "Mrs. Singh is also wanting her coffee."

"Oh. Sure," the lieutenant said. "Tell her . . . uh . . . ask her to come on in."

He stood and extended his hand to me across the table. "A pleasure, Ms. Mullins. I'm sure I'll be talking to you again."

I stood also and shook his hand. "You might as well call me Phoebe," I said with resignation.

"Right," said the lieutenant. "Hal."

I caught a self-satisfied look on Ben Solliday's face which I pointedly ignored.

At the end of the hallway I met Portia, who said, "Is the damn coffee drinkable?"

I nodded. She put her hand on my arm. "Sorry about you bein' in the middle of this, Phoebe. But nothin' to worry about, y'know."

My aunt was dressed formally, for her, in a long grey wool skirt with a rose-colored silk blouse and a fringed, deep-red Indian shawl draped around her shoulders. I watched her solid and upright body as she made her way slowly to the kitchen door, and hoped to God she was right.

16

Oh rash, that judgest
From half, the whole!

BETWEEN THE MOMENT IN POOH-BAH'S DRESSING ROOM when I'd jumped to the horrifying conclusion that Portia Singh had just stuck a knife into the back of E. Foster Ballard and the one where I'd told myself not to be an idiot, barely thirty seconds had passed. Now, as I walked briskly along a path in a park a few blocks from Portia's house, I went carefully over the thought processes of that half-minute, testing them for gaps in logic.

After leaving the kitchen, I'd felt a powerful need for head-clearing air, for exercise to loosen muscles knotted with tension, above all for solitude. I consulted Anandi.

"Child's Park," she replied with no hesitation. "It is very still, very beautiful, I often go there myself. Will be perfect for you."

Anandi's eyes were ringed with fatigue. Because she was still recovering from her own bout with that ubiquitous bug, she had not gone with us to the theater last night, and I didn't know how much Portia had told her. I sensed that despite her customary air of calm she was deeply worried. I dispensed with easy reassurances. The best thing I could do, I decided, was to get my own thoughts into some sort of order.

Anandi'd been right: the park, spread over the equivalent of a dozen or so city blocks, consisted mostly of trees and broad lawns and was blessedly quiet. Despite an overnight change in the weather that had produced a near cloudless day and above normal temperatures for November it was, except for a few solitary walkers such as myself, virtually deserted. The peak of the fall color season now being a distant memory, only a muted dab of russet or gold here and there punctuated the deep greens of pines and firs, the blacks and browns of stripped limbs. But the sun was warm, the grass still brightly green and enlivened by the crisscrossing of a multitude of grey squirrels.

As I entered the park from Elm Street, I was greeted by a small white sign on a wooden post that announced in black letters, DOGS ON LEASH AT ALL TIMES. Next to it, a similar sign bluntly reminded dog owners of the city code that required them to REMOVE AND DISPOSE OF CANINE FECES. I surmised that more euphemistically worded directives had failed to do the job. Grateful for the moment to be dogless, I shoved my hands deeper into the pockets of my grey wool car coat, struck out along the paved drive that curved among the trees, and got down to some organized reflection.

A: How *could* Portia have done it, physically handicapped as she still was? The information that made it back to us that night was that Pooh-Bah had been first hit from behind at the base of the skull with a baseball bat, then stabbed as he lay prone on the floor. Portia's left arm, newly released from its cast, was still extremely weak. Grab a heavy wooden bat and swing it with enough force to stun a grown man into insensibility? I didn't think so. And then stoop down, balanced on her cane, to thrust a dagger inches deep into a man's back? The picture was absurd.

She had barely managed to bend over and feel for

the carotid artery—whence the blood on her sleeve.
"Had to make sure, y'know. That he was past help.
Thought for a minute I was goin' to fall on top of 'im."
But she'd been able to pull herself upright, and the re-
sult of that effort had been the labored breathing I'd
heard.

B. *Why* would she have done it? What possible resentment, sustained over more than forty years, could
have led to such a violent and self-destructive act? I
couldn't imagine any. Nor had I seen any sign, in all the
eagerness of her anticipation before leaving for the theater, of anger or brooding—nothing at all that would
hint at lethal intent. The sort of thing, I thought, for
which Lieutenant Griffith might well be probing at this
very moment. I wondered what Portia was telling him.

What she'd said to me was, "Just wanted to talk to
'im, Phoebe."

After running to yell up the stairs for one of the remaining stage crew to call the police, I'd returned to
lead Aunt Portia to a chair in the central dressing area.
She was beginning to shake, and I got her a glass of
water from the women's lavatory. She drank it down,
and then sat slumped in the chair, slowly rubbing her
left arm.

"I knew he hadn't gone, y'see. I'd been watchin'
from the back of the theater and he hadn't come out either from backstage or from that other stair at the side."

"Nobody was supposed to use that one," I explained.
"Except in an emergency."

"Well, those two youngsters used it—Yum-Yum and
Peep-Bo. Came out gigglin', almost fell over the chair
with the sign on it an' then put it back how it was
s'posed to be. Looked guilty when they saw me. I asked
'em if they'd tell Dr. Ballard I was waitin' to see him
and they said he'd already gone. I knew it wasn't true,
thought they just didn't want to be bothered, but I let it
go. Later on, after it seemed just about everybody'd left,
I decided to go down there."

"But Aunt Portia," I protested, "why didn't you ask me to look for him?"

Her eyes met mine, then lowered. The pile of snowy hair, so carefully arranged in honor of the occasion, had come loose and was listing to one side. I had an urge to fix it—I didn't want the police seeing her like this. But more important at the moment was to hear her story.

"Felt like a fool," she muttered. "Thought he was avoidin' me. Didn't want to make a big deal out of it." She raised her head and looked directly at me. "But it was important to me, Phoebe. A matter of layin' old ghosts."

Although tempted, I didn't follow up on this statement. Old ghosts later, I thought, facts now.

"Once you'd gotten down the stairs, what made you think he was in his dressing room?"

"Saw the light. Those curtain things had been pulled aside enough so you could see the door and I knew it was his room from you talkin' about it."

Saw, in other words, exactly what I had seen. Meaning that someone else had gone to Pooh-Bah's room between the time I'd last been downstairs and Portia's discovery of the body. The person who had turned the light on and left the door ajar.

Assuming, that is, that Portia was telling the truth. Which (C) I did assume, because . . . well, because she told me so. (Okay, some might point out here a breakdown in strictly logical thought.) In that awful moment as we stood together over Pooh-Bah's body, my face must have betrayed my fears, because the second thing she said was, "I didn't do it, Phoebe. Found 'im like this. Don't worry, m'dear."

Elliptical, disjointed, yes—a liar, no. There might be things Portia Singh wouldn't tell you, but what she did tell you was the truth, I'd bet my life on it. So I believed her without question. Not worrying was another matter.

"Aunt Portia, do you have any idea who—"

And then the first contingent of the Law had descended.

By the time we and the two goggle-eyed and patently thrilled-to-pieces teenage members of the stage crew had told our stories to the third level of authority it had been after midnight. It was plain from the relative intensity of the questioning that Aunt Portia had instantly become a prime suspect. But at last, she having surrendered her bloodstained blouse and been outfitted with a makeup smock borrowed from Lydia's dressing room, we'd been told we could go home. An elderly and exhausted woman with a bum hip was evidently not considered a flight risk. Still, a police car followed us to the house and waited until we had gone inside.

It wasn't until I was in my own room, taking off my shoes, that I made a no doubt inconsequential discovery. The crunchy object I'd stepped on on my way to Pooh-Bah's dressing room hadn't been any kind of makeup stick. Trapped in the ridged rubber sole of my sensible canvas stage-manager shoe were the mashed remains of a piece of yellow chalk.

Chalk? My monumentally weary brain refused to come up with a logical explanation, though no doubt there were several. The thing was, I thought I would have noticed during my previous sweep of the basement a piece of yellow chalk lying on the floor. Or maybe not. Anyway, the chances that it had any significance, I decided, were slim to none.

I rounded a curve in the park drive and came in sight of a woman with flyaway white hair wearing a bulky brown sweater-coat. Ahead of her ran a small, rather unkempt, and defiantly unleashed black poodle. She gave me a nervous glance, and looked relieved when I bent to pet the dog, which had come up to yap at me and sniff my ankles.

"I only let her loose when there's nobody around," the woman said apologetically. "But they can be pretty sticky about it—the people who run the park."

I assured her I was totally pro poodle freedom and not about to snitch. The dog, not having found any smells worthy of interest on my socks, trotted on, followed by her rule-breaking companion. I turned onto a footpath that wound through a small copse thick with rhododendrons, and resumed thinking.

Just how sticky were the police likely to be about Aunt Portia? I forced myself to look at the bare facts from their point of view: Here was a woman found standing over a corpse with the victim's blood (Portia had readily confirmed this) on her sleeve. Sure she was in her sixties and partially disabled. But she'd had enough determination to make it down a twelve-step staircase—obviously her motivation was strong. Who was to say that motivation hadn't included—or escalated into—a fury that resulted in a brief, superhuman physical effort? If they could only unearth the motive . . . again, I couldn't make my imagination produce a scenario of murderous anger nurtured for nearly half a century—not one involving the woman I knew.

It had not occurred to us to lie about the circumstances of finding Pooh-Bah's body. All right, it had occurred to me. But when I'd suggested to my aunt that perhaps the two of us had come down to the basement together, Portia had said a firm No. "Only make things worse, Phoebe. Better to tell the truth. Be all right, don't worry."

I wished she'd stop telling me not to worry. It made me think she hadn't grasped how deep was the shit into which she had landed. After all, with such a convenient suspect virtually dropped in their laps, how hard would the local police—in conjunction, I'd gathered from last night's experiences, with the state cops and the D.A.'s office—be looking elsewhere? I hoped I was doing them a collective injustice. Lieutenant Griffith, for instance, hadn't seemed like a jump-to-conclusions type.

And then there'd been the Bear in his, to me,

mysterious role as watchdog to the accused. I recalled
the look he'd exchanged with the lieutenant as I bab-
bled about how Pooh-Bah took his coffee. The look
that said, See, what did I tell you? And the lieutenant's
follow-up observations about my part in the Varovna
Colony murders—surely he didn't suppose there'd be
any chance of enlisting me in an effort to prove my
aunt's guilt? Which must mean he still had an open
mind.

I had been aware last night, as various officers of the
law came and went—stringing yellow crime scene tape,
dusting for prints, taking pictures, examining and then
removing E. Foster's body, interviewing and finger-
printing my aunt and me—that others were being dis-
patched to track down and question the rest of the
company. I had provided my list of names, addresses,
and phone numbers, and pointed out that most of the
cast and crew were probably at the party being held at
Harry Johns's house. Beyond that, I had been too busy
coping with my own state of shock to give much
thought to anyone else. Except to note, as the time
wore on, that Harry had not, as I'd half hoped, rushed
back to the theater in support of his . . . well, his stage
manager if nothing else. Then I told myself not to be
silly, obviously the cops weren't going to allow anyone
to go haring off into the night, and especially not back
to what was now a major crime scene. Besides, for all
Harry's sterling qualities, I'd had ample evidence that
Young Lochinvar he was not.

The path led to a clearing containing a shallow pond,
its surface obscured by a counterpane of floating dead
leaves. Sunlight splashed warmly onto the pond's opposite bank. It seemed like an invitation. I skirted the
reedy perimeter, tucked the tail of my coat under my
bottom, and sat, drawing my knees to my chin.

Maybe sitting down had been a mistake. Exhaustion,
both mental and physical, suddenly enveloped me. My
head drooped, my thought processes seemed to have

assumed all the clarity of the leaf-choked water before me. Oh, come *on,* Phoebe, this is really not the time for murky thinking. I gave my head a vigorous shake.

Okay, here was the central question: If not Portia, then who?

Well, for starters there was Portia's niece. Who better placed than the stage manager, with her unquestioned access to all areas of the theater, to pop into a dressing room, eliminate its occupant, and slip out unnoticed? *I* knew I hadn't done it, but my name must inevitably appear on any list the police might now be drawing up.

The same reasoning applied, of course, to Harry Johns and Derek Bowles. That the director and producer of the show should be circulating throughout the dressing area bestowing hugs, kisses, and lavish congratulations was not only expected but downright obligatory. Who would be able to say for sure where either had been for the entire period during which the murder must have taken place?

I considered Harry, acknowledging to myself again how little I actually knew about him. What was the phrase I'd overheard: ". . . hardly the one to go around talking about assault"? And then, "I wonder just how much your employers at that so-called college of yours know . . ." A serious threat or simply another bit of characteristic nastiness on Pooh-Bah's part? After the show Harry had seemed his usual levelheaded self, smiling broadly, looking mightily relieved, but calm. Was it possible that that coolness could extend to showing no sign of a recent bout of homicide?

Presumably in the face of the universal euphoria, he had dispensed with the usual giving of notes. And I was pretty sure he'd left the theater ahead of many of the company, since he was hosting the cast party. He'd sought me out to apologize for leaving it to me to close up the theater. Had he then actually gone home? And had I seen Pooh-Bah after Harry (presumably) left? Not that I could remember.

If Harry had been his usual collected self, Derek Bowles's customary high spirits had been revved to a point just shy of hysteria. I pictured him as he'd been last night, still in his outlandish getup as Ko-Ko, whirling through the dressing areas like a miniature cyclone, grabbing first this one then that: "You were marvelous, absolutely marvelous!" "Did you hear the laugh when you . . ." "Darling, did you *hear* the applause?"

I had gone down to collect a couple of fans which, despite repeated instructions to leave all props on the backstage prop table, had inevitably been carried off to the basement. Derek paused in his jubilant path long enough to plant a hand on each side of my face and pull it down to deliver an enthusiastic smack on the lips. "Thank you, Phoebe! Absolutely couldn't have done it without! My God, Portia must be happy! I haven't seen her yet, have you?" No, but before I could say so he pulled me close again and murmured confidentially, "Have to confess, for a bit there last night I was getting just a smidgen worried." Then, the boyish face all smiles, "But it all worked! God, what a show!" and he was off. Sure, he could have done it, but why?

Who next? Well, I supposed the police would feel obligated to consider Beth Rosario's father, as someone who had actually issued a threat against Pooh-Bah, albeit of a lawsuit rather than mayhem. But for me he was a nonstarter. The rule barring the basement area to all but cast members, the director, and the stage manager had been followed pretty much to the letter. Even the Cougher had made an ostentatious point of not putting a foot beyond the top step of the back staircase. The stage crew had been so offended by E. Foster's implication that they were responsible for the broken mirror that Carl had had to do some fancy cajoling to persuade them not to quit en masse. They wouldn't have gone near the place on a bet. The front stairs had been, as I'd told Portia, declared off-limits to everyone. There was a basement door to the outside, but since

Derek had had the locks changed I was pretty sure that only he and Harry had keys. And for the performance itself the edict had gone out that after curtain calls the actors were to go directly downstairs to remove costumes and makeup. Family, friends, and other admirers would have to wait for them in the auditorium.

An edict, I recalled, flouted only and inevitably by E. Foster. I remembered seeing him, on my return from the lower depths, standing just below the stage in full Pooh-Bah regalia receiving congratulations from a circle of men and women in the kinds of outfits that to the young people of the company would have seemed like quaint relics of yesteryear—in other words, suits and cocktail dresses.

Which explained, I now realized, why Pooh-Bah had still been in costume when he'd been struck down. I started trying to work out a timetable. Say Foster had been schmoozing with his cronies for ten, perhaps even fifteen minutes. By the time he'd gotten to his dressing room, most of the cast would have been removing the last vestiges of their makeup, getting into their party clothes, even starting to leave. It must have been soon after he sat down at his dressing table that the murderer, unnoticed—or at least unnoted—had entered the room, killed him, and left, turning off the light and closing the door.

How many people, I wondered, had trooped past that closed door on their way up the stairs, either assuming that Pooh-Bah had already left for the party, or in obedience to his strictures on privacy? And hadn't I done the same on my penultimate check of the basement? No, I realized now with a shudder, I'd actually given a quick knock on each dressing room door in passing. All had been closed and silent. So who had subsequently opened Pooh-Bah's door and turned on the light?

I gave it up. This was the sort of thing the cops could do far better. And perhaps, once they'd put together all their interviews, one person would emerge as the only one who could have been at the right (wrong?) place at the right time. I thought of the hubbub of that basement scene and shook my head. But even allowing for the general chaos I was sure of one thing: No member of the public, let alone an avenging father breathing fire, would have gone unnoticed. Mr. Rosario was definitely out of it.

A woman pushing a sleeping toddler in a stroller and accompanied by a boy of about five entered the clearing. They stopped by another of those white signs, on the opposite side of the pond from where I sat. This one read: PLEASE DON'T REMOVE WILDLIFE FROM POND AREA. The woman rummaged in the bag that hung behind the stroller and produced a paper cup which she gave to the little boy. Then she pulled out a book, sat down, and began to read. The child ran to the pond's edge, squatted on a flattish rock, and began pushing the leaves aside with a stick. He eyed the water intently, paper cup poised.

What was it about rules, I wondered, that brought on the urge to flout them, even here in law-abiding Northampton? Oh well, I didn't think the kid would find anything still moving in the chilly water, and in any case I wasn't here as Protector of Pond Life. I was here to put my mind to the problem of who, in Pooh-Bah's case, had flouted the biggest rule of all.

The kid was already making sounds of frustration. He abandoned his post and started around to the sunnier side—my side—of the pond. I decided I could think better on my feet anyway, rose, and ceded the field to him. Following the continuation of the path I'd come in by, I wandered on through the trees.

And came now in my mind, reluctantly, to the three people who, to my certain knowledge, held grudges against E. Foster Ballard: Lydia Hicks, Carl Piquette, and Irene Polaski.

In Lydia's case, the cause was clear. She was still in

love with the man she had married—what, thirty-five or so years ago? The man who had left her, married twice more, and gave no sign of any regard for the feelings of his former partner, let alone any residual affection. Why had she stayed in Northampton? Why, for God's sake, had she taken the part in *The Mikado* when she knew he was going to be involved? Was it some neurotic need to probe the wound? If so, what a waste of a life!

And then that sudden change after the rehearsal where she had displayed her heart to the world and Pooh-Bah had laughed. The alteration had been dramatic—gone were the sarcastic remarks, the sniping, the air of belligerence, the nightly sloshings. Instead, she had become a laid-back Lydia, a Lydia who gave every indication of being at peace with herself. Was this because she had, at that traumatic moment, been released from the thrall of an old and hopeless love? Or was it the calm of the tormented victim who has finally resolved to end her humiliation in the most direct and ultimate way?

For Irene and Carl I had no such concrete scenarios at hand. I was certain, to my own satisfaction, that each bore a dislike amounting to hatred for their late colleague. But since that certainty was based on nothing more than my own observations of behavior and emotional climate, it didn't amount to anything resembling evidence. Perhaps by now the cops had ferreted out a pair of motives for Irene and Carl anyway. Or, remembering I was in Small Town country, perhaps their stories were already common knowledge. For the time being, I filed Irene Polaski and Carl Piquette under Motive Unknown, At Least To Me.

Come to that, a slew of other unknown motives could be lurking out there, E. Foster having been, in my book, a sort of walking engine of provocation. Still, there was no getting away from it: logistics dictated that the killer had to be a member of the company.

I had come out of the trees and onto another section of the drive. I turned left, which I figured should circle me back to where I'd come in. On my right, a low-to-the-ground, green-painted sign instructed in faded gold lettering:

PEACE AND QUIET PLEASE
NO ORGANIZED GAMES

Nothing, happily, against organized thoughts. I wondered if mine had done me any good—they certainly hadn't brought me to any conclusions.

There was one conclusion, though, that I had reached long before my walk in the park. Even though a connection would automatically remove Aunt Portia from suspicion, I was convinced that Pooh-Bah's murder was not tied in to the incidents of the coffee, the book, and the mirror. Those had been petty acts, deliberate, and designed to embarrass and harass. The murder had been, in my reading of the scene, not planned but an act of spontaneous passion, committed with objects at hand. I didn't see those two types of acts emanating from the same psyche.

For Aunt Portia's sake, I hoped I was wrong. But I didn't think so.

17

Is it but a world of trouble—
Sadness set to song?

WHEN I GOT BACK TO THE HOUSE, BOTH LIEUTENANT
Griffith and Ben Solliday had left. It was after twelve,
and Portia pronounced it lunchtime. Further, she declared the subject of the murder off-limits until after
we'd eaten. Consequently, as we spooned tomato soup
and munched on tuna sandwiches, conversation was
sparse. I spoke of the delights of Child's Park. Anandi
relayed her latest gleanings from the *Gazette:* beaver
dams were creating flood problems for some riverside
residents, leading to the inevitable confrontations between the animal-rights people and those whose base-
ments were under two feet of water; the Town Council
was struggling with the yearly decision on whether or
not to buy snow insurance; the parking problem in
Northampton was becoming critical. Beyond the occasional "hmm" or "ah," my aunt said nothing at all.

Despite her repeated instructions to me not to
worry, it was clear from the deepening of the lines in
her broad forehead and the tightening of the muscles
around her mouth that Portia was feeling the strain. I
told myself that however secure she might be in her

own innocence it would be surprising if shock and exhaustion were *not* having their effect. Still, an air of abstraction and something like a wince of pain that from time to time flickered over her features told me her mind was occupied elsewhere and that the thoughts were not pleasant.

After our few plates and glasses had been consigned to the dishwasher, Portia faced Anandi and me and heaved a large sigh. "C'mon," she said. "Let's have our coffee in the livin' room. Be sunny there. Somethin' I need to tell you."

Portia indicated that I should sit on the velvet settee, then lowered herself to sit beside me. Anandi placed the tray with three coffee mugs on a low table and went to perch on the very edge of the leather recliner, back straight, hands clasped tightly in her lap. She was wearing a sari in shades of lavender that emphasized the shadows around her eyes.

Again I was facing the end of the room that housed the gold harp. The sight brought home to me anew how little I really knew of my aunt's life. I tried to picture her as a young woman, yellow-haired and slim, her hands moving gracefully across the strings.

The picture abruptly dissolved. For all I knew, the harp belonged to Anandi, or had come with the house. What I was doing, I admitted, was distracting myself from the fact of sitting here beside my very somber aunt, scared to death as to what she might be about to tell me. Even worse, she had taken my hand in hers and was absently patting it. Omigod, whatever it was must be really, really bad.

"I already told this to the police," Portia said. "Figured I might as well or they'd go pokin' around, get it wrong. Now I'm goin' to tell you two. Anandi knows some of it, not all."

She glanced over at Anandi, who was staring at her sister-in-law with an expression approaching panic and whose small hands were occupied in twisting the several gold rings on her fingers as if trying to melt them down.

"Pete's sake, Anandi, go get your knittin'," she said. "Givin' me the heebie-jeebies." And while Anandi went gratefully to retrieve her carpetbag from a chair by the door, she added with some impatience, "F'God's sake, I'm not about to confess to killin' the son of a bitch, I didn't. Even though some people might think I had a reason to. Ridiculous, a'course, they'll find that out soon enough."

Oh, sure. My heart took a dive to the vicinity of my lower intestine. Was it possible that Portia had actually sat there and calmly detailed for the police a motive for a murder for which she was already a prime suspect? Could she, for all her years, be so incredibly innocent?

Anandi resumed her seat on the recliner, her hands now busy with a large section of some garment in electric green mohair, the muscles of her face several degrees less rigid. Portia had relinquished my hand in favor of one of the coffee mugs and sat nursing it, looking straight in front of her with a slight scowl on her face. I picked up one of the other mugs, then put it down again. The last thing my nerves were calling for was more stimulation. Anandi's cup, also, sat untouched on the tray. There was a brief silence during which I sensed a scream making its inexorable way toward my vocal cords.

A harrumphing sound from Aunt Portia rescued me. "Lotta this is damn embarrassin'," she said. "So don't interrupt, just let me get it over with."

Embarrassing? Embarrassing didn't sound so bad. My spirits rose marginally. Perhaps Portia had exaggerated the impact of her story.

Anandi's needles glided in and out; I kept my eyes on Aunt Portia's face; Aunt Portia kept hers determinedly focussed on the middle distance.

"My junior year, his senior, we were in *The Gondoliers,* Eddie and I. At the high school."

Eddie? I thought, momentarily at a loss. Oh, right. Eddie Balcowicz, E. Foster Ballard's former incarnation.

"Reason I was at the high school at all—Helen had done the whole boarding school thing—was that my daddy was beginnin' to think about gettin' into local politics, maybe run for the school board. Daddy was a lawyer, y'know."

Had I known that? I must have. Why was it only now striking me with force how little I'd been told about my maternal grandparents?

"Thing was, he couldn't very well run for the school board at the same time he was sendin' his kid off to some fancy prep school. So I got t'go to the high school. Couldn't believe my luck. By then I was beginnin' to get pretty sick of the whole upper-class wannabe, white glove, what'll-the-neighbors-say kind of life. Wanted to get out an' meet the 'real people,' y'know, was turnin' into a regular Baby Bolshie. 'Course I kept it under wraps around Mum and Dad."

She paused to grimace and shift her weight on the settee. Anandi and I obediently said not a word. For my part, I was practically holding my breath. It had taken Pooh-Bah's death for me to start hearing the family things I'd longed to know. I could almost feel grateful to him.

"Eddie played the Duke of Plaza-Toro. I was the Duchess."

Okay. Back to *The Gondoliers.*

"Eddie was a popular kid. 'Cept for the people who couldn't stand 'im." She shot me a glance. "Guess that hadn't changed much."

I nodded. You could certainly say that.

"Good lookin', too."

I tried and failed to picture the young Pooh-Bah. My face must have telegraphed my doubts, because Portia

said, with a grim little smile, "Well, he was. Take my
word for it. And there I was, tall and skinny and awkward, never'd had a boyfriend. Gettin' that part in *The
Gondoliers* was the best thing that'd happened to me up
to then. Because it turned out I was good. Eddie and I
were the hit of the show. And Eddie started lookin' at
me differently. An' then he asked me to go to a movie
with him."

She took a long sip of coffee, looked at Anandi and
me and said, with a touch of humor, "Guess you've
gathered I didn't like my parents much. Sorry, Anandi,
but that's the way it was. Thought they were narrow-
minded, thought they were awful snobs. Which they
were, a'course. And I knew my goin' out with Eddie
would give 'em fits. Prob'ly one of Eddie's charms for
me. But after what they did to Eddie when he came to
pick me up that first time . . . after that, I really hated
'em."

She had turned away again, but I could see the
knuckles of the long fingers clutching the coffee mug
whiten as she talked.

"Sat him down in the livin' room. Said, 'Balcowicz?
Is that Polish? And what does your father do, Mr.
Balcowicz? Ah, tobacco farming. And your uncle runs a
garage? How interesting.' An' this was postwar, too.
Long past the time when Polish farm girls were hirin'
themselves out as household maids at six dollars a
week. Defense factory jobs put an end to that. Polish
boys had fought an' died for us. Poles were goin' into
the professions, into politics. But for folks like my parents the old snobberies died hard. To them, Eddie was
from the local peasant class an' he had no business
messin' with their daughter."

Anandi's needles had slowed. She was shaking her
head and she murmured something I didn't catch.

Portia, as if picking up on some wavelength inaudible to me, said, with an edge, "Yes, Anandi, in India

that would've been the end of it. But in America we don't go in much for arranged marriages. Even back then."

Anandi's eyebrows rose a fraction, but she made no comment.

Portia waved an impatient hand. "Well, anyway. After what they did—humiliatin' Eddie right in front of me while he just sat there gettin' redder and redder—after that, it was like a big black cloud that'd been followin' me around just burst open. When I got home that night after the movie I told Mum and Daddy I was goin' steady with Eddie Balcowicz. Not that he'd asked me—I just wanted to really rile 'em up. An' boy, did it work! They said no, I wasn't, in fact I wasn't goin' to see him anymore at all. Used words like 'unwise' and 'inappropriate' and 'not our class a'people.' " She gave a little bark of laughter. "Too bad Ann Landers wasn't around back then to point out to 'em what a mistake *that* was. Phoebe, give me a hand up, my hip's killin' me."

I transferred her coffee mug back to the tray and helped my aunt to her feet. She grabbed her ebony walking stick, shook off my proffered arm, and stumped to the end of the room and back. She stopped by an antique pine hutch opposite the bay window enclave and began absentmindedly straightening its display of Quimper pottery plates. She heaved another large sigh and faced around to the window, leaning against the hutch, her good arm braced on its broad lower shelf.

" 'Spose you can imagine what happened next. I started lyin', sneakin' out at night to see Eddie. And I started sleepin' with him. Give him credit, it was as much my idea as his. Let's just say he didn't turn me down. Thought I was gettin' away with it, too. Some neighbor must've tipped my parents off, though, and they caught me one night climbin' out of my window."

To my amazement, she gave out a hearty chuckle. "My God, what a scene! My mother came right out and

asked, as she so quaintly put it, if I'd 'lost my virginity.'
I said, yes, and it was the best thing I'd ever done. They
said I was a bad, shameless girl. I said they were damn
prigs an' hypocrites and how I hated everythin' they
stood for. An' you know? I looked in their eyes and I
saw fear. They were afraid of me! Biggest rush of
power I ever felt. Huh!" She gave another short laugh.
"So they had me committed."

"They *what*?!" Shock had overcome my promise of
silence.

"Private sanitarium outside Boston. They gave me
shock treatments."

I gasped. "They gave you *shock treatments*? Because
you'd had *sex*?"

Anandi's needles had stopped moving altogether and
she was staring at her sister-in-law with pity and incredulity. Evidently this was the part of the story she'd
never heard.

Portia shrugged, took up her stick, walked back to
the settee, and resumed her place beside me. She patted
my knee, shook her head at Anandi, then turned again
to me.

"Don't think too hardly of 'em, Phoebe. Y'have to
understand. This was somethin' they had no idea how
to deal with. In their world, nice, well-brought-up,
middle-class young girls just didn't behave the way I
was behavin'. So it must be some kinda mental illness,
and they sent me away to be cured."

Think too hardly! What would be too hard to think
about what Portia's parents had done to her?! If it had
been Mum and Dad who now lay dead, murdered by
an unknown hand, I would have had to agree that my
aunt belonged at the top of the suspect list. But what
did this have to do with E. Foster Ballard, the former
Eddie Balcowicz? Unhappily, I was about to find out.

"I am not," my aunt said firmly, "goin' to talk about
those treatments. 'Cept to say they were god-awful and
I was terrified of 'em. Terrified. All I could think and

plan about was how to get out of there. And then one day Eddie showed up. By then the doctors figured I'd calmed down some, so I was allowed to walk in the grounds and so on."

She looked down at her hands, now clasped in her lap, and shook her head wonderingly. "Never occurred to me to ask Eddie how he knew where I was, how he'd gotten on the visitor list. Just took it as provin' how much he loved me. I had my plan all worked out by then, where I'd hide, how I'd get past the gate. But I'd need money. Eddie promised to bring it."

Icy fingers began performing maneuvers on my spine. I did not, *did not,* want to hear what was coming.

"Next day, the doctors decided I hadn't been doing as well as they thought. Took away my privileges. Kept me there for another month of . . . treatments."

She turned directly to Anandi and me. "All I wanted last night was to ask 'im why he did it. What did they promise, what did they give him? Just wanted to know." Her lips made a wry twist. "Guess I'll just have t'go on wantin'."

I pushed away the implications of what I'd just heard. "What happened after you left the sanitarium?" I asked.

"Never saw Eddie again. He went off to college, I think. Sometimes wonder if Mum and Daddy had somethin' to do with that. Did my senior year of high school, never said boo, was a model kid. Three days after graduation I turned eighteen. Packed a suitcase and walked out of the house. Didn't even leave a note."

Suddenly my aunt's shoulders slumped and her facial muscles went slack. It came to me what an effort it must have been for her to relate this sad and awful tale. I scooted over, took both her hands in mine, and pressed them to my cheek. My cheek, I found, was wet. "I'm glad you finally came back," I said.

Anandi had risen and come to bend over her old friend and pat her hair. "They were wrong, your parents," she said. "Very, very wrong." I had the sense that she had just made an enormous concession.

Aunt Portia straightened. "No need to fuss," she said. "Thought you ought to know. Don't need to speak of it again."

All very well to say, but the truth was that Portia's story had provided what up to know I'd found it impossible to imagine: a motive for murder conceivably strong enough to survive the passage of half a century.

18

To ask you what you mean to do,
We punctually appear.

THAT MORNING, I HAD GOTTEN A PHONE CALL FROM
Harry. It had come only minutes before the arrival of
Lieutenant Griffith and the Bear, so there hadn't been
time for much more than an exchange of commisera-
tions and expressions of disbelief. Harry had barely
gotten started on a description of the descent of the police on the cast party when the doorbell rang and
Anandi was brushing past me on her way to answer it.

"I have to go," I said. "Call me later when—"

"Wait. What I'm mainly calling about . . . Derek
wants everyone at the theater tonight. Eight o'clock. He
seems to think it's something we should do."

"I see. Well, tell Derek I'll think about it. It depends a
lot on how Portia's feeling," and I said a quick good-bye.

Mainly calling about? As in, Otherwise I wouldn't
have bothered? Forget Young Lochinvar, the man
wasn't even one of those bumbling wooers Hugh Grant
kept playing. What was it about him I continued to find
appealing?

·   ·   ·

By the time Portia, Anandi, and I had reached the Old Church Theater at about five minutes to eight that evening, most of the company were already assembled in the auditorium. Portia had insisted on going, and Anandi was consumed with curiosity to put faces to the people she had been hearing about over the past weeks.

If the occasion had been less solemn, I had the feeling our entrance would have been greeted with applause. As it was, Derek galloped up the shallow steps of the center aisle, followed more deliberately by Harry, to escort my aunt to a seat in the front row. Portia, however, demurred and chose the pew behind the first four rows of the center section, which was pretty well filled. I was glad. In the front row, I wouldn't have been able to observe individual reactions to the goings-on, whatever they were to be—a point that had hardly been made clear by Harry's phone message. "Something we should do" was, to say the least, open to a number of interpretations. Were we there to mourn? To compare notes? To be interrogated? (I saw no sign of police presence.) To turn in our scores?

Derek said to Portia in a hushed voice, "We're just waiting for Jane Manypenny. She said she'd definitely be here." He looked toward the swinging door that led to the lobby. "Maybe I'll go take a look," and he trotted on up and disappeared through the door.

Harry said, "Can I sit with you?"

Portia had entered the pew first, followed by Anandi and me. I squeezed over to make space at the end, into which Harry sank with a grateful look.

"Do *you* know why we're here?" I said.

Harry shook his head. "Derek's idea. Something to do, I gather, with 'closure.' Told him if I heard that word again I was out of here."

I smothered a laugh. Harry took my hand and held it, resting it on the red velveteen cushion in the minimal space between our two thighs. My tummy flipped pleasantly.

As I looked over the assemblage, it occurred to me that if what we were participating in wasn't some sort of funereal gathering, people had certainly dressed as if it were. Brown and black, blue and beige was the predominant palette.

Lydia Hicks, sitting in the front left pew, was wearing a black, boat-neck sweater over grey slacks. Her red mop, though, was held in place with salmon pink combs. She sat straight, shoulders squared, and when she turned around to look toward the lobby door, impatiently, I thought, I could see that her face was fully made up, effectively hiding any signs there might have been of strain or grief. She saw me, nodded, and turned back. What could Lydia be feeling? I wondered. She didn't have the appearance of a woman who had suddenly lost the love of her life to a macabre death. Nor, on the other hand, did she seem like one who had been the engineer of that death.

I stopped myself. If I had learned anything from last summer's experience, it should have been not to expect a murderer to go around conveniently exhibiting signs of guilt.

Sitting beside Lydia, Irene Polaski had dropped the peasant look in favor of a tailored navy blue dress. She was sitting directly under one of the auditorium lights, which brought out silvery glints in the fair braid wound around her head and anchored with the familiar floral barrette. Given how she felt about the late E. Foster, what was Irene doing here? Come to that, what were any of us doing here? And most of us had elected to come.

There was Carl Piquette, sitting, not with Lydia and Irene, but at the right-hand end of the third row of pews. Was there any significance to that? A falling-out, perhaps, a distancing?

Nadine Gardner, no doubt from force of habit, had taken up her place on the piano bench. She had given me a small smile when I came in, which I had returned. I was discovering that the punch to the gut brought on by each encounter with Nadine, by the fact of Nadine, was becoming progressively less severe. With the assistance of recent events, I had managed to push Nadine and what she represented in my life somewhat to one side. But I well knew I couldn't keep her there. Sooner or later—probably the sooner the better—Nadine and I were going to have to have a talk. But, my cowardly self pointed out with relief, not just now.

Mitchell Kim was here, seated in the middle of a clutch of female choristers. Beside him was Ardys Feldman. I didn't catch any significant glances between Mitchell and Nadine. If anything I'd have said they were avoiding making eye contact. That particular romance aboard the good ship *Mikado* seemed to have foundered with more than usual speed.

Ardys's sidekick Beth Rosario, though, was missing. I assumed that Mr. Rosario, his misgivings about his daughter's association with the Northampton Repertory Company having been justified in spades, had finally put his foot down.

The Mikado himself, Arnold Zimmer, deprived of his borrowed finery and the authority it had bestowed, sat alone looking dazed and apprehensive.

I counted up the chorus members. All but two had come, as had four of the technical crew, three of Nadine's pit band, and Cynthia the Cougher.

I returned to the question I'd posed to myself earlier: why were we here? What had propelled each of us to answer Derek's vaguely defined summons to return to a scene which, if not to most of us a scene of horror, was at least one of tragedy and shock?

We had, I decided, all been wrenched too suddenly and with too much finality from an ongoing activity which, for better or worse, had made us into a kind of family. We needed to see each other again. We needed, if possible, to form some sort of consensus about what had happened. We needed someone to articulate—or try to—what we felt.

We needed . . . um (my hand twitched guiltily in Harry's) . . . closure.

The door to the lobby whooshed inward and Derek reappeared, ushering in Jane Manypenny. As they came down the aisle Derek put his arm around her shoulders and murmured a few words, to which Jane answered with what looked to me like a reluctant nod. She took a seat in the pew across the aisle from ours and Derek trotted on down the steps.

I turned toward her, intending to exchange at least a nod of sympathy and support. But either she didn't notice me or she didn't want to. In contrast to her usual neat little outfits, she was wearing a rather wrinkled denim jumper over a white blouse, and white running shoes. I thought she looked as if she hadn't slept much—her face was white except for brown smudges under her eyes. The auburn hair, usually so smooth and neat around her pretty face, needed a comb. But it was her expression—lips set, with downturned corners; brows drawn in, the vertical lines between them so deep as to appear black—that surprised me. I would have expected Jane Manypenny to look sad, shocked, perhaps bewildered. But she didn't. She looked angry.

Derek's voice said, "I think everybody's here now who's coming, so we can begin."

He was sitting on the lip of the stage, his short legs, encased in neat navy blue slacks, crossed at the knee, his hands gripping the narrow molding that ran along the platform's edge. Under a cream-colored V-neck sweater, he wore a white shirt and sober maroon tie. Behind him, the black flats were still festooned with branches of cherry blossoms and lengths of silk fabric colored rose and green and gold. The final set piece of the production—a tree with arching, drooping branches and artfully disguised platform where Ko-Ko had perched to sing "Tit-Willow"—remained in its designated spot, up left of center.

Derek's face, like Jane's, looked pale and weary, but

in his case the expression was one of simple wretched-
ness. Poor Derek! With Pooh-Bah had died, at least for
now, his dream of the tremendous success that would
launch the Northampton Repertory Company on its
way to becoming a fixture in the community. How
much energy, both physical and emotional, he had
poured into this initial venture! And it had paid off!

And then, with one horrendous act, it had all been
taken away. I wondered whether he would have the
heart—or the finances—to try again. Aunt Portia hadn't
said a word about the money she had now no hope of
ever recovering, and I truly didn't think she cared. But
neither did I think she'd do it again. Had Derek himself
put money into the company? And if so . . .

"I asked you to come here," Derek said, "because
what happened last night was so . . . shocking and so
sad that I thought if we all came together one last time
it might help us deal with our feelings. At least I knew it
would help me."

He spoke with a conversational simplicity devoid of
any hint of bombast or theatricality, and I sensed a general relaxation among his listeners: they were not, as
they might have feared, going to be subjected to a performance or expected to produce one of their own. His
voice, even though thinned with fatigue and stress,
reached easily to where we sat, reminding me again of
the remarkable acoustics of the Old Church. What, I
wondered, would become of it now?

"Don't worry," he gave a small smile, "that I'm going
to launch into some kind of eulogy, I wouldn't presume
to. Many of you here knew Foster far longer and better
than I did. And let's be honest, I also know that some of
you didn't particularly like him. I mean, Foster could be,
in some ways . . . difficult."

A few murmurs from the company, whether in
agreement or protest I couldn't tell, but no one spoke.

"But I don't think," Derek went on quickly, "that
there's any argument that Foster was a marvelous

performer. And at the risk of being sentimental, I think we can be glad to know that his last performance may have been one of his best and that he enjoyed every minute of it."

Except for the bit where he got slugged with a bat and then stabbed with his own dagger, I thought. Was Derek planning to deal with that detail at all? Where, exactly, was he going with this? From a certain restless shuffling I gathered there were similar thoughts circulating among my fellow company members.

"However, there's one important thing about Foster— important to everyone here—that you don't know."

The shuffling stopped.

"You don't know it because Foster didn't want it generally known. But, second only to Portia Singh," he acknowledged my aunt with a rueful smile, "it was Foster Ballard who made this production of *The Mikado* possible."

He paused, and I adjusted my assessment of his performance. Because I could see now it *was* a performance, albeit a low-key one. In his defense, I decided he probably couldn't help it. He was, after all, an actor.

Having milked his hesitation for maximum suspense, Derek said, "It was Foster who owned the church, owned this building. He was the one who agreed to let us have it at a rent we could afford. If it hadn't been for him . . ." he trailed off. The shoulders of the cream-colored sweater rose and fell in an expressive shrug.

This time the murmurs were more substantial.

Beside me, Harry exclaimed under his breath, "Son of a bitch! Nobody told *me* that." I glanced across at my aunt, who was frowning in disbelief. Anandi put her hand on Portia's arm and whispered something to her. On the other side of the aisle, Jane Manypenny muttered to herself.

For my part, I was abruptly enlightened as to Derek's

coziness with Pooh-Bah. No wonder he'd been so concerned with "keeping him sweet," so unwilling to join
Lydia and the others in Foster-bashing.

Carl Piquette said, "Then who owns the building
now?"

"I don't know," Derek said. "I mean, I guess we'll
find out soon, but that's not really why we're—"

"I know who owns it," Lydia Hicks said loudly. "I
do."

Derek's head swiveled to where Lydia sat, an expression of mingled doubt and hope on his face. "You do?
Are you sure?"

"Yup," Lydia said. She had been sitting stiffly and
staring at the floor while Derek talked. Now she swung
one arm over the back of the pew and shifted around to
face the rest of the company. "Not that I had any idea
the place was his. Must have been one of his front companies. Foster loved having his little secrets. But if it
was his, yeah, I get it. I get everything. Unless, of
course, the cops decide I was the one who sent my
beloved ex to his reward. In that case, I expect I'd get
zip." She crossed her legs and smiled pleasantly.

Derek had abandoned his grip on the edge of the
stage and was running his hands through his hair—a fu-
tile gesture, since the silky forelock fell immediately
back over his forehead after every pass, but one that I
had come to learn indicated agitation. Ignoring the
open-mouthed astonishment that had greeted Lydia's
announcement, he began eagerly, "But if the place is
yours, Lyd—"

"For God's sake!" A woman in the second row had
risen to her feet. It was the chorus member with the
Theda Bara bob—the one who, during the last couple
of weeks, had been singled out for special attention by
the great (late) E. Foster. "Why are we talking about
buildings? I thought we'd come here to . . . to remember
a man who has died, someone we all knew." Her voice

began to choke. "Someone that some of us had a great respect and . . . and fondness for. Not to talk about buildings and," she glared at Lydia, "make flip remarks!"

Whereupon she started to cry, put her hands to her face, and dropped back into her seat.

"Oh dear," Lydia said dryly and with a distinct lack of empathy. "Worked his well-known charm on you too, huh? What, you thought he was going to make you Mrs. Doctor Ballard number four? Sorry to disappoint you, dear, but he stopped marrying 'em long ago."

"Oh!" shrieked Theda Bara. She jumped up, gripping the back of the pew in front of her. Mascara-dyed tears made their inky way down her thin cheeks. "If you hated Foster so much, why couldn't you leave him alone? He told me all about how you harassed him, how you kept trying to get more money out of him. Now you've got it all, and I hope you're satisfied! Was that why you killed him? Or was it just because you couldn't bear to see him happy with someone else?"

Fresh sobs overtook her and she acceded to the urging of the women on either side of her—one of whom, I observed, was the Cougher—and again subsided onto the red pew cushion.

A momentary flush in Lydia's cheeks indicated that some, at least, of Ms. Bara's barbs had hit home. But she only said, in measured tones, "Slander isn't nice, dear. Fortunately, I'm not one of those litigious types. But if I were you I'd watch my mouth."

Derek, who had been alternating his gaze helplessly between the two women, said, "Hey, guys, come on! We're not here to—"

"Well, why the hell *are* we here?" It was the erstwhile Mikado, Arnold Zimmer, who had lumbered to his feet from his solitary position on the far side of the right-hand aisle. He surveyed the gathering, an expression of indignation on his pumpkin face. "A man's been murdered!" he said. "He didn't just die, somebody killed him. And as far as I can see, we're all suspects. Isn't that what we should be talking about?"

There was a babble of assent, cut through by Harry's voice raised in firm directorial mode: "*No,* it isn't. It's what the police should be talking about."

He gave my hand a quick squeeze, got up and strode down to the stage to stand beside Derek. "What we— all of us—should be doing is remembering everything we can about last night, telling the police if we think it might be significant, and answering their questions. Not speculating among ourselves or making wild accusations."

"Absolutely right!" Derek said. He was looking, I thought, somewhat miffed that the meeting had veered away from whatever script it was he had designed for it. Whether he appreciated or resented Harry's effort to restore civility, I couldn't be sure. "Anyway, what I hoped we could do—"

"But the cops *do* think it was one of us that killed Foster." It was the Cougher, and she added dramatically, "Someone in this room!"

"Hey, what about the WAGS?" said a male voice. It was one of the chorus men who had been a Pooh-Bah acolyte. "They're the ones who've been making trouble all along."

This was greeted with cries of "Don't be ridiculous!" and "How could they have gotten in?" and "Oh sure, blame the feminists!"

Carl Piquette stood up, his face a picture of disgust. "STOP IT!" he said in a voice no doubt cultivated over years of high school teaching. He turned to the stage. "I'm sorry, Derek, but whatever it was you thought this meeting would accomplish, it's not working. The rest of you can do what you want, but I've had enough." He picked his coat up from where it was draped over the pew's back and started putting it on.

Derek shook his head sadly. "I guess you're right,

Carl." He slid off the stage and stood forlornly looking over his little company, most of whom were following Carl's example with alacrity. "I'd thought we were . . . I'd hoped . . ." He shrugged, and began to study the carpet at his feet.

"Just a minute, please," Irene Polaski called out. "The police have said we can go downstairs again, and I'd appreciate some volunteers to help me pack up the costumes. Maybe tomorrow afternoon?"

A couple of hands were raised, and on that note of practicality the meeting adjourned for good.

Portia, Anandi, and I waited for the aisle to clear. Derek and Harry were the last ones up. Derek said, "God, Portia, I'm sorry it turned out like this. What a mess, huh?" He managed to produce a shadow of the old ebullient grin, but I thought his eyes were wet.

Harry offered his arm to my aunt, and we proceeded slowly up and into the lobby. There Harry said, "I'm going to help Derek close up." To me he said, "Call you tomorrow?" I nodded, and he went back through the swinging door.

Outside, at the top of the steps leading to the front door of the Old Church Theater, we found Jane Manypenny standing, wearing the same frown I'd observed in the auditorium. She was staring into the darkness, perhaps at the people dissipating in the direction of their cars, perhaps at something only she could see.

Without acknowledging our presence, she said distinctly, "It's not right! It's just not right!" before marching down the steps and into the night.

As the three of us negotiated the same steps and made our way to our car, I reflected that Harry should at least be pleased about one thing: Whatever had been achieved by Derek's ill-advised meeting, it certainly hadn't been closure.

19

. . . corroborative detail . . .

I STUDIED THE LIST OF NAMES THAT BEN SOLLIDAY HAD placed on the kitchen table atop a clutter of sections from two Sunday newspapers: *The New York Times* and the *Springfield Sunday Republican*. A glowing review of *The Mikado* on page six of the Springfield paper was everything that Derek Bowles, as producer, could have dreamed of. All, alas, turned to dusty irrelevance by the real-life drama which had made the front page, where the headline read: NORTHAMPTON MAN SLAIN IN BIZARRE BACKSTAGE MURDER. Reporters had done their best, dwelling at length on the irony of the victim's having been stabbed with his own dagger. But details were skimpy and boiled down to "Police are pursuing a number of leads."

As indeed they were. The list, jotted onto a sheet of lined notebook paper, read: Portia Singh; Phoebe Mullins; Lydia Hicks; Harry Johns; Jane Manypenny; Irene Polaski; Derek Bowles; Carl Piquette; Mitchell Kim. Though I'd been well aware, in theory, that my name as well as my aunt's must appear on any preliminary list of suspects, actually seeing them there still gave me a nasty shiver. A napkin-wrapped plateful of blueberry muffins rested on the *Times* Book Review. I reached for the comfort of a still-warm muffin and passed the list on to Anandi.

Last night Portia and Anandi and I had sat over tea and Oreo cookies—according to Portia, the food she had missed the most during her life abroad—and discussed the evening's events. Portia hadn't contributed much beyond characterizing the participants as a "pack a'fools." But I could tell she was upset by the way her fingers periodically drummed the kitchen table and the fact that she absently squeezed half a lemon into her tea and had to throw it out and start over.

Anandi, on the other hand, questioned me closely about each of the players in the evening's drama. She made few comments, but those she did make carried a certainty I began to find a mite irritating. "She doesn't care about the money," she said of Lydia, and when I pressed her simply shook her head and said "I know it." Of Jane Manypenny she stated, "She has a strict morality, that one. Which some person has betrayed."

Perhaps I should sic Anandi on the lieutenant, I thought somewhat sourly, since she seemed to be sure of a lot more than I was.

After a while, still too keyed up to sleep, we adjourned to the TV room. Anandi made it through the middle episode of a Masterpiece Theater drama and a rerun of *Seinfeld,* but drew the line at *Saturday Night Live* and retired to bed. *Saturday Night Live* held a peculiar fascination for my aunt, who was alternately delighted and appalled, and I stayed to keep her company, so it was one o'clock when we turned off the TV.

"By the way," Portia said as she heaved herself to her feet, "Ben Solliday is comin' around in the mornin'. Get us up-to-date on the investigation."

I gave an inward groan. She couldn't have mentioned this before keeping me up to all hours? Besides which . . .

"I don't understand," I said. "What's the deal? Why is the lieutenant letting Solliday in on this?"

"Used to be on the force," my aunt said. "Ten years, I think. Quit when his wife and son died, opened up the shop."

With which pregnant piece of information she said good night and stumped off to her room.

What? Died how? And why the leap from cop to storekeeper . . . what had Anandi said . . . "Objects from India, from China"? And an opera buff? What was that about?

But since I was left with no one to question, I went up to my own bed.

Not, however, to sleep, desperately tired as I was. In spite of my best efforts to screen them out, a whole new set of pesky questions buzzed irritatingly behind my clenched eyelids. What was Ben Solliday's real purpose in regard to Aunt Portia? Was he a friend to be trusted, or—once a cop, always a cop—a spy cleverly planted in our kitchen? Him with his sticky buns! But no, that was way before the murder. What was his interest, then? Renting a garage was hardly automatic grounds for personal involvement. Did the relationship with my aunt perhaps predate her move back to Northampton? I pegged the Bear at his middle forties . . . no, he couldn't have been more than an infant, if that, when Portia left home. Then what possible . . . on the other hand . . .

I fell into a fitful and dream-filled sleep, interrupted by sudden awakenings. Toward morning I dreamt I was holding a teddy bear that suddenly turned its fuzzy head to me and bared its fangs.

How embarrassingly obvious, I thought as I rose reluctantly in response to the chattering of the alarm clock. Why couldn't I have dreams that at least involved a modicum of interpretation? Still, before going down to breakfast I made a gesture in the direction of armor to the extent of substituting jeans and a sweatshirt for the blue chenille bathrobe.

·   ·   ·   ·

"How did the police arrive at this list?" I said to the Bear.

He sat opposite me at the table, and judging from the tinge of pink in the whites of his eyes had not slept any better than I had.

"Interviews, cross-checking statements. Basically, the people using the big central area as dressing rooms were able to account for each other during the relevant time period. And everyone swore there was no way an outsider could have been down there without being noticed."

I took the list back from Anandi, who had been studying it closely with a frown of concentration. What it boiled down to were the people in the two dressing rooms besides Pooh-Bah's: Lydia and Jane in number two, and Derek, Carl, and Mitchell in number three. Add to those the director, Harry, the stage manager, me, and my aunt. Wait.

"What's Irene Polaski doing here? Didn't she dress with the other women?"

"Yes, but evidently she was in and out checking on costumes that needed attention before the next performance."

"But," I protested, "that must be true of other people as well—going in and out, I mean, to the bathrooms and so on."

The Bear nodded patiently. "The amount of togetherness seemed unusual to me, too. But I think you can trust that the questioning was detailed and very thorough."

I thought back to the arrangement of that sheet-partitioned area. On the one side the eight members of the women's chorus plus Ardys and Beth; on the other the seven Gentlemen (Carl Piquette, who as Pish-Tush also sang with the chorus, having opted for the relative privacy of dressing room number three), and Arnold

Zimmer. As I recalled, during the final days of costumed rehearsals the curtains dividing the sexes and those facing the three principal dressing rooms had generally remained closed. But the ones on the sides, hanging between the performers and the only sources of the water needed for applying makeup and cleaning up afterwards, had quickly been seen as nuisances and shoved aside. I grudgingly conceded the possibility of no one being out of somebody else's sight (or at least ken, while in the bathrooms) during that time.

"How about Mitchell and Carl?" I persisted. "I know Derek was all over the place, but the other two were in the same small room, why can't they alibi each other?"

"Because it seems that Mitchell—that would be Mr. Kim?—disappeared from his dressing room for a good ten minutes in the middle of removing his makeup. He says he went upstairs to speak to the young woman who was the music director—Nadine Gardner—but she was busy so he waited a short time and then came back. She says she didn't see him."

It came to me that Ben Solliday must have spent considerable time to familiarize himself to this degree with the police reports. No wonder his eyes were bloodshot.

"And I suppose it must be the same sort of thing with Jane and Lydia?" Even to me, my voice sounded antagonistic. Tough. To my surprise, I was experiencing an emotional circling of the wagons, as in, How dare these outsiders come in and start pointing fingers at members of Our Gang? I pushed aside the thought that finger-pointing was exactly what I had been attempting to do during yesterday's walk in the park, and that clearing Aunt Portia would inevitably involve nailing someone else. Where was it written that Phoebe Mullins was compelled to be reasonable on a twenty-four-hour basis?

The Bear gave a reluctant nod. "Jane Manypenny, according to her account and Lydia Hicks's, removed her makeup and changed her clothes very quickly. She then

went up to the backstage room where the big coffeemaker is kept, she says, to be sure it was packed and
ready to be taken to Harry Johns's house for the party.
She says that on checking, she discovered that the plug-
in cord was missing and it took her some minutes to
find it. Mr. Johns corroborates that he had arranged to
borrow the coffeemaker. However, the detective who
interviewed—" He broke off to take a sip of the coffee
that had been cooling in front of him. The brown eyes
blinked rapidly and he said, "Whew! Anandi, could you
slide that milk pitcher over here?"

I tasted my own brew. It wasn't too strong. Whatever the Bear had been about to say, he'd obviously
thought better of it. Fine. If he could censor his information, so could I. I expected that he would question us
about the meeting last night and tried to think of some
item that I could possibly withhold. At which point the
childishness of my thinking caused me an inward
blush. I had also conveniently forgotten that I had not
gone to that meeting unaccompanied.

Aunt Portia said, "Hand me that list again, Phoebe."
She pulled her reading glasses out of the pocket of the
maroon robe, perused the sheet of notebook paper
briefly, removed the glasses and said to the Bear with
something like a twinkle, " 'Spose I should be glad to
find myself with plenty'a company. Any special significance to the order here?" She tapped the paper with her
spectacles.

"No, no, certainly not," Ben Solliday said hastily.

"How 'bout motives?" my aunt continued. " 'Cause I
have to say, in defense of my niece here, I don't think
even Eddie—'scuse me, Foster—could drive a person to
murder in that short a time."

The Bear looked distressed. "You have to understand,
this list is based solely on opportunity, nothing else. Hal
wanted you to see it in case anything . . . um . . . you
know, as a starting point."

Huh! It couldn't have been that "Hal" thought seeing

my aunt's name, not to mention mine, heading a list of suspects might fuel my enthusiasm for "helping the police with their inquiries."

"A'course, could be that some of those people who were keepin' such a close eye on each other were lyin'," my aunt observed.

The Bear said gently, "In the case of eighteen people's statements—that is, all the names not on that list—being compared and cross-checked it's possible, I suppose. But really not likely." His gaze shifted to take in the three of us. "And as to motive . . . the, ah . . . police are hoping that you might be able to help out there. Especially Phoebe." He looked at me with a hint of apology. "Considering you've been in a position to observe everyone, you know, interacting over the past weeks. And knowing that you are a . . . an observing sort of person."

I sighed. Wasn't this what I'd heard last summer? And hadn't it earned me a load of sorrow? Ah, well. "Look," I said, "of course I want to help if I can. I know *I* didn't murder Foster, and I know Aunt Portia didn't, and the sooner everyone knows that the happier I'll be. But I'm not going to report on a bunch of impressions or guesses or feelings. If I come up with a fact, it's yours. Or the lieutenant's or the D.A.'s or whoever."

Anandi said quietly, "From what I have seen last night, I am thinking that there were many feelings, strong feelings, about this Dr. Ballard. And that it will have been the strongest feelings of all that have led to this killing. You must look"—she directed her gaze to the Bear—"for the one with the most emotion. Perhaps also with the most to lose."

It seemed to me that this pronouncement smacked of an obviousness not redeemed by the aura of subcontinental wisdom lent by Anandi's calm manner, not to mention the accent. Ben Solliday, however, received it gravely, and I chided myself for being unkind.

Portia appeared to be of my mind. "Forget emotion,"

she said, "what about money? Last night the Hicks woman said she gets it all. Do the cops know that?"

Yes, it seemed they did, since Lydia had made no secret of it during her interrogation. Not only did she get it, she'd known she was going to get it. Had this been one reason why Aunt Portia was not under arrest? Who benefits? was, I understood, a primary consideration in investigations of murder. If the late Dr. Ballard had lived up to his wheeler-dealer image, the benefit in this case was presumably large.

And as for "the most emotion"! Who more qualified than Lydia the Scorned? Discounting, naturally, her recent switch to Lydia the Laid-back. As public as Lydia had been about her former (if it was former) resentment of her objectionable ex, I couldn't imagine the police were unaware of it. In any case, I had no intention of contributing another layer of gossip to the mix. Facts were what I had promised, and at facts I drew the line. According to the police timetable, Lydia had had opportunity to pop next door and deliver the fatal blows. I hoped she hadn't, I liked Lydia.

Which brought me abruptly back around to the central fact: Portia hadn't done it, so someone else had, and if I were to be any help at all in clearing my aunt my likes and dislikes had no standing in the matter.

I became aware that conversation had stopped and that the Bear was looking at me with an inquiring expression.

"Oh, sorry. What?"

The Bear smiled. "Just wondering if you have any more thoughts you'd like to share before I go."

I shook my head, and as I did so my glance went past the Bear's shoulder to the chalkboard on the wall beside the pantry door. From some association I couldn't pin down, it reminded me of a question.

"Are you allowed to tell us . . . that is, what's the feeling about those incidents with the coffee and the mirror and so on? I mean, obviously if the lieutenant was convinced there was a direct relationship between those and the murder, Aunt Portia's name wouldn't be on that list. Do they have any idea who . . ."

Ben Solliday looked at me with, I thought, renewed interest. "No. And as to a connection, you're right, the question's wide open. Any ideas of your own?"

I shook my head slowly. "No. That is . . . no."

The Bear's expression turned grave. He leaned toward me across the table. "Because if you do—at any point—think of anything, let me know, or Hal Griffith. Right away."

My hand was resting on the table, and he reached to cover it with his own, which was large and warm. "Because if you were put in any danger because I've . . . urged you to get involved, I'd never forgive myself."

"Of course," I said, taken aback. "Don't worry, I'm not the thrill-seeking type."

The Bear removed his hand hastily, rose, thanked my aunt for the coffee, waved away Anandi's offer to wash the muffin plate, said a quick good-bye, and was out the back door.

When I looked at my aunt, she had an odd little smile on her face. "Prob'ly in a hurry to get to his store," she said.

I didn't bother pointing out it was still Sunday morning.

Anandi returned to her interrupted perusal of the *Republican*. I turned to my aunt.

Up to now, I had practically made myself into a corkscrew trying to avoid questions that might embarrass Aunt Portia. This one time, at least, I was going to untwist and ask the one that to me was the greatest mystery so far.

"Why did you tell the cops about what your parents and Eddie Balcowicz did to you?"

Portia looked surprised, but after a short hesitation she said, "Ben knew. Ben's daddy was our family doctor, a real nice man. He was appalled when they talked about havin' me committed, tried to talk some sense into 'em. Never forgot it. Years later when he was talkin' to Ben about how times had changed, back when he was still hopin' Ben would go to medical school, he brought it up. Ben told me soon after we met, thought I should know he knew—he's a real moral man, Ben is."

And also, I thought angrily, the reason for Portia's current precarious position. How could he betray a confidence like that? Moral, my eye!

"He wouldn't have said anything, a'course," my aunt continued. "But I wasn't goin' to put him in that position."

Well, okay. But still it was because of Ben Solliday—

"An' if it hadn't been Ben it would've been someone else."

My God, was my face that transparent?

My aunt gave me a kindly smile. "Have to remember, Phoebe, this is a small town. Hard to keep a secret in a place like this, somebody always knows. Better to get there first, not seem to be hidin' somethin'."

She reached for her cane. "I'm goin' to get dressed. No, Anandi, now I've got m'arm back I can perfectly well start doin' for myself."

After Portia had left, I poured myself another cup of coffee and grabbed a second muffin. (I might still be harboring a certain resentment against the Bear, but he sure knew how to make a muffin. If the man had wanted to open a store, why hadn't it been a bakery?)

Was what my aunt had said really true? I wondered. Was it that difficult in a town like Northampton to keep highly personal information under wraps? If so, finding motives for the murder of E. Foster Ballard should be a snap. Someone, presumably, would know the reasons for Irene Polaski's and Carl Piquette's hatred of the deceased. And for Lydia's ostensible turnaround. And what Jane Manypenny had meant when she'd said, "It's just not right!" Also, I thought with a twinge, what was behind Pooh-Bah's remark to Harry about assault and "that business." And God-knew-what possible connection between Pooh-Bah and Mitchell Kim. All the cops had to do was to find those someones. And for that they certainly didn't need me.

With which sensible thought I suddenly remembered another question I'd been meaning to ask.

I cleared my throat apologetically. "Anandi?"

She lifted her head, while keeping her finger on a Dear Abby column headlined "Busybody Neighbor Out of Line."

"I'm sorry," I said, "but I was just curious . . . last night when Derek told us that Foster owned the Old Church you whispered something to Aunt Portia. I just wondered what it was. If you don't mind telling me."

Anandi's brow wrinkled, then cleared. "Ah yes. I was saying only that Dr. Ballard had recently bought also the house next door to the church."

It was my turn to frown. "The rooming house? The big white one?"

"Yes, yes, that one. I saw this in the Property Transfers list in the *Gazette*. Only, until we went to the church I did not recognize the address."

"Oh. Well, thanks."

Anandi went back to her newspaper. I sat dabbing stray crumbs off my plate with a moist finger and wondering what possible significance there might be in Pooh-Bah's acquiring yet another piece of property. Probably nothing, I finally decided. But still . . . I filed it away under You Never Know.

20

Modified rapture!

I HAD NOT YET SEEN MUCH OF THE SMITH COLLEGE campus, and Harry, phoning true to his promise, suggested a walk through the grounds. Not quite a candlelit dinner for two, I mused as I pondered what to wear. But still, it was our first contact that wasn't directly as a result of involvement with the Northampton Repertory Company. It could be considered progress.

The day was a true Indian summer one, all blue with sky and yellow with sun but cool enough to remind you that fall was already over a month old. I settled on tan twill slacks and a cotton turtleneck topped with a heavy fisherman's knit sweater, checked in the mirror and added a gold and green silk scarf. My hair, fresh from the shower and as yet untamed, was, I noted, approaching perilously close to afro stage. I was either going to have to get a haircut or grow it out. I gave it a severe brushing, pinned it back, and decided to use the gold and green scarf to hold it in place, Grecian fashion, allowing a few tendrils to escape in front. Tendrils, I noted on closer inspection, with a generous sprinkling of silver. More than I'd arrived with a month ago? I decided to believe they gave me distinction, and went on to wonder idly just how old Harry Johns was.

"Of course I wouldn't have had it happen like this," Harry said. "But truthfully it's a relief to me that it's over—*The Mikado,* I mean."

We were sitting on a bench overlooking a waterfall cascading from a small man-made lake into the rocky bed of a shallow stream below. The stream flowed on under an arched footbridge with red-painted railings in an oriental-flavored geometric design. Across the stream stretched the college athletic fields, their greens ranging from pale to emerald to forest.

From the college music building to our left, the sound of a violin, from time to time, depending on the vagaries of the breeze, penetrated the rush of the waterfall. The player was practising the solo violin part of Vivaldi's *Four Seasons*—the middle movement of "Summer," I thought, though I've always had trouble keeping them straight (one listener's sleeping shepherd, I've always thought, being just as easily another's dripping icicle).

"Oh?" I said. It was the first mention of *The Mikado* by either of us since we'd left Portia's house and begun our ramble through the grounds of Smith. Mostly we had been occupied in identifying the buildings according to a campus map Harry had brought along, and trying to put names to an astonishing variety of trees and then giving up and reading the little metal labels conveniently attached to most of them. I had the uncomfortable thought, from a certain hesitation in Harry's manner, that what he was about to say now might be the real reason for our little get-together.

"I have a full-time teaching job, you know," he went on, naming a community college in a nearby town. "Lucky to have it, too. Half the faculty are adjuncts—no security, no benefits, it's a rotten system. As it happens, this fall they're doing a complete renovation of the only available performing space, so we couldn't put on our usual first semester show. That's why, when Derek asked me, I agreed to do *The Mikado*. But it's been a stretch."

He'd been staring out across the river, both arms lying along the bench's back. Now he turned to me with his wry grin. "A lot more intense than I'd expected, even before"—he flapped an encompassing hand—"all this." The hand dropped to my shoulder. "What we'd have done without you I cannot imagine."

A warm sensation proceeded from my shoulder downward. Damn! What kind of pathetic pushover had I become? I took a moment and then said, keeping the tone determinedly light, "It was a pleasure for me to be doing something I never thought I'd have a chance to again. Choreographing and . . ."

"And stage-managing?" Harry said with an apologetic grimace. "I'm really sorry about that."

"No, no," I protested. "It was fun. All of it. Except," I added, remembering, "for the parts that were . . . not fun."

Harry's other hand—the one that was not resting so agreeably on my shoulder—reached to tug at his earlobe. Uh-oh, I thought, what now?

"Can I ask you . . . and if I'm stepping where I shouldn't, just say so and I won't mention it again . . . what happened between you and Nadine?"

To my horror, I felt the tears well up and start to spill down my cheeks with a suddenness that left me gasping.

"Oh God, Phoebe, I'm sorry, I'm sorry." Harry's arm tightened around my shoulders and I found myself with my face buried against his chest and creating a large damp spot on the lapel of his tan corduroy jacket. "I shouldn't have asked."

Beyond the sound of my own hiccups, I heard the approaching voices of a party that included a baby and at least one dog. I pulled myself upright, fished in the pocket of my slacks for the tissue experience had taught me never to leave home without, and blew my nose.

The family group had drawn parallel to our bench. It included a small girl whose piping voice rose clearly. "Why is the lady crying, Daddy?" They hurried on by.

"*I'm* sorry," I said. "I guess it's because I've been sitting on it for so long—well, it seems long—without talking to anyone . . ."

Harry said hastily, "You certainly don't have to tell me either, if—"

"No," I said, "I want to."

And so I did, keeping my eyes fixed on the falls, laying out the facts as calmly as I was able, feeling more and more as if I were narrating the plot of a particularly unlikely soap opera: Husband has brief affair in Britain with a married woman at the same time that his unsuspecting wife is still mourning the death of their unborn child. Twenty-one years later, a year and a half after husband dies, clueless wife and daughter of adulterous union meet in small town in another country. Daughter reveals herself. Wife is devastated. Then there's this murder . . .

I heaved a large sigh, gave my eyes a final blotting, and tucked the soggy tissue back into my pants pocket. I turned my face to Harry. The grey eyes were regarding me with an empathy that almost undid me all over again. Not wanting to spend the remainder of the afternoon sobbing on a public bench, I bit my lip hard and then produced a shaky laugh. "Who'd believe it?" I said. "If you put it on stage, I mean. *I* wouldn't."

Harry shook his head. "It must have been god-awful for you."

"Uh-huh." Now that I'd actually gotten the words out, I found that for the present that was enough.

"Have you talked to Nadine? Since then, I mean?"

"Not really. I will, of course." I turned my gaze back to the bucolic scene before us, relaxing into the curve of Harry's arm. "But not today."

For some moments we sat silently. The violinist had moved on to the *presto* section of "Summer" (or whatever), and was having trouble with it. The notes broke off, restarted, tripped over a tricky passage, started again. I was just beginning to wonder when, if ever, my cautious friend was going to offer to kiss me when he gave my shoulder a quick squeeze and stood up, pulling me along with him.

"Come on," he said. "Let's go that way," pointing, "and we should come to the gardens and the greenhouses."

I bit back a comment about the joys of wandering through a garden in November and meekly fell into step beside him. He reached for my hand and held it as we made our way back toward the center of the campus. Was hand-holding, I wondered, as far as this particular relationship was destined to go? Was it unseemly of me, a woman approaching the august half-century mark, to fantasize something a bit more . . . well, more?

After we had been strolling for a minute or two, during which I was aware that Harry's left earlobe was getting a particularly heavy workout, he said, as if having reached a decision, "There's something I need to tell you."

My imagination leapt into instant overdrive: a fatal (communicable?) disease? a secret life as a cross-dresser? a wife?

"When you were coming down the stairs that night, when I was . . . talking to Foster in his dressing room. I thought you might have overheard something of what we were saying. Specifically, something Foster said."

My spirits plummeted. Was that what this was all about? What it simply Mr. Covering-His-Butt that I had been indulging in romantic fantasies about? On the other hand, it wasn't as if I hadn't been curious about that little exchange.

"Yes," I said. "Foster mentioned an assault. It sounded as if he meant it to be a threat. I didn't mention it to the police, by the way. I had no idea what he was talking about and I figured if there *was* anything the cops would dig it up anyway."

And basically, I added to myself, I didn't want to think it could have been you.

I was beginning to wonder now if that had been altogether wise. We had reached the gardens, predictably deserted, and were wandering the paths between beds of dead and dying flowers interspersed with the occasional splash of purple, yellow, and red from late-blooming mums. Oh, get a grip, Phoebe! This is Harry the Gentle we're dealing with. What do you think he's going to do?

"It was in New York," Harry said. "I was appearing in an Off-Broadway show and giving acting classes during the day. My wife had just left me and filed for divorce. Decided after fourteen years she wanted stability. And kids, which I thought we'd agreed in the beginning . . . well, anyway. Not a good time in my life."

We turned into a narrow pathway that wound up and around a miniature rock garden landscape.

"There was a woman in one of my classes who developed a . . . well, I guess you'd call it a crush, though it was much more than that."

"Like the Cougher," I said.

"Who?"

"Uh . . . Cynthia. Sorry, I tend to give people handles as memory aids. Comes from the days when I had to keep dozens of people straight in my mind while we were touring."

Harry chuckled, but shook his head. "No, not like Cynthia. Cynthia backed off when she saw how the land lay." He gave me what I interpreted as a significant glance, to which I responded with what I hoped he interpreted as a cool one. Before I allowed myself to get any more carried away I wanted to know where this was going.

"No, this woman—Joyce was her name—was a

full-blown obsessional. I made the mistake of meeting her for lunch once, at her invitation. After that she started phoning me several times a day, coming to every performance of the play I was in, hanging around afterwards. I didn't know what I was dealing with at first, tried to be polite, you know. If I went out after the show with the cast she'd tag along to the restaurant or whatever and sit with us."

Oh yes, I could imagine that well enough. Good Lord, the man made his living representing strong emotions—what happened when it came to making his own feelings clear?

"Then she decided that I was getting too . . . friendly with another cast member, started phoning her, telling her to let me alone, I belonged to her, Joyce. Making vague threats. Naturally my friend got upset and insisted we go to the police. Turned out they knew Joyce, she'd done this kind of thing before, not any real danger, etc., etc. One of your friendly neighborhood paranoid schizos. They'd contact her social worker, make sure she got back on her meds."

We had reached what I judged to be the midpoint of the rock garden. Harry had picked up a stick fallen across the path and was using it to flick aside the occasional dead leaf. His gaze remained fixed on the ground.

"Well, they didn't succeed—or not quickly enough. The next day I found her sitting in the hallway outside my apartment door. She'd managed somehow to get buzzed in." He shook his head and sighed. "Stupidly, I lost my temper. I hauled her up and marched her down the two flights of stairs and out the front door. On the stoop, she tried to put her arms around me and I . . . shoved her, and she fell down the steps. It was a warm day, she was only wearing a cotton dress, and she scraped herself up pretty well and then hit her head on the bottom step."

"Was she seriously hurt?"

"No, but she was bleeding a lot. A couple of people

had seen it happen, Joyce started yelling. What a mess! She marched right down to the police station and charged me with assault." He stopped and turned to me with a rueful smile. "And that's the story of my criminal record. What Foster was talking about, though naturally he didn't have all the facts."

I looked into those level grey eyes, now fixed so searchingly on my face, at the fine laugh lines radiating from their corners, at the grey-and-brown curls, wind-disheveled and in need of a trim. Then, as my stomach went into its old acrobatic routine, I reminded myself that I was standing in a sheltered area with a man who might have murdered another for possessing the very information I now had. Ridiculous, I didn't believe it for a minute. Still . . . I resumed walking, with a somewhat brisker pace than before. Since Harry had never stopped gripping my hand, he came along.

"So what happened?" I said. "With the assault charge?"

"I was arrested. God, it was humiliating. The two women who'd seen it happen painted a pretty ugly picture so the cops really had no choice. But when it got to the D.A. and all the facts came out they decided not to prosecute. Not before my name got in the papers, though. I suppose that's how Foster found out. But, my God, it was more than three years ago!" He gave a short, humorless laugh. "What a shit the man was!"

Not, I thought, the best sort of sentiment to be expressing in the circumstances. And hadn't Foster said something about his employers?

Harry's mind must have been running along the same lines because he stopped again, turned to face me, and said, "And no, I didn't tell the college. Why should I? The charge was dismissed. And yes, I prefer to keep it that way. But I didn't kill him, Phoebe. I swear to you."

His face, looking down at me, was filled with distress and something more . . . pleading? I steeled myself against any reaction that might be less than objective and made a judgment. This man was not a murderer.

"I believe you," I said.

"Thank God," he said.

Okay, was that it? I wondered as we strolled on. Had Harry accomplished his purpose and would he now hurry to deposit me at home? Had the "Thank God" been because he cared about my opinion, or was he naive enough to think that the police were not even now raking through all our backgrounds with the proverbial tiny combs? He hadn't told me not to tell. Was he assuming I wouldn't? Not that (see above) it mattered anyway.

Harry had tucked my arm under his. I could feel the heat of his body and smell the comforting combination of aftershave and warm corduroy. We didn't appear to be hurrying anywhere. Jeez, Phoebe, just for now forget the damn murder.

Our path had led us between a row of greenhouses and the perimeter of a reed-rimmed pond. Another few steps took us to the door of a low brick building which a hanging sign identified as the Lyman Plant House. A cardboard placard in the window said OPEN.

Inside, the sudden and welcome warmth made me realize that the afternoon had been steadily cooling and that my sweater would soon be completely inadequate for the walk home. But through a door directly ahead I could see brilliant flashes of color, along with the irresistible smells of fresh loam and moist greenery. Whatever my suspicions might be of Harry's motive for this little outing, here at least was something I could enjoy for its own sake. In answer to Harry's questioning look, I nodded, Harry stuffed a couple of dollars into a glass donation box, and we entered the first greenhouse room.

Slender aisles separated a broad central waist-level planting area from the narrower ones lining the glass windows. We sauntered down one side, admiring a spread of begonias, exclaiming over grapefruit-sized lemons hanging from the branches of a dwarf "ponderosa," bending down to struggle with the latin names written on little white popsicle sticks, touching the tiny fringed leaves of a sensitive plant *("Mimosa pudica")* to watch them curl tightly in on themselves. A scattering of other Sunday visitors were doing likewise, their murmured voices swelling and receding as they passed by on the opposite aisle.

From that room we went on to one with a pond displaying papyrus and sugar cane and dotted with lotuses in full bloom. By the time we reached the third room, a tropical forest whose ceiling soared to double the height of the preceding ones, I was beginning to feel as if we were actually enjoying a purely social occasion.

In addition to the aisle around the perimeter, a curving path led into the center of the "forest" and past a slatted bench. By mutual, unspoken consent, we went in and sat on the bench. Over our heads the enormous leaves of a banana palm swept the glass ceiling. Water dripped from leaf to leaf to the dark earth below. The saturated air smelled at once of growth and ripeness and decay.

And it was here, in this ersatz rain forest, that Harry tilted my face to his and kissed me most satisfactorily on my shamelessly willing lips.

When we arrived back at Portia's house, I was wearing Harry's jacket, with the green and gold scarf, which had somehow fallen off, tucked into its pocket. As we passed between the wrought-iron posts and into the drive, I stopped short. In the parking area, Harry's green Honda had been joined by a police car and Derek Bowles's blue Rabbit.

"Oh God! Portia!" I said. I dropped Harry's hand and ran for the front door.

21

From three little maids take one away . . .

THEY WERE GATHERED IN THE LIVING ROOM: AUNT Portia in the recliner but sitting upright, straight-backed, feet on the floor; Anandi on a low hassock by her side, Derek Bowles hovering just behind her; standing on Portia's other side, Ben Solliday; and facing her on the velvet settee, Lieutenant Griffith.

I had burst into the room and stopped short, taking in the scene before me, panting, barely able to get out the words "What is it? What's happened?" The five faces turned to me, and Hal Griffith stood up. "There's been—" he started, but was interrupted by Derek, who burst out, "Oh, Phoebe! Jane Manypenny's dead! She was shot to death last night!"

For a moment my head swam, and I must have staggered because Harry, coming up behind me, put an arm around me and led me to the chair Ben Solliday had rushed to pull over and place next to my aunt's recliner. There was a babble of concern, a glass of water was thrust into my hand, and I caught a look of serious annoyance on the lieutenant's face and on Derek's one of worried apology. The Bear had moved to stand behind

Portia and he also looked annoyed, though evidently not at Derek, since he was staring beyond me to where Harry stood by my shoulder.

What I was not about to explain to anyone was that my momentary giddiness had been brought on not by shock and distress but by sheer relief. I thought the police had come to arrest my aunt. Instead, they had brought news of a second murder which Portia could not possibly have committed. Ergo she must be innocent of the first one. I could berate myself on grounds of callousness later. For now I concentrated on trying not to look as gleeful as I felt.

"I'm *so* sorry," Derek said, whether to me or the lieutenant I wasn't sure. "I shouldn't have blurted it out like that." With one hand he swiped at the recalcitrant forelock; the other was gripping the back of Portia's chair. "It's just . . . what a nightmare! Foster and then Jane. What's happening?" Then, with a catch in his voice, "How could it have turned out like this?"

"Assuming," Lieutenant Griffith said rather loudly, "that Ms. Manypenny's death was also connected with your . . . um, show."

"What?" I cried out. "How couldn't it be? I mean, what kind of coincidence . . . how many murders do you usually have around here in the course of a year anyway?"

The lieutenant acknowledged my outburst with a nod of his nearly naked head. "Which is why I'm here," he said. "Not meaning that we're not also looking in other directions. However, for the record"—again the notebook appeared from the breast pocket—"where were you, Ms. Mullins, last night between eleven and midnight?"

"I was watching television. With my aunt." I directed a fond glance at Portia. Thank God for her addiction to *Saturday Night Live*!

Hal Griffith nodded and made a couple of squiggles. "And you, Mr. Johns?"

"At home, asleep."

"Anyone to vouch for that?"

"No," Harry said drily. "Unhappily, I was alone."

Derek nodded in sympathy. "As was I, worse luck! Saturday night, dateless and loveless—how pathetic! Of course, what we all *thought* we'd be doing was the second performance—"

"Wait a minute," I said. "Where did this happen? And why did it take so long for anyone to find her?"

Derek opened his mouth eagerly but the lieutenant frowned him down. "It happened in the front hallway of her house. It looks like she answered the door, the killer came in, shot her once in the chest with a twenty-five-caliber pistol, and left. A neighbor heard the shot but didn't identify it at the time. Besides, all the doors and windows were closed, it wouldn't have sounded like much more than a pop. Since Ms. Manypenny is another one that lives alone it wasn't until she didn't show up for church that anyone got worried. A fellow church member phoned, got no answer of course, was concerned and went to the house. The door wasn't locked."

The lieutenant's official facade showed a hairline crack as he added, "Poor woman was still hardly coherent when we got there. But she'd had the presence of mind not to touch anything."

The horror of what had happened to Jane Manypenny was finally beginning to override my initial, less than empathetic reaction to the news.

"Poor Jane!" I exclaimed. "Why her? And to go to her door like that and be . . . she must have known whoever it was if she let them in. What could she possibly—" I turned to my aunt. "What was it she said last night? Something about not being right?"

Portia nodded, and Lieutenant Griffith flipped a page of his notebook and read out, "It's not right, it's just not right." He raised his eyebrows at me. "That how you remember it?"

"Yes, that was it." In hindsight, I thought, a phrase rife with possible significance, not to mention pathos. But in terms of hard fact, ultimately useless.

"I should be going too," Derek said.

After urging us to dredge our memories for anything about Jane Manypenny's behavior or movements, especially on the night of Pooh-Bah's murder, that we might not have considered before, Hal Griffith had taken himself off. The Bear, after a quiet word with my aunt, had followed him.

Harry, admitting to a neglected pileup of preparatory work for the coming week of classes, left soon after. I walked him to the front door. In the vestibule he caught up my two hands, looked into my eyes with great seriousness, and said, "I want you to know . . . about this afternoon . . . that I don't take this sort of thing . . . lightly."

Since "this sort of thing" amounted to one kiss in a quite public setting, I found the seriousness a tad alarming. Had I hit upon the one man in the free world who would now consider us to be engaged?

The alarm must have showed because he laughed and said, "Not to worry, Phoebe, I'm not about to ask you to leave your nearest and dearest and fly with me. Just to say that I'm not much of a flirt and that I . . . like you a lot."

With which he bent, gave me a quick one on the lips, and was out the door.

Okay. I could live with that.

Now Derek moved restlessly about the big room, seeming, despite his expressed intention, unable to make up his mind to actually leave.

I sensed that Portia was only waiting for his departure to tell me something. But she observed him kindly and finally said, "Come and sit down, boy. You're givin' me a crick in the neck tryin' to keep track of you."

Anandi had moved from the hassock to the settee and taken up her knitting. Derek obediently came and, at Portia's indication, took Anandi's place. But the restlessness continued to show itself in a nervous rocking movement as he sat, hugging his knees and looking thoroughly miserable.

Aunt Portia put a firm hand on his shoulder. "No point in makin' yourself a wreck," she said. "Nothin' you could've done."

Was that true? I wondered. I looked at him and tried to picture Derek Bowles as a murderer.

He was, after all, very much on the list—that list from which, barring the possibility of some colossal coincidence, Portia and I were now eliminated. In fact, in terms of opportunity, Derek should be at the very top. Who better than the show's producer to be bopping in and out of dressing rooms with nobody giving it a thought, or even conscious notice? When I had last seen him that night—or at least last remembered seeing him—he had been in a state of euphoria that, even knowing what a good actor he was, I would have staked my life was real. What could conceivably have happened between then and the time— twenty minutes, half an hour later?—that Pooh-Bah had encountered the business end of that antique aikuchi dagger? And then there was the fact that E. Foster turned out to have been a second angel to the existence of the Northampton Repertory Company. What possible reason could Derek have for eliminating one of his main benefactors?

At which point I was startled back to the present by hearing Derek moan to Portia, "Who knows what will happen to the Old Church now? God, those acoustics! Now somebody'll probably snatch it up and turn it into a goddam warehouse."

"What about the Hicks woman?" my aunt said. "If she knew what she was talkin' about last night the place belongs to her now. Maybe she'd be willin' to keep it goin' as a theater."

Derek shook his head gloomily. "The way Lydia hated Foster? She'll probably sell it just to spite him in his grave. Besides, the place needs work. There's two upper floors, you know. Foster was going to turn them into rental offices with a couple of condos on top. We'd even started drawing up the plans. But you're talking a big investment there."

"Did Jane say anything to you when she first came into the theater last night?" I said abruptly.

Derek, torn from his not entirely unpleasurable (I suspected) wallow in the Slough of Despond, turned to me with a bewildered frown. "Jane?"

"Yes. I thought you spoke to her as you were coming down the aisle together. As if you might be answering something she'd said."

The frown turned thoughtful. "She was terribly upset, of course. What *did* she say? . . . oh yes, something about almost deciding not to come. She sounded somehow . . . angry about it. And I told her not to worry, she'd see that the meeting would be helpful. Hah!" He made a self-deprecating grimace. "*Not* one of my better predictions."

He rose to his feet and said, with an attempt at his usual animation, "Now I *am* going. Thanks, Portia, and you too, Phoebe, for putting up with my blathering. And Portia, thanks again for . . . everything." Then, with a wistful smile at my aunt, as if seeking the only comfort left to him, "It *was* a good show, wasn't it?"

After Derek had left, my aunt said to me, "Ben's asked us to supper. Anandi's begged off. She's tired, wants to go to bed early. So I guess it's just you and me."

I longed for my own bed, or at least some quiet solitude to mull over the emotions of the day. But since Anandi had gotten there ahead of me, I expressed as

much pleasure as I could muster and with a good deal
of resentment toiled up the stairs to change my clothes.
Why couldn't the Bear just have retired to his cave and
left us alone?

At least, I consoled myself, we might learn more
about which way the Law was leaning. Though now
that Portia was—*must* be—out of the picture, the question, for me, had become considerably more academic.

22

Your anger pray bury,
For all will be merry . . .

A VELVETY BEEF STROGANOFF, A BIG TOSSED SALAD WITH artichoke hearts, and for dessert bits of melon, grapes, and strawberries drizzled with an apricot liqueur: it was clear the Bear's culinary skills were not confined to baking. Had he really whipped this up off the cuff, or was the seemingly last-minute dinner invitation part of some prearranged plan, perhaps involving Lieutenant Griffith and/or other levels of Massachusetts law enforcement?

And *why,* I puzzled, did my subconscious (or whatever) persist in sending out impulses of suspicion about this outwardly very nice man?

I looked at him as he sat, elbows on the table, chin resting on folded hands, chatting with Portia about the recent history of some family she had known in her girlhood. The bearlike first impression still held, I decided, on account of the hair—on his head thick, springy, and dark, on his face grizzled. And the size of him. He could stand to lose some weight, but the burliness, I thought, did not translate to fat—as I should know from our first encounter outside the garage. It was not a pillow I'd walked into, more like a well-upholstered rock.

When we'd first arrived, the rock had been swathed in a mammoth, no-nonsense white apron. Now he wore a tan herringbone jacket over a dark green shirt and a brown tie that would have been sober if it hadn't been sprinkled with yellow poodles. A man, I decided, who could laugh at himself.

I watched as he spoke to my aunt—face alive with interest, a smile that broke through its surrounding thicket like a beacon in a briar patch and extended to deepen the laugh lines at the corners of his eyes. Yes, definitely a nice man.

Too nice? Was that my problem? Too decent, too thoughtful, too self-effacing, and therefore automatically suspect? Good Lord, had I really become so cynical?

Relax, I told myself. Not the time for character analysis and introspection. Stomach full, taste buds celebrating, a nice buzz from two glasses of a really good cabernet—and not one mention of murder.

It was Portia who brought up the subject.

We had moved from the round table in the lee of yet another Victorian bay window to a sitting area in the same big room defined by an assortment of comfortable chairs and a sofa arranged to face a white-manteled fireplace complete with fire. The Bear had just stirred the embers, added another log, and reseated himself in the larger of two brown leather armchairs. I was in the other, my aunt on the sofa. Each of us was nursing a brandy.

"Your friend Hal," my aunt said, "how c'n he think that poor woman's death wouldn't be connected with Foster's?"

"I don't believe he really does," Ben said. "It's just something they have to consider. Seems that Jane Manypenny was a therapist and also active in a lot of self-help groups. Including one that dealt with the rehabilitation of released prisoners. A stereotype, maybe, but they have to look at that angle."

"What about the list?" I said. "The list of suspects for Foster's murder. Have you heard yet if they've interviewed—"

"Oh, yeah. Soon as they found her. Starting with the little guy—Derek Bowles. Who immediately afterwards hared off to your aunt's."

"Really upset," Portia said with a touch of defensiveness. "Needed to talk."

"Well." The Bear swirled his brandy thoughtfully, but didn't drink. "Anyway, as you heard, he has no alibi for the time." He glanced at me. "And it seems the same holds true for your . . . friend Harry." Then hurrying on: "Mitchell Kim was with a group of friends at a bar in Amherst, so that lets him out. Irene Polaski lives by herself in the apartment over her shop. Says she went straight back there after the meeting at the theater and didn't go out again. Lydia Hicks stopped for a large coffee to go at the Cumberland Farms opposite Cooley Dickinson Hospital before, she says, driving home to watch a video of *Four Weddings and a Funeral*. So no verification for either of them. And Carl Piquette was home with his wife. The two teen-age kids were out—one at a sleepover, the other with a one o'clock curfew. Thing with him is, he lives two streets over from Jane Manypenny. His wife had gone to bed early, he was downstairs, where he says he fell asleep watching television. He could have done it."

Ben Solliday's pipeline to the P.D., I thought, was looking more like an eight-lane highway. What, truly, was his interest? I decided to give him the benefit of the doubt and assume it was the protection of his parents' old friend.

Which thought he now echoed by smiling widely and saying, "As for Mrs. Singh and her niece, they were together and watching *Saturday Night Live*."

"Unless we were in cahoots and giving each other an

alibi," I said, in what I thought was the same light-hearted vein.

"In which case," Portia put in with a chuckle, "we'd've come up with somethin' more respectable to be watchin'."

The Bear said, "Fortunately, Anandi couldn't entirely escape the sounds of the TV and the two of you laughing. She also heard you both going to your rooms."

I felt a chill. Clearly, the possibility of collusion between my aunt and me had been given consideration. The idea brought home to me the ugly fact that two people had been killed in connection with our production of *The Mikado,* that the forces of the Law were not fooling around, and that Portia and I were, willy-nilly, involved. But, I reminded myself, thank God no longer prime suspects.

"What about the forensic stuff?" I said. "What about fingerprints?"

The Bear shook his head. "You saw the carved handle on that knife." Then, reflectively, "A stunning piece, as it happens. But," brisk again, "no good for prints. Besides which, thanks to all the cop shows everyone knows enough to wipe the murder weapon. Only smudges on the bat. Ditto the light switch. A few identifiables on the door, but none that couldn't have been there quite legitimately."

I waited a beat, but evidently the Bear was not choosing to be more specific. Okay. "What about the angle of the blow from the bat?"

The Bear nodded, settled back further in his chair and crossed his legs. "You're thinking of the height of the swinger," he said with a note of approval. "But it's iffy. Was the victim sitting or standing? Or even in the act of rising? Was the person with the bat standing erect or crouching? The blow wasn't lethal—enough to raise an egg, enough to stun, but not to kill. The way we read it, Ballard was sitting facing the mirror, in which case he'd see what was about to happen. He starts to turn, maybe to get up, but he isn't quick enough. He manages to get to his feet, then blacks out and falls straight forward on his face—his lip was cut from the inside. After that, of course, height doesn't enter into it."

There was an enthusiasm to his delivery of this analysis that made me wonder if Ben Solliday didn't miss his days on the police force quite a lot. And wonder again what had brought about the radical change of vocation.

As if acknowledging an unbecoming exuberance, the Bear added, with a sheepish smile, "That's the long version. The short one is that we . . . they . . . can't really tell how tall the perp . . . person was."

Sure. And if "we . . . they" *could* tell would you be passing the news along? Somehow I thought not.

Seeming to feel that murder had intruded long enough on an otherwise tranquil evening, Ben said to Aunt Portia, "My mother tells me you have a wonderful singing voice. She saw you in *The Gondoliers* at the high school."

Flash! The Bear had a mother! And one with whom he was on gossipy terms. Definitely too good.

Portia looked pleased, but hmmphed, " 'Had' is more like it. Don't sing anymore. Too old."

"Don't say that!" the Bear protested. "Come on, I've got a whole collection of duets I haven't sung in years. We'll give Phoebe a little after-dinner music."

He put down his brandy glass, rose and grasped Portia's hand and guided her, only mildly protesting, to the baby grand at the far end of the room. With one part of my mind I listened, amused, to their gentle bickering ("Here, perfect! Schubert's 'Serenade.' " "You kiddin'? I can't sing that high!" "Wait then, I may have it in a lower . . . yes, here." "C'n you play this stuff?" "I'll take the left hand, you do the right." "Well, don't blame me . . ." etc.). With the other I appreciated anew the Bear's digs.

The house was on a street that paralleled Portia's but at a higher elevation. To reach it, we had gone behind Portia's garage and up a steep and well-worn dirt path to the side door that was the entrance to Ben's apartment. The apartment itself had been carved out of the part of the house that originally included a big main living room, similar to Portia's. But here a section of the second floor had been removed, so that the back-facing half of the room rose two stories. A metal spiral staircase led to a loft over the front section that appeared to be the Bear's office space. A gallery along the inner wall gave access to two doors, presumably bedrooms or bed and bath. Off the big room at first-floor level were a kitchen, powder room, and den. I saw no reason not to stand by my first reaction, which had been: Wow! What a marvelous place!

After several false starts, Ben and Portia had gotten going on Schubert's "Serenade," which they were singing in German—the Bear in a resonant bass, my aunt in a robust alto that, while rusty, gave evidence of a fine natural instrument. As a nonsinger perpetually in awe of those blessed with beautiful voices, I wondered what had led each of them to follow paths so removed from those gifts. Ben Solliday a *cop*? His voice was more than good—smooth, flexible, not growly. What a great Mikado he would have made! He was not, I was relieved to observe, an expert pianist, or even a very good one (enough is enough). Nor was Portia. But between them they were managing to keep an accompaniment of sorts going. Altogether, I mused indulgently, the sort of performance that is most satisfying to those doing the performing. Anyway, my aunt and the Bear seemed to be having a rare old time.

I searched the room for more clues to Ben Solliday's personality. Books up the wazoo, crammed into floor-to-ceiling bookcases complete with a library ladder. A few paintings on the white walls, most of which looked like originals by good but not famous artists. Scatter and area rugs on the maple flooring, some oriental, all well-worn. A few knickknacks, but not the accumulation of artifacts I would have expected from the owner of an import business. On one of the end tables by the sofa, an eight-by-ten photograph of a pretty woman with long, fair hair and a boy of about six. The boy was blond, like his mother, but with the Bear's dark eyes. The woman smiled broadly, but the boy gazed soberly at the camera, as if conscious of the importance of having his picture taken. Not a studio photo, I thought, but an enlargement of a snapshot taken on a sunny day. By the Bear? And when? My aunt hadn't said how long ago Ben Solliday's wife and son had died, or how, and I hadn't gotten around to asking her.

The duo at the piano had moved on to Offenbach's "Barcarolle." Their two voices rose and fell in parallel thirds, soothing, almost soporific. I contemplated the very small amount of brandy at the bottom of my glass and allowed my thoughts to wander. Which they did, in the way of thoughts unwisely given their liberty, straight back to the subject of the murders.

What had been the relationship between Jane Manypenny and E. Foster Ballard? On her side, I would have said, deference and admiration; on his, little more than tolerance. But last night, at the meeting, Jane had seemed different: upset, yes, but also angry. Angry at what or at whom? Had she been killed for the same motive that lay behind Foster's murder? Or because she knew something dangerous to the murderer? What had been the significance, if any, of their both coming out of that downtown office building?

Now that the police would surely be questioning everyone again, with the emphasis on Jane's mood and movements on the night of Pooh-Bah's death, maybe some small new recollection would shed light. Had *I* noticed anything about Jane that night? No, I decided. She had seemed to me the same bustling Jane, helping with makeup, turning in her usual competent performance, fussbudgeting about the coffeemaker. If I now remembered a frown deeper than her usual worrywart expression, it was probably after the fact. It was Lydia who shared a dressing room with her. If there was anything to notice, Lydia would be the one . . .

The Bear's duet collection was an eclectic one. They had now launched into Victor Herbert's "Sweethearts," giving it their schmaltzy all.

Sweetheart, sweetheart, sweetheart,
Will you love me ever?

Ah, and wasn't *that* the question?

To my surprise, the brandy glass was now empty. I put it on the end table, nudged off my shoes, and tucked my legs under me.

What was really going on between Harry and me? Was I seriously thinking of him as a possible life companion? Was I just a randy forty-something looking for sex with a touch of romance thrown in? An embryo Katisha? Or was my attraction to him based on nothing more than getting back at the dead husband's betrayal? An "I'll show you and I hope you're watching" thrown up to the Great Beyond. No, it had started before that, from the first time we'd met, at Portia's . . .

Sweetheart, sweetheart, sweetheart,
Though our paths may sever . . .

Death, the Great Severer, had done the job for Mick and me. Taken him away and left me to face, alone, the living evidence of his faithlessness. Living evidence, I reminded myself, that I still needed to meet with, to talk to. If people would just stop getting themselves bumped off . . .

To life's last faint ember
Will you remember . . .

Oh yes, dammit, I'll remember. Mick . . . Nadine . . . Harry . . . I think maybe I should have said no to the brandy.

> *Springtime,*
> *Lovetime,*
> *May!*

bawled Ben and Portia.

The concert, it seemed, had come to an end. I clapped, they beamed and gave exaggerated bows. How really nice of Ben, I thought muzzily, to give Aunt Portia such a good time.

Portia headed, with a steady step, for the powder room. Since she had had fully as much to drink as I, she must have a far stronger head.

Ben turned off the piano light and said, "Come and see the view of your house."

I joined him at one of the two large windows flanking the baby grand. There indeed, a looming hulk in the darkness, was Portia's house, down the hill and slightly to the right, its roof, from this vantage point, at about eye level. And there was my bedroom bay window lit with a faint yellow glow.

"Oh, dear," I said, pointing it out. "Caught wasting electricity again. Could have sworn I turned that light off."

"That's your bedroom?" said the Bear.

"Yes."

There was a silence as we continued to gaze out at shadowy, crisscrossing tree limbs, the dark shapes of other houses on the street below, with here and there light streaming from a window or around the edges of a drawn curtain. And in the far distance, barely discernible, the black curves of the Holyoke range. I began to be aware of the Bear's solid presence beside me, exuding scents of brandy and woodsmoke and to find it oddly comforting.

He said hesitantly, "There's something I've been wanting to mention. None of my business in a way, but still. .... It's about Harry Johns."

I stiffened, and turned from the window to face him. "Yes?"

The Bear looked pained, but continued, "I just think you should know that he was arrested, three years ago in New York, for assault on a woman."

"I *know* that," I said. "He told me himself. And also that the charge was thrown out."

"Yes, but—"

"The woman was a nut. She was stalking him."

"That's true, but—"

"Well, Phoebe," my aunt cried gaily, emerging from the powder room, "Don't know about you, but this old gal's ready for bed!"

"Absolutely!" I said, and went to retrieve our coats from the rack by the door.

Ben Solliday insisted on accompanying us down the path and to our back door.

"Thanks, m'dear," Portia said. She reached up to pat his cheek. "Haven't had that much fun in a long while."

I shook the Bear's hand and expressed gratitude for a lovely evening.

In the kitchen, Portia gave me a quizzical look, then remarked, "Sweet on you, y'know."

I stared at her. "Don't be silly!"

"Huh!" Portia said.

Alone in my room, I contemplated my aunt's pronouncement. Could it be true? If so, my antennae needed a tune-up. And if so, too bad! In this light, the Bear's implicit warning against Harry took on new and complicated meaning. Obviously, the police were considering Harry a serious suspect. And the Bear would be in no mood to challenge that theory.

Ergo, my only slightly tipsy brain informed me, it was up to me. With Portia in the clear, whatever

sleuthing abilities I had would be in the service of exon-
erating Harry Johns.

I fell into bed and dreamed that I was Joan of Arc and
Harry was the Dauphin. It was only in the morning that
I reflected uncomfortably on what had come of *that* re-
lationship.

23

It's an affecting tale, and quite true.

DUE TO THE HEFTY PILE OF RESENTMENT I'D MANAGED TO work up overnight, Ben Solliday was the last person I wanted to see when I dragged myself down to the kitchen breakfast table. But there he was, though without any baked offering. He had a scrap of paper in his hand and was in the midst of explaining to Portia that he had only dropped by to ask one quick question.

I mumbled a "good morning," pulled my ratty bathrobe closer around me with what dignity I could muster, and went to pour myself a cup of coffee.

Portia, in her usual place and looking not at all the worse for last night's mild debauchery, said, "Shoot."

The question, the Bear explained, involved Ardys Feldman's statement taken immediately after Pooh-Bah's death. She had mentioned hearing Jane Manypenny talking to someone in the utility room off the backstage corridor.

"Ardys and the Rosario girl, Beth, had gone up to-gether to return their parasols to the prop table. The door was closed, but Ardys says in her statement that they recognized Jane's voice, and that she was saying something about"—he referred to his scrap with a puzzled frown—" 'the horse and buggy thing.' Ring any bells?"

Portia snorted. "Y'mean that fool idea about paradin' around town dressed up like G 'n S?"

Since the Bear continued to look unenlightened, I explained about Derek's obsession with his proposed publicity stunt. "He wanted to hire a horse and carriage and drive around dressed up like Arthur Sullivan with Harry as William S. Gilbert. Harry wouldn't do it, so he tried to rope Foster in. But Foster refused too, and anyway Aunt Portia looked into the cost and decided it would be too expensive. But what that could have to do with Jane Manypenny . . ."

"Yes. The thing is, that in her statement Ms. Manypenny made no reference to any such conversation. And when she was asked about it later she said the girls must have been mistaken, she'd only been looking for the cord to the coffeepot and might have been talking to herself, as she said, 'in exasperation.' "

The Bear, who I thought had been avoiding looking at me, now did so.

"Phoebe, you had a rapport with the two girls. How reliable would you say Ardys Feldman is?"

I had been leaning against the kitchen counter, coffee cup in hand, trying to look cool if not downright chilly. But I found, in lifting the cup to my lips, that my hand was shaking, so I joined Portia at the table. Ben Solliday, as if emphasizing that his visit was to be brief, remained standing.

"What did Beth say?" I asked.

"She more or less agreed with her friend. Said that Jane had been talking to somebody, though they didn't hear the other person, and that it was about the horse and buggy."

"They were interviewed together?" I raised a questioning eyebrow.

The Bear frowned. "Uh . . . yes, I think they were."

"Well, Beth is the one with the real smarts. I don't think she would have backed Ardys up if it weren't the truth. So I'd say they heard something, yeah. Whether it was what they thought it was . . . I can't think of any reason why Jane would be rehashing that idea. As far as I knew it was dead in the water, and in any case it had nothing to do with Jane."

An hour later I was on my way to downtown Northampton, driving my own car. I had told Portia I wanted to do some shopping, which wasn't strictly true. (Okay, it wasn't true at all. My aunt might be incapable of telling a lie but I was not.) I salved my conscience in this case by arguing that, in a way, I was shopping. Not for goods, but for answers. For all my self-protestations about not wanting to become involved in another murder investigation, that was exactly what, off my own bat, I was now doing. To clear Harry, of course, but also because I just wanted to *know*.

As I saw it, the suspect list had shrunk dramatically. With Portia and me out of it, Jane dead, and Mitchell alibied for her murder, it now read: Lydia Hicks, Harry Johns, Irene Polaski, Derek Bowles, Carl Piquette. Since my ruminative walk in Child's Park, and allowing for certain interruptions, I had continued to rack my memory for details, evaluate my observations, put this together with that—and when my conscious mind was otherwise engaged, my subconscious must have been clicking along because certain ideas were beginning to take shape. I was on my way now to check out one of them.

Irene Polaski's store was called The Natural Crafter and was located on a narrow street off Main. Since every street parking space within a half-mile radius of my destination seemed to be occupied, I left my car in the downtown parking garage. A three-minute walk brought me to the door of the shop.

To the left of the narrow door was a display window featuring a chalkboard on which was printed: EVERY ITEM IN THIS SHOP IS MADE FROM NATURE'S OWN RENEWABLE RESOURCES. The board was surrounded by an assortment of artfully placed objects that included knitted and crocheted afghans, scarves, and sweaters, a patchwork quilt, carved wooden toys, rag dolls, and a pottery vase filled with an arrangement of pink and white silk cherry blossoms.

The door opened, to the accompaniment of clanking cowbells, on an area roughly half the size of Aunt Portia's living room. Floor-to-ceiling shelves made of wood from an old barn—or wood made to look like wood from an old barn (oh, Phoebe, you *are* a cynic)—a couple of tables, a quilt rack, held merchandise of the sort promised by the window. On a wall-to-wall wooden counter at the back were some small racks displaying jewelry, notecards, and the like, with at one end a vintage cash register.

A dark-haired young woman with a patient expression was waiting on a couple who were choosing notecards one at a time, each choice occasioning a deliberation at least worthy of a panel on world disarmament. Apparently summoned by the cowbells, Irene Polaski emerged from a door behind the counter. She was wearing a pink smock over black slacks. A measuring tape hung around her neck.

"Phoebe!" she exclaimed with a smile. Her expression quickly sobered. "Isn't it awful about Jane?"

I agreed that it was indeed awful about Jane, and broke off to admire the shop. This exchange was enough to bring me up to the counter, where I said quietly, "I have something I want to talk to you about."

A hint of wariness crept into Irene's face. After a momentary hesitation she said to the dark-haired girl,

"Annie, hold the fort, will you?" She raised a hinged section of the counter to let me pass, then opened the door to the back of the premises.

I followed her into the room with my heart beating faster than I would have liked. I'm not big on confrontations, and a confrontation was exactly what I was about to launch.

Just inside the door I stopped short. The back room was a workroom, equal in size to the front, stretching away to a big square window with a view of an areaway and a brick wall. A high cutting table occupied the center of the room, its surface mostly hidden under a length of ruby wool fabric pinned with brown paper pattern pieces. Along the side walls were a sewing machine—no, two of them—a couple of dressmaker's dummies, an ironing board, and another table piled with bits of colored silk and lengths of wire.

"I didn't know you were a dressmaker," I said.

"Yeah, well, I didn't mind doing the flowers but I didn't want to get stuck making all the costumes—I've got more work than I can keep up with now. The shop is more of a hobby. Most of the stuff is on consignment. But I like having a place where I actually get to have contact with people."

She was leading me, as she spoke, to an area at the back of the room where a coffeemaker sat on a small metal table. Two worn armchairs, here and there leaking stuffing, were arranged on a piece of beige and blue carpeting. She gestured apologetically at the chairs. "One of these days, slipcovers. But you know how it is—the shoemaker's children, etc. Have a seat, Phoebe. Coffee?"

I nodded, and Irene filled two mugs, taking a container out of a dorm-size refrigerator under the table and adding milk to one of them, which she handed to me.

She then sat, fixed her pale, round eyes on my face and said, with a little lift of the chin, "Okay, Phoebe, what was it you wanted to talk about?"

If I was going to do this at all, I decided, I might as well get it over with. I took a shaky breath. "It was you, wasn't it, who broke the mirror."

I don't know what I'd expected, but what I got was nothing. No guilty start, no indignant denial. Irene said levelly, "What on earth makes you think that?"

"You don't go in for glitter," I said.

"What?"

"That night when they discovered the broken mirror, you were sitting on the edge of the stage and the light was hitting something sparkly in your hair. At the time I thought it was some kind of jeweled barette. It was only later that I realized you never wear that kind, it's always the silk-flowered ones. So it must have been a piece of glass that got caught in your hair when you . . ." I made a bat-swinging gesture. Irene said nothing, and I added gently, "You're lucky you didn't get any in your eyes."

Irene placed her coffee mug carefully on the floor, briefly closed her eyes, and drew her thumb and index finger slowly across the lids. Her hand dropped and she raised her head.

"I *was* lucky," she said. "Had no idea the glass would splinter that way. I thought I'd gotten it all off my clothes. It wasn't as if I'd planned to bash his silly mirror."

"You were there early to bring back the men's costumes you'd taken to hem up," I said.

"Yeah. Derek had given me a key to the side door. Afterwards I went out the same way and waited out of sight until Derek came and opened the front door and then I just went in with the rest."

"And the book? And the ipecac in the coffee?"

She stared. "What, were you looking over my shoulder?"

I shrugged. "Just . . . putting things together. Why did you do it?"

The round eyes narrowed. She rose abruptly, and I

thought for a moment she was going to ask me to leave, in which case, of course, I would have no choice but to do so. Instead, she moved over to the window and stood for some moments with her back to me. When she turned around, her face was set and she had obviously come to a decision.

"I'm not really clear what business this is of yours," she said. "But for some reason I find myself wanting to explain it to you. What I did to Foster was . . . childish. I'm not proud of it. Maybe I just need to say it out loud. Convince myself and possibly some other person that I'm not a total nut."

Since this was more than I'd had any right to expect, I figured my best course was to keep my mouth shut. I nodded and sipped my coffee.

Irene didn't return to the chair, but wandered over to the cutting table and leaned her forearms on it. I thought she looked unutterably sad, this plump, fortyish woman in the pink smock with her greying braid and round face with its hints of youthful prettiness. What was it she'd said about a place to have contact with people? Why was she so lonely?

"As soon as I found out he was going to be in the show I should have dropped out," she said. "But then I thought, This is my try at getting involved, getting to meet people. Why should I let him spoil it for me? I didn't realize at first how much I still hated him."

Her finger began to trace its own patterns on the ruby fabric. She glanced at me and then away again. "I'm going to make this brief, because . . . well, just because. Eighteen years ago I was married and living in Northampton with my husband and our little boy. David was five. He was never a strong kid—lots of colds and earaches and strep throat and naturally I worried about him. My husband said I coddled him. Foster was our pediatrician. One Saturday David woke up with a fever and headache. I called Ballard's office and he gave me the 'Now, now, little mother' routine. Give him an aspirin, and if he's not better by Monday, etc.

"Well, he didn't seem to get much worse that day. Just slept a lot, wanted his room dark, said the light hurt his eyes. David was . . . a very good little boy. Very patient, not a complainer."

Irene's voice broke, she took a deep breath and continued. "But by late that night I could tell this was something different. The fever didn't go away, he said it hurt to move his eyes, and he started vomiting. I called Foster's service and when he didn't respond I called him at home—even though my husband tried to stop me. It wasn't done, you know, 'bothering the doctor' in the middle of the night for a kid with the flu. This time it was 'little lady' instead of 'little mother,' which meant he was really pissed. He told me there was a flu going around and that David would just have to wait it out, 'like a hundred other little boys.' I wanted to take him to the hospital right then, but my husband talked me out of it."

She looked straight at me, with an almost beseeching expression. "You have to remember, Phoebe, I was so young! And here were these two men, the big authority figures in my life, telling me I was overreacting. My husband even said I was scaring David by making such a fuss. So it wasn't until noon on Sunday when David started crying in pain and talking irrationally that he got scared too and we got in the car and drove like hell to the hospital. It was too late, of course. What he had was meningitis and he died that night."

Still leaning her elbows on the cutting table, she buried her face in her hands. Her shoulders shook.

I sat frozen, feeling like the lowest sort of reptile. God, Phoebe, how could you make her go through this? What gives you the right?

Abruptly, the paroxysm passed. Irene lifted her face, grabbed a handful of tissues from a box on one of the

sewing machine tables, and blew her nose. "Sorry. I
didn't realize . . . I don't talk about it much."

"*I'm* sorry," I said. "I shouldn't have . . . how incredibly awful for you! Did you sue the bastard?"

"My husband wouldn't do it. He was building up a
business—plumbing and heating—and Foster was already heavily into real estate, big man in the business
community. He didn't want to alienate him. Besides,"
with a shaky laugh, "when I'd recovered to the point
where I could think straight, I didn't want to sue the
bastard. I wanted to kill him." She shot me another
look. "But I didn't—then or now. I divorced my husband, moved to Springfield and set up as a dressmaker.
I'd married right out of high school and that was my
one skill. Turned out I was good at it and at business,
too. When I heard last year that this shop was available
with a nice apartment upstairs I decided to go for it."

She moved back to the armchair and dropped into it
wearily. "And then I had the brilliant idea that community theater was the way to make new friends. At the
first rehearsal there he was, E. Foster Ballard, big as life.
I went up and introduced myself, and you know what?
He had no idea who I was! That slimy, pompous shit
who'd ruined my life didn't even remember me!"

"Was spiking his coffee with ipecac supposed to jog
his memory?"

"No. It was just . . . supposed to humiliate him
and . . . let him know that somebody out there despised
him. To make him sweat a little, wondering who it
could be. I'm sure he knew, afterwards, what had happened. He was a doctor, after all. I thought he'd make a
big fuss, start accusing people, maybe even leave the
show."

"So when he didn't, you got even more obvious—
with the book and the mirror."

And when that didn't work, murder? I thought but
did not say.

Again Irene's eyes narrowed. Was she, perhaps, regretting having told her story to a relative stranger with an unknown agenda? She said with some belligerence, "Yes, but I didn't kill him. I've *said* what I did was childish, but that's all it was."

Childish, yes . . . a thought that had been nipping at the back of my brain made it to the front. I said, "You came down to the basement that night, after everybody had gone. You were the one who pushed Foster's door ajar and turned on the light. You had a piece of yellow chalk with you—the same color as you use on the blackboard in your window. What were you going to do? Scribble insults on his wall?"

Irene said harshly, "You know so much, you tell me." Then in a swift transformation her face crumpled, her hand flew up to cover her eyes. "God, Phoebe, it was ghastly. I had a flashlight. I was going to write on his door—something, I don't know what, maybe a threat. But when I pushed on it it started to open and I saw him, I saw the dagger, I knew he was dead." She lowered her hand. "What could I do? I couldn't be the one to find him! I mean, I hadn't killed him, but it was almost like I had, can you understand that? I'd hated him. And there I was, sneaking back into the theater by the side door after I'd left and told people I was on my way to the party. So I turned on the light so somebody'd be more likely to notice, and got out of there."

She was looking at me pleadingly now. A sad, frightened woman who had been through hell, who had lashed out foolishly at the man she blamed for that hell. Who had also, I reminded myself, allowed another woman to be suspected of a terrible crime when she could have cleared her with a word. If she was telling the truth. I rather thought she was, but I wasn't bringing the jury in yet.

I said, "I don't suppose you've mentioned any of this to the police?"

Irene shook her head.

"Well, you'd better believe they're picking through

all our backgrounds with great care. They're going to find out about your son and Dr. Ballard. If I were you I'd get there first."

"Suppose I don't?" she said, with another flash of truculence. "Are you going to tell them?"

This, I reminded myself tiredly, was the very reason I had given myself that good advice about not getting involved.

"Just do it," I said.

24

The fact appears to be as you've recited.

I ARRIVED HOME WITH AN ARMFUL OF SILK CHERRY BLOS-
soms for my aunt. Also a heart full of sorrow and empathy for Irene's story, and a mind kicking itself for the
questions I hadn't asked. There she'd been, vulnerable
and in confessional mode and I hadn't followed through.
How well had she known Jane Manypenny? Had she
really been at home on the night of Jane's murder? Did
she have an idea as to the murderer's identity, and if she
did, would she tell?

The problem, I decided, was an insufficiently developed instinct for the jugular. Which, in a general way, I
was glad about, but it didn't exactly make me a killer
interrogator.

Portia accepted the bouquet with pleasure tempered
by a look of skepticism. I explained that I'd stopped by
Irene's shop and she'd suggested that Portia might like
the cherry blossoms as a souvenir. I didn't convey
Irene's exact words, which had been, "Please, take the
damn things, I never want to see them again."

Portia regarded me thoughtfully, and when, an hour
after lunch, I poked my head into the TV room where

she sat reading and announced that I was going for a walk, she only nodded and said, "Good idea. Lovely day." And then, as I turned away, "Take care, Phoebe."

My aunt, I thought with chagrin, was quite aware that I was not being wholly candid but she would never pry. I wished I could confide in her. But her coziness with Ben Solliday made me reluctant to bring up Harry's name. And I suspected that if I told her about Irene her native directness would mandate an immediate report to the Law. I was pretty sure Irene would go on her own, and besides, I wasn't at the moment in a cooperative mood. In any case, Irene's confession, I reasoned, had served only to clear away some irrelevancies; if and when I found real evidence pointing to the murderer, of course I'd go to the police. Of course.

Northampton High School was a large brick rectangle situated across from Child's Park. I got there several minutes before school let out and took up a post near the string of yellow buses at the curb from where I could keep an eye on the front exit doors. I was waiting for Beth Rosario.

By the time the Bear had finished asking his question about what Ardys and Beth might or might not have overheard, it had been too late to call Beth at home. Besides which I had no desire to hazard an encounter with Rosario *père* even at the other end of a phone line. So I'd decided to take a chance on intercepting her as she left school. If unsuccessful, I could at least go for a nice stroll in the park.

But I was in luck. The raucous sound of the school bell had hardly faded before I spotted Beth, dressed in jeans and a Day-Glo pink zippered jacket with a navy blue knapsack strapped to her back, emerging amid a gaggle of students from the door nearest to me. She ignored the buses and turned onto the sidewalk, walking in my direction. I waved, her face broke into a big smile, and she came loping toward me, arms wide.

"Phoebe! Hey! What're you doing here?" She gave me a hug which, overbalanced as she was by her backpack, almost landed us both on the sidewalk.

I laughed and hugged her back. "Hey, yourself! Actually, I came to see you."

I looked beyond her to where streams of kids were climbing into the buses or separating into couples and clusters and heading down the sidewalk. "No Ardys?"

Beth wrinkled her nose. "Ardys and I are not, like, as tight as we were. I found out she was the one who told my dad about Dr. Ballard. What a dork!" Her round, pretty face took on a look of disappointment. "Was it Ardys you wanted to see?"

"No, no," I said hastily, "it was you. Look, could we go somewhere and talk for a few minutes? Maybe over to the park?"

"Sure," Beth said with enthusiasm. As we made our way across Elm Street, she chattered on, "Gee, Phoebe, you don't know how glad I am to see you! My dad's being, like, Neanderthal about the whole thing. He wouldn't let me go to that meeting, you know, and when I wanted to call Derek he, like, had a fit. And then when we heard about Jane Manypenny I thought maybe I'd get to, like, talk to the police again, but my dad said did I have anything new to tell them and of course I really didn't. Do you know anything? Do the police think they know who did it?"

We had reached the park now, and come to a bench at the side of the drive.

"Let's sit down," I said, "and I'll tell you why I specially wanted to see you."

Beth unslung her burden, dropped it onto the grass, and sat, turning to me expectantly. Having achieved my goal with such unexpected ease, I realized I hadn't completely figured out just how I was going to put my question.

"A . . . friend of my aunt's," I began cautiously, "is an ex-police officer who's . . . sort of in on some parts of the investigation. And he mentioned that in your statements after Dr. Ballard's murder you and Ardys said you'd heard Jane Manypenny talking to someone in the utility room backstage."

Beth's big brown eyes regarded me with a combination of awe and shrewdness. "You're in on it too, aren't you?"

"Well, not exactly, I—"

"You're trying to find out who did it so they won't arrest your aunt! People say . . . well, my dad says she must have done it because of something Dr. Ballard did to her long ago. But I told him don't be silly, Mrs. Singh is, like, an old lady, I mean she can hardly even walk! Sure, I'll help if I can. What do you want to know, Phoebe?"

I pushed aside the unpleasant thought that "people" were speculating God knew what about Aunt Portia. "What exactly did you and Ardys hear Jane Manypenny say?"

"I already told the cops—"

"Yes, but it sounded to me more as if Ardys talked and you went along with it. I want to know what *you* remember."

Beth looked chagrined and said, "Yeah, I do tend to do that, don't I? Did, I mean. Not anymore, though. Let me think, it was . . ."

"Something about the horse and buggy idea," I prompted.

"Yeah, but not exactly . . ." She squeezed her eyes shut. "We were, like, coming down the hall and . . . it wasn't buggy . . . it was carriage!" The eyes flew open. " 'He's going to fill a carriage!' Something like that. Or 'bill a carriage'? But that doesn't make sense. Well, neither of them do, really. But that's what she said, I'm pretty sure of it now."

"And you think she was talking *to* someone? Did you hear another voice?"

Beth shook her head. "No. But she must have been, mustn't she? I mean, she said, 'he,' talking about a third person, so there must have been, you know, a second person. Phoebe, do you think it could be, like, important? Are you going to tell the cops?"

I nodded. "They'll probably want to talk to you again."

Beth grinned. "My dad's gonna have another fit."

And not the only one, I mused after Beth had gone. Whichever detective had questioned the girls was going to be on the receiving end of someone's quite justifiable anger. But in the end, did Beth's "pretty sure" impression amount to all that much? "Fill a carriage" . . . I tried and failed to link the words to anything I knew or could speculate about the circumstances of Foster's murder.

I got up from the bench and paused, undecided whether to go directly home or take a brisk circuit of the park. The Indian summer weather was still holding, I was going to miss my ballet class today and could use the exercise. I had made up my mind to the second alternative when I heard my name being called.

It was Carl Piquette, coming toward me down the drive. His dark wool topcoat was unbuttoned, showing beneath a teacherly sweater vest, shirt, and tie above fawn slacks. A leather cap sat jauntily on his balding head and he carried an old-fashioned soft leather briefcase. He too seemed glad to see me, though after the initial warm greetings his face sobered.

"My God, Phoebe, Jane Manypenny! What the hell's going on?" The very clear blue eyes regarded me with a friendly concern. "Bet you didn't bank on getting involved in this kind of mess!"

Nice man, I thought. Nice, reliable, pleasant Carl Piquette. Of them all, he was the one I could least imagine succumbing to the kind of violent anger that I had read into the scene in Pooh-Bah's dressing room. Then I remembered the implacability of his ignoring of the man away from their necessary interaction on stage.

"I was about to take a walk," I said. "Care to join me?"

"My car's parked just over there. Let me go dump this thing in it," indicating the briefcase, "and I'll catch up."

I strolled on slowly, wondering why Carl appeared so ready to take time out of his no doubt busy day to chat with Phoebe Mullins. Was it my irresistible charm? A simple need to talk? Or was there something he hoped to learn?

"I saw you talking with Beth," he said as he rejoined me.

The unasked question hung blatantly. Well, why not? I thought. If he were guilty and saw significance in what I'd learned he might betray the fact. Or if not, he might at least have an opinion.

"I wanted to clarify what she and Ardys heard Jane say on the night Foster was murdered," I said, and recounted what Beth had told me.

" 'Fill a carriage'?" Carl said in a tone of bewilderment. "Means nothing to me. And even if she was referring to the horse and buggy idea, what did that have to do with Jane Manypenny?"

I shrugged. "Not a clue. Maybe the cops will be able to make a connection."

Again, the tactful Carl's unspoken question dangled between us.

I glanced at him and then away. "The police still think Portia may have murdered Foster," I said, crossing mental fingers. "And I thought Beth might talk to me better than . . ."

"But weren't you and Mrs. Singh together when Jane was murdered?" And at my look of surprise, "Oh yes, Derek's been on the phone practically nonstop. Gives him something to do, I suppose, poor guy. Anyway, I thought you two were out of it."

"Oh. Well . . . the cops seem to think Jane's murder may have been unrelated. Have to do with one of her, uh, clients."

"Yeah, sure." To my relief, he didn't press me on how I knew what the cops were thinking. Instead, his thoughts had traveled elsewhere because he said, "I, on the other hand, have no alibi for either Foster or Jane." He shook his head. "Poor old Janie. What a rotten thing."

"Not 'poor old Foster'?" I said.

Carl stopped and turned to me. "Don't play coy, Phoebe, it doesn't become you. I'm not as blind as some of my colleagues. I'm quite aware that you were one of the few people in our little company capable of looking beyond yourself and taking note of what was actually going on. Picking up, for instance, on the fact that I couldn't stomach that son of a bitch Ballard."

I had the grace, I think, to look abashed, but only said, "I thought you controlled yourself pretty well. Especially since you had all that interacting to do on stage."

He shrugged and resumed walking. "Thing is, I'd thought I was over what happened between Foster and me. Old history, I thought, won't bother me now. People change, etcetera, etcetera." He gave a brief, humorless laugh. "But not Foster. I saw him and my hackles went up and everything came back like yesterday."

The direct approach had worked with Irene. I might as well try it again. "What was it?" I said. "The 'everything'?"

We had reached, at a more leisurely pace than I would have chosen had I been alone, a rock-walled rose garden where a few stalwart blooms still glowed against the general decay.

Carl said, "Want to take a look?" and without waiting for a response mounted the three shallow stone steps that led into the garden. I followed, and for a few moments we strolled between the rectangular beds, pausing to appreciate a delicate pink blossom here, a warm peach or splashy ruby there. It struck me that I was spending a lot of time lately in dying gardens. I wondered if it were an omen and thought that, if so, it couldn't be a good one.

Carl interrupted these morbid reflections by saying, "It's an extremely unoriginal story. A goddam cliche even. But if you really want to know . . ."

"Yes," I said, "I do. I mean, the more I know about Foster, about how he operated, about, well, his character I suppose, the better I might be able to figure out . . ."

Under Carl's appraising stare, I broke off. Shoot, I should've stopped at "yes."

He said, "Playing detective in a big way, are we? Well, why not? From what I've observed of *your* observing ways, you're probably a natural. So . . . Foster's character, is it? Yes, I think I can be of some help there," with a grim little smile. "Fifteen years ago, you see, I was working for a small chemical company in Holyoke. Plastics. We made parts for a number of the appliances the great American consumer can't do without. Had a nice little lab where I puttered away until one day I came up with a way to bring even extremely thin plastic pieces to twice the strength of the stuff we were turning out. Went to the owner of the plant who was also, I thought, my friend. Showed him what I had and reminded him of our verbal agreement for a fifty-fifty split on any patents resulting from my efforts in his lab. True, says my friend, but what I didn't tell you was that

I have a silent partner in the business and I'm going to have to run this by him."

"Oh my God!" I exclaimed. "Pooh-Bah!"

Carl raised two fingers to his cap brim in a mock salute. "By G, I think she's getting the picture! Lord High Everything Else in person. Sometimes I wonder why he bothered with the doctor business—probably couldn't resist giving himself at least one legitimate title. Anyway, you can imagine the rest. 'Nothing in writing? Tsk, tsk. And done on company time? Afraid it's no go, my boy.' " He grimaced. "Naturally the company made a bundle. By the time I'd finished suing—unsuccessfully I hardly need say—I was out of a job and broke with a family to support."

"What an incredible shit!" I observed.

Carl chuckled. "Neatly put. But you know, Phoebe, thanks to the incredible shit I got into teaching and found out I love it and I'm good at it. Basically, I suppose, I should thank him."

We had stopped at a small rectangular concrete pool at one end of the garden. Under its leaf-dotted waters glinted a scattering of coins, mostly pennies.

Staring at the water, Carl said, "But when I saw him again at the first *Mikado* rehearsal, still throwing his weight around, still pulling the same sleazy crap, still somehow snowing people—God, I would have loved to pull him down a peg or two." He gave me a direct look. "But I didn't. Didn't pull the dirty tricks and didn't kill him."

"Any ideas about who did?"

"God, no. Well, I always assumed it was Lydia who smashed the mirror and so on. But murder? Not Lydia. Incredibly, she was still fond of him."

I wasn't at all sure about that, but said nothing. "Have you told the police about your . . . history with Foster?"

"I didn't exactly raise my hand and jump up and

down. But I answered their questions. And anything I didn't tell them I'm sure they'll have no trouble discovering."

He gave me a genuine smile. "Oddly, even knowing I'm on the short list I'm still naive enough to have faith that since I didn't do it I have nothing to fear."

As we started to leave the garden, he turned back, dug in his pants pocket and produced a couple of coins which he tossed into the pool.

His smile this time was self-mocking. "And me a scientist. Still, it couldn't hurt."

25

From our intention, well expressed,
You cannot turn us!

"PHOEBE!" DEREK BOWLES EXCLAIMED AS I PUT MY HEAD around the kitchen door. "Come on in!"

I had been drawn there by sounds of if not quite revelry at least relative cheerfulness. Gathered around the big table besides Derek were Aunt Portia, Anandi, Harry, and the Bear. A gallon jug of chianti reposed on the table's oak surface and as I made my appearance Derek was in the act of raising his glass as if for a toast. My curiosity as to what had occasioned this motley assembly took a distant second to the absurd surge of pleasure I felt at seeing Harry. I took the chair beside him and he reached for my hand under the table. I turned my resultant broad smile to Derek. If there was something celebratory going on I was certainly in the mood.

"What's the occasion?" I said.

"I talked to Lydia," Derek crowed. "About the Old Church, whether we could keep the theater going there. And she didn't say no!"

I offered congratulations and accepted a glass of

wine, though not saying no seemed to me a pretty thin premise for general rejoicing.

"Besides," Derek went on, "I couldn't take any more gloom and doom. Decided we needed a break, called Harry, made him come with me, Portia said okay . . . and here we are!"

Hmm, let's see. A gruesome death on Friday, another on Saturday, and here it was Monday already. Derek's gloom and doom capacity, it seemed to me, was singularly small. Then I looked at his face, thinner, I thought, even than it had been on Saturday night, the strain lines around the eyes betraying the fact that he was not, after all, a boy but a man in his thirties. A man who had suffered a crushing disappointment no doubt greater than anyone's. I remembered guiltily our own partying of the night before and decided to forgive him.

Ben Solliday, sitting across from Harry and me, said heartily, "And I had the good fortune to drop by at just the right time." The heartiness didn't extend to his eyes; they were watchful, and I wondered precisely how accidental the dropping by had been.

"What exactly did Lydia say?" I asked Derek.

"Oh, you know the kind of thing. Too soon to say, so much to sort out, lawyers, details, all that stuff. But all being equal, she wouldn't rule out the company being able to stay put. *Well,* I tell you, *what* a relief. I'd been convinced she wouldn't wait to sell up, grab the money, and run. I mean, the way she felt about Foster."

There was an uncomfortable pause, as if we had all recollected at the same moment that Lydia was a prime suspect in her ex-husband's stabbing. Nothing like murder, I thought, for creating awkward social situations.

Anandi's quiet voice said, "I am seeing in the *Gazette* that Dr. Ballard's funeral is to be held on Wednesday at three P.M." There was a hint of reproach in her tone.

Derek turned to her immediately. "Of course! The funeral! Thank you Anandi, I hadn't heard." He reached to touch her arm with his small hand. "You must think I'm terribly callous. It's just . . . I guess I still have moments of not believing these awful murders have really happened. Naturally I'll be there. I'm sure we all will."

Harry said shortly, "Not I, I'm afraid. I have classes all that afternoon. Can't cut them, the school's already not best pleased about having a murder suspect on their faculty."

Aunt Portia said nothing.

I gave a mental sigh. Another job for Diplomacy Woman. When at a loss, change the subject.

"What about Jane Manypenny?" I said. "Has a service been scheduled for her?"

"Her sister's coming from England," said the Bear. "I imagine she'll make the arrangements. As soon as the coroner's office releases the body."

"My God!" Derek burst out. "What more do they need to do to her? The poor woman was shot, wasn't she? No big mystery, why can't they just—" He broke off, shaking his head.

At the other end of the table, Aunt Portia murmured, "Doin' their best, I'm sure, Derek." No one else chose to contribute.

Okay, bad subject.

After a quick recon of the pros and cons, I took the plunge. "I went for a walk up to the park and happened to run into Beth Rosario. She . . . happened to mention" (nice going Phoebe, do you imagine anyone's buying this?) "something she and Ardys overheard Jane say the night of Foster's murder. Something that sounded like 'he wants to fill a carriage,' or maybe 'bill a carriage.' I just wondered if—"

"Oh, that!" Derek said. "The cops already asked me about that! The girls thought she was referring to my publicity idea about G and S in a horse and buggy," he gave Harry a mock-defiant look, "which I still think was *absolutely* brilliant. Though after that review and word-of-mouth, we'd hardly have needed . . . ah well, promised myself not to wallow. Anyway, even I had given up on that. Besides, what could it possibly have to do with Jane?"

Harry said, "You actually ran into Beth by herself? I thought she and Ardys were joined at the hip."

I explained Beth's new-found independence. Aunt Portia nodded and said, "Good for her!" Then, with an undertone of amusement, "Guess school was just lettin' out, huh? You runnin' into her like that."

She wasn't within reach for me to kick under the table, but anyway it was clear from the thoughtful frown Ben Solliday was directing at me that he, at least, wasn't buying the casual coincidence angle.

Also that he had picked up on the relevant fact. "Carriage?" he said. "She was sure?"

"Yes. Though it's probably not important. Still doesn't make sense, I mean."

The Bear said nothing more but remained thoughtful and shortly thereafter took his leave.

So did Harry, explaining that he had an evening scene-study group he couldn't put off. I saw him to the front door where I collected a quick but fervent kiss and a promise to phone later.

When I went back to the kitchen, Derek was still sitting at the table, now looking distinctly forlorn. Portia, at the other end of the table, and Anandi, who was at the sink managing to make a good deal of bustle out of washing three wine glasses, each had the look of a hostess who is just restraining herself from mentioning that the party is over.

Derek, however, either oblivious or too low spirited to care, poured himself another glass of chianti, held out the bottle and said, "Join me, Phoebe?"

"Sure," I said. It was the bottom of the bottle and I've never been fond of chianti dregs, but I thought if I refused he might cry.

The same message must have reached my aunt because she said, "Want to stay for supper, Derek?"

"Oh, could I, Portia? You're an angel! You can't know how I dread going back to my place alone with nothing to do but brood."

Shoot, *I* might cry.

Not my aunt, though. She gave Derek a considering look, then rose briskly. "All right, the two of you clear out, give Anandi and me some cookin' space. No, Anandi, it's high time I started doin' somethin' besides sittin' around lettin' people wait on me. Not you, Phoebe, you take Derek off and cheer 'im up."

As Derek and I, glasses in hand, made our way to the living room, I reflected it might be a kindness to drop a hint that if he wanted a prayer of any more theatrical support from Mrs. Singh self-pity was not the way to go. Then I decided the hell with it, it was his lookout.

However, as long as I had him here there were a couple of questions . . . wait a minute. Had that been Aunt Portia's plan in sending Derek and me out of the kitchen? Did she perhaps have a pretty shrewd idea of what I was trying to do and was she, in her understated way, lending her tacit support?

Derek sank with a sigh onto the velveteen loveseat in a lounging position, crossing his legs and throwing back his head; I took the small armchair. Interesting, I thought, that Portia's recliner seemed so profoundly hers neither of us had apparently considered sitting there. Or could it be that Derek was aware of how charmingly the rose-colored upholstery set off his creamy bulky-knit sweater, neat grey slacks, and blondly (now palely) boyish good looks? Not especially for my benefit but as a matter of instinct? Of all the company, I thought, it was Derek who was theatrical to the bone. Not in itself a bad thing, but it made him difficult to read.

I took a sip of wine, suppressed a grimace, and put the glass down on the coffee table.

"If you don't mind my asking," I said (silly phrase meaning Even if you do I'm going to ask anyway), "what were your real feelings about Foster? I mean, you seemed to get along with him where a lot of people didn't. Was it just . . ." how to put this tactfully . . .

Derek rescued me. "Was it just brown-nosing because of what he'd done—could do—for the theater? Oh sure, that was part of it." Elbow propped on the arm of the loveseat, he was holding his wine glass by its rim with his fingertips and he gave its contents a whirl or two. "But Foster wasn't all bad. He could be good company— funny, you know. And I understand he gave away a good deal of money to charities and so on. Mostly anony- mously. Like with the Old Church, he was letting us have that for a song."

"A song indeed," I said. "And in return he got to play his dream part and show off for all his buddies."

"Hey, wait a minute, Phoebe, that's not fair! Harry and I never would have cast him if he hadn't been— well, you saw him." He shook his head sadly. "Foster was the best amateur actor/singer I've ever run across. Better than a lot who claim to be professional."

"True," I conceded. "But apart from that I have to say I thought he was an odious man."

Derek pulled himself to an upright sitting position, glanced at me, looked away and back. "Your . . . mas- sive friend Ben, I gather he has some connection with the cops?"

"Well, yeah, he—"

"Because this isn't anything I *know,* just *suspect,* and I wouldn't want it getting around."

I shook my head earnestly, figuring he could take it any way he chose. It seemed to do the job. He leaned forward in a confidential manner.

"About those nasty tricks—the mirror and the book and I guess the coffee too. It might surprise you to know, whether he was right or wrong, I got the strong impression that Foster thought Lydia did them. And that's why he didn't raise a stink and carry on the way you'd have expected. He was protecting her."

My immediate response was to pooh-pooh the very idea; my second was to consider it. Was it possible that the relationship between Foster and Lydia was more complicated than I'd understood? And supposing Foster *had* thought Lydia was behind the tricks, was it residual affection that had led him to protect her or a reluctance to impair his dignity by a public airing of the family laundry?

For now, unanswerable questions, but I did have a more immediate one. "Do *you* think Lydia did those things? And if so, do you think she killed him too? And Jane?"

Derek's eyes widened. "Me? I haven't got Clue One. Hell, Phoebe, I still can't believe it's all really happened, let alone that one of the company was involved." He leaned back against the cushions and added, with a hint of his former roguishness, "However, as you've pointed out, Foster was not universally beloved. It does rather leave the field wide open."

Several hours later, I replaced the receiver of my bedroom extension phone with warm and agreeable feelings somewhat compromised by guilt. Harry and I were (I was pretty sure) working on the idea of a weekend for two at a bed and breakfast in Vermont. At least I knew that "weekend" and "two" and "Vermont" had come up in the course of the conversation. This time I couldn't entirely blame Harry the Deliberate. My own sense of caution was kicking in big time. I very much didn't want to make a bad mistake.

Since Mick's death I had not had a lover. I liked Harry, he turned me on; we had, I thought, many of the same attitudes, laughed at the same things. I could even imagine us, in my more extended fantasies, going through life together—a very different life from what I had known, simpler, quieter, but wasn't that what I was looking for? Or maybe not? Was I ready for this?

Jeez, Phoebe, what are you looking for? Lightning flashes, a colossal finger reaching down from the clouds to point at Harry Johns, a booming voice urging, "Go, my child!"? Well, yeah, that would be nice.

The guilt stemmed from the fact that I had not been entirely forthcoming with Harry about my recent activities. We had discussed Beth's statement, what she had heard and what it might mean, arriving at no conclusions. I had mentioned bumping into Carl Piquette and also my visit to Irene's store. But I hadn't shared the important stuff, the questions I'd asked, the revelations, the pieces of the puzzle I was gathering and which would, I fondly hoped, begin to fit together into a picture of the one possible murderer. Unless, I mused, the puzzle turned out to be one of those two-sided ones where the pieces may fit but be part of the wrong picture . . . oh please, Phoebe, don't add complications. Anyway . . .

If the man was in the running for true companion of my heart, shouldn't I be confiding all? Did my reluctance indicate that I still wasn't a hundred percent sure that he was not also in the running for First Murderer?

Nonsense! In the first place, what Irene and Carl had told me were confidences. I had no right to go blabbing them to anyone. Except the police? whispered my inconvenient, law-abiding self. Shoot, the police most likely already knew. And if not . . . well, I'd think about that one tomorrow.

Basically, I decided, having gotten this far I wanted to finish the job myself. Like a puppy with one end of a towel in its teeth, I didn't want to let go and I didn't want anyone telling me to let go—not Harry, not Portia, not the Bear, not Lieutenant Griffith. I wanted to find the answer and I wanted to find it on my own.

If I had paused to recognize this sentiment as hubris and to remember what hubris is generally agreed to lead to, I could have saved myself a lot of grief.

26

To our prerogative we cling . . .

MY PLANS FOR THE FOLLOWING DAY, AND THE TWO
phone calls I'd made to set them up, were another
matter I hadn't shared with Harry.

On Tuesday morning I was looking forward to both
appointments with a good deal of nervous anticipation.
Therefore, I was not best pleased when an hour before I
was due at the first one, Anandi came to tap on my bedroom door and tell me that "Mr. Ben and the policeman" were on the premises and wanted to speak
with me.

Rats! *Not* what I needed while still in the process of
persuading myself I was doing the right thing.

I finished brushing my hair and then, on a sudden in-
spiration, rummaged in my top bureau drawer and retrieved a small amber bottle labeled "Self-Confidence."
It had been a parting gift from a large and imperious
contralto last summer at the Varovna Colony. I had put
it into my bottomless life-on-a-strap shoulder bag and
only recently rediscovered and reconsigned it to Top
Drawer Limbo. Along with the gift had come an
earnest lecture on aromatherapy involving the terms

"neurotransmitters" and "limbic area of the brain." On the theory that it seemed to have worked for her, and further that just because you didn't believe in something was no guarantee it wasn't true, I dabbed a bit behind each ear and went downstairs to face my gentlemen callers.

Aunt Portia had brought the visitors into the kitchen, which was warm with morning sunshine. I got the impression from Hal Griffith's determinedly unsmiling demeanor that he would have preferred the greater formality of the living room. He refused an offer of coffee. The Bear, however, as if attempting to lighten the atmosphere, accepted heartily the stewed remains of that morning's pot, and even drank some, which I couldn't help thinking showed a heroic nature.

We sat at the table—Portia in her usual place, the Bear at the opposite end with Anandi on his right, the lieutenant and me across from each other on either side of my aunt. Hal Griffith said without preamble, "Irene Polaski came to me late yesterday afternoon and told me about your visit, Phoebe. I thought it was understood that you were to come straight to me with any ideas that occurred to you. May I ask when or if you intended to let me—let the police—know what you'd discovered?"

"I encouraged her to go to you," I said. "And I was pretty sure she would. I thought it would be better coming directly from her."

"I see," the lieutenant said. "And you *assumed*"—the word dripped with quotation marks—"that she would tell us everything you'd talked about?"

The Bear cleared his throat but I was on a roll and in no need of rescuing. "Yes," I said calmly. "But then, I don't know what she told you."

Hal glowered, but pulled a notebook from his pocket and read out a pretty good account of my conversation with Irene that included all the relevant information.

"Yup, that's it," I said.

"And it didn't occur to you to come to me . . . us," with a glance at Ben Solliday, "with your suspicions, rather than running off to tackle this woman by yourself?"

Hey, excuse me! I thought. Aren't we overlooking the fact that it worked? Aloud I said, "Come to you with what? Some yellow chalk dust and a barette that might or might not have had rhinestones on it?" Hot damn! I could practically feel the confidence radiating from behind my ears.

The lieutenant's glower turned a shade darker. "You seem to presume that I, not to mention the state police and the D.A., are incapable of the deductive process or properly questioning a witness."

"Speaking of which," I said smoothly, "did someone get in touch with Beth Rosario?"

A flush appeared on the lieutenant's pale skin. Smoke didn't quite come out of his ears but it was a near thing.

During this exchange, Portia's head had been swiveling back and forth like an umpire at a Ping-Pong match. I thought she'd been trying not to smile. Now she said mildly to Hal Griffith, "Doesn't seem to me m'niece has done any harm. Even helped some. Shouldn't you maybe be thankin' her, 'stead of readin' the riot act?"

The lieutenant turned to my aunt, met her large intelligent blue-eyed gaze, and turned back to me. He heaved a sigh, planted his elbows on the table and rubbed his forehead with his fingertips. "Your aunt's right. What you've turned up has been helpful. But from now on, Phoebe, I want you"—he backtracked— "I'm *asking* you, to leave this kind of thing to us."

" 'This kind of thing,' " I countered politely, "meaning . . . ?"

"Oh, come on, you know what I'm talking about. Questioning witnesses, for God's sake! Did you ever stop to think that could be a dangerous thing to do?

When I implied that you could help us I was thinking in terms of your . . . people skills, of things you might have noticed and could pass on to us. Not that you'd go haring off on your own—"

He broke off, probably stopped by my expression, which I could feel growing stonier by the moment.

"I had a couple of conversations," I said, "I'd hardly call that 'questioning witnesses.' I can't help it if people choose to tell me things."

Hal Griffith gave me a look that said I had just insulted his intelligence, which I probably had. He ran his palms back over the eighteenth-of-an-inch stubble on his head, sighed again, and when he spoke his voice was several degrees less belligerent.

"Look, Phoebe, I'll lay it on the line for you. You were quite right, our thinking is that the person who killed Dr. Ballard also killed Jane Manypenny. She was shot at almost point-blank range and there's no evidence of a struggle. A deranged or hostile client doesn't fit the scene. So it was someone she knew well and trusted. Which lets you and your aunt right out of both murders, since you were home together while Jane was being shot. Just in case, I mean, you felt you were acting in Mrs. Singh's defense."

From the other end of the table, Ben Solliday said, "We're worried about you, Phoebe. Whoever committed these killings has got to be pretty desperate and if he—or she—thought you were getting too close . . ."

Hal said, "So please, anything you remember or put together in your mind—like the barette, now that was clever thinking—come to me or Ben with it. But don't go out looking. Believe me, there are plenty of people already doing that."

Hmmm. Double-teaming *and* flattery. What could I say?

I said, "Fine. I won't go out looking."

The lieutenant's face cleared. "Thanks."

My aunt's expression, on the other hand, could only

be called skeptical. Fortunately, Hal Griffith was not looking at her.

He started to rise, but paused and said, "By the way, any ideas about what the Rosario girl now says she heard?"

"No. I've been trying but . . . no."

"Well, if you think of anything . . ."

"Oh!" I gave a guilty start. I *had* thought of something.

The lieutenant's eyes narrowed. "Yes?"

"I . . . uh . . . suppose you know about Carl Piquette and the chemical company and so on."

Hal shook his head in disbelief, started to say something, checked himself, took a breath. "Yes, we do. As I mentioned, there are a large number of professional people investigating this case."

Huh! No need for sarcasm. I said meekly, "Oh . . . well, then . . ."

A moment after the two men had disappeared through the kitchen door, the Bear came back. He stood just inside the door, fixed me with a look of deep concern, and said earnestly, "Phoebe, please take what Hal said seriously. You need to be careful of . . . trusting people."

He ducked out again without waiting for a reply. Well, I knew what *that* was about. Harry was still a suspect. It was he I was being warned against. The knowledge made me feel less guilty about my next move.

Anandi's hostessing instincts had propelled her out the door with the two men. I turned to my aunt.

"I have a coffee date with Lydia Hicks in"—I consulted my watch—"twenty minutes. I don't see any reason why I shouldn't keep it. I mean, I consider her a friend and she probably needs one right now. If Ben or Hal Griffith choose to misinterpret a perfectly ordinary get-together . . ."

Portia produced the grin she'd been suppressing and held up a hand. "Don't have to convince me, Phoebe.

You're a grown woman, can make your own decisions. Don't need my permission or anyone else's. Want you to feel free to come an' go as you like, not feel you have t'check in with me, and vice versa. Speakin' of which"—as Anandi reentered the kitchen—"tomorrow night Anandi and I'll be goin' on a jaunt. Signed up for it weeks ago, before you came. A Senior Citizen thing," with a grimace, "but it sounded like fun. Dinner at an Indian restaurant in Amherst an' a sitar concert or some such. They come to pick you up in a van."

As Anandi went into the pantry, she added in a low tone, "Doin' it for her, really. She misses home, y'know."

I picked up the shoulder bag I'd had the forethought to bring downstairs with me and went to grab a jacket off the coatrack in the hall on my way out to my car. Too late now to walk downtown, which was what I'd been planning.

Before I could get out the door, Anandi materialized at my side. It was evident from her sober gaze that there was something on her mind. I waited.

She gave a soft little cough and said, "Our small trip tomorrow—Mrs. Portia has been looking forward to it. She is missing India, you know."

I nodded. I didn't think that was it.

Anandi put her small hand on my wrist. "I hope you are forgiving me, Phoebe, but . . . you truly must be very careful. Some one of these people you think are your friends is a person without conscience. A dangerous person."

Oh, Please! On top of all the other warnings I'd been given, I certainly didn't need an additional dose of Anandi's quasimystical pronouncements. I put on the best smile I could muster, said I would certainly take great care, and went quickly out the door.

27

. . . they don't understand the delicacy
of your position.

LYDIA WAS DRESSED IN AN OVERSIZED ROLL-COLLAR turquoise sweater and purple stretch pants. The strawberry blond hair had received a recent touch-up—the words "fierce and bold in fiery gold" from Yum-Yum's big number came to mind. Her expression couldn't be called jubilant, but she hardly looked like a woman in mourning.

She settled back in the wooden booth and said, "Thanks for suggesting this, Phoebe, your timing was perfect. I've just been talking to the priest at Foster's church about funeral arrangements and I really need someone looking at me who isn't reeking of disapproval. So—how the hell've you been?"

We were in the coffee shop called Bart's which, as I'd hoped, at eleven A.M. was not crowded. The booth to which we'd brought our lattes and muffins was in a section deserted except for a young couple at a small round table by the front window who were holding hands and whispering.

"I'm okay," I said noncommitally. "More to the point, how are you? This must be a pretty awful time for you." I assessed Lydia's humor quotient, decided it was high, and added, "Not to mention awkward."

To my relief, she broke into a genuine and hearty laugh. "You mean receiving condolences from people when half of them think I was the one who did the old so-and-so in? And not even sure I'm the one they should be condoling in the first place, but numbers two and three aren't around, so who's left? Sure it would be awkward if it wasn't so damn funny." She gave me a direct look. "And if that close stare you've been giving me means you're wondering the same as everyone else, then the answer is no, I didn't kill Foster."

"I'm sorry," I said. "For staring, if I was. But that wasn't what I was thinking. I was thinking you look as if you've been going through hell."

It was true. Below the fiery hair, underlying the green eyeshadow and the mascara and the crimson lipstick and the rest was the hollow-eyed face of a woman who had recently received a major life blow.

Lydia blinked, and her eyes filled with sudden tears. "Damn it, Phoebe," she said. "Every time I have an encounter with you I end up blubbing." She picked up a paper napkin, dabbed at her eyes and blew her nose.

"I *am* sorry," I said.

"Don't be. You're the first person that's . . . everyone seems to assume that I hated the poor bastard. Which I didn't. Oh, I hated it when he dumped me after twenty years—would you believe for his nurse? What a cliche! Damned embarrassing! And I'd begun to see through him long before that. I knew he was pompous and arrogant and self-deluded. But I knew something about what made him that way." She raised a questioning eyebrow. "I suppose your aunt has told you about Foster's background . . ."

I nodded.

Lydia sighed. "Of course I didn't realize when I married him how much those early experiences had soured him. Warped him even. I only found it out gradually.

My family—my dad was a doctor—had just moved to Northampton when I met Foster. He didn't even let on that his parents still lived nearby until we'd been married a year."

Unable to stop myself, I said, "You're kidding!"

Lydia said, with a mixture of anger and pleading, "Well, picture it, Phoebe! Here's this boy, very bright, very proud, and he learns early on that a lot of people are going to judge him for his last name—for his ethnicity, for what his parents do for a living. So he sets his mind to escaping that. And he does a damn good job!"

I thought of what Eddie Balcowicz had done to the young Portia, and why, and was not impressed.

Lydia's tone became less defensive. "Well, okay, maybe he overdid it. But God, Phoebe, in the end it didn't matter to me. I really really loved him." She gave me a defiant look. "Foster wasn't all bad, you know, in spite of what some people like to think. There was a side not many people saw. He did a lot of private charity—scholarships and paying medical bills. He'd hear about some kid who was up against it and he'd arrange to help. I know he sent at least three kids to Manypenny—you might not believe it but she was a pretty good therapist."

That, I thought, at least explained Jane's reverent attitude. But how could Lydia—

"He thought it was me, you know, pulling those stupid tricks, that's why he didn't raise a fuss. Didn't believe me when I said I wouldn't lower myself. So you see, ol' Foster was still fond of me in his way."

Yeah, sure, I thought.

She said fiercely, "Oh I know, not enough to make up for all the shit that went down . . . I can hear you thinking, 'How could the woman have kept on making a fool of herself over that bastard for so many years?' Jesus, who knows? But I did. I kept on loving him, no matter how much I tried not to."

Okay. I couldn't understand it, but I believed it.

"Yes, I could see that," I said. "Right up to the moment you sang 'Hearts do not break,' and Foster didn't even notice."

Lydia gave me a long look, took a large and deliberate bite of her muffin, chewed, and brushed the crumbs off the bosom of the turquoise sweater. Finally she said, not entirely amicably, "You're an observant little . . . person, aren't you? And people talk to you, don't they? Well, hell, why should I be any different? Not that I can see it's any of your business, but now that you bring it up . . ."

She folded her arms, leaned them on the table, looked away, and back at me. "It was the damndest thing, Phoebe. When I thought about it afterwards, it was like somebody threw a switch. One minute I was in love—angry, hurting, wanting him, not able to let go. And the next it was all gone. I looked at him and all I saw was this faintly ridiculous, sad, oblivious old guy. Talk about your proverbial straw! And he didn't even mean it! To insult me, you know. It was just Foster being clueless. And then I looked at myself and I thought, my God, Lydia, you poor stupid bitch, this is what you've wasted your life for? Well, after I finished crying over that, I decided I could at least be glad I wasn't going to waste it anymore."

She leaned back and said, with the shadow of a mischievous grin, "And boy, am I gonna have a lot of money! That Foster! Finger in more pies than you could believe. I had no idea."

"The other wives don't get anything?"

She paused in the act of raising her coffee cup to wave a dismissive hand. "Both remarried. And the three kids—all mine, by the way—they're doing fine. Plus they'll get it all anyway when I kick off." She peered at me over the rim of the cup. "I had a damn good divorce lawyer."

"What about the theater?" I said.

"The Old Church? Oh yeah, the Twerp's been onto

me about that." She shrugged. "I dunno. Foster's deals were so convoluted it's going to take a while to sort them out. I put him off—Derek, I mean. To tell the truth, I was kind of disgusted to find out the reason for all the ass-kissing. I'd thought maybe he was being friendly to the old guy just to . . . well, be friendly."

So much for Derek's hopes, I thought with a twinge of pity. I sure wouldn't want to have to be the one to tell him.

"Not many people were, you know," Lydia continued. "Most of them wanted something. I used to hate to see it and wonder if he knew."

She heaved a sigh and again her eyes grew damp. "I may have been over him, but you can't just wipe out thirty-five years of memories, and there were some good ones. Just because I didn't love him anymore doesn't mean I'm not mourning the poor bastard. As you've been practically the only person to notice . . . damn!" She swiped impatiently with her index fingers at the soft flesh below her lower lids and picked up the shoulder bag she'd dumped beside her on the bench. "Time to go, before I make a complete friggin' spectacle of myself. Thanks, Phoebe, for listening. I guess."

And as we made our way together toward the door, with a hand on my arm, "No, really. Thanks."

As we emerged onto the sidewalk a tentative voice said, "Excuse me?"

I would never have recognized the voice, but the face I knew immediately. It was the Head WAG. She drew us over to one side of the broad walkway—even on a Tuesday morning pedestrian traffic was brisk—and addressing Lydia said, "I just wanted to say how sorry I am about the loss of your . . . that is, of Mr., um, Dr. Ballard."

I began to appreciate fully the difficulties Lydia had outlined.

Before the (ex?) widow could do more than nod, she went on, "It was so terrible, what happened, and of course we had nothing to do . . . well, the police saw that very quickly, of course. But I didn't want you to think that we were in any way *glad* about what happened."

Lydia said with an ironic grin, "Did the job for you, though, didn't it?" At the sight of the other woman's expression, her own softened and she said, "Hey, don't worry. You gals gave the old boy something new to be clever about in his last days. I'm sure, in his way, he was grateful."

The Head WAG shook her head and said, with some dignity, "I'm sorry to see that you still think our protest was just a big joke. If you'd only try to understand—"

"Hey!" Lydia said, "we understand! We even think you're right, don't we, Phoebe? W. S. Gilbert had a shitty attitude toward women. So you're going to assume that nobody but you can recognize that? You're going to throw out all that gorgeous music, all that comedy, all that great satire? What else do you want to throw out? *Shrew? Merchant of Venice?* What about *Romeo and Juliet* with all those high-handed, bloodthirsty Italians? You gonna tell the high schools they can't do *West Side Story,* for God's sake, because it might offend Poles or Puerto Ricans or gang members or New York City cops? Get a grip!"

Lydia's voice had risen during this minitirade and at its end there was a spatter of applause from the occupants of the tables outside Bart's and several passersby who had paused to observe this bit of street theater.

The Head WAG stared at Lydia with the injured expression of one who has offered the hand of friendship only to have it bitten off at the elbow. "I only meant," she began, faltered, looked around her, raised her hands in a gesture of defeat. "Anyway, my condolences," she said stiffly, and walked away.

28

Each a little bit afraid is . . .

AT TWO O'CLOCK THAT AFTERNOON I SAT ON YET AN-
other bench on the Smith College campus waiting for
Nadine Gardner. This one was situated by a fountain
near the botanic gardens and behind the library where
Nadine had said she'd be working. The fountain was a
concrete bowl perhaps twenty feet across. In its center
stood a bronze statue of a young woman with long hair
dressed in a neo-Romantic gown that draped to her feet
in graceful folds. She gazed soberly down at a pedestal
at her side where water bubbled from under the extended fingers of her right hand and trickled to the pool
below. From her other hand dangled a half-open book.
On one side of the statue's square base a legend carved
in relief read, "In Memory of a Beautiful Life."

Harry and I had passed near the fountain on our
stroll on Sunday, but I had barely registered its presence, my mind being otherwise occupied. Now I stared
from my bench at the sweetly sentimental idealization
of young womanhood standing isolated in the middle
of her gently rippling pool and found it almost unbear-
ably poignant. Who had she been? How had she died?

Wasn't there something else inscribed there on the base?

I got up and took a closer look. Yes, a name and dates. She'd been twenty-two. Nadine's age. The age my daughter would have been if she'd lived.

Suddenly, the poignancy became wholly unbearable. My throat felt as if I'd swallowed a fistful of pencil shavings, the statue, the water, the bench, the trees, wavered and dissolved.

Damn, Phoebe! I thought you were over this! Or at least in control. The last time you had a significant conversation with Nadine you threw up under a streetlamp. This time, hysterics? To quote Lydia, Get a Grip!

I dug my fingernails hard into the palms of my hands, forced my throat to swallow down the ache, took deep breaths. Shortly, I was able to return to the bench, where I sat looking expectantly toward the back of the library, away from the girl in the fountain.

When a few minutes later I saw Nadine come out of the library's back door and start toward me across an expanse of still green lawn, I came close to losing it again. Her cascade of burnished hair was caught back high on her head and floated behind her like a red wave. She was dressed in jeans and a loose-fitting plaid shirt whose tails flapped in rhythm with her long-legged stride. My God, she moved like him, too!

Think of something else! I told myself fiercely. Think of the fact that here's one interview Hal Griffith and Ben Solliday can't possibly object to because it has zilch to do with the murders—is absolutely nobody's business but mine and Nadine's. By the time she reached the bench, I was no more than understandably nervous and able to greet her with an easy smile.

She swung a denim backpack off her shoulders and sat at the opposite end of the bench, plopping the backpack down between us. Being as body-language-literate as the next guy, I took it that I was not the only one in a state of nervous wariness.

"Whew!" Nadine said, "do you believe this weather? Sixty degrees! That's why I thought it'd be nice to meet outside."

Okay. Weather. That always works.

"Yes," I agreed. "I had no idea it could be like this in New England in November."

Nadine rummaged in her pack and pulled out a container of cherry yogurt and a plastic spoon. "D'you mind? I worked right through lunch."

"Of course not. What's the project?"

"Victorian Lit." She licked off the top of the yogurt container, wrapped it neatly in a napkin and stowed it in her pack. "I decided to take the course when I knew I'd be working on *The Mikado*. I've really gotten into Christina Rossetti. You know her poetry?"

" 'Goblin Market'? I've always loved that one."

"Yes, and there's another called 'The Prince's Progress.' All about this prince who has a big problem with commitment. Dillydallys and screws around on his way to claiming his princess and when he finally gets there years later she's dead. Quite funny." She'd gone to work with the plastic spoon and now paused with it halfway to her lips to give me a quizzical look. "Makes me think Christina must have known someone like Mitch Kim."

"Ah!" I said. "I did notice at Derek's meeting that you two didn't seem to be . . . together anymore."

She shrugged. "I got tired of all the eager competition. And Mitch might have looked like he didn't notice but he did and he loved it. Besides, it turned out that except for the sex he was really, really boring. Took me a while to notice, what with one thing and another, but when I did. . . . Oh well," with a quick grin, "another learning experience I guess."

At this indication of an ability in Nadine to laugh at herself I felt a lightening of the spirit. I had been afraid she was one of those young people so focussed and driven as to be terminally sober.

"By the way, what are you doing here at Smith? I thought you went to Hampshire College."

"I do. But there's a big cooperative thing with the five colleges in the valley. If your college doesn't have a course you want you can take it at one of the others. I study piano with a Smith professor, too. One of the reasons I came to the area. Besides wanting to get out of England, that is."

She had reached the bottom of the yogurt cup and appeared to be studying it with interest.

I said gently, "When did you find out that Mick . . . that Michael Mullins was your father?"

Nadine put the cup down on the bench and turned to me. Her eyes had lost some of their caution, I thought, as they met mine.

"Not until last year," she said. "Not until after he was already . . . had already died. My mother told me. I couldn't believe she hadn't told me before. My father—that is, the man I'd always thought was my father—had died when I was fifteen."

"It must have been a shock."

"Oh, it was. Awful. I'd just come home for a couple of weeks during the summer break. I had no idea. None."

"Why did she tell you then?"

"She knew she had cancer. She thought I ought to know. I ended up staying the whole summer. She died at the end of it."

Oh dear Lord, I thought, what messes we humans manage to create, and to pass along to our hapless offspring.

Nadine said hesitantly, "You know who my mother was?"

I nodded. I could see her clearly, slender like Nadine but fair, blue-eyed, with the porcelain skin that is supposed to be a product of all that nasty fog and damp—a regular goddam English rose. There had been a party. "Darling, you must meet George and Sybil Gardner.

George is producing the BBC broadcasts . . ." I hadn't gone to many parties during those, what—three weeks? four? I was still recovering. Mick had a full concert schedule. I remembered there had been a lot of flowers.

I thought of all the things I wanted to know, all the questions I ached to ask. How much, I wondered, had the dying Sybil confided to her daughter?

Nadine said, "Mother didn't tell me a lot. Only that their time together was very short and that she had loved him. And that he never knew. By the time she was telling me all this she was awfully sick. But I read everything I could find about my . . . about Michael Mullins—Mischa, didn't some people call him? And of course I listened to all the recordings."

She crumpled the empty container in those deceptively delicate-looking fingers, tucked it into her backpack, and moved the pack to her other side so it was no longer between us. She leaned forward, hands clasped between her knees, eyes fixed on my face. In a tone half command, half pleading, she said, "Phoebe, please, tell me about my . . . about my father."

I nodded. "Well, to begin with, he would have been terribly proud of you . . ."

I didn't add what I was reasonably certain of: that he would also have been terribly relieved at not having had to go through the actual raising of a child with all its attendant demands and subsequent diverting of focus away from him and his needs. Delighted instead to be presented with the end result, this striking and deeply talented young woman, a colleague now, a proud reflection of his own talent. And he'd never known of her existence. I could almost—almost—feel sorry for him.

I pushed the thoughts away. This was Nadine's time, a time for her need to know, not for any bitterness I might be feeling. Time for the good stuff.

So I told her about Mick, about his Russian mama and Irish dad, about how we'd met, how handsome and warm and funny and smart he'd been. About the early struggles, the failures, and then the successes.

By the time we realized that the sun was approaching the level of the greenhouse roof and even an unseasonably warm November day was becoming nippy, we had laughed and cried ourselves into a state of relaxed familiarity that I, at least, found astonishing.

"Oh, gosh," Nadine said, checking her watch. "I'll be just right for the next bus if I hurry."

"I'd offer you a ride," I said, "but I walked here. Anyway, I thought you had a car."

"Yeah, but where am I supposed to park? Smith has been talking for years about building a parking garage but it hasn't happened, and God forbid you should park on campus without a sticker. Besides, the bus is free."

We had both risen, and after only the briefest of hesitations she put her arms around me and hugged me. "Thank you, Phoebe. I know it's been . . . I guess awful for you in a way. But thanks."

Well, yeah. She had that right. And yet, in the end, not as awful as I'd feared.

When she had hoisted the backpack into place, I tucked my arm into hers. "I'll walk you to the bus stop."

After I'd waved Nadine off, I walked home, grabbed my leotard and slippers, got in my car and drove downtown to the dance studio. After an hour of barre and then floor work, including, if I do say so, a pretty nifty series of *fouettés,* my endorphins had kicked in to the point where the day's emotional turmoil was subsumed in the rosy feel-good of an exercise high.

As I prepared to take my body home to its own comfortable shower, the owner of the studio asked if I'd be interested in teaching a couple of classes. Since I had at the moment no idea what direction my life would be taking me in the next couple of days, let alone beyond, I had to say thanks and I'll think about it.

Which I did all the way home, still in my state of sweaty, loose-muscled semieuphoria. Would this turn out to be the place I wanted to live, these the people I wanted to live among? Would Phoebe find happiness in a small New England town? Love? A job? Tune in tomorrow.

29

So in spite of all temptation,
Such a theme I'll not discuss . . .

BY THE TIME I SWITCHED OFF MY BEDSIDE LAMP THAT
night, the euphoria had dissipated and my thigh muscles were pointing out to me crossly that I'd really gone
too far this time. But I congratulated myself that I was
able, at intervals, to contemplate the fact of Nadine,
even the prospect of her presence in my life, with
something approaching equanimity. I had told Anandi
and my aunt about our meeting and suggested that it
might be nice to ask Nadine to the house sometime
soon. Anandi had heard my tale with great interest and
had mercifully refrained from offering any nuggets of
Asian wisdom. Aunt Portia, I thought, was greatly relieved at my ability to talk about the situation without
any messy emotionalism.

The mess I could save for my own bedroom, as at-
tested by a wastebasket brimming with soggy wads of
Kleenex. At least I could spare Portia my swings from
anger to sorrow to burgeoning affection to self-pity to,
in an especially low moment, a cynical contemplation
of a parade of Nadine half-siblings ambushing my life
to its end.

It was this last that had brought me to tell myself firmly to Cut it Out. Enough was enough. For now.

I had also told Portia and Anandi about my conversation with Lydia. Did they think it was credible, I'd asked, that Lydia had, as she claimed, come out from a lifetime under Foster's spell in that one defining moment? Portia had come down firmly on the "Yes" side. Anandi hadn't been so sure.

I had the grace to tell Anandi I thought she'd been right about one thing, though—that Lydia didn't care about the money. "Oh, she'll enjoy it all right. But if she did kill him, it wasn't about the money."

Up in my bedroom, when I'd finished wallowing, I called Harry. The instantaneous stab of pleasure I felt on hearing his voice let me know definitively, if I'd doubted it before, that something special was going on between us. I found myself pouring out the details of this highly emotional day. Harry listened patiently, commiserated, discussed, laughed, understood. I felt warmed, I felt comforted, I felt—had I dared to acknowledge it—loved.

I felt all this even more when Harry said hesitantly, "Phoebe darling, all these people you've been talking to. I get the impression that you're trying to do the police's job. And it worries me that you might be putting yourself in harm's way. No, listen to me. If you're concerned that they could be zeroing in on the wrong person, don't be. Please. Leave it to the pros."

How sweet! I thought, conveniently ignoring that others who had offered the same advice had been interfering/patronizing/bossy. Harry cared. He'd called me "darling." I murmured reassurances into the phone. I hoped he wouldn't notice that they contained nothing that could be construed as a promise.

Now I lay in the dark, willing myself to sleep. Portia, to my surprise, had decided she would go to Foster's funeral the next afternoon. Since I have been known to fall apart at the funerals of total strangers, I figured my best defense in this case was the strengthening effect of a good night's rest.

Who else would be there? Lydia, of course . . . jeez, I didn't need that top blanket. I flipped it to one side. Irene? I doubted it. Harry had already said he couldn't make it. I bet Derek would come, if for nothing else than to remind Lydia of his existence, his hopes . . . the window! I hadn't opened the window, no wonder I was uncomfortable.

I padded over to the curving bay, pulled open the curtains and raised the center sash. Moonlight brushed the tops of the hedges separating Portia's house from the one next door and glinted off an attic windowpane. Someone in the neighborhood had a wood fire going; the clean, pungent smell of the smoke drifted deliciously past my nostrils as I leaned on the sill. The air had turned cold enough to raise a sprinkle of goose bumps on my arms and cause a pleasant shiver. From a few houses down, a dog was barking to be let in, or maybe out.

Leaving the curtains open, I crawled back into bed, pulled the covers over my shoulders, and lay staring at the moonlight now touching my windowsill. Overstimulated, my mother would have said, and would have been right on. Should I go down to the kitchen for a cup of Ovaltine? Or make use of the enforced wakefulness to attempt some organized thinking? I decided in favor of thinking.

Sure, I hadn't made any promises to Harry, and the one I'd made to Hal Griffith I didn't count, it having been made under duress. But in fact, what more, in the way of gathering facts, could I do? And had the ones I'd already gathered led to any important conclusions?

Okay, I'd established that Irene was responsible for the tricks on Foster, but that was about it. Otherwise all I had was a bunch of motives and background information, most, probably all of which were already known to the police. Was it still possible that I'd missed something?

Start with my most recent (suspect) encounter—Lydia. I had been quite sincere in what I'd told Anandi: with Lydia, it wouldn't have been about the money. Lydia had never given the impression of being hard up; I was sure the "damn good divorce lawyer" had seen to that. No, with Lydia it would have been . . . anger? hatred? a final boiling over of the hurt and frustration of years? Perhaps something that had happened between them even after the incident of Katisha's song, a final insult, a final twist of the knife. Sure, Lydia *said* she had had an epiphany, been released from her ex-husband's emotional thrall, eliminated his ability to hurt her. But was such a sudden reversal credible? Portia thought so, but for myself I had no idea. For all I knew, Lydia could be laying a clever smokescreen.

But in the end, I acknowledged, there was no solid evidence against Lydia. None.

Irene, now—*there* was not only motive but admitted hostile acts against the victim. But I had not changed my early opinion that dirty tricks and murder were the result of two very different psyches. And if Irene had killed Foster, why on earth would she risk discovery by sneaking back afterwards with her bit of chalk to write insults on his door?

The dog down the street had segued from an intermittent bark to a soulful howl. A male voice that sounded as if its owner was leaning out a window shouted, "For God's sake, will someone muzzle the damn dog!" Another howl and then shortly the sound of a door slamming shut, and silence. Apparently the dog had been "muzzled." Or had the voice said "muffled"?

My thoughts drifted to Beth and the engimatic sentence she'd overheard. "He's going to fill—bill?—a carriage." I played with the words, trying to make sense of them. Carriage? Marriage? Going to fill . . . kill . . .

bill . . . how about *build* a marriage? Could it have been Lydia Jane was talking to, in which case "he" would refer to Foster, perhaps to his plans in regard to Theda Bara? Or had she indeed been talking about the horse-and-buggy plan? In which case the "he" would be Derek. The listener one of the others whose exact movements on that night were unknown—Irene, Harry, Carl, me (being scrupulously fair), Foster himself. "Fill a carriage"? Fill it with what, and who would care?

The moonlight was now flooding the window, silvering the pattern on the border of the Indian rug, piercing even my closed eyelids. I could get up and pull the curtain. Or I could just turn over. I turned over.

What was Harry doing at this moment? Was he perhaps also unable to sleep? Did he wear pajamas? Was his bed wide or narrow? Was there any conceivable reason that Jane would have been talking to Harry about a carriage/marriage there in the utility room? No, and if there had been he would have told me. There is such a thing as instinct, as trust—as knowing in your gut that a person is incapable of murder. I knew that about Harry. Forget Harry.

Derek, on the other hand, I had no instinct about. Further, I knew practically nothing about his background, where he'd come from, what his life had been prior to his appearance in Northampton. But Harry did, I suddenly remembered. Harry had been the reason for Derek's initial visit. Why hadn't I thought to ask Harry about Derek? Well, I could certainly remedy that oversight the next time we talked. But in any case why on earth would Derek want to kill his very own golden goose? I was at least sure that Derek's enthusiasm for his fledgling company and especially for the Old Church Theater was twenty-four-carat genuine. What would he do now, with Foster gone and Lydia indifferent? I gave a mental shrug. I could feel pity, but it was not my problem.

Who was left? Ah yes, Carl. So easy to forget Carl.

Carl the high school teacher—nice, reliable, husband-and-father, ordinary Carl. And yet not so ordinary. A man with the intellect and talent of an inventor, cheated out of the fruits of that talent and then financially ruined by failed lawsuits against those richer and better connected than he. Could he really mean it about Foster having in effect done him a favor? Suppose, I mused, that I'd had a chance at becoming a prima ballerina and had it snatched away from me. Would I then be grateful for the chance to teach others perhaps not as talented as I had been? Uh-uh.

I flopped over again to face the window. The moon had risen higher, so its light no longer splashed through my open window. A delicate breeze, hardly more than a current of air, still smelling faintly of the wood fire, cooled my face and made me hug the covers around my shoulders. My leg muscles, I found, had begun to relax. Really, all this thinking was too much. And in the end, it had gotten me nowhere.

The hell with it. What had made me think I was so special, anyway—my one success last summer, which was now beginning to seem several lifetimes ago? What had been my excuse? . . . first Aunt Portia and then Harry. Since I knew for sure they hadn't done it, what did I expect, some kind of massive frame-up? Don't be stupid, Phoebe. Give it up, forget it. Leave it to the authorities. Leave it to Lieutenant Griffith and his cohorts, leave it to the D.A., leave it to. . . .

30

I thought it would come sooner or later!

"FOR MAN WALKETH IN A VAIN SHADOW, AND DISQUI-
eteth himself in vain; he heapeth up riches, and cannot
tell who shall gather them," the minister intoned.

Oh, Lydia! If it was you who chose this particular
Psalm, what a naughty old girl you are! Or maybe I'm
doing you a disservice and it's only my own antic sense
of irony working overtime. From what I could see of
Lydia's profile as she sat in the Episcopal church's front
pew, across the aisle and several rows down from
Portia, Anandi, and me, her expression was appropriately sober. She was wearing a grey jersey dress and
small black hat. On either side sat what I assumed to be
her children, a blond woman all in black and two dark-
suited men, one blond and pudgy, the other dark and
with his father's characteristic slouch of the shoulders.

"Deliver me from all mine offences; and make me
not a rebuke unto the foolish . . ."

Arnold Zimmer was there, I observed. And two
rows ahead of us Derek, his head barely visible over the
back of the pew. What effect might it have had on him,
I mused, that small stature? Another few inches and,

given his talent and looks, he could have made his way easily from handsome juvenile to leading man . . .

By golly, there was Lieutenant Griffith, sitting alone. A mark of respect for the deceased? Or a further scoping out of suspects? If so, he must be disappointed—neither Harry nor Irene nor Carl had chosen to appear. Perhaps after the service I could put his mind at ease on at least one point: he no longer had to be concerned about Portia Singh's rash niece—she was decisively bowing out of the investigation.

"For I am a stranger with thee, and a sojourner, as all my fathers were . . ."

Who were all these people—sober-suited, the women hatted for the most part, here and there furred—filling the pews in quite respectable numbers? Pals? Friends? Business associates? The atmosphere was solemn but hardly emotional.

No—there, sitting with two other members of the *Mikado* chorus, the Theda Bara look-alike was sniffling and blotting at her eyes. I felt grateful for this evidence that the dead man was being remembered at least in one quarter with genuine sorrow.

A hymn was being called for. The congregation thumbed through their hymnals, rose:

> *Once to every man and nation*
> *Comes the moment to decide*
> *In the strife of truth with falsehood*
> *For the good or evil side . . .*

Actually one of Foster's favorites, as the minister had declared? Or Lydia's choice? Or was I again reading significance where none was intended?

I murmured along in my back-row-of-the-chorus voice. Not the tune I was familiar with, but a good one. I checked the composer's name: Arthur S. Sullivan.

Beside me, Portia was taking the second line in her strong alto. Just behind us, a sweet soprano sounded so

much like Jane Manypenny that I caught myself in the
act of turning around to check. Where's your head,
Phoebe? Still trying, I supposed, to catch up with an
overload of traumatic events. Besides, the voice behind
me was wholly American, with no trace of Jane's
plummy accent.

The hymn continued inexorably through its four
verses. My mind wandered . . .

Though the cause of evil prosper,
Yet 'tis truth alone is strong—

. . . and came to a jolting stop. You idiot, Phoebe! You
incredible idiot! Of course!

By the concerned looks I was receiving from Anandi
on one side and Portia on the other, I realized that my
bolt of enlightenment had been visceral as well as
mental. That strangled squeak I'd heard must have been
mine. I muttered reassurances and returned my eyes to
the page of the hymnal.

But I saw nothing, my brain being entirely occupied
in following the insight I'd stumbled on, trying to trace
it to some sort of logical conclusion. When Portia
tugged gently at my arm, I realized the music had
stopped and I was the only member of the congregation
still standing.

Everyone said afterwards that the remainder of
E. Foster's funeral "went off very well"—with dignity,
beauty, and no direct mention of the unpleasantness that
had brought it about. I had a few vague memories—of
the children rising one by one to speak about their father;
of a lot of getting up and down as prayers and hymns
succeeded each other; of Lydia's drawn and, for a moment, tragic face as she watched her ex-husband's coffin
being carried up the aisle.

Beyond that, my mind was in quite another place,
clicking over at a furious rate, floundering, leaping,
coming up short. If that's what she meant, what

possible . . . and why would she . . . when Nadine
said . . . didn't Anandi tell us. . . . And finally, how had
Jane Manypenny known, and what had been her connection with E. Foster Ballard? I thought of the one connection I had seen for myself. I would start there.

"I'm terribly sorry to bother you, and I'm sure this will
seem to you like a very trivial matter . . ."

The woman behind the small desk, which looked
rather like a raft set adrift on a sea of oatmeal, gave
me a look worthy of a castaway to her rescuer.
She was middle-aged and stout with a broad, florid
face and pale yellow hair curled like a poodle's into
tight little ringlets all over her head. When I'd entered
the office door which listed a Ph.D., a specialist in
Somato-Respiratory Integration, a Certified Professional ReBirther, and Jane Manypenny, M.S.W., she
had been tapping the eraser end of a pencil against her
desk blotter and frowning at the rubber plant that
provided the only relief in an otherwise unbroken
palette of windowless white wall and beige floor. Several closed doors in the white wall presumably led
to offices. From behind the nearest one came a faint
murmur of voices. To my right a doorless archway led
to a corridor. The room was redolent with the sweet,
pungent scent of fresh wood and the chemical one of
newly laid carpet.

The blond poodle said, "Oh, do come in," half rose,
made a gesture as if to offer me a seat, realized there
wasn't one, sank back into her chair, and added plain-
tively, "Would you believe the furniture was supposed
to be delivered last week?"

"It's always tough when places are being redeco-
rated," I said. "But I can see it's going to be very nice.
Excuse me, but are you the receptionist for all these
people?" gesturing toward the door.

The Poodle nodded and said glumly, "For now, at

least. There's really not enough for me to do, so they'll probably let me go soon."

"Business not brisk?"

"Too darn many therapists in this town, you ask me."

"Then why all this redecorating?" I said, looking around.

"Oh, that's the building owners. Put in a whole new heating and air-conditioning system." Her voice fell to confidential level. "Now they'll be able to jack up the rent and this lot will be out on their ear I shouldn't be surprised. Jane Manypenny was the only one who had a solid clientele and now—" she broke off and gave me an inquiring look. "You know what happened . . ."

"Yes," I said, "and actually that's why I'm here. I'm . . . I was a friend of Jane's. That is, we were in the *Mikado* production together, my name's Phoebe Mullins."

The woman stuck out her hand. "Flo Potter. Oh, Jane was so excited about that show! Especially being English, you know. She talked about it a lot, how she was enjoying it. Oh, dear." She withdrew her hand from my grasp, retrieved a tissue from a desk drawer, and dabbed at her eyes. "I was really quite fond of Jane. It was such a shock."

"Yes it was," I said. "Terrible. Which is why I feel kind of awkward even asking this. You see," improvising rapidly and trusting that the Poodle would be ignorant of how these arrangements worked, "I was in charge of the rentals, the playbooks, you know, music scores. And it's my responsibility to get them all back before we're charged extra. But I never got Jane's book. And I was wondering—"

"If it could be here in her office? Well . . ." I was aware of being scrutinized anew and was grateful to be still dressed in my ultrarespectable, suitable-for-serious-occasions, navy blue dress and jacket and pumps. "I don't suppose it would hurt to take a peek."

Looking almost eager now, Flo rummaged in another drawer, found a key attached to a round cardboard label, and heaved herself to her feet.

"Of course the police were here—on Sunday, right after they found her. I had to come down and open up, the owner was out of town. But if her playbook was here I don't imagine they would have taken it. Here we are."

We had gone through the archway and turned left along a short hallway to a door at the end. The Poodle wielded her key and we entered a medium-size room with two large windows overlooking Main Street three stories below. A desk and chair in one corner, two padded chairs with wooden arms, some wooden file cabinets, a tall bookcase, half of its shelves empty, that bland ubiquitous oatmeal carpeting. No plants, no pictures on the walls—for a therapist, I thought, strangely uninviting.

"Sad, isn't it?" my guide observed. "After all those months of sharing offices and lugging stuff around—her files and all, you know—not to mention the dust, poor Jane had just gotten her office back. Last Friday she was just moving her things back in—oh, shoot! There's my phone! Wouldn't you know?"

"Go ahead," I said. "It doesn't seem there's much here. I'll just have a quick look through the books."

"Well . . . all right," and the Poodle hotfooted it back down the hall.

I surveyed the office with acute disappointment. What were my chances of finding anything in this barren environment—a diary entry, a hastily jotted memo crumpled up and tossed in a wastebasket—to back up my theory? Besides which, the police had already searched the place. True, they hadn't been looking for what I was looking for . . . the Poodle's voice in one-sided conversation still drifted from the reception area . . . oh heck, as long as I was here . . .

I tried the file drawers—locked, of course—then

went over to the desk in the corner and made a quick search of its surface and drawers: on top the usual desk paraphernalia, in one drawer two boxes of tissues— necessary equipment in the therapist's trade—in another a supply of various types of insurance forms, a small Bible, a package of Twinkies. No diary, no address book—well, naturally the police would have those. I turned my back on the desk. I'd been a fool, made myself into a lying snoop for nothing. What had I expected, anyway, some—

"Hey, what are you doing here?" said a voice, faint but distinct, above my right ear.

For one eerie fraction of a second I wondered how my conscience had suddenly acquired a voice and why the voice was male. Then it continued: "Good to see you!"

A second voice said "Took a chance you'd still be here. I've just picked up those contracts we talked about and thought I'd drop them off."

"Sure, let's take a look . . ."

I had whipped around and was staring at the blank white wall above Jane Manypenny's desk. Blank except for a louvered metal vent set just below ceiling level. It was from here that the voices were drifting— distant-sounding, somewhat tinny, but perfectly discernible.

I left the room, barely holding myself back from a flat-out run, and regained the reception area as the Poodle was replacing the phone.

"It wasn't there," I said hastily, "but thanks so much anyway. I really have to run, I . . . have another appointment."

Just shy of the door another thought struck me. "Has anyone else been using Jane's office since . . . her death?"

The Poodle shook her head. "Oh, no. Her sister's coming, you know. From England." Her tone became slightly defensive. "Nobody's touched anything."

"Heavens, I didn't mean to suggest . . . anyway, thanks again."

Down one flight, turn right toward the front of the building. To the door on the left lettered "Carlton G. Lattimer, Attorney at Law."

I took a deep breath before turning the handle. This one was a lawyer, not a bored receptionist who had probably inhaled too many unvented new-carpet fumes.

The door opened on a minuscule lobby already crowded with two straight chairs and a standing coat-rack. Before I had time to take a seat and give my pounding heart a chance to slow, the inner door opened and two men emerged. The shorter of the two gave me a curious glance, opened the door for the other, and said good-bye. He turned to me. "Yes? Can I help you?"

Attorney Lattimer (at least I sure hoped that's who it was) was a stocky man of fifty or so in shirtsleeves and vest. He had a smooth face, a smooth manner, and small hands, one of which was weighed down by a gold signet ring roughly the size of a teacup. The tone of his brief question—insinuating, but this side of actionable—helped me decide my approach.

I smiled sweetly and gave my eyelashes a bat or two. "Oh, Mr. Lattimer, I *know* I should have made an appointment, but, well, it has to do with something an acquaintance of mine—Dr. Ballard—was talking to me about before he—we were in the operetta together, you see, and we got to be such good friends and he was telling me about this opportunity, only he said I mustn't mention it to anyone else—"

By now we were in the office, the Sleaze behind his desk, me in a client chair so low that my skirt was riding inexorably up my thighs.

"And I know it must seem just *terrible* for me to be coming to you so soon after . . . but, you see, Dr. Ballard was *so* encouraging about my possibly joining in this project of his and I do have a little extra money at the moment . . ."

Just what project was that?

I told him.

The Sleaze shook his head regretfully. That project, he explained, had only been in the preliminary stages and was now extremely doubtful. The person I should really talk to was Dr. Ballard's beneficiary, Lydia Hicks. But if I were interested in investing, he could steer me to a couple of good things. Would I like to make an appointment? Or get together for a drink? Only (with a frown at his watch) unhappily not tonight, since he had an engagement.

I said brightly I'd certainly think about that, struggled out of the chair, and made it out the door with my virtue, if not my dignity, intact.

The Sleaze would discover without my help, I decided, the security breach represented by the ductwork in the new heating and air-conditioning system.

31

Well, a nice mess you've got us into . . .

WHEN I HAD DROPPED ANANDI AND PORTIA OFF AT THE
house after the funeral, I'd told them I had a couple of
errands to run downtown and would be back in a jiff.
Now, as I drove slowly home through what passed in
Northampton for rush hour, I reflected on the really ex-
cessive amount of fibbing I'd been doing of late, and
that it was time to stop. I would tell my aunt what
I had discovered, and then tell the Bear and/or Hal
Griffith and have done with it.

What would I tell? That I knew who had murdered
Foster and Jane and I knew why. No proof, of course.
No evidence that could even be called circumstantial.
Only a compelling motive. Only the one solution that
made sense. Only, I told myself sourly, in police terms
damn-all.

Nevertheless . . . I would be a good girl. After I'd
talked things over with Aunt Portia I would take my
twig, so to speak, and lay it reverentially at the feet of
Authority.

But I arrived home to find my aunt and Anandi already in their coats awaiting the van that would pick

them up for their evening of Indian food and culture in Amherst. It arrived, I sent them off with assurances to Anandi that I was perfectly capable of feeding myself and went to the kitchen to make a sandwich, pour a glass of milk, and battle an unreasonable feeling of having been ill-used.

I had been clever, hadn't I? Not to mention enterprising. I had figured out something that, to my knowledge, no one else had, and I'd been looking forward to sharing it, testing it out, with Portia. Now she was gone, not to return until ten-thirty. Too bad! She was not my only confidant. I called Harry, got his machine, and left a brief message: "I know who did it. Call me." Then I took my sandwich into the TV room.

I clicked around, found a *Law & Order* rerun, and watched as Briscoe and Logan's search of the suspect's car was declared illegal, once again leaving McCoy with a bunch of damning but useless evidence. "At least you *had* some evidence," I said crossly to the screen. "And everybody knows the guy's guilty and why he did it."

Scene shift to the D.A.'s office: Adam Schiff instructing wearily, "Motive is not an element in proving a homicide."

Exactly. Couldn't put it plainer than that. If motive alone *were* an element, any of the suspects in our case could now be under arrest—pick one. My conviction that the motive I'd uncovered was the strongest, the best fit to the facts, was perhaps interesting, but by itself worthless.

Hah! The judge has allowed in one smidgen of the formerly suppressed evidence. The suspect's lawyer asks for a deal. In McCoy's office, under his relentless prodding, the suspect breaks down.

I, on the other hand, was smidgenless. And my suspect, having played a part brilliantly so far, was unlikely to break down.

I turned off the TV, took my plate and glass back to the kitchen, and was suddenly overwhelmed with weariness. My suspect might play a part with relative ease, but I had played two today and found it exhausting. I climbed up to my room, ditched the heels, the pantyhose, the dress, wrapped myself in the familiar comfort of my blue robe, and lay down on the bed. Harry might be calling at anytime, but until then I could at least shut my eyes. . . .

I was so deeply asleep when the phone shrilled in my ear that it took me a moment, even after hearing Harry's voice, to remember where I was and why I had called him. Just as quickly, it all came roaring back, and, in a rush of relief at finally having someone to confide in, I said, "Oh, Harry, it was Derek! Derek killed Foster and Jane, I'm sure of it!"

I heard a quick intake of breath and Harry said, "But it couldn't—Phoebe, *why?*"

"Because Foster was planning to tear down the Old Church and build a parking garage! He'd already bought the property next door—the white clapboard building, the rooming house—so he'd have enough space. And Jane found out because her office was above the lawyer's—Foster's lawyer—and she overheard—"

"Hold on, Phoebe. This is . . . have you gone to the police yet?"

"No, because all I have is the motive and that doesn't count with them. They need evidence and I haven't got any. But I'm sure, Harry. Think of how Derek must have felt when Jane told him that night—opening night when he was so over the moon about the success of *The Mikado*! What a shock! He must have gone right down to Foster's room and—well, you can imagine."

"Phoebe, you really should . . . you haven't told this to anybody?"

Dear Harry! So concerned for my safety!

"No, but don't worry, of course I'm going to. At least it'll point the police in the right direction. I just wanted to talk to Portia first—and you. See if we could come up with anything concrete now that we know. But Portia

and Anandi are out, so . . . can you think of *anything,*
Harry, anything at all? To do with the timetable,
maybe? With something you saw but didn't register at
the time?"

"No, I don't . . . I can't . . . wait a minute!" Harry's
voice became animated. "There was something! At the
theater—damn! Why didn't I realize . . . Wait right
there, I'm coming to pick you up, we'll go together. No,
better, meet me in the drive, okay?"

"What is it?" I said. But Harry had hung up.

Fifteen minutes later I was pacing the driveway in a
state of mind that ricocheted between excited curiosity
and annoyance. The theater? What kind of evidence
could possibly have been overlooked at the theater by
the time the lieutenant and his cohorts had finished
searching every corner? And why the big rush? Why
not tell me more on the phone? On the other hand, I
was waiting for my (almost) lover to join me in pursuit
of . . . well, whatever it was that might enable me to
present the Bear and the lieutenant with a complete
case rather than just another motive. Harry wasn't
stupid. And he wouldn't be hauling me off at (I glanced
yet again at my watch) 10:25 at night without good
reason.

Because I trusted Harry and that was that. Which
didn't mean I hadn't left a hasty note propped on the
vestibule table: "Gone to Old Church with Harry. Back
soon." Aunt Portia, I told myself, deserved not to be
worried unnecessarily by an unaccountably missing
niece.

Ah, here was the man himself, pulling into the
driveway with a flourish, leaning across to open the
passenger door. I jumped in, noting that Harry's dome
light was on the fritz, and was still buckling my belt as
he backed out through the wrought-iron gates and
headed toward Elm Street.

A van was coming toward us, the narrowness of the

street causing both vehicles to slow down in preparation for maneuvering past one another. "Hey, that must be Portia's group coming back," I said, and gave a wave in case she or Anandi happened to recognize the car.

Once we'd negotiated the passage with inches to spare, I turned to Harry. "*Now*," I said, "tell me what we're going to look for. I'm dying of curiosity."

"Oh dear, how appropriate," said a voice from the backseat.

Only my seat belt kept me from connecting with the roof of the car. Only the sudden constriction of my throat muscles turned what wanted to be an all-out scream into a strangulated squeal. The voice belonged to Derek Bowles. So did the hand that had appeared in the space between Harry and me holding a gun so small that in other circumstances I would have assumed it was a toy.

How many emotions can a human being sustain at once? I only know that at that moment the adrenaline rush of fear—terror, actually—was jockeying for space with a fury so intense that it felt as though successive waves of fire and ice were using my body as a convenient beach.

When I could command my voice again, I said evenly, addressing Harry, "Let me be sure I have this right. You came to my house and got me into your car even though you knew there was a shithead with a gun in the backseat."

"Hey, no need to be rude," Derek said.

"Shut up, Derek. Well? Does that about cover it?"

The knuckles of Harry's hands gripping the wheel whitened. He stared ahead, grim-faced. "He had a gun on me. We all know he had no problem using it before."

I gaped at him, while in the back of my mind the answer to one question became radiantly clear. Aunt Portia had been right and Lydia had told the truth: it *was* possible in an instant to go from love—or love's illusion—to indifference or worse. In this case, much worse. Who *was* this man? And—my God!—had I actually contemplated going to bed with him? I just managed to keep myself from retching.

"Jesus, Phoebe, put yourself in my place! He was with me when I came home. He heard your message on the machine. 'Hey, great! Call her!' he says. I swear, I had no idea. And then you blurted out his name first thing. Next thing I know he's got the gun at my head and he's mouthing at me what to say."

" '*Blurted out his name*'? You . . . you unspeakable worm! Are you trying to make this into *my fault*?"

"Well, if you'd gone straight to the police like everyone's been telling you to do . . . And damn it, Phoebe, the guy was threatening to shoot me! What would *you* have done?"

"I would've said no! I would've called his bluff! What good would it do him to shoot you? I'm the one that was the real threat, and now he's got us both!"

"I hate to interrupt you two lovebirds," Derek said, "but we're almost at the theater and I need to tell you what's going to happen next."

I noted with a shiver that his tone had now lost all trace of playfulness and, even more ominous, of theatricality. It was flat and purposeful.

As Harry made the turn onto the street that would bring us to the Old Church, Derek went on, "As you so neatly put it, Phoebe, I have you both. If either of you tries something cute I won't hesitate to shoot the other. As it happens, I'm quite a good shot, so I could probably get you both. And at this point, you see, I have nothing to lose. Just so you know."

I thought I'd detected the slightest of tremors in the *nothing to lose*. I might as well give it a try.

"Derek," I said, "You can't really want to do this. What would killing Harry and me possibly do besides dig you into an even deeper hole? It wouldn't take the police long to find out where I've been today and come to their own conclusions. Why make things worse for yourself?"

We had by now cruised half a block past the Old Church and Derek instructed, "Here, take this spot. It's the closest we're going to get." And as Harry maneuvered the Honda into the barely adequate space and turned off the ignition, "Okay, listen up. You're both going to get out on the passenger side and start walking—not too fast, not too slow—up to the church door. I'll be ten paces behind you. Go ahead."

We got out of the car. The fact that Derek had completely ignored what I'd said chilled me even further. It was as if, I thought, he was on some sort of cruise control for which there was no braking system. I turned around for one last attempt.

Derek had exited the car on the street-side and now lounged against the bumper of the vehicle parked behind Harry's. In dark jeans and a short, navy blue ski jacket, a black knit watch cap covering the telltale hair, he was almost invisible. His right arm was held close to his body. The gun, almost hidden even in his small hand unless you'd been looking for it, was pointed steadily in our direction. His face was barely discernible in the darkness between the two nearest streetlamps, but as I started to say "Derek—" I saw his head move infinitesimally from side to side and the gun start to rise. I turned back and, side by side with Harry, started walking.

This was the place, I thought, where if it had been a movie I was watching I'd have been muttering at the screen: "*Do* something, you idiots! Don't just walk in there like sheep! Scream! Make a break for it! Do you think once he's got you in there he's going to let you walk out again? Catch each other's eye, turn, duck, rush him, knock the gun out of his hand!"

Oh right. One thing if, supposing it doesn't quite

work out, there's always another take. Entirely something else when a wrong calculation could get you
dead. Let alone being partnered with Mr. Pushover.

We were passing the run-down rooming house so recently purchased by E. Foster Ballard, its broad wraparound porch now deserted. Where were those guys
when you needed them? Ten-frigging-forty-five at night,
not even all that cold, and the damn street was empty.

A car drove by, its headlights sweeping over us: a
companionable couple out for a nighttime stroll. I had
no doubt that Derek was ducked down out of sight.
Whatever scenario he'd cooked up obviously involved
two people, not three, entering the Old Church, assuming that anyone happened to notice.

How long might it take for Aunt Portia to start wondering why her niece was gone for so long and what she
and Harry were doing at the Old Church in the first
place? I remembered with a pang that cheerful little wave
I'd given the van as we passed. Phoebe out with her
beau, why should anyone worry? Derek at that point no
doubt still concealed on the floor of the backseat.

And, most painful thought of all—Harry was right, I
should have gone immediately to the police. What a
fool I'd been! Damn, damn, damn, damn it all to hell!

We turned in at the walkway, mounted the steps,
reached the door, turned around—to no sign of Derek.
His voice came from the shadows in the angle where
the staircase met the wall: "Open the door, Harry, and
go on in. I know you have your key." And when Harry
had done so, there was Derek, quick as a whippet, up
the steps and slipping in at the open door behind us.

As it closed, he leaned his back against it and felt
with his left hand for the switch that turned on the
lobby lights. As they came on, he gestured with the
gun. "Into the theater, please. There's going to be a little
drama."

32

. . . it places us in a very awkward position.

WE STEPPED THROUGH THE SWINGING LOBBY DOORS INTO
a theater lit only by the lurid gleam of the EXIT signs.

"Hold it!" Derek said. He found the rheostat switches
for the chandeliers, pressed the center one, and adjusted
the light down to a soft glow. "Ah, perfect! Just the atmosphere for a romantic tragedy. Down the steps now,
you two. Sit there," indicating the front pew. "No, no,
together. Closer. That's good."

He put his left hand on the stage and vaulted effort-
lessly up to sit on its edge, a good ten feet from Harry
and me. He had taken off the watch cap, and the silky
fair hair gleamed against the background of black flats
now denuded of their cherry blossoms and swaths of
brilliant silks. The "Tit-Willow" tree had been shoved
downstage right, probably to get it out of the way of
the crew who had stripped the flats.

The theater was cold, the thermostat set on the
minimum to prevent pipes from freezing, and after
only—what, four, five days?—the smell of mildew was
returning. In response to Harry's urgency, I had thrown
on jeans, a sweatshirt, and my green wool cape without

taking time to check the outside temperature. Now I was shivering for real, but when Harry put his arm around my shoulders I shook it off.

"Oh, dear," Derek observed drily. "Our hero has turned out to have feet of clay. Poor Phoebe. *Quel* disappointment! But not a patch on what you'll feel when you find out that he's also a murderer—oops! I'm forgetting that you're not going to be around to suffer that particular shock."

"For God's sake, Derek!" Harry burst out. "Whatever you've got planned you have to know nobody's going to believe it! You'll only end up accountable for two more deaths and no hope for any kind of leniency. Obviously, you killed Foster in a rage, you were provoked, that has to count for something!"

"Very cogent, Harry. Unfortunately Jane Manypenny is another matter. Dear little Jane was shot, as they say, in cold blood. Though why they say that I can't imagine. *I* was in an absolute sweat."

"She was going to tell, wasn't she?" I said. "What she'd overheard."

"Yes, she was. Stupid woman. And by the way, Phoebe, just to satisfy my curiosity, how did you come by all this information?"

Screw you, was my first thought, followed by No, you idiot! Talk! Talk is good. Talk is a lot better than getting shot.

"It started at Foster's funeral—well, long before that of course, all these bits messing around in my head. Anyway, at the funeral we were singing a hymn and the woman behind me had a voice so much like Jane's that it startled me. But I realized right away it was quite different because she didn't have Jane's accent—somehow I'd completely lost sight of the accent. So I started to think about what Beth said she'd heard, and there it was. Not 'bill a carriage' but 'build a garridge'—the way Jane would have pronounced *garage*. I think the idea had already been planted the day before when I had a conversation with Nadine and she mentioned that Smith was always promising to build a parking garage. Except Nadine's accent wasn't as exaggerated as Jane's so with her it came out *ga*-rahge, the same as we say but with the emphasis on the first syllable."

"Excuse me," Harry said, "but how did you make the leap from building a garage to Foster to Derek?"

I bit my tongue as it was starting to spit out "How do you think, dummy?" Harry, I admitted grudgingly, was trying to help.

"Who in that bunch would be wanting to build a garage besides wheeler-dealer Lord High Everything Else himself—the person we now know owned the Old Church and had just bought the building next door? And why would Jane be upset about it to the point of spilling the beans to someone else in the company, unless that someone else would be vitally affected? Someone who had no idea what was going on. You didn't know, did you, Derek?"

"No, I didn't know! You think I would have spent all those weeks dancing attendance, kissing that ghastly man's ass, if I'd known?"

Derek's voice had lost some of its icy control, but his gun hand, I observed, maintained its implacable focus.

"My God, what the man promised me! *Promised me!* A jewel of a theater! Me the General Manager! Northampton had just been named Best Small Arts Town in the country. It was ready for its own rep company. Start with the local talent, more would come. What I'd wanted all my life! Jesus, no wonder I believed him!"

He jumped to his feet and started pacing back and forth along the edge of the platform, never taking his eyes off of Harry and me.

"Do you realize how much *talent* I have? How much I *know* about the *theater*?" He reached Ko-Ko's tree and in one fluid movement was standing on its platform. "How much goddam *training* I've had? And you know how many road shows I've been offered of fucking *Peter Pan*?"

He jumped down and resumed the pacing. "I'm thirty-eight years old, folks, and I ain't no Peter Pan. I can act circles around ninety percent of the guys I see but what do you know, I'm *short*! I'm small! I'm a goddam freak!"

"That's not true—" I began, but Derek interrupted with a snarled, "Don't start! Don't trot out your goddam Joel Greys and Michael J. Foxes. Let's just leave it that what I wanted I couldn't have. And now, by God, someone was giving me a theater! And then he was taking it away!"

Harry said, "How did Jane find out?"

"Sheer bloody chance," Derek said savagely. "Something to do with renovations in the building where she had her office. She overheard Foster talking to his lawyer in the room below hers."

"What did Foster say when you confronted him?" I asked.

"He said"—Derek stopped his pacing and his voice took on an eerie resemblance to E. Foster's oily tones— " 'My dear boy, I'm sorry you had to find out just now, but you must realize I'm a businessman. Northampton's desperate for parking space, I provide it, I make a bundle. It's been fun, but there's no money in theater, dear boy.' *Fun!* It was my damn *life*! He was just going to raze it, tear it down—this gorgeous space, this ambience, these incredible fucking *acoustics*!"

His unexpectedly rich baritone rang to the far reaches of the sanctuary. Would somebody hear? If they did, would they think to investigate the sound of shouting in the Old Church Theater late at night? Derek seemed, for the moment, to have forgotten his immediate purpose in bringing us here in favor of a need to vent his outrage.

"So you hit him with the bat," I prompted.

"Hardly knew I was doing it. He saw me, of course, in the mirror, but he couldn't move in time. It only stunned him. He staggered up out of the chair and turned and started toward me. God, it was terrifying—like something out of a zombie movie. And then he fell on his face. The only thing I could think was that I couldn't let him live now, after what I'd done, he'd ruin me. So I grabbed the dagger off the dressing table. Ugh! Like sticking a knife into a grapefruit. Except with that heavy silk kimono to soak up the blood there wasn't any squirting. I wiped the handle and the bat and turned out the light. When I was sure there was nobody outside I walked out and went to my own dressing room."

"Why didn't you padlock the door? The lock was hanging right there on the hasp. That way you could be sure that everyone would assume he'd already left."

"Couldn't take the time. Someone was coming down the stairs."

He was leaning against the tree now, elbow braced on the platform. His face was shadowy in the dim light from the chandelier, but the gun picked up silver glints as it drooped in a now careless-looking hand. His tone had become almost conversational.

Harry said, "Why the hell did Jane Manypenny feel she had to tell you about Foster right then? Why couldn't she have waited?"

Derek gave a bitter little laugh. "Why indeed? Dear, stupid Janey! She'd been shocked, you see, *shocked*. To find out that her idol was a liar and a weasel. She'd been in on some of our little post-rehearsal gatherings when Foster expanded on his plans for the theater. God, the man was good! He wanted to be sure, you see, that while he was running around sounding out members of the zoning board, having his slimy lawyer deal with any inconvenient legalities, that no bleeding-heart, artsy opposition groups had a chance to organize. Well, poor Janey! When she overheard Foster laying it on the line with his lawyer she practically had a heart attack. It was all so awfully uncricket, so non-U, so *unfair*. She thought I had a *right* to *know*."

"Why didn't she tell the cops?" I said.

"I got to her at the cast party, after we'd gotten the news but before they started interviewing. Swore I hadn't done it, pointed out how bad it would look for me. Made her agree to hold off for a couple of days. By that time, for her, Foster was the anti-Christ, I was the good guy, it wasn't that hard. Janey had a highly developed moral sense."

An echo came to me . . . Anandi's voice . . . "She has a strict morality, that one. Which someone has betrayed." Shit, was it going to turn out that everyone else had been right and I wrong? And if Derek carried out whatever plan he had in mind, which surely involved Harry and me ending up dead, what would it matter? I had the feeling that this current spate of garrulousness would not continue much—

"The thing is," Harry said thoughtfully, "that the chances of Foster's ever getting to actually build a garage in this area I'd say were pretty slim. I don't care what his connections were, Northampton isn't—"

Shut up, you fool! the scream went up inside my head, at the same moment that Derek jolted upright, the gun once more grasped firmly and pointing at our corner of the front pew.

"You think I don't know that, asshole? You think I don't know that I've lost everything—*everything*—because for one black second I lost my temper? My God, you think I haven't gone *over* it and *over* it! And then that *stupid* woman calling me and saying she'd decided it was only right for her to tell the police what she knew, because after all she was sure I hadn't done it, so it would clear out some of the underbrush and didn't I think it had to be Lydia?"

He walked to the lip of the stage, both hands on the gun now, eyes narrowed. "But you know, there *is* one possible way out and that, my friends, is why we're here. A tragic murder-suicide. Nosy girlfriend discovers the awful truth. Cornered murderer shoots her and then himself. With the very gun that killed Jane Manypenny. Case solved." He dropped to sit on the edge of the stage, raised the gun. "So, Phoebe, if you'll move just a hair closer to Harry . . . and I have to say I really am sorry about this . . ."

Sorry? And move closer to that lily-livered polecat? If I had to die it was going to be standing on my feet and not according to anyone's direction. Besides . . . I was sure I'd heard a catch in Derek's voice when he'd said he was sorry. I didn't believe he was beyond persuasion.

"No," I said. I stood up and walked deliberately to the far end of the pew.

"Hey, get back!" he yelled. "I'm not kidding!" The gun wavered from me to Harry and back.

I turned to face him squarely. "For God's sake, Derek, have some sense! So you shoot me first, then what? Harry's going to stand quietly while you put the gun to his head? It'll never play! The police will see through your little scenario in a New York minute! You'll have killed us for nothing, just the way you killed Foster and Jane for nothing!"

I could feel him hesitate, see the indecision play across his face. I started toward him with my hand outstretched.

"You don't, you can't really want to do this, Derek. Let it be over. Let it be—"

At this point, several things seemed to happen at once. The remarkable acoustics of the Old Church Theater reverberated with the sound of a loud report. Something hit my shoulder hard, causing me to sit down suddenly on the red velveteen pew cushion. Simultaneously, the doors to the lobby exploded inward and something large, hairy, and bellowing plunged down the aisle straight at Derek. Through a curtain of tiny dots brought on by my shoulder being on fire, I saw Derek's eyes widen in shock, saw him raise the gun again, heard a second report seconds before the large intruder leapt onto the stage, landing with a thud and a cracking noise on top of his quarry, who began shrieking in pain.

I had only time to formulate the thought, "Jeez, the little bastard shot me!" before the place was swarming with law enforcement types, several of whom were telling me not to move, which was the last thing on my mind. Over one of their shoulders I saw Harry approaching, his face puckered with concern, only to be armed aside by a large presence who addressed him as "you useless son of a bitch" and then the Bear was kneeling beside me, warming my cold hands in his immense paws and repeating, as if he would never be able to stop, "Phoebe, Phoebe, Phoebe!"

33

So adventurous a tale
Which may rank with most romances.

BETWEEN BEN SOLLIDAY ROARING, PORTIA (WHO HAD demanded and received police transportation to the hospital) pulling out all the stops as the eccentric and highly agitated aunt of the victim, and Lieutenant Griffith hovering and swearing nonstop under his breath while they dug the bullet out of my back, the emergency room personnel at Cooley Dickinson couldn't clean me up and get me out of there fast enough.

Nor could a succession of types in white coats, after examining my X rays, keep from commenting about how incredibly lucky I'd been. The bullet had hit below the left shoulder bone, cracked a rib, been deflected, and lodged neatly just under the skin halfway down my back without messing up any vital organs. Being still in a disoriented state brought about by shock and the injection of some delightful drug, I struggled to explain that it was all very well to talk about luck, but my very favorite green wool cape had been *completely ruined*.

Hal Griffith calmed me down by promising that the NPD would return my cape to me cleaned and mended once it stopped being evidence in an assault. Thus comforted, I did my best to answer his questions about the evening's sequence of events until Portia and the Bear put down their collective feet and demanded to take me home.

Before leaving, and while still in a mentally less-than-sharp state, I demanded to know what was happening to the poor man being treated in the curtained bay at the far end of the room and why two policemen were lurking nearby. It wasn't until the next day that I fully understood that my fellow patient had been Derek Bowles having his broken arm set.

In fact, there was a lot I didn't know until the next day. I didn't know that, once at home, Portia and Anandi had taken it in turns to sit by my bedside all through the night. Or that the Bear, denied this particular duty, had found an outlet for his feelings by rising at dawn to cook enough dishes to keep our little household in meals for a week. Or that by the time I came to in the mid-morning, wondering dazedly what my aunt was doing in my room and why my shoulder was all wrapped up and ached like blazes, the *Mikado* grapevine had been zapping its tendrils around town as if fueled by some kind of bio-atomic fertilizer.

Beyond a couple of pain pills, gulped down in deference to the fire raging in my shoulder, I refused breakfast in bed, suddenly as wide awake and wired as I'd previously been groggy. So while Anandi and Portia between them picked out and got me into a pair of navy wool slacks and a loose-fitting blue silk shirt that set off nicely the white sling I'd somehow acquired the previous night, they filled me in.

Anxious phone calls (not counting inquiries from the press) had been logged from Lydia Hicks, Carl Piquette, Irene Polaski, Beth Rosario, Nadine Gardner, and Harry Johns. In addition, Lydia, Carl, and Irene had sent flowers.

On my making a snorting sound at the mention of

Harry's name, Portia looked at me quizzically and noted, "Poor man sounded really miserable." I considered the question of whether Harry Johns being miserable affected me in any way and decided the answer was no.

And speaking of last night . . . "How did you know—how did Ben know—that we were in trouble at the church? And how did the cops get there so fast? And why—"

"Breakfast first," Portia said firmly.

Down in the kitchen, where three extravagant arrangements of fall flowers crowded the surface of the Welsh dresser and filled the air with the tart scent of crysanthemums, the Bear was in the act of taking a pan of popovers from the oven. Popovers! I hadn't tasted popovers since my mother made them. I looked at their golden brown tops ballooning over the rims of the iron muffin pan, smelled the toasty, eggy aroma and felt my eyes fill with tears of nostalgia, and gratitude for still being in a position to smell popovers or anything else. Clearly my emotional state was more fragile than I'd realized.

I hoped nobody had noticed, but when my aunt insisted that I take her chair, which had been draped with a poufy blue comforter, I almost lost it again. Portia gave me a panicky look and pronounced, "Th'girl needs somethin' to eat!"

So I was plied with fresh orange juice and oatmeal sprinkled with cinnamon sugar and milky, sweet coffee (this last Anandi's contribution as appropriate invalid food). In deference to my one-armed state, the Bear himself slathered butter on popovers and watched with satisfaction while I scarfed down two of them.

I had just gotten my hand around a proper cup of coffee and was preparing to ask the first of my flock of questions when the doorbell chimed. Anandi went to answer it and came back with Nadine in tow. Nadine's expression on seeing me (profound relief) and the fervor of her embrace (even though necessarily gentle) made me realize the place I had, willy-nilly, assumed in this young woman's life. In the course of that life she had already lost a mother and two fathers. Guess who, I thought with some misgivings, had been elected? Ah well, I'd have to grapple with that one later.

As coffee and popovers were pressed on the newcomer, I gazed around the table and thought about my good luck. About the fact of my being here, surrounded by people who were all treating me as if I were some kind of heroine instead of all kinds of a fool who, if Derek's aim had been as good as he claimed, would have gotten no better than she deserved. Realizing that these musings were leading inevitably to another unseemly display, I swallowed and turned to the Bear, who was sitting at my right, and put my hand on his arm.

"I haven't actually thanked you for saving my life," I said. "So let me do it now."

Ben covered my hand with his own. "My God, Phoebe, when I think it almost didn't happen . . . and it was my fault, of course, I shouldn't have—"

"Hey!" I said, "If we're going to talk about fault, let's get it straight. It was entirely mine. No"—shaking my head at the Bear—"it was and I apologize to everyone. If I had listened—"

The doorbell chimed again. This time Anandi returned with a sheaf of red roses, which she placed on the table while she went to find another vase. The Bear had not relinquished my hand and, all things considered, it seemed churlish to pull it away, so when Portia picked up the card in its white envelope and raised her eyebrows at me, I nodded.

She peered at the card through her reading glasses then, over their rims, at me. "Harry Johns," she announced.

"Oh, please," I said.

Nadine glanced at the bouquets on the dresser and back to the roses. "Late again?"

I began to feel I could definitely warm to this girl.

"Take 'em away," I said wearily.

The Bear, no doubt feeling in the circumstances he could afford to be magnanimous, said, "Johns did try to alert the van driver."

"What van driver?"

"The one bringin' all us senior types home," Portia explained. "Seems Harry was flickin' his lights on and off. Driver mentioned it, wondered what the deal was. But it was Anandi who thought she saw somethin' that mighta been a person in the backseat."

"It was because, you see, I was sitting by the window," Anandi said. "And looking down. But I am thinking, Why would a person be lying on the floor? So I mentioned it only to your Auntie Portia when we got back to the house. And she—"

"Smelled a rat," Portia broke in. "If someone was on the floor it was either a corpse or was hidin'. Didn't look good either way. So I called Ben here—"

"But we didn't know where you'd gone," the Bear said.

"What about my note?"

"Didn't see it at first," my aunt explained. "Must have gotten shoved off the table when I plopped m'bag down, ended up on the floor underneath. Anandi found it later. Said she didn't believe you'd go off without leavin' a note, went lookin'."

My debt to Anandi, I reflected ruefully, was getting larger by the second.

"But by that time," Anandi took up the tale, "Mr. Ben has already gone off in his car looking for you. Right away we called him on his cell phone."

"Fortunately, I was only a couple of blocks from the Old Church. I'd already alerted Hal, now I called to tell him where you were and to send the troops, but quietly since I didn't know the situation. When I got in—"

"How did you get in? We didn't hear a sound."

"Johns had left the keys in the door. I'm surprised Derek Bowles didn't notice."

I thought back to that quick, surreptitious entry. Okay, Harry hadn't been completely without wits. It still didn't matter.

"Derek Bowles," I said, "was performing the ultimate improv. Entirely made up as he went along, no wonder he missed a detail here and there."

"He came close to not missing you," the Bear said grimly. "When I looked through that little square of glass in the door he was pointing the gun at you and you were standing there trying to talk him out of it." He shook his head at me with an expression that I read as combining disbelief, admiration, and deep—very deep—affection. Oh dear. Another item for my Grapple-With-It-Later list. While I was not in love with Ben Solliday, there's something about a man risking his life for yours that puts him, at the very least, into a special category.

"You could have gotten shot," I said.

The Bear waved that one away. "The bullet didn't come near me. All that stuff Bowles gave you about being such a good shot must have been part of the improv."

I frowned. "How did you know about what Derek said?"

"Hal Griffith," Portia said. "Remember him yammerin' at you in the hospital?"

"Oh, yeah. Vaguely. Good, at least I won't have to—"

The doorbell again. I pulled my hand away from the Bear's in order to attend to my need for caffeine. I bet I knew who it was.

While Anandi scurried once again to answer the summons, I glanced at Nadine. She had been following the conversation—or trying to—with a bewilderment that reminded me that the information provided via the grapevine had doubtless been long on sensation and short on facts. I gave her a reassuring smile, being pretty sure that Mr. Facts himself was about to put in an appearance.

It was indeed Hal Griffith, bearing, by golly, a bouquet of yellow mums, white carnations, and baby's breath. I relaxed. Surely an offerer of baby's breath couldn't be about to deliver the stern lecture I couldn't help feeling I deserved. Of all the people whose good advice I'd ignored, it was Hal, I thought, who had the most right to be pissed off at me. Unless it was the Bear, who could have been killed on my account. Or Anandi, whose on-the-nose insights I'd rather arrogantly dismissed. Or Aunt Portia, whose hospitality I'd rewarded with at least one night of heart-stopping anxiety.

The lieutenant sat down between Ben and Anandi and accepted a cup of coffee. I decided to jump in first.

"Without going into how much of an idiot I feel, I just want to apologize for . . . creating such a mess."

Hal tilted his head. "Hey, you gave us the little guy on a platter. The gun was the one that killed Jane Manypenny—a Colt twenty-five—so we've got him on that as well as the assault on you and Ben." His gave me a look both sober and direct. "However, you can imagine how relieved we are not to be dealing with another murder."

I gave him an equally sober look. "I promise," I said sincerely, "that I'll never be that stupid again."

"Good." Hal reached into his jacket pocket and pulled out the notebook. It looked like the same one as before only a lot grubbier. "I'm afraid this isn't entirely a social call. I just need to go over what you told me last night."

As he read off the gist of that conversation, I was surprised at the relative coherence of my account. "Yes, I think that's everything."

Nadine asked, "What exactly did you say to the lawyer?"

I assumed the nauseating simper I'd employed on

the Sleaze. "That *dear* Dr. Ballard had *confided* to me that he was planning to build a parking garage on the Old Church site and that even a *small* investment on my part would guarantee *big* returns. As soon as he started to explain to me that the project had been iffy at best and now was probably defunct, I knew I'd guessed right."

"But why," Nadine persisted, "if he knew that, didn't he go to the cops? He must have recognized a big motive in the idea of destroying the church."

I shook my head. "No, he wouldn't. To him it was just another building. He wouldn't have understood about the acoustics and the atmosphere. Unlike Jane Manypenny, he wouldn't have had a clue that anyone could be passionate enough about a theater to go momentarily crazy when he heard it might be torn down. To him, it was simply another real estate deal. That's what it's all been about. A little piece of real estate."

Murmurs and nods. A brief silence.

"Want to stay for lunch?" the Bear said to Hal.

Lunch? I, for one, had barely begun to digest breakfast. According to the clock, however, it was definitely afternoon. Well, maybe just a taste . . .

Hal declined with regrets, but Nadine, on being asked, accepted with alacrity. Hal took his leave. The Bear and Anandi put their heads together in front of the open refrigerator door. Portia and Nadine had somehow launched into a discussion of "The Prince's Progress."

I sipped my coffee and tried to pin down the feeling I was experiencing. The question that had for the most part been pushed aside since my arrival in Northampton—what I was going to do with the rest of my life—was no nearer being answered. I was emphatically out of love with Harry Johns. Ben Solliday and Nadine Gardner at this point only represented new unanswered questions.

Portia was laughing her deep guffaw at something

Nadine had said. Behind me I caught fragments of an exchange between Ben and Anandi that involved the relative merits of mushroom and split pea soup.

I nodded, adjusted my sling, and settled more deeply into the blue comforter. I had identified the feeling. It was the feeling of being home.

ABOUT THE AUTHOR

KAREN STURGES lives in Western Massachusetts
with her husband and a small dog.